HALLOWEDDREAMS

MAPLE HILL CHRONICLES
BOOK THREE

ELIZABETH R. ALIX

Hallowed Dreams
Maple Hill Chronicles
Book Three

Elizabeth R. Alix

Printing History: First Edition, February 2023.

Paperback: ISBN 13: 978-0-9985243-7-5

E-book: ISBN 13: 978-0-9985243-6-8

Cover illustration and layout by 100 Covers https://100covers.com

Supported by Palouse Digital Press, Pullman, WA USA: http://palousedigitalpress.com/

Distributed by IngramSpark

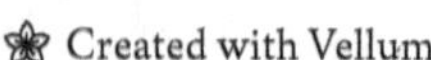 Created with Vellum

*To Austin, Kelton, and Orion
who are always there for me.*

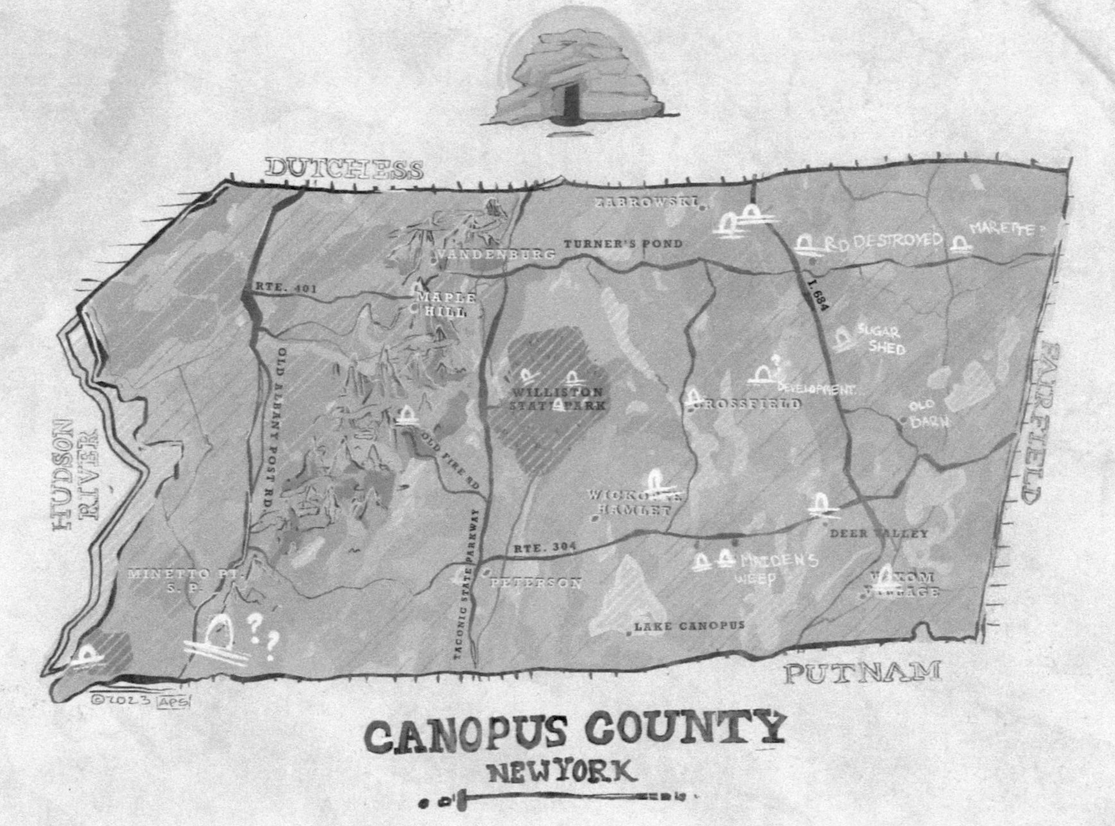

CANOPUS COUNTY
NEW YORK
DUTCHESS
PUTNAM
FAIRFIELD
HUDSON RIVER
ZABROWSKI
TURNER'S POND
VANDENBURG
MAPLE HILL
RTE. 401
OLD ALBANY POST RD.
OLD FIRE RD.
TACONIC STATE PARKWAY
WILLISTON STATE PARK
WICKOPEE HAMLET
RTE. 304
PETERSON
MINETTO PT. S.P.
LAKE CANOPUS
MAIDENS WEEP
DEER VALLEY
RD. DESTROYED
MARETTE
I. 684
SUGAR SHED
DEVELOPMENT
CROSSFIELD
OLD BARN
WATOM VILLAGE
©2023 APS
??

CHAPTER 1

 here were her dead friends?

Marianne surveyed Maple Hill Cemetery. Leaves rustled in a wind that mourned summer, dancing in a kaleidoscope of red, gold, and orange. None of the resident ghosts swayed with them. Not the pale woman who flitted, translucent against sentinel oaks that towered over the oldest section of the cemetery. Not the bagpiper who piped a tinny, spectral tune lost on mundane ears.

Instead, it was eerily quiet.

Her brow creased. *Is it just too bright a day for them?* Ghostly energies were often faint and harder to sense during the high-energy bustle of midday. *Or is it the time of year?* Halloween was around the corner. Did ghosts slumber at Halloween? Marianne had only started seeing ghosts since she arrived in Maple Hill two months ago. Maybe Halloween was a thing.

With a quick nod she decided to ask Sarah. She would know. She'd been able to see ghosts all her life.

Desiccated leaves crisped under her feet, releasing a spicy scent of decay, as Marianne walked among the headstones, enjoying the last kiss of summer sun on her shoulders. Mediterranean ancestry several generations back made her long for sun drenched landscapes. She shifted the potted plants in her arms to a more comfortable position.

She owed Sarah her sanity. Two months ago when ghosts began to haunt her new Maple Hill home, Marianne had been convinced she was losing her mind. Sarah had assured her she wasn't and become her guide to all things otherworldly.

Who would have thought a lawyer would be the local expert on ghosts? She shook her head. A particularly prickly, intimidating lawyer at that. Prickly with her anyway. Sarah's partner, Kelly, showered her with warmth and affection for a reason. Marianne just couldn't see it.

Escaping to the cemetery was a welcome break from days of unsuccessful job hunting. Much more peaceful than staring at her discouraging computer screen. Her visit also indulged the nagging feeling that she needed to check on things at the cemetery. In the last couple of weeks, she'd taken to visiting all the places she had met spirits. It was important to know where one's ghosts were.

Most people who died went off to an afterlife or whatever their beliefs had laid out for them. Sometimes people stuck around, confused about their death. Others remained because they had unresolved issues that needed addressing before they could move on. She'd met both kinds of spirits and was grateful most people moved on. It would be annoying and crowded to meet dead people at every turn. Sarah had told her to treat the dead with the same courtesy and respect as she would the living. So she was bringing flowers to the ghosts she had met in person.

The newest plots stretched up to the top of the hill and the oldest huddled next to the old county road at the bottom of the hill. Halfway down in the 1970s, she arrived at an imposing monument chiseled with the name Rutherford. George and his wife Anne were buried together here. They'd been the first ghosts she'd ever seen. They'd both invaded her dreams. Anne, anxious and sweet, had played the Pachelbel Canon on Marianne's piano. George had simply scared the hell out of her.

Marianne visualized the dark-haired, pale woman with cat eye tortoiseshell glasses. "Anne, I hope you're happy where you are. I think of you every once in a while. You can come back and play my piano again, if you want." She knelt and placed a small pot of brown and gold mums at the foot of the Rutherford headstone.

She couldn't prevent the image of George's florid face with his bushy beard and searing, angry eyes from leaping into her mind. She frowned. "You, George, are never welcome in my house again."

Standing, she scanned the immediate area with her eyes closed, swinging her head from side to side. She often saw spirits better with her eyes closed. Somehow that removed all other visual distractions, leaving only the spirits behind. Now she saw nothing but darkness inside her lids. She started walking again this time focusing her attention down.

Under the shade of the trees by the road the oldest graves resided. Weather stained, their engraving was blurred by time. A few rows up from the road she found the one she was looking for. It was a tiny, flat rectangle next to a larger monolith with 'Eddy' inscribed on it. The forlorn little stone bore the name Samuel Eddy Jr. 1905. Marianne smiled. She'd helped Anne return a stuffed toy rabbit to her little brother. The rabbit was gone, likely it had disintegrated with all the rain over the last few weeks, and John Irving, the caretaker, had removed it. She laid another pot of orange and brown mums between the tiny headstone and that of his parents. "Rest In Peace, little Sam," she murmured.

She picked her way through the stone markers to the other part of the cemetery. The place always felt like a quiet town: the headstones were like houses and the coffins, caskets, and urns below were like beds for the residents. Some graves had a little flicker of energy but most were quiet. She imagined them all safely asleep. Grandpa Clare Singleton was buried in the other section of the cemetery under an elegant black marble headstone.

She laid her last pot of mums next to it and brushed away a few leaves.

"Hi, Grandpa. I saw Grandma recently. She looked well." She closed her eyes and scanned the area again, but it was ghost-free. She opened them, wishing that her dad's grave was here as well. He was laid to rest up in Hyde Park where Mom lived. Pneumonia had claimed him when Marianne was five, and she and Mom had gone on alone. Her memories of him were few and faded like postcards from an old trunk. A smile and outstretched arms from a dark haired, clean shaven man. An impression of comfort. She'd never seen or felt her grandfather either, but Grandma Selene assured her he was happy on the other side.

She sighed. "Grandpa, if you see Dad, tell him I said hi."

She patted the sun warmed stone and continued her walk, following the gravel access road away from the river. She hadn't explored this part of the cemetery before and wanted to check it out. It was a good excuse to avoid going home just yet.

There weren't too many headstones back here. There was a good view of treetops but no river. A little like being seated near the kitchen at a restaurant, she thought with a smile. Maple Hill and the surrounding communities were not large, so the final resting place of residents who had passed on was only a few acres in size. John had told her once that roughly five-thousand souls were buried along the hillside between the trees and the county road.

On the back side of the public area, the road ended in a large pile of brush. It was probably cheaper and faster for John to burn it than take it to the dump. The beat of a mower made her look up. John was headed down the hill in her direction riding his agile zero-turn-radius machine. She waved and he raised his hand.

She continued exploring. A dark opening on the other side of the brush pile caught her eye. Curiosity drew her closer. Two stacks of rough cut stones obscured by vegetation framed a doorway, leading straight into the hillside. She walked nearer and a scent of lifeless dust and something metallic like rust assailed her nostrils. Stone steps led down into the dark, criss-crossed by spider webs. Huge stone slabs roofed the chamber. It reminded her of passage burials in the British Isles. Maybe it was a cold cellar from the early days of settlement? Maybe it had once been a Native American burial or ritual place?

She rested her hand on the stone support and peered inside for a better look. Immediately, her hand tingled as if she'd touched a live current, and she felt a wave of dizziness. She braced herself between the two stones to keep from pitching forward and felt the vibration through her whole body, drawing her downwards. She did not want go down the steps, but her feet moved forward of their own accord.

A hand grasped her upper arm and pulled her firmly away. She fell back panting slightly, her head clearing as the tingle disappeared.

"Don't go down there unless you know what you're doing." John Irving released her arm as she regained her balance. The caretaker was old and sun beaten, with an awesome Mark Twain mustache and a shock of white hair. He'd served her tea once when she was wrung out from ghost wrangling. He was her go-to for questions about the cemetery.

"Thank you for catching me," she said. "What's down there?"

His blue eyes stared at her as he considered what to say. "It's an old stone passage from before Europeans arrived. If an ordinary visitor went inside, nothing would happen. You're a little different. Ask Sarah about it. She'll tell you, if she wants."

"John, do you know what happened to all the spirits? They're not here today. Is that a time-of-year thing?"

He shrugged. "I don't know. Jesse might have an idea. He and Jason are in the machine shed."

He got aboard his mower and backed out carefully, turned, and spun the blades back up. Marianne noticed skid marks in the gravel that hadn't been there when she arrived. How had she missed the sound of a mower arriving at full tilt?

Her vertigo completely gone, she wondered if she'd overreacted. The dark entrance with its cold breath of dust stood a few feet away.

Don't go down there unless you know what you're doing. She shivered. No problem there. She headed back to the parking lot. Passageway? To where? What would happen if she went in there?

She dropped by the machine shed where John kept his mower and other tools. It was an old carriage building made of rounded stones with a tile roof. An array of lucky horseshoes were nailed over the doorway. She stepped into the deep shade of the interior.

"Hello?" She called. "Jason? Jesse? Are you here? I just came by to see how you're doing." As her eyes adjusted to the gloom, she saw movement in the back.

Hey Marianne! Long time no see. Jason's pale, lanky figure glided out of the dark. She closed her eyes to see him better. His spirit glowed as he half walked, half floated toward her. A hoody covered his mane of pale hair, and he sported a roguish grin.

"You're looking well, Jason." She returned the smile. "I'm really glad." He'd been depressed and fading from existence when she'd brought him here. For a ghost, he looked in the bloom of health.

My man Jesse has been showing me around and teaching me how to do stuff.

"Bet he doesn't play a lot of punk music," she teased. He'd been on his way home from a sludge metal band when he'd been killed by a drunk driver outside of Maple Hill. He'd lingered for four years before she found him and offered to help.

Nah, but Jesse says he'd listen if the Melvins played the cemetery, and that's cool.

"What are you learning?"

You know, stuff. How to move things in the physical world. Watch this!

Marianne watched him reach up and close his translucent

fingertips over the lapel of her light jacket. She felt a definite tug and gave a little yelp of surprise.

Hah, gotcha! He said with a grin.

She stepped back out of his range. "That's amazing, Jason." *And I'm so glad I brought you here. The last thing I need is you showing up in my bedroom again knowing you can do that.* "What are you using this new talent for?"

He shrugged his pale shoulders. *We help John out. He's the only one taking care of the whole place and doesn't always get everything done. I'm not great at it yet, but I'm learning to focus.*

"I'm kind of jealous. It's nice to know old ghosts can learn new tricks." She was glad he was no longer sad about not finding his parents.

His playful bump on her arm passed right through like an icy breath, and he pulled his arm back.

Dang. If I don't really concentrate, it doesn't work. The only bummer about being here is there's no girls! He gave her an impish smile and a wink.

"What about the lady in white at the bottom of the hill?"

Too old for me.

"Well, I can't solve that one for you," she chuckled, rubbing the chill off her arm. "Maybe someone will come along."

I can hope. Oh, gotta go. Jesse needs me. See ya 'round.

"Wait! I noticed that most of the spirits I see here usually aren't around. Do you know anything about that?"

He shrugged. *Mostly I stay here with Jesse. I don't hang out in the graveyard. It's a little depressing.*

"Do you think Jesse would know?"

Maybe. I could ask.

"Would you?"

He flitted off into the darkness, and she waited with a slight smile. Jason found the graveyard depressing. He certainly wasn't Goth or Emo. He returned a moment later.

He says it's better to stay indoors for now.

"Why?"

Jason shrugged again. *Plenty to do here. Learning to move things around.* With an expression of concentration he tugged her jacket sleeve again. She was ready for it this time.

"Do you know anything about the stone doorway on the hill?"

He frowned. *It's really creepy. I stay away from it.*

"I'll say. Thanks, Jason. Good to see you."

He gave a wink and faded. He was such a flirt.

She sighed. It was mid-afternoon, and she couldn't delay anymore. Time to go back and put in another couple of hours job hunting. Ruari was coming by after work for a movie and dinner at her place. He'd been busy the last couple of days, and she couldn't wait to see him. Besides, Oscar, her big orange tabby, would be wanting to come inside for a snack and a nap.

Time to call Sarah.

Marianne plunked down on her couch and tucked her feet up. Dialing Sarah's cell number rather than her work number was beginning to feel like raising the Bat Signal or calling a hotline. Oscar hopped up next to her and began an elaborate grooming ritual with one leg thrust in the air.

After a few rings, Sarah picked up. "Hey, Marianne? Everything okay?" Sarah always got right to the point.

"Mostly yes. I just had a couple of ghost questions if you have time."

"I have a meeting in ten. So yes, if they're short."

"Okay, I was out at the cemetery today and noticed there weren't any ghosts around. Except Jason and Jesse. That seemed really strange to me. Do they just settle down around Halloween?"

"Not that I know of. Are you sure? They don't always show up."

"I didn't see the bagpiper or the white lady under the trees by the road. When I went looking for some of the others I know about, they seemed to be asleep. Do you know what's going on?"

"No. I've never noticed that."

"Okay, what do you know about the stone doorway on the backside of the cemetery?"

"Why do you ask?" She replied sharply.

"John told me to ask you. I had the strangest experience today. I got really dizzy and nearly fell down the stairs. John pulled me back."

Sarah was quiet for a moment. "How about you come for dinner the day after tomorrow? I'll tell you what I know then."

"I guess I could. Would it be okay if Ruari came?"

She hesitated for a microsecond then said, "Sure. I have to go." And she hung up.

Did Sarah not want Ruari to be there? Well, it had been a little presumptuous of Marianne to ask if he could join them. She almost texted her back to say, never mind, he doesn't have to, but she let it go.

She spent the rest of the afternoon making phone calls to old history department colleagues in the city to see if they needed help, but they were training undergrads and new grad students and didn't need an old postgrad. Feeling a little desperate, she decided to try Mrs. Caldwell at the local library tomorrow, in case she had anything. Mrs. C had helped Marianne on several research projects but was an unsmiling grump most of the time. Marianne was willing to work for her all the same.

Ruari knocked on the door a little after six, and her heart leaped. She opened it with a big smile. He was a head taller than her, broad shouldered, wiry and muscled from a life of active work. A light trace of freckles sprayed across his cheeks under a thatch of sandy red hair. An answering smile lit up his face.

Stepping back, she said, "Come on in. Dinner's about ready. Are you hungry?"

Oscar immediately twined around his ankles, making his greeting.

"Starving!" He gave Oscar an affectionate noogie on his head, then enveloped her in a big hug. "Mahri, have I told you how much I love coming here instead of spending the night at my empty studio?"

She laughed. "You could shower here too, you know. You don't have to go home first."

"Guess I'm not ready to inflict my stinky, sweaty self on you yet." He followed her into the kitchen.

She gave him a big kiss. "Don't worry, you're fine."

"Remember, I can tell when people are lying!" He teased.

"It's true!" She protested. "I really do like how you smell."

"Do you now?" He leaned her against the counter and pressed his lips to hers. They were soft and warm. Her breath quickened. Maybe dinner could wait…When they broke apart, his grey-blue eyes were inches from her own. She said a little breathlessly, "Dinner first or later?"

His stomach made a questioning growl, and he chuckled. "I think I'm outvoted. Dinner first."

Over dinner she told him about her unsuccessful job hunt and her escape to the cemetery. Ruari had worked with an ancient tree spirit in his wood studio, and he understood about the ghost side of her life.

"Don't worry," he said. "Something will come up. You know, if you're struggling with the rent, I can help."

"I appreciate that. I'll let you know." She wanted to have every chance to make it on her own before relying on someone else.

He took another bite of pasta carbonara and smiled. "You're the only person I know who calls going to the cemetery 'escaping.'"

"Most of the time it's really peaceful. Did you know there's a stone doorway at the cemetery?"

"Where?"

"It goes off into a hillside on the back of the property."

He thought for a moment. "If it's the one I'm thinking of, kids in high school used to dare each other to go in it at night. The caretaker boarded it up so people wouldn't get hurt. Why do you ask?"

"It's not boarded up now. Don't laugh, but I nearly fell down the steps."

"What happened?" He asked. The concern in his eyes warmed her heart. Her ex would have called her a klutz.

"It was the weirdest thing. I came over all dizzy for a moment. I didn't hear John coming, but he must've seen me and stopped by to make sure I was okay. He kept me from falling."

"Are you okay now?

"I'm fine."

"I wonder why it's not boarded up anymore?"

"I don't know. John said something odd. Something about not going down there unless I knew what I was doing."

"What does that mean?"

She shrugged. "He told me to call Sarah, so I did. She promised to explain over dinner the day after tomorrow. You can come too."

He looked thoughtful and nodded. "I can be there."

Ruari had gone to high school with Sarah and her partner Kelly. They'd had a reputation for being weird and not been very popular people. "Great. How was work?"

"The usual. Getting rentals ready for winter."

"And the terrible Casey?" His young assistant hindered more than helped more often than not.

"If he could just focus, he wouldn't be half bad. Today's distraction was telling me about a play audition that's coming up."

"Really? I hadn't pegged him as a drama type."

"I don't think he is. I got the impression he was making up a school credit."

"So, has he moved on from dating the pizza girl?"

"No, he was busy texting her and setting up the next date."

She rolled her eyes. "Good grief. Can't you take his phone away?"

"I'd like to, but he's the owner's son. So, I've taken to handing him tools and making him do as much as possible, so he doesn't have any time to text."

"Good strategy."

He washed down another mouthful with a swallow of hard cider. "Halloween is coming up. Do you want to do something fun together?"

Although she'd never been a die hard Halloween fan, she hadn't minded pumpkin season. But now that she could see the dead, it might as well be Halloween every day as far as she was concerned. "What did you have in mind?"

"The high school does a haunted house fund raiser. We could go there."

She raised her eyebrows.

"It's a fundraiser so the marching band can get new uniforms this year. Besides, it won't actually be spooky, right? It'll be fun!"

She laughed. She didn't need his ability to see when people told lies to know he was being truthful. "Okay, let's go. Anything else?"

"And The Dutch is having a holiday special. If you come in costume, there are free snacks and a drink."

The Dutch was his favorite watering hole, shabby and off the tourist track. She'd been a couple of times with him, and it was nice. But a big party? With people she didn't know in a close space, many of them drinking or drunk? She'd been to many a work party with her ex and gotten pinched or groped by his colleagues too often to be excited about that.

But he looked so earnest and hopeful. Maybe this would be different. She took a deep breath, smiled, and said, "Do you have a costume in mind?"

His eyes twinkled. "I have a kilt and the whole regalia for the Allen clan."

"Really? I need to see that! You'll have to model it for me ahead of time."

He grinned. "I could arrange that. Do you have anything that would go with that?"

"What are the colors?"

"Dark blue, green, and red or black."

"Hmm." She mentally flipped through her wardrobe. "No, but I can go to the thrift store and put something together. I'll definitely find something."

Their plates were empty.

"Want help cleaning up?" he asked.

"You bet." Help in the kitchen was a novelty she hadn't grown tired of.

They watched a romantic movie and made out, kissing like teenagers, on the couch. When it grew more intense, he picked her up and carried her into the bedroom. Oscar vacated the bed just in time.

CHAPTER 2

$\mathcal{A}$fter Ruari left for work the next day, Marianne tidied up. Ruari had stayed overnight now about half a dozen times. It was nice to wake up with him in the morning, and his genuine concern for her well-being felt so good after years of being told she was an idiot. Ruari's offer of help with the rent was very dear. It made her a little nervous, though. Geoffrey had always expected something in return for any favor.

Rats. Why was her ex on her mind so much? He was long gone, and Ruari wasn't anything like him. *Because Geoffrey casts a long shadow,* she told herself, and she still needed time to get out from under it.

I need to be able to handle things on my own. I don't want to be dependent on Ruari to come to my rescue all the time. When I can do things for myself, I'll be ready to commit to a full time relationship again.

Time to see if Mrs. Caldwell had anything. Marianne had left her a message and planned to follow up today with an in person visit the old dragon couldn't ignore.

She was on the verge of going out the door when her cell phone rang.

"Hi Gillian, how are you?" She answered cautiously. Dr. Gillian Braithwaite was a history professor at NYU, and Marianne had hoped to co-teach a class with her next semester on "Victorian Influences in America." But the job had fallen through disastrously. Marianne had emailed her weeks ago about it. What did she want?

"Hey, Marianne. I haven't heard from you in a while. How's the class prep going?"

Her stomach plunged. "Dr. Plank nixed it, remember?"

"He mentioned that your lectures were not at a level he expected. But he said you could rework them. Haven't you done that yet? The deadline is tomorrow!"

"I'm sorry. I thought you got my email."

"I thought you were kidding! I can't believe you're just going to let Dr. Plank push you around. He's tough but he's fair. If you pull an all nighter, you could resubmit them—"

"Gillian, I'm not going to do that. To be honest, he wasn't supportive at all. I don't think my style of teaching would be a good fit for his department."

Gillian made an exasperated sound. "Marianne, you have to get used to people not being openly supportive. You're not a grad student anymore and don't need handholding! Academe is a tough world, but you can make it if you have the nerve to pursue it."

She thought of her colleague teaching four classes in a semester, vying for tenure, sitting on two committees, shepherding a couple of grad students, and trying to write an article for a peer review journal. If Marianne tried to do all that simultaneously, she'd explode. "Truthfully, I don't think I want to work for Dr. Plank."

The snort of derision was audible. "What are you going to do instead?"

"I'm not sure. I'm working on it."

There was a knock on the door in the background, and Gillian covered the receiver, "Come on in, be with you in a moment." Then she was back. "Sorry, Marianne, I have a student. Good luck, bye."

Wow, I did all the prep work, and all you tell me is I'm a big pushover and don't have the nerve to work in academe. Thanks, Gillian. Maybe I'm applying for teaching jobs because that's all I know? But what else can I do? How is a degree in history useful to anybody? Maybe I should just learn to do computer coding or medical billing.

She snorted aloud. "Yeah, I'd hate that."

There has to be something better. Maybe a nice quiet research position in a local historical society? I could do genealogies and write pamphlets. Make people smile, get them excited about history. Time to see Mrs. C.

She let Oscar out and maneuvered around him where he sat surveying the cul-de-sac, his crooked tail tapping gently. She patted him and kissed his head one more time. Her backpack bumped comfortably over her shoulder as she walked into town with a couple of copies of her resumé.

Maple Hill was not too busy mid-week. The autumn foliage seeking Leaf Peepers would come for the weekend and fill the inns and restaurants. She made her way toward the far end of town where the library and the Avery Theater stood side by side. The old section of the library was built of rough fieldstone with windows around a central entrance. A modern addition connected by a glassed in walkway had been built with climate controlled book preservation in mind. The local historical society was appropriately housed in the basement of the old building.

Halloween was a little over a week away, and the library was getting into the spirit. Strings of paper leaves and cheery cutouts of pumpkins and witches were stuck to the windows and draped around the entryway.

Marianne descended the stairs into the room that held the historical collections. A couple of heavy, mismatched tables and chairs occupied the center. A microfiche and microfilm reader stood off to the side and rows of shelves held local records, early diaries, old newspapers, cemetery records, and more. Mrs. Caldwell was the keeper of the lore and oversaw the whole room from her vantage point at a counter across from the stairs. Her iron gray hair bound in a firm bun, she was somewhere between fifty and seventy in age. Her sharp, dark eyes fixed on Marianne as she entered.

She gave the old librarian a bright smile and approached the counter. "Hi Mrs. Caldwell, how are you today?" Marianne had an ongoing personal challenge to get her to smile. So far, no luck.

"Miss Singleton." She gave a short nod, but her dour expression didn't change.

Oh for five, Marianne sighed.

"Are you here for another of your local projects?" Mrs. Caldwell inquired. She had helped Marianne research both the ghosts in her house and the identity of hitchhiker Jason, though Mrs. C hadn't known the exact nature of the research.

"Actually yes, but it's more personal." She decided to prostrate herself at Mrs. Caldwell's feet and hope for the best. "I'm looking for a job. Do you know of anyone who needs a historian?"

The woman regarded her with sharp brown eyes. "You want to be a librarian?"

"No. I have a PhD as a historian and specialize in the Victorian era both in Britain and the U.S. I don't know a lot about Maple Hill or Canopus County per se, but I could learn quickly. Please, if you can think of anything at all, I'd be grateful." She hoped she didn't sound too desperate.

"Are you aware that the city council decided to cut our budget and has eliminated several positions? Even simple things like book shelving have gone to volunteers."

Marianne's spirits fell. "I was afraid of that. You must have contacts with other libraries in Canopus County, though. Maybe you could ask around?"

Her nostrils flared and she looked affronted at being asked to do such a thing. "I am extremely busy."

Marianne nodded. "Of course. If you hear of anything, I'd be glad to work at a historical society, tourist attraction, or anything having to do with history."

Mrs. Caldwell's expression didn't change much, but Marianne thought she saw a flicker of something. She hadn't said no outright, so Marianne placed a copy of her resumé on the counter between them. "Thanks. My contact info is at the top." She turned to go.

The dry old throat cleared behind her. "I have one little project. If you're interested."

Marianne turned back, hope rising.

"It isn't much, but it does need to be done. I could pay you minimum wage out of discretionary funds."

"What is it?"

"I have a bunch of old maps that need to be organized and filed."

That sounded promising. She nodded. "I could do that for you. I'm not a conservator, but I could file them for you."

Mrs. Caldwell sniffed. "Come back tomorrow, and I'll show you what I have."

Marianne gave her a broad, relieved smile. "I'll be here. Thank you."

The thin lips softened and twitched. "Don't thank me yet."

Feeling optimistic for the first time since her failed teaching application, Marianne decided to check on some of her other ghosts. There were two little boys who haunted the stacks near the reading desks in the main library. After her visit to the cemetery yesterday, she wanted to know they were there.

The new library wing was quite festive, draped in orange and black crepe paper and dangling letters proclaiming 'spooky' and 'boo' at regular intervals. The windows had clinging gel spider webs and cartoonish grinning black spiders. She made her way past the children's books to adult fiction and the reading tables where she'd encountered the boys before. A few people sat reading the paper and using the computers, but otherwise, the section was quiet and deserted.

She sat quietly, and let her mind run through the happy gyrations of, *Mrs. Caldwell has a job for me! Minimum wage isn't great, but it's a start. Old maps sound cool. I have a job tomorrow!* When that calmed down, she closed her eyes and listened with her mind. The boys loved whispering and giggling just out of sight whenever she was here. She'd shushed them on a couple of occasions, and they'd laughed and run away, but they always came back.

They weren't here today.

She sat for a few minutes longer to see if they'd show up, but nothing happened. *Curious. I wonder where ghosts go when they're not here?*

On the way home, she stopped in at Brown's Hardware and walked up and down the aisles looking for the ghost of the man who had been looking for fuses. He wasn't there either, but that was less surprising. She'd helped him find the fuse he'd been looking for, and he'd disappeared happily. He might have simply moved on of his own accord.

Strange. Of all the local ghosts she knew, only Jason had turned up.

Marianne was waiting for Mrs. Caldwell in the entrance to the old library at eight-thirty the next morning.

"You're punctual at least," Mrs. C said as they proceeded down the stairs to unlock the door to the historical section. A large wooden case with wide shallow drawers stood in a corner. "I had the custodian bring it out of storage after you left yesterday."

Marianne stowed her pack behind Mrs. C's counter and followed her down a short hall to a closet. The old librarian unlocked the door and opened it. Marianne was surprised they weren't ambushed. The small space was full of maps: rolled in tubes, leaning haphazardly against the walls, and folded on shelves, waiting to tumble out.

"These are part of a bequest we received several years ago and haven't had the time or space to manage," Mrs. Caldwell explained. "We recently acquired an old flat file cabinet and have agreed these could go into it. I'd like you to bring these into the main room, flatten them out, log them into our system, label them, and put them away."

"I can do that." Her eyes sparkled at the prospect of handling such old documents. Original materials carried an aura of history, significance, and a connection to the people who made and used them. They were rather like ghosts but less scary. She couldn't wait.

"First you'll have to fill out paperwork as a temporary, part-time worker. Then you may proceed."

Half an hour later, her paycheck assured, Marianne returned to the closet and got started. She extracted a pair of cotton gloves from her pack and put them on to keep the natural oils of her hands from marring the old paper. Mrs. C raised her penciled eyebrows. "I know they're blue," Marianne said, embarrassed. "They're from an old garden party." Mrs. C snorted and Marianne couldn't tell if she was amused or disdainful.

She brought out five maps at a time and gently spread them out on the big wooden tables. They represented Canopus County and its surroundings at different times over the last two hundred and fifty years. Some were very detailed drawings of particular settlements while others showed the county in context with the river and neighboring areas. The paper was often brittle, and Marianne felt guilty every time a piece flaked off. She carefully described each map and took pictures with her phone for the record, planning to download them to the library catalog when she was done.

One document was more artwork than map. Someone had painted tiny representations of buildings and people in the margins of a plat map of the county seat, Crossfield. She stared in fascination at the detail of each miniature until a throat clearing interrupted her. She looked up apologetically to see Mrs. Caldwell point with her eyes at the clock. It was mid-afternoon. She'd catalogued fifteen maps and had a long way to go. It would take another couple of days to finish at this rate.

Marianne worked industriously for another hour before she came across a brown, stained, flat pouch. It was made of oilcloth with a deep flap and ties to keep it shut. This was likely to be a map made for use on the road. Excited, she opened the flap and drew out a folded document. It was also made of linen but wasn't oiled. When she teased the stiff folds apart and spread it out, it showed a network of lines criss-crossing an early representation of the county. Gently she pressed the edges and folds flat so she could see it better.

By now she had a pretty good idea of the locations of the original towns and settlements and the roads between them. On this map they were marked in black ink. She would have categorized it as the equivalent of a road map in an early traveler's saddlebags, a well preserved example, but nothing special. Except for a second network of lines in faded sepia tones that had been overlaid. The end point of each line showed a little half circle or rectangle open at the bottom. They didn't necessarily correspond to settlements or towns, though some them did. She looked more closely and could see numbers alongside each line, perhaps noting travel times? There were nineteen such locations.

I wonder if those are the equivalent of Ley lines? Alfred Watkins had come up with the idea of secret, straight roads between prominent locations on the English landscape in the early twentieth century. Since then, they'd been discredited as mere coincidence. However, the idea that old, prehistoric locations were somehow connected had persisted. Wouldn't that be interesting if this was Canopus County's equivalent of a Ley line map?

She took her obligatory photos, described the map, and gave it a number.

As the last action of the day, Marianne asked Mrs. C to give her a hand to carry the larger maps to the case and lay them out in their drawers. The edges curled stubbornly on some. "Do you have any metal rods we could use to hold these down? Glass would probably be better in the long run, but you might have to order those."

"Yes, I see what you mean. I'll see what I can do." Mrs. C closed the drawer and said, "Thank you for your work today."

"You're welcome. I'm sorry I get so distracted looking at things, but it's hard not to. Some of them are so beautiful."

Mrs. C's lips twitched. Was that a smile? "The library discretionary fund is not big enough for you to spend more than a couple of days doing this. See that you finish quickly. You can always come back and look later."

Marianne grinned. "True enough. Thank you, good night!"

As she left feeling tired but exhilarated, her cell phone rang.

"Hello?"

"Hi Marianne, it's Kelly."

"Hey, what's up? You sound really down."

"I'm fine. Sarah wanted me to remind you about dinner at our place tonight. You can still make it, right?"

"I suppose so. You sure nothing's wrong?"

"I'll explain when you come over. Mr. Hot Stuff is welcome," she added with a hint of her old self.

Marianne grinned. Kelly liked teasing her about Ruari. "Thanks. Can I bring anything? Drinks, side dish, dessert?"

"Nope, just yourselves. See you around six."

"Okay then!"

"What happened to you?!" Marianne exclaimed when Kelly opened the door for her and Ruari a little later. She stood balanced on a pair of crutches, her leg in a cumbersome boot below the knee.

Kelly gave them a wry smile and let them in. "Short story: I broke my leg rock climbing last weekend."

Ruari winced in sympathy, and Marianne hugged her carefully.

Kelly led them into the living room, an open plan with the dining room and kitchen, and seated them on the couch.

"Hi everybody," Sarah called. "I'm on kitchen duty till Kelly gets better."

"What would you like to drink? We have wine, tea, beer, something stronger?" Kelly asked.

"I'll take a beer," Ruari replied.

"Glass of white wine sounds good," Marianne said.

"Coming right up." Kelly swung herself into the kitchen.

"Do you want help?" Marianne offered.

She hesitated, then said, "Sure."

Marianne carried an opened bottle of beer and a glass of white back to the living room.

Kelly lowered her tall, athletic body into an easy chair and propped her booted leg up on a pillow on the coffee table with a sigh. She took a swallow of water.

"So, the longer story is: I went on the last climb of the season to the 'Gunks last weekend with my climbing buddies. It was a trad route we'd climbed a bunch of times before, and I went up to check the bolts. They were solid for the first twenty feet or so, but the next one I put my hand on pulled loose, and my partner didn't pick up the slack in time. So, I landed badly, and I'm stuck in this stupid cast for six weeks." She gestured at her leg.

"Your buddy Chip is on my shit list," Sarah called.

"To be fair, he feels awful about it."

"Can I say, 'I don't care?' You're the one in the cast," Sarah responded. The sound of the oven opening and closing was accompanied by the savory smell of roasted beef and potatoes. "Come serve yourselves."

Kelly shrugged. "Climbing is mostly safe but not without risks and that's part of the reason I like to go. Much more exciting than cutting and coloring hair all day!" She gave them a wry grin.

Marianne and Ruari filled their plates with meat, potatoes and carrots, pan juice, and green beans and sat at the table. Kelly stubbornly served herself, but Sarah's watchful eye never left her. When the plate bobbled as a crutch caught the edge of a chair, Sarah reflexively reached for it.

Kelly scowled. "I got it."

After the first few mouthfuls, Sarah asked, "How are things going?"

Marianne sighed. "Still job hunting. The teaching job I hoped for fell through, so I'm sending my resumé out to more local places that have a history angle. I'm filing old maps at the library right now, but that'll be done in a couple of days. I don't know as it will lead to anything else."

"You never know."

Kelly told an entertaining story about a client at Hair Magic who'd come in with fly paper stuck to her hair. Nothing worked until she Googled the problem and got out an can of paint thinner from a stash in the back room. "Voila, no more stickiness. It took five washes to get the smell out, though!"

Marianne waited for Sarah to bring up anything in the realm of magic or ghosts, but she remained conspicuously bland. Maybe it was more of a dessert and coffee topic.

When it came time to clear the plates, Marianne and Ruari immediately offered to help, but Sarah said, "Sit, you're our guests. We've got this. Coffee? Tea?" Sarah ferried the plates to the island that separated the kitchen from the living room while Kelly got the tea kettle going and maneuvered plates and silverware.

A lull in kitchen activity made her glance up. Kelly and Sarah were conferring in soft voices. Sarah's back was to her, but Kelly's face was clearly unhappy. The exchange lasted only a couple of seconds, but Marianne wondered what was going on.

Maybe Sarah thought Kelly was doing too much? Kelly's expression turned to a smile as returned to the table.

"We have apple crisp for dessert," she announced as she sat down with a stifled groan.

"You okay?" Ruari asked.

"Pain meds are wearing off."

"We probably shouldn't stick around too long after dinner," Marianne said.

"No worries. It's been great to have you."

Sarah returned with a bowl of whipped cream and an oven dish that smelled like brown sugar and apple heaven. She gave everyone a portion and passed the cream.

"Marianne, I have a proposal for you," Sarah declared.

Marianne was intrigued.

"I have a history related job that you'd be perfect for, if you're interested."

"Are you working on a case at your law firm that needs some research?" That wasn't an avenue she'd thought of exploring, but of course, there might be instances where historical research was needed.

"Not exactly. It's more of a personal project. How would you like to go on a little road trip with me?"

"I thought you worked full time?"

"Yes, but I always take about a week or ten days off at this time of year. Kelly and I get out of town for a few days. She can't come this year for obvious reasons, but I can show you the major historical sites in Canopus County, and you can do a little networking."

"I don't want to horn in on your vacation!" She protested. "Don't you want to spend it here with Kelly?"

Kelly gave a dry laugh. "I'll be fine. Sarah, quit beating around the bush and just spit it out."

She cleared her throat. "It isn't really a vacation. It's more of a magical necessity." She gave Marianne a frank gaze. "Kelly and I are the magical protectors of Canopus County. Each year we drive around the county and cast a spell to protect it from bad influences. Kelly can't go, and I need a second pair of hands. You're the obvious choice."

"But I don't know how to do magic!"

"Don't worry, I'll teach you as we go along. Since you already can see ghosts, it's not a hard or particularly dangerous task. We meet a bunch of spirits and lay protective charms in all the communities. Kelly and I have done it for five years and never had a problem."

"But, I need to get a job. I can't really afford to take that kind of time."

"Let me sweeten the pot. I'll take you to all the major libraries and historical societies. You can drop your resumé and network."

Marianne wavered. She'd considered driving to those places herself. If she helped Sarah out at the same time, that was okay. Ruari's knee pressed against hers. Marianne looked his way and saw a slight crease between his eyebrows in his otherwise bland expression. What was he trying to say?

"How about this," Sarah said, "I need some historical research done. I'll pay you fifteen dollars an hour. That way you won't feel like you're losing paid time."

"It's tempting. Is your trip related somehow to the stone passage in the cemetery and the missing ghosts?"

Sarah nodded. "Yes. I don't know why the local spirits are laying low. They aren't affected by Halloween and the thinning of the veil. If anything, they are usually more active. I plan to investigate that. You're good at ghosts. You can help me. The stone portal is a lot more complicated. Suffice it to say, it's part of the spell to shut out unwanted entities."

"I'm not sure I'm your gal. It made me dizzy."

Sarah's serious expression lightened. "That's a good sign. It means you're magically sensitive and I can train you."

"Can she think about it and get back to you?" Ruari asked. She looked at Ruari. His knee pressed against hers again, and she wished they could step outside and talk without offending their hosts.

She was immediately annoyed with herself for feeling like she had to ask the man in her life for permission. Her ex had run her life so thoroughly that she'd gotten used to him making all the decisions. She cleared her throat. "It sounds okay. Do you need me this week?"

Sarah answered, "Time is running out. We have to close the spell by Halloween night and need all the time we can get. If you can commit to this tonight, it would be a big relief to me."

Ruari said mildly, "It's a big favor to ask. She needs to check her calendar at the very least."

Sarah frowned. "Like I said, I'm running out of time. I need you to get back to me sooner rather than later."

Nettled by Ruari's interference, Marianne made up her mind. "I'm pretty sure all I have is job hunting for the next week. I do have to finish the library job, though. After that, sure, I can go with you."

Ruari sat back and his knee moved away. His withdrawal stung, but it was her decision, not his. It was her life. They'd talk about it on the way home.

Sarah looked relieved. "Great! I'll send you an email later with the things you'll need to bring. I'll pick you up first thing in the morning the day after tomorrow."

"Okay then."

They made their departure shortly after that. On the way home in Ruari's truck, Marianne said, "I get the feeling you're not happy. What's wrong? This is my choice. If this will help me get a job, then it's worth doing."

He stopped at a red light and said, "I've got a bad feeling about it. She wasn't telling us the whole story."

"How do you know? Did you see black smoke?" That was his signal for lies.

"No, I just felt like there's something more. Sarah was being pretty pushy."

"She said she was in a time crunch and sounded worried about it. She was probably just wanting to have it settled as soon as possible."

"Yeah, but something about this this doesn't feel totally legit." He accelerated again.

A wave of stubbornness washed over her. It was easy for Ruari to tell her not to go when he was secure in his own profession, on the verge of starting a new business. Besides, she could take care of herself. Geoffrey had been overprotective and jealous of other men. She knew Ruari wasn't like that, but she didn't want him to start thinking he could run her life. She lifted her chin. "I'll be fine. It's only for a few days, a week at most. Getting my resumé out there is really important to me, and helping Sarah is a bonus. She's done a lot for me. If I don't like it, I can just come home."

He pulled up in front of her house and parked. The engine ticked quietly. "Can't you just tell them something came up and you can't go?"

She felt her heels digging in. "It'll be fine," she repeated. "Would you take care of Oscar for me while I'm away?"

He breathed out audibly. "Sure. Please call me if you need to come back. I'd absolutely come get you."

Her heart unclenched a little. "Thank you. That means a lot to me. You want to come in for a bit?" She was half afraid he wouldn't.

They watched a little TV before heading to bed. Instead of making love, they curled up together, his arms around her. She squashed any hint of alarm by telling herself that she'd made the right decision.

CHAPTER 3

After an intense day, Marianne finished the map project and finalized her own plans to be away for several days. Once she'd made up her mind to go, Ruari had refrained from trying to convince her otherwise. He'd limited his commentary to worried looks which she found both endearing and exasperating.

Sarah rang the doorbell at eight in the morning as Ruari was leaving for work. At the door, he hugged her hard and murmured in her ear, "Please take care of yourself. Call me if you need anything. Here," he pressed something into her hand, "this will keep you company."

The carved likeness of Oscar lay in her palm. He'd made it when they were in London a couple of weeks ago and must've grabbed it off the mantlepiece. "Thanks. I'll be back soon, hopefully with some new contacts!" She kissed him and turned to open the door.

"Hey, Sarah," Ruari said as he stepped out. His expression was neutral but Marianne heard a hint of steel. "Take care of her. See you in a few days."

Unfazed, Sarah answered, "You bet. Hi Marianne, are you ready?" She had pulled her hair into a French braid and was wearing jeans and a T-shirt with a light jacket over it. Her usual solemn expression was firmly in place.

"I got your list and put together what I had. Why the sleeping bag?" Marianne took the bag she'd borrowed from Ruari, a pillow, her research pack with a couple dozen resumés, and a rolling suitcase out to Sarah's car. She'd managed to keep her selections to one modest bag. The last time she'd packed for unknown weather she'd upended a couple of drawers into a steamer trunk sized suitcase. She felt better prepared this time.

"We'll camp out one night," Sarah said. "Besides, you never know with hotel rooms."

Marianne stopped short on the sidewalk. "Wait, what? We're going camping? I haven't been camping since I was a kid!" Flustered, she turned to go back inside. "I need different clothes."

Sarah stopped her with a hand on her arm. "Don't worry. I have everything we'll need. You'll be fine."

Feeling wrong footed, Marianne stepped into the house one more time, grabbed a hat, scarf and gloves and one more sweater. She absolutely hated the cold. Oscar had already gone out for the day, and Ruari would be back in time to feed him in the evening. She locked the door behind her.

Sarah was tucking Marianne's things into the back of her old white Volvo station wagon. Marianne was surprised there was any room at all. Several boxes of different sizes, a pile of camping gear, a large duffel, and a metal tool box had been pushed aside to make room for her suitcase and sleeping bag.

"What's all this?"

Sarah tipped one of the boxes, showing hundreds of small cloth bags. "Charms for laying the spell."

"That's…a lot."

"We have to drive every road and leave them behind as part of the spell."

That sort of meshed with Sarah's description of protecting the county. "What's in here?" Marianne indicated a smaller cardboard box.

"Those are specialty charms."

"And this?" She indicated a metal toolbox that had been painted black with white, blue, green, red, and yellow symbols on it.

"Magical gear. Don't mess with that unless I tell you to." She slammed the back hatch and stepped over to the driver's side.

Marianne opened the passenger door with a stiff creak, and the strong scent of coffee mixed with something floral and herbal wafted out. Sarah had always had tea when they'd been together, and Marianne had assumed she didn't do coffee. A folded towel sat on the passenger seat. She moved it discreetly to the back seat. As she slid into the front seat, she noticed the travel mug carefully standing in a hiking boot secured to the front bench with the center seat belt. The aged Volvo predated cupholders, and someone had gotten creative.

"Marianne, meet Natalie." Sarah patted the dashboard. "Natalie, this is Marianne."

"Hi Natalie." She'd named her mother's little Ford Escort The Flea, so she was only a little surprised. She'd never thought to introduce her to new passengers, though.

Sarah started the engine, put the car into first gear and rolled it forward around the cul-de-sac. "Okay, we're headed for Crossfield. Have you been there?"

"Not yet."

"It's the county seat for Canopus with a library and a historical society."

"Perfect!"

They passed through Maple Hill quickly and got to the road that led down to Route 9. It was fairly steep with several switchbacks, and Marianne had not been looking forward to driving it in winter. Sarah paused at the top, took a sip of her coffee and put the mug firmly back in its boot holder before turning down hill. They gathered speed, and Marianne gripped the seat, trying to stay upright while Sarah veered tightly around the first turn in the road. Marianne's foot pressed an imaginary brake pedal through the floor, and she felt the springs of the old seat through the thin padding. The next curve came quickly and Sarah down-shifted and took the corner way faster than Marianne would have.

Holy crap! She drives like a maniac. I might not survive the week if this keeps up. She glanced at the speedometer. Sarah was casually doing sixty in spite of signs indicating that forty-five was prudent.

"Sarah," Marianne ventured, "are you okay?" The lawyer's usual shuttered expression had transformed into one of unholy glee as she concentrated on the road. "Sarah!" she said more sharply.

"What?" Sarah upshifted and gunned the engine on the straightaway towards the next turn.

"You're driving a little fast," Marianne said carefully, not wanting to upset the caffeine-fueled crazy lady at the wheel.

"Fast? It's not that fast." She rolled the window down and let the chilly October wind rip through her hair. "This is fast!" She downshifted, taking the next corner tightly as Natalie groaned. Marianne felt her body pulled heavily toward the outside of the turn. A car suddenly appeared coming up the hill.

"Oh my God!" Marianne breathed and closed her eyes. She heard the car pass them and imagined the doppler shift of sound.

Reaching the bottom of the hill after a long glide, Sarah hit the brakes and laughed like a little kid. "Wow! I love that road!"

Marianne released her death grip on the seat cushion, flexing her sore fingers, and unbracing her legs. Suddenly she could feel the springs under her butt and thighs and the purpose of the towel was clear. "I had no idea you were a speed junkie!" She tried to keep her tone light. "You must be a fan of roller coasters too."

Sarah laughed again. "Kelly keeps saying she's going to get me high performance driving lessons for my birthday. And yes, I love roller coasters!"

Marianne didn't think Sarah's learning to drive faster was a good idea.

They pulled onto Route 9 more sedately. The traffic was thinner south of Fishkill and Poughkeepsie.

"How's Kelly feeling?" Marianne said when her heart rate had returned to normal.

"She's getting better. Leg still hurts, but she'll bounce back in no time."

"I'm glad. Crossfield is one of the oldest towns in Canopus isn't it?" Marianne remembered the little black dot on the far side of Canopus County from the earliest maps she'd looked at.

"Yup."

"I noticed there were a couple of other historic register places as well as an old homestead that had become a state park near there. I'd like to stop there so I can leave my resumé."

"Yup."

"You mentioned doing some historical work for you?"

"Yeah, I have a couple of projects I could use a little more information on."

"Great! What are they?" Marianne reached for her backpack at her feet and pulled out a yellow notepad and pen. She could do some preliminary work with her phone as long as they had a good signal and generate some questions and topics to look up when they got there.

Sarah glanced over. "You ready?"

"Shoot."

"Okay, could you find out more about Turner's Hope Mine, Williston State Park, and Minetto Point Preserve."

"You got it. What specifically do you want to know?"

"General history for now."

"Okay. Mind if I get started? I'll keep track of my hours as I go."

"Go for it."

Grateful she didn't get carsick easily, Marianne used her phone and dug into research, finding her happy zone.

They arrived in Crossfield mid-morning having driven through gorgeous fall foliage. Canopus County wasn't large but it had a series of low ridges that ran roughly parallel to the Hudson in the west half and then a lot of freshwater lakes nestled in trees and fields in the middle. The eastern half was flatter and drier as it neared the Connecticut border. Consequently, there were only two major north-south roads, the Taconic State Parkway and Route 684. The east-west roads were smaller and more winding, accommodating the terrain challenges. Half the time there were no direct roads between two points.

And, it turned out that cell reception was spotty, making internet research difficult. *Makes me grateful for my connection at home. If I get a job in Crossfield, I'm going to spend a lot of time commuting. That could suck big time especially in winter.*

Crossfield was a mix of old and new, a bit like Maple Hill, but bigger. The downtown area had a couple of modern glass and steel buildings, though they were only four stories tall, a nod to strict zoning laws preserving the older feel of the town. Most of the architecture was a mix of brick and clapboard structures, including some grand "Painted Ladies" from the Victorian era. At the other end of the historic spectrum were three sturdy stone buildings from the earliest days. Marianne smiled remembering the little paintings in the margins of the map she'd filed a couple of days ago.

Sarah pulled into a parking spot near one of the stone buildings, and Marianne shouldered her backpack. After sitting in the car for forty minutes, jouncing along on the barely padded springs, she was feeling a little bruised. She'd have to remember to put the towel padding back in place before they got going again or it was going to be a long, sore day.

"You go ahead, I'm going to get another coffee. Want one?" Sarah offered.

"No thanks. I don't really like coffee."

The Canopus County Historical Society had much posher digs than the old basement in Maple Hill. She opened the glass door and stepped inside. A woman at a desk in the foyer looked up and said, "May I help you?"

Marianne smiled and introduced herself as a historian. "I don't know if you have any positions open now or might open in the near future, but I'd like to leave my resumé for the head of the historical society."

The woman stood, offered her hand and said with a smile, "I volunteer here. It's nice to meet you, Miss Singleton." She took the resumé and glanced at at. "Your specialty is the Victorian era? That sounds interesting. I'm afraid we don't have anything open at the moment. It's been a tough couple of years. But I'll certainly pass along your CV to the director."

Disappointed, Marianne shook the woman's hand and said, "I'd appreciate that. Thank you."

"I'm sorry you drove here all the way from Maple Hill for nothing. Why don't you take one of our brochures? We also have a website that lists our holdings for researchers and our events."

Marianne thanked her and took the pamphlet. *One down, two dozen to go,* she thought. *Well, at least I'll have some names of people and what their collections have in case I need to do research in the future.*

Sarah was waiting for her by the car, sipping a fresh latte. "Any luck?"

Marianne shook her head. "No, but I left my resumé just in case."

"Come on. I have another place to show you."

Sarah wedged the new drink into the hiking boot and angled the old Volvo out into the flow of traffic. A couple of blocks away she pulled into a parking lot adjacent to a small park with a war monument. Several meticulously maintained flowerbeds full of fall flowers bordered the tapered column set off by a chain draped partition. The plaque held the names of locals who had been in WWI and WWII. It was all very ordinary. What wasn't ordinary was the entrance to a stone chamber behind it.

Stacks of dry fitted stones held up several large slabs that formed the roof just like at the Maple Hill cemetery. However, instead of penetrating a hillside, leading to a mysterious other realm, the hill had been carved away, making the stones look more like a kid's fort. The plaque beside it said it had been preserved as the town grew and remained a testament to the prehistoric past.

Sarah beckoned to her. "Follow me, I want to show you something." She disappeared into the shaded interior.

Marianne touched the upright stone gingerly with her finger tips, but there was no answering hum or vibration. There was no tugging sensation either and it smelled like dry stone and earth.

Go on, follow her before she thinks you're a complete wuss.

She stepped down into the darkness after Sarah. The passage was short, barely ten feet long and five feet wide. A scatter of dry leaves clustered at the far end of a concrete floor. Graffiti had been scratched and painted on every flat surface.

Sarah said, "Could you give me a boost?"

"A boost?"

"I need to reach up there." She pointed to a little crevice in the ceiling near the back wall. "Kelly says I'm only as heavy as the last bagel I ate," she laughed.

Marianne put one knee down and steadied herself while Sarah stepped up onto her thigh. Sarah was slightly taller than Marianne and even though she was neither thin nor fat, she seemed to be dense. Sarah's boot was hard on her thigh. The lawyer stretched, rising up on tiptoes, and murmuring something Marianne couldn't hear.

"Ouch," Marianne grunted. *Lay off the bagels, lady!*

A moment later Sarah hopped down. "Sorry about that. Kelly usually just lifts me up."

Marianne rubbed her leg and straightened. "I'm not as tall or as strong as she is. What's up there?"

"This." A dirty muslin pouch about three by four inches lay in Sarah's hand.

"What's that?"

"Last year's charm. I put in a fresh one."

"Everybody and their sister comes in here. How can you keep it from being removed?"

"I put a 'don't see me' spell on it. Works every time." She dropped the old bag in Marianne's hand. Four polished stones and a dusty crumble of herbs tumbled out, smelling faintly of Angelica, echinacea, and something sharp and sulfurous.

"Why do you need to put a charm here?"

"I'll tell you over lunch. Are you hungry?"

"I guess." It was early and Marianne had a dozen questions, starting with wanting to know more about the stone passageway.

They exited into sunlight and returned to the car.

In the early days, Crossfield had been a nexus of trade in lumber, iron ore, and goods, and carriage travel between western Connecticut and places like Albany, New York City and the Hudson River. At the crossroads, the Pheasant and Tankard Inn prospered and grew from a coach stop into a destination. It survived the Revolutionary war, and today it was a beautiful place for weddings and getaways. Three stories tall, it had a widow's walk supported by white columns, and black shutters framed each window.

They were led into a dining room with crisp white linen tablecloths and fall flower bouquets on each table. The maitre d' seated them, and a woman with a confident, possessive air approached their table.

"Sarah! It's wonderful to see you again. Tony told me you were coming." She leaned down and gave Sarah a quick peck on the cheek. Sarah gave her a brief one armed hug.

"Rebecca Stanton, this is Marianne Singleton," Sarah said.

"Nice to meet you." She shook Marianne's hand and turned back to Sarah. "Where's Kelly?"

"She's laid up with a broken leg but sends her regards. She loves your crab cakes, and I promised to bring her back soon."

"I'm so sorry to hear that! Wish her a speedy recovery for me. Let me get your server." Rebecca bustled off and sent a young man with menus.

Marianne looked at the selections and gulped. The food looked marvelous, but the prices made her blanch. Sarah's expression was mild and didn't seem phased by the double digit entrees. *A lawyer's salary must be much better than I thought. If I just have an appetizer, it won't go over twenty bucks. I'll have to push for fast food or mom and pop diners for the rest of the trip.*

"What looks good to you?" Marianne tried to gauge her companion's selections.

"I'll have the lobster bisque and scallops Florentine, I think. How about you?" She folded the menu.

"The soup and salad look good."

Sarah's mouth quirked into a small smile. "Surely you're hungrier than that. Kelly always eats like there's no tomorrow. Pick what you want."

"I can't afford to eat like this every meal," Marianne admitted with some embarrassment. She *had* eaten like this every meal when she'd lived with Geoffrey. But she'd reverted to much humbler fare since her divorce.

"Don't worry. We'll eat pizza and hamburgers everywhere else, I promise."

"If you say so." She chose the seared Ahi tuna.

As expected the meal was delicious and Marianne enjoyed it with guilty pleasure. It was a nice change from take out from the Maple Hill Co-op. "You said you'd explain what we were doing at the park."

Sarah carefully cut her three large scallops into bite sized pieces before answering. "I swapped out the old charm and put in a new one. It needs to be refreshed every year."

"Is that what you meant by laying charms?"

"Yes."

Before Marianne went to Scotland, Sarah had provided her with charms to protect her and Ruari from a possessive fey woman. "Are you guarding against fey beings? Is that what you meant by bad influences?"

"Not exactly. The chamber here has been deactivated and the charm keeps it that way."

"Deactivated? It looks like a glorified cold cellar."

"Some say that's what the stone chambers were built for. Others say they were ritual locations for Native Americans or Celts who arrived before the Mayflower."

"What do you think?"

"They're originally closer to sacred sites, though undoubtedly the people who came across them later used them for storage."

"So they're magical in some way?"

She nodded.

Just then Rebecca Stanton returned. "How was your meal, ladies?" She inquired with a pleasant smile.

Sarah returned her smile. "Delicious as always."

"Wonderful. I'll be at the hostess station whenever you're ready."

"Thank you." She turned to Marianne who reached for her wallet. "Not right now. We have work to do."

They left the table, taking their things, and Sarah led them to the stairs behind the hostess desk in the foyer. Marianne followed her up to the guest room area, down a pale yellow corridor to the far end.

Sarah loved this room. It had a simple, elegant dignity she'd always admired. A rich Wedgewood blue adorned the walls, and layered wood moldings framed a high ceiling. A delicate four poster bed and canopy drew the eye with a white quilted bedspread. The highboy dresser and secretary desk with a spindle backed chair completed the look. It was spotlessly clean and tidy. Three wingback armchairs were arranged in front of a small fireplace. A polished silver tray with a cut glass decanter and several glasses contained the tawny color of port.

Sarah drew the curtains, laying the room in twilight.

It was very weird having Marianne here instead of Kelly. Marianne wasn't a client, wasn't a paralegal, and certainly wasn't a lawyer. Her law firm occasionally hired outside experts like researchers to help with cases but not often. Sarah didn't have any friends who weren't in one of those categories, and she felt uncomfortable. The idea of being in close quarters with Marianne for a week made her edgy, though she wasn't sure why. Maybe because she seemed so unsuitable for this task much less becoming a protege.

Marianne was looking around the room. Pretty and petite, she was so feminine. She had no sharp edges and lacked Kelly's biting observations and earthy humor, much less her other skills. How was Sarah going to rely on this timid woman to watch her back?

One step at a time. Focus on the objective: protecting the county. Marianne might have hidden depths and pick up magic readily. At least she was okay with ghosts.

"We need to talk to some of my friends," Sarah said. "I'll introduce you but let me do the talking." She gestured to one of the chairs and said, "Do you like port?"

Marianne grimaced slightly. "It's not my favorite."

"Have a seat then. You don't have to drink."

They sat across from each other, Marianne looking uncertain. Sarah took several deep breaths and centered herself.

"Mr. & Mrs. Wallace, I request an audience with you," Sarah began. "Will you share a glass of port with me?"

She waited a minute or so and asked again. While she waited, she pondered what to do about Marianne. The woman had talent and unrecognized potential for magic use, but she'd been intimidated by George Rutherford, requiring Sarah's help to banish him from her house. Granted, George had been a piece of work, and Marianne was new to speaking with ghosts, but ghosts were just humans who'd transitioned to death. If Marianne was intimidated by overbearing people in general, it was going to be hard to teach her to be a guardian.

Gods, she wished Kelly were here instead.

Protecting Canopus County required balls and tenacity. Even though Kels couldn't see ghosts, she was the perfect person to watch Sarah's back while she focused on the unseen. Force of will alone went a long way to protecting the living from the dead and the county from worse entities than angry ghosts. Her magical backup was added fire power. Sarah had learned that the hard way.

Perhaps Sarah should've left Marianne out of this meeting, but being immersed was the best way to learn. Byron Mandell had taught her with a mix of rote exercises and throwing her in the deep end. It had worked for Sarah. Marianne was a grown woman, not the child Sarah had been when she started. She would be fine.

Sarah felt a presence gently pressing on her skin. Ghosts were a lot like soap bubbles, if you moved too fast, they vanished.

"Mr. & Mrs. Wallace, it's Sarah Landsman. I'd like a few minutes of your time, if I may."

Mr. Wallace's pale figure drew closer. He was a portly man, straining the buttons on his waistcoat, his hair pulled back in a queue. Mrs. Wallace was nearby, but she was more reserved, and Sarah rarely caught a glimpse of her. She heard Marianne's sharp intake of breath and glanced at her. She was doing the weird eyes-closed thing. Marianne claimed she could see ghosts better that way. Bizarre.

Sarah stood and gave him a short bow. "Good day to you, sir. May I introduce my colleague, Miss Singleton."

Marianne had the good sense to rise and nod at him in greeting. He bowed slightly at each of them.

Good day to you, ladies. His voice had been a rich baritone, but it had faded after death.

"The Stanton's have laid on good port for our meeting. Please have some." Mr. Wallace's hand swept through the glass on the table and picked up a ghostly version of the same. He raised the glass and Sarah toasted him. They both drank. Sarah noticed Marianne's fleeting grimace. Too bad. It was very good port. Sarah felt the mellow fire burn down her throat and appreciated that Tony and Rebecca were willing to spend $75 to keep this room ghost free for a year.

Thank the innkeepers for the excellent port, Mistress Landsman, Mr. Wallace said.

"I shall. I appreciate your coming. It's almost All Saint's Day."

Yes, we can feel the thinning of the veil.

"Thank you for keeping an eye on this part of the county for the last year."

It is our duty as American patriots to be ever vigilant against Loyalists and Monarchists who would degrade our freedoms and tie us back to the crown.

"Of course." Sarah sighed internally. The departed rarely understood the march of time and often were stuck in their own era. The fact that the Wallaces were willing to adapt a little made them useful allies. "Do you have anything to report from the last year? Any disturbances?"

He frowned. *Something has been growing since the end of summer, but I cannot tell from what direction. The portal here is still deactivated thanks to your intervention, so I don't think that is it.*

"What does it feel like?" She wished Mr. Wallace were more forthcoming.

He shook his head. *It feels like something is growing, pushing. It reminds me a little of the secret, house to house rumors of rebellion before the war.* He tilted his head to the side and listened. *Are you sure, my dear? Very well.* He turned back to

Sarah with an apologetic smile. *My lady wife wants me to tell you it feels like hunger.*

"Hunger?" She let her words hang in the air. Poetic descriptions were not particularly enlightening, and Sarah wished they would speak more plainly.

Yes, she can't be more specific. He shrugged. *Perhaps it is a female thing.*

Sarah bit back her annoyance at his casual sexism. "Please thank her for me. I respect her thoughts." She sipped again. "I've come to ask if you are willing to watch this corner of Canopus County again this year. Will you come to our aid if we should call?"

He nodded and drank his spectral port with apparent gusto. Sarah didn't know how but appreciated his ability to taste it. It made her job easier when she could offer such a gift.

We shall come to the defense of this young nation should the need arise.

"Thank you, Mr. & Mrs. Wallace."

He polished off his glass and set it on the tray before nodding to them both again and vanishing. Gone in a blink.

"Wow!" Marianne breathed, her face animated. "I've never met an eighteenth century ghost before! That is so cool. I wonder if they'd let me interview them? Think of the possibilities for historical research!"

Sarah chuckled. "I don't think you'd learn much. They're remarkably limited in their scope. Like most of us, they don't have much of an understanding beyond their day to day affairs."

"All the same." She shook her head, her eyes still shining with amazement.

That was the most interest Marianne had shown all day. Maybe Sarah needed to trigger her historical interest to get her to take an interest in magic?

"How did you meet the Wallaces?" Marianne asked curiously.

"Kelly and I stayed here several years ago and overheard a couple of guests complaining about their room. We figured it might be haunted and offered to stay there and see if we could suss out what was going on. Mr. Wallace appeared in the middle of the night shouting at us indignantly that we were in his bedroom. I explained the situation, and we came to an agreement. The Stantons keep the room in period furniture and only rent it out when all other rooms are full. They provide good port once a year, and the Wallaces agree to keep an eye on things in Crossfield."

"What was all that about something feeling like hunger and rumors?"

"Honestly, I have no idea. It may be nothing. I'll have to think about it." The most important news was that the portal remained deactivated, and the Wallaces were willing to continue at their post.

They were halfway back to Natalie when Marianne turned with a stricken look on her face. "Sarah, we forgot to pay our bill!"

"No worries. It's on the house."

CHAPTER 4

Marianne discreetly replaced the towel on the passenger seat. It fit the depression perfectly. Her butt was happier. She wished Sarah had said something earlier about the meal being gratis. She would have felt better about it. Sarah started the car and pulled into traffic.

"I'd really like to stop at the other two places that are on the Historic Register, if you don't mind," Marianne said.

"Sure, just don't take too long. We have a lot of miles to drive today."

They stopped at an eighteenth century fieldstone building that had been the residence of a well to do Revolutionary War family and then at a late nineteenth century post office. Marianne left her resumé in both places. Neither was hiring, and she hoped her papers would at least go into a file of prospects instead of the circular file at the side of the desk. She added their phone numbers to her list of people to follow up with next week.

After that they began driving through neighborhoods. They parked on a side street of clapboard houses, single family homes and duplexes with narrow spaces between them. Sarah opened the back hatch and pulled the larger box of linen bags to her. She handed Marianne several.

"What's in these?" Marianne asked, curious. She pulled the top open on one and saw four slivers of polished stones, and a mix of herbs and flowers.

"A piece of obsidian, sunstone, quartz, and chrysocolla. Plus a dried Angelica floweret, a little bergamot, a couple of cloves, some cumin, dill, and a bit of orange peel."

"I wondered why I kept thinking of tea and soup," Marianne said with a smile. She pulled the drawstring shut again.

"You'd be surprised how effective kitchen herbs are. Each bag is an amulet to protect the area from negative energies and connects to all the other amulets we leave behind."

"Where do you put them?"

"Wherever we can tuck one. At least one every few blocks or group of houses."

"Why doesn't someone just find them and throw them away or keep them?" She could just picture kids messing around or curious residents looking after they'd left.

"The 'don't-see-me' spell usually works."

Marianne looked up and down the block. "I don't see where…"

"Don't worry. I'll take care of these. You run interference for me. That's Kelly's job. She's really good at deflecting questions." Sarah took a handful of charms and began strolling down the block.

Run interference? Already Marianne felt like they were doing something slightly nefarious or illegal, like she was the lookout for a robbery or something. She followed Sarah several paces back trying to watch what she was doing and keep an eye out for pedestrians or people watching them from windows or passing cars.

We're just trying to protect the county. No one will be hurt by these charms if they find them or not. It just feels really weird.

A woman stared at her from a second story window. Marianne smiled and waved. The face pulled back from the sill. At least people are more embarrassed being caught watching than by staring. They walked several blocks. Marianne tried to look like she was just out for a stroll through the neighborhood on her way to somewhere else. She pulled out her phone and looked for a nearby café. That way if someone challenged her, she could say she was lost. She lost track of Sarah for a block.

"What are you doing?"

Marianne jumped. Sarah had come back. "Looking for a café or something in case someone asks. You're done?"

"Yup." They headed back to Natalie.

They drove a few other places within Crossfield, and Sarah declared them done, steering out of town. Marianne was surprised they bypassed the developments on the outskirts of town.

"What about them?"

"We'll catch them another time. We need to get to Centerburg today."

Centerburg was halfway back across the county. If Marianne had been driving, she would have done everything at the farthest east part of the county next to Connecticut and worked her way back towards Maple Hill on the shores of the Hudson, like working her way through the grocery store.

"Nice idea," Sarah replied. "Doesn't work that way. We're creating a spell to catch as many places as we can."

"But it seems so disorganized."

"Stop thinking books and research. Too linear. This is magic. It's organized in a different way. Trust me, it works."

They pulled Natalie onto the shoulder of the road between Crossfield and Centerburg twice more to leave a little charm bag at the base of a guard rail. Sarah murmured an incantation each time.

"How did you learn magic? Are you self-taught?" Marianne asked during a stretch when there was no internet and the silence between them grew uncomfortable.

"I was failing chemistry and not doing well in history in high school. My parents hired a tutor from a nearby college. They were afraid I wasn't going to get into Harvard."

"Did you get into Harvard?"

"Nope. My older brother did, and my parents thought it would be nice if we both went Ivy League." Her voice had an edge to it that made Marianne think Sarah was bitter about something.

"Ivy League isn't everything. There are lots of good colleges out there."

She snorted. "Yeah. But SUNY Binghamton didn't have the same cachet. Where did you go?"

"Vassar."

"Lucky you. If I'd gotten in, we might have met earlier."

"So how did tutoring in chemistry and history teach you magic? Did Binghamton have a minor in magic?" She was kidding but…

" 'Course not. My tutor was Byron Mandel. He was a fellow ghost speaker, and he taught me magic. I studied with him for two and a half years till I graduated and went to college. Then I studied on breaks and during the summers."

"How did you figure that out? I got the impression that you didn't share your ghost abilities with too many people."

Sarah smiled. "True. I gave myself away. There was a ghostly janitor who showed up periodically, and Byron happened to see him and was surprised. I said something about the janitor not hurting him, and we ended up in conversation about being able to see ghosts."

"Wow. So he taught you magic?"

"Yup, everything I know. And when he went to Europe to study more, he handed me and Kelly the Protector gig. I'd done it with him several times before, and it's been a cinch since then."

"Does Kelly do magic as well?"

"Not so much. She knows how to put charms together but doesn't really feel or channel magic. She watches my back when I'm doing magic."

"Cool." Well, at least Sarah knew what she was doing. If she'd had a good teacher, then Marianne was probably in good hands. She still wasn't too sure how magic worked but had seen enough success to believe that it did work. Maybe she'd learn the how's and why's.

When they pulled into the parking lot of Holy Family Catholic Church outside Centerburg, it was mid afternoon.

"What's here?" Marianne asked. She'd expected Sarah to be more Wiccan than Catholic.

"Father Williams," she answered. She got out and opened Natalie's rear hatch where she rummaged around in another box. Marianne heard the clink of bottles. "He's an ally of ours and is kind enough to bless some water for our work."

"That's unexpected." Marianne helped pull a couple dozen small bottles that formerly had held herbs and spices and put them in Sarah's capacious purse as directed. Interesting way to recycle. She closed the hatch gently, remembering Natalie was an old vehicle. The latch didn't catch, and the door popped open. She closed it more firmly, not wanting Sarah to admonish her for hurting her car. The latch still didn't take.

"Just slam it," Sarah called over her shoulder as she headed for the front door of the church.

"Sorry, Natalie," Marianne murmured as she slammed the door. The latch held. She hurried to catch up.

Holy Family Church was quiet in the early afternoon. There was a faint smell of votive candles and a little flicker of light from the right side transept. Marianne noted one person sitting quietly in a front pew. Churches always made her a little nervous. She'd attended church with her mother only on holidays and always felt vaguely guilty that she wasn't more observant. In the last few years she was aware that her mother had become more devout and was glad it worked for her. She hadn't personally felt the compulsion.

"I'm going to find Father Williams," Sarah said. "Stay here."

She headed toward a side door, leaving Marianne standing behind the last row of pews. The hush was heavy. She walked down one side, looking at the stained glass across the nave. Lots of colorful depictions of Biblical figures. A sound of muffled crying reached her ears. The vaulted ceiling made the source hard to locate. Automatically, she looked toward the figure kneeling in the front pew, running her hands through a rosary. Her head was bowed. Marianne gave her a wide berth for privacy's sake and headed back up the aisle.

The sound of crying was louder in the back, but she saw no one. She supposed sounds might carry easily from the front and tried not to listen. Strolling over to the marble baptismal font, she turned and looked back at the stained glass on the opposite side. Someone close by sniffed and gave a stifled sob. A woman in a white kerchief was sitting in the corner of the back pew. She must have slipped in when Marianne wasn't looking. She sounded like her heart was breaking.

Marianne couldn't help it. With a glance in the direction Sarah had disappeared, she knelt next to the crying woman and said, "Excuse me, is there anything I can do for you? Would you like me to find the Father for you?"

The woman looked up, tears streaking her cheeks. *Oh no, thank you. He won't see me.*

Really? That's just rude. Why wouldn't the Father tend to a parishioner who was clearly in distress? "Would you like me to just sit with you? My friend will be back soon, but I can sit with you until then."

She gave Marianne a watery smile. *That would be really nice. Thank you.*

Marianne settled herself on the pew next to her. "I'm Marianne by the way."

Astrid Delaney. Nice to meet you.

She put out her hand, and Marianne felt a chill touch her palm. The hairs on her scalp prickled. She radiated cold the way Jason did. Perhaps this was why the good Father wouldn't 'see' her.

"Astrid, how long have you been coming here?" Marianne asked gently.

Since I was a little girl. Are you new here?

"I'm just visiting for today. May I ask why you're crying?"

Tears welled in her eyes again. *My little boy Benny is missing.*

"That's awful! What happened?"

We went to the park together after church just like always. He was playing on the swings and running around with some other children. I looked away for just a minute. When I looked back he was gone. I swear it was only for a minute! I looked all over the place, but he'd just vanished.

"Did any of the other kids see what happened?"

One of them said Benny had gone with a man, and they drove away.

"Did you report it to the police?"

Of course. They looked everywhere, but the kids could only say the man was tall and drove a dark colored car. There was no ransom, no demands. He just vanished. They kept the case open for ages, but there were no leads.

Marianne's heart twisted in sympathy. "How old is he?"

Benny's five. She began sobbing quietly again.

"I'm so sorry." How could the police give up on a child abduction so easily? When had this happened? Marianne couldn't recall any recent news about missing children. If Astrid Delaney was a ghost, she might have a skewed sense of time the way Jason had when she'd met him. He thought he'd been hitching for a ride for a few hours when in fact he'd been out on the road for four years.

"Mrs. Delaney, this sounds like an odd question, but what year is it?"

Astrid gave her a confused look, like Marianne was out of her mind.

"Please humor me," Marianne said with a little smile.

I-it's 1953, of course.

Well, Benny Delaney was either alive and very old by now, or he'd met his end soon after his abduction. That's how those things usually went. What chance did Marianne have of finding out what had happened to him? She didn't have friends in the police department in Centerburg or know any detectives. But maybe she could call and find out.

"Mrs. Delaney, I hate to tell you this, but it's quite a bit later than that. It's 2009."

Shock and disbelief broke through her tears. *That's ridiculous! Why, it's 1953, of course. Ask anybody!*

Marianne waved her hand in a calming gesture. "You've been coming to this church for a long time right? Maybe every week? Are there changes to the church that you can't explain? Carpeting, the staff, Father Williams?"

Astrid looked down at her hands. They were very pale in the filtered daylight. *I guess, there might be. Father O'Malley was helping me for a long time but he left. Then there were other priests, but they never seemed to have the time for me. Father Williams gives a good sermon, but he's very busy.*

Making up her mind, Marianne said, "I'm not sure what I can do for you, but I can look into where the case is at and get back to you."

Astrid dabbed her damp cheeks with the heel of her hand. *He's been gone for months but the police have no leads. I don't have any money to hire a detective to keep looking for him.*

"I'm not actually a detective. I'm a historian. I'll look into it and get back to you. Promise."

A look of dawning hope lit up her face and her eyes welled with fresh tears. *That would be wonderful. I miss him so much. He must be so scared without me.*

"Mrs. Delaney, I'm kind of busy this week, but I'll put it at the top of my list for next week. I swear." If no one would hire her as a historian, she could do this in the interim. She'd deal with how she was going to get paid later.

You're so kind, Marianne. God bless you!

A throat cleared nearby and Marianne looked up. Sarah stood with a faintly exasperated look on her face, shaking her head slightly. "Father Williams has the goods. C'mon."

"Mrs. Delaney, I have to—" Marianne began, but Astrid had vanished, leaving traces of a cold spot behind.

"That's not going to work out," Sarah said flatly as they headed for a side door where the church offices were.

"What do you mean?"

"You know that most dead people who hang around have unfinished business."

"Yes."

"You can't help them all."

"I don't need to help all of them. I don't know what I can do for her, but I'm willing to give it a try. She's so scared and sad. Why wouldn't I help her?"

Sarah frowned and said, "We'll talk about this later. Right now we have to pick up the holy water before the Father's next appointment at three."

Father Williams was short, with neatly combed black hair and a homely face. His genuine smile of pleasure transformed his features. "Miss Singleton, it's wonderful to meet another person doing the Lord's work."

Marianne felt embarrassed heat rise into her face. "It's nice to meet you as well. I don't—I mean, I'm not a—"

"Regular church goer?" He laughed. "You can still do the Lord's work without sitting in a pew every Sunday. Sarah tells me you have a lot of promise. This," he gestured to two gallon-sized milk jugs filled with water on his desk, "is the least I can do to help you out."

Marianne nodded. They spent the next twenty minutes transferring consecrated water into the herb and spice jars. Sarah put them back into her bag and thanked the Father.

"May I offer you a quick blessing?" He asked.

"Certainly." Sarah nodded.

Marianne awkwardly clasped her hands in front of her and bowed her head. Sarah did the same.

Father Williams intoned, "Oh Lord, your agents come in many forms and guises. Please look after these two women as they work to keep the forces of darkness at bay. Walk beside them as they go and bless their way." He recited the Lord's Prayer and finished with, "In the name of the Father, the Son, and the Holy Ghost, amen."

"Amen," they murmured in response.

Marianne felt her spirits lighten as they returned to the car. She wondered if Father Williams considered ghosts 'forces of darkness' and what he would say if he knew a ghost sat in the back pew every Sunday. Sarah stowed her precious water bottles in another little box in the back.

How were all these pieces going to fit together to protect an entire county of people? Marianne wondered.

"You can't help every needy soul you come across," Sarah said as she pulled the old white Volvo out of the parking lot and began driving down the streets of the nearby developments. Pumpkins and jack-o-lanterns clustered on porches and piles of raked leaves lined the roadside.

"Her little boy was abducted, and they never found him. She's been looking for him since 1953."

"All the more reason to just encourage her to pass over. He's probably already there waiting for her."

"Maybe," Marianne said stubbornly. "It won't hurt for me to look into it. I can do a little research and see what I can find out. I can come back and tell her."

Sarah shook her head. "Do you know what the number one killer of psychics and clairvoyants is?"

"No, other than you, I don't know any real ones."

"Cancer. Autoimmune diseases like MS."

"Really? Why?" That was not the answer she'd expected. Interacting with ghosts gave you cancer? That was a new one on her.

"Because they spend so much energy they don't leave enough for themselves. Their personal energy runs down trying to help others, and that leaves them vulnerable to disease."

Marianne was taken aback.

"That's why I protect myself and ignore a lot of needy dead people. They'll eventually cross over on their own or not. I want to be around when I'm ninety, not die by the time I'm fifty."

"Sarah, her child was five! She spent the rest of her life in agony wondering what happened to him. I have to do what I can."

The lawyer shook her head. "You can't be too sentimental in this job. You're going to have to learn to be really selective and choose your battles."

How could Sarah wanted her to ignore someone like Astrid Delaney? What was so much more important? This magic spell she said they were casting seemed to take only a week to do. Besides she'd responded to Marianne's haunted house problem. How was that different?

"Sarah, why did you help me? If you're supposed to conserve your energy, why did you bother to help me?"

"You were local. It was a fairly standard haunting. And you did most of the work finding out who the spirits were. All I had to do was help you confront them. Digging into this woman's problems will take a lot more time, and you may never be able to solve it. She might end up haunting you personally, pestering you to help her or getting angry if you can't."

"Sarah, I'm not employed right now. All I have is time. If she ends up hanging around, I'll deal with that later."

"Whatever," Sarah scoffed and muttered something that sounded like, "such a soft touch."

Marianne was determined to help Astrid whatever it took.

They pulled off the road. Sarah said in a more normal tone, "Will you help me find and replace the next couple of bags?"

"Fine." Still fuming, she grabbed three cloth pouches out of the box and tucked them into her jacket pocket. "Where are we looking?"

They were in a stretch of road between two developments. Sarah cast around, looking like she'd dropped her wallet. Eventually, she found a little cairn of rocks behind a tree. She unstacked the rocks down to the dirt. There was nothing under it.

"Huh," she said.

"Is that where you put it last year?"

"Uh huh." She scanned the area and said, "Let's move it there," and pointed to a different tree on the other side of the road. "Maybe that'll keep the little buggers from stealing my stuff." They carried the stones across and formed a new cairn with a bag at the bottom. Sarah murmured a chant under her breath.

"What are you saying?"

" 'By Earth and Sky and Fire and Water, protect Canopus for another year.' It activates the amulet. Here, can you feel it?" She grabbed Marianne's hand and pressed it against the stones.

The cold edges of the stone pressed against her palm, but she felt nothing special. "What am I supposed to feel?"

"It's a little different for everyone. Sometimes it's a color or an impression in your mind, or a vibration, or a sound, maybe even a taste. It takes practice to feel it and not everyone can. You're sensitive to spirits and felt the vibe at the Maple Hill cemetery doorway. I assumed you'd be able to feel this as well."

She shook her head. "Nothing, sorry."

Sarah stood and wiped her hands on her pants. "Keep trying. You'll get it."

They returned to the car and got moving again.

Marianne's stubbornness turned into questions. "What exactly is magic? I picture Harry Potter and fantasy novels. But what you're doing doesn't fit that."

Sarah turned onto another road before answering. "Physics tells us everything is made up of atoms and molecules, and they vibrate at different frequencies, right?"

"Yeah."

"Magic is just the word for being able to manipulate that energy using your mind and your own energetic field."

"That's possible?"

"Absolutely. Is it easy? No. It takes practice and focus. Some people have a leg up in being able to see the energetic fields around everything. They see auras, for instance. Sometimes little kids can see ghosts because they haven't been told they can't or shouldn't. Usually, they close that sense down if it becomes too frightening or the adults around them convince them it's bad. Sometimes an older person gets their senses opened to energy fields through an extraordinary event like being struck by lightning or having a near-death experience. I'm not sure where you fit in."

Where did she fit in? The only catastrophic event had been being divorced from her horrible ex. And having that spark jump between her and Ruari when they first shook hands. Ruari's fey artistic partner had intimated that she'd given him the ability to see auras, but the spark between him and Marianne had catalyzed it somehow. Maybe that spark had catalyzed her senses as well, like a lightning strike?

I wonder if he could do magic? Maybe he should be here instead of me.

Seeing ghosts she was sure of. That had happened often enough and been enough in her control that she believed it. Manipulating the energetic vibrations of the world around her was another thing entirely. Ruari could see auras. He'd described them enough to her that she believed that was possible. She couldn't see them, though. If she couldn't see what she was supposed to learn about, how could she manipulate it?

"You're awfully quiet," Sarah said.

"Just trying to digest what you said. So, I get that living things could have energy fields representing the atoms they're made of sort of jumping around. How come people have different colored auras then? Shouldn't they have the same because they're humans? And then animals and maybe plants would have their own auras?"

"The human body is just one part of the aura. The mind and its emotions affect the vibration rate and thus the aura color. So you can see auras?" Sarah sounded interested.

"No, Ruari can. I never really tried."

"When did that happen?" Sarah sounded surprised.

"I thought I told you?"

"No."

"Oh, sorry. His fey partner gave him that ability. He's still figuring it out."

"Huh." Sarah stored that away for later. "Maybe you can learn too. For now, you spend a lot of time reading other people's emotions, right? Someone who's happy feels different from someone who's depressed or secretive or confused, right?"

Marianne nodded.

"Auras are just a visualization of that. Like I said before, magic feels different to each person. You just have to be aware and look for the new feeling. When we stop for tonight, I'll give you some exercises to help you focus on it okay?"

"Okay."

The rural suburbs had given way to the old mill town of Centerburg. Strip malls on the outskirts surrounded a familiar mix of new and old architecture. Overall, it was more run down and industrial looking than Crossfield. Sarah piloted Natalie to a quiet side street where a clapboard, two-story building proclaimed 'County Records.'

They alighted and Marianne grabbed a copy of her resumé. It was nearly five o'clock, and she hoped to find someone before they closed. The main window had a high counter with a small office behind it.

An older woman with a beehive hairdo looked up. "May I help

you?"

"I hope so. I'm job hunting and wondered if I could leave my resumé here?"

The woman glanced to a large clock on the wall and said in a bored, end-of-the-day voice, "Is there a particular department you're looking for?"

"I'm not sure. I'm a historian. I do research. I specialize in the mid-eighteen hundreds to early nineteen hundreds."

The woman nodded at the counter. "You can leave it there. I'll check around and see who might be interested."

Marianne gave her a polite smile. "Thank you, I appreciate it." Well, that was probably going to hit the can as soon as she left. Oh well. She should have done more research for Centerburg and found a particular person to leave it with. Maybe next week.

Out on the sidewalk, Sarah was waiting for her, arms folded, leaning against Natalie's hood. "All good?"

She shrugged.

"Great. Next stop: Centerburg Cemetery. I want you to meet some more of my ghost allies."

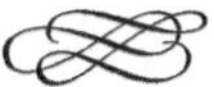

CHAPTER 5

They drove to the edge of town where a sizable cemetery lay. Sarah parked and opened Natalie's rear hatch. She rummaged in a box that looked like a thrift store donation bin and pocketed a few items.

"Grab a couple of charm bags would you?" she asked Marianne and walked away.

Suppressing her irritation that Sarah was in such a hurry that she couldn't wait a couple of seconds, Marianne hastened after her. Long shadows darkened the cemetery, marking the impending twilight. It was bigger than the Maple Hill Cemetery, surrounded by trees and full of gravestones. Marianne shivered. It didn't feel nearly as personal and homey. Out of habit, she paused long enough to read a few dates and names. Mid-twentieth century mainly, and a mix of surnames from Anglo ones like Smith to Farjoo, Gonzalez, and Mancini. The usual polyglot of immigrants. She looked up and angled toward Sarah.

She'd stopped in front of a headstone from the 1970s: "Trompenter, Daniel and Lisa and their beloved son, Richard." Marianne stood slightly behind her mentor and waited.

Sarah said, "Mr. and Mrs. Trompenter, this is Sarah Landsman. I ask you to speak with me, please." She stood quietly waiting for them to manifest.

Marianne blew out a breath and pushed aside her frustration, opening her senses to whatever ghostly presences might be nearby. Minutes passed as the shadows lengthened and the light steadily dimmed. She scanned the area, searching for anything. A little flicker of something a couple of rows away caught her attention. She closed her eyes to see it better.

Sarah sensed it as well and placed a handful of silk flowers at the foot of the grave, stuck a small American flag next to it, and put a little purple matchbox truck on the top of the headstone.

The flicker of presence strengthened, and Marianne saw a white mist coalesce and drift closer. It looked like a slowly flaming column, not like a person at all. The hairs on her arms prickled, and she tensed. The ghosts she'd seen before were more human looking, and this was a first for her.

Sarah said, "Thank you for coming. I hope you've been well this year. I've come to ask you to renew your offer to watch over this corner of Canopus County."

Marianne was unprepared for the wash of emotion that blew over her, and she gasped. Fear followed by anger. A fast gabble of unintelligible words from which she picked out, *...them...no... us alone!*

The mist stopped three headstones away.

Sarah seemed surprised as well. "What's wrong? Please tell me! I can help you."

A male voice said clearly, *Go away!* accompanied by a flare of anger. The mist solidified.

Alarm bells began ringing in Marianne's head. "Sarah, I don't think they want to talk to us. We should leave." She pulled the lawyer's arm.

She pulled her arm free of Marianne's grasp. "No, I'm not leaving until they tell me what's going on. Please tell me why you're upset. I can help you."

An indistinct man's shape appeared. He was tall and built like a line backer. Marianne took a step back. Menace filled his form. He was protecting his family with every fiber of his being, and Sarah was his enemy.

"Sarah," she hissed. "Let's go."

Reluctantly, Sarah said, "Let me leave you a charm of protection at least." She bent and pulled a little white cloth bag out of her pocket. Scraping a shallow hole in front of the gravestone, she buried it with a murmur of "By Earth and Sky and Fire and Water, protect the Trompenters."

Marianne caught a flicker of movement from the corner of her eye and saw his arm draw back. She grabbed Sarah's jacket shoulder and pulled her as the arm swung forward. The ghostly fist missed Sarah's head by a hair's breadth, but a gust of wind sprang up in its wake. Daniel's form twisted and melted into a dust devil swirl that flung the silk flowers several headstones away.

Together they hurried away from the graveside and back toward the car, shoulders hunched under the shower of small pebbles, bits of leaves, and grass. Something sharp struck the back of Marianne's head.

"Ow!" She yelped. She glanced back and saw the little purple matchbox truck lying on the ground behind her.

They made it back to the car and slammed the doors, grateful to be inside.

"What just happened?" Marianne exclaimed, rubbing the back of her head. "He wasn't very friendly at all!"

"That was strange," Sarah said absently, staring out at the darkening cemetery the way they'd come.

"No, that was frightening," Marianne corrected.

Sarah started Natalie's engine. "Well, too late to do anything more here. We'll have to come back tomorrow."

"I don't think he'll feel any different tomorrow."

"No, I mean to lay some charms. It's not particularly safe to do this work after dark if we don't have to." She put the car into drive and turned to Marianne. "You want Mexican or Greek? I know a great little diner here."

She might be new to ghosts and magic, but Marianne was dead certain something was very wrong.

❧

They got souvlaki and gyros at Julie's Diner in Centerburg proper. Marianne was full of questions and tired of being put off. The diner was crowded and noisy, but their little booth was insulated by the red vinyl seats.

"Sarah, what is it you're not telling me? Surely the visit with the Trompenters wasn't what you expected."

"Did I tell you they were killed with their little boy in a car crash? Their older daughter, Carly, survived and was raised by Lisa's sister. I met Carly through work. She was consumed with survivor's guilt. So, here's a time I helped someone. I was able to tell Carly her family was fine. They were waiting for her to live her life, and when it was her time to go, they'd cross over together. Daniel and Lisa were grateful to be able to ease their daughter's pain and agreed to help watch over this corner of Canopus for me. They've been doing it for about four years. I'm not sure why they changed their minds."

Marianne widened her eyes. "Couldn't you feel it? Something scared them badly. Daniel was protecting his family from whatever it was."

Sarah's brows contracted in a frown. "But why didn't he just tell me what it was?"

"He didn't seem overly articulate in the moment. I don't have a lot of ghost experience, but I've never heard of a ghost who was scared of something." She took a bite of gyro. "What would scare a ghost?"

Sarah, apparently lost in thought, didn't reply. She ate her souvlaki, mopping up tzatziki sauce with pita.

Anger at being ignored or not taken seriously welled up inside her again. Geoffrey had done this to her time and again.

64

Only instead of feeling small, right now she was mad. This day had not gone at all like she'd planned. She'd gotten a couple of resumés out, but no networking had happened. Sarah had been maddeningly vague any time she asked questions. She'd done some research, but Sarah hadn't cared about the outcome. Worst of all, Sarah seemed to be comparing her to Kelly and coming up short. The only half positive thing was meeting Astrid Delaney. At least if Marianne was able to find out what happened to her and her child, Astrid would care. If it worked out, maybe Marianne could open a new business focused on helping ghosts. The hell with Sarah's so-called warnings.

She could have an office and devote her historical research skills to solving ghost problems. Maybe she could even work with the police in some capacity. That would be cool. She'd have to find someone who believed her ability to communicate with the departed, though.

"Marianne?" Sarah interrupted her thought stream.

"What?" She heard the irritated edge to her voice and tried to quell it.

"You asked if there were things that could scare ghosts. The answer is yes. I just don't know if that's what's going on. I need to check on a few things tomorrow and give you a clearer answer then. We have to check into a motel for the night. Are you done?"

"What kinds of things could scare ghosts? Are we talking demons, poltergeists, devils, monsters, djinns, something Native American? I need to know. Maybe I can do some research."

Sarah frowned, looking distracted. "Demons maybe. Poltergeists are just really riled up ghosts. There's no record of djinns in the area. Maybe something Native American, I just don't know what."

While it wasn't super helpful, Marianne at least had something to go on. "Okay, I'll look some of that up."

As they climbed back into Natalie, Sarah said, "Don't worry about it until I know more. Kelly and I have protected the county for the last five years, and the spell has been very effective. I have to assume that we're on track. As long as we do everything in order like we always have, it'll be fine. We have to teach you how to feel magic so you can start using it. That will be the best way you can help me."

They checked in to the two-story Canopus Motor Inn not far from the diner, got their keys, and brought their suitcases in for the night. There were two full-sized beds with garish geometric bedspreads and a faint smell of cigarettes. Marianne had just dumped her bag on a bed when her phone rang. It was Ruari. Sarah had gone into the bathroom and shut the door so she was temporarily alone.

"Hi, Ruari."

"Mahri, how are you doing? I've been wanting to call you all day."

His concern washed over her in a welcome wave. She sighed. "I'm okay. We're in Centerburg at the Canopus Motor Inn for tonight."

"How was your day? Did you get some resumés out?"

"A couple." He'd warned her that Sarah wasn't being entirely truthful. Would he just say, 'told you so'? She really didn't want to hear it. "We went to Crossfield and checked out the library and historical society there. Sarah tells me we'll hit all the major places. We've laid a bunch of charms in residential areas. I'm supposed to start learning magic tonight."

"Wow, that sounds cool. Oscar's good. He's right here. He misses you. I miss you."

"I wish I was at home instead of in a hotel. Thanks for looking after him. At least my guys are keeping each other company. How was work?"

"Same old, same old. I saw Erin today. She's having some trouble—"

Sarah had stepped out of the bathroom and pulled some things out of her bag. She looked pointedly at Marianne and made hand motions that Marianne took to mean cut the phone call, they needed to talk.

"I'm sorry, Ruari," she broke in, feeling bad for interrupting. "I have to go. Time for magic lessons 101. Tell Erin I said hi."

"Oh, okay." He sounded disappointed. "Can't wait to see you when you get back."

"Me too. I'll try to stop in a thrift store or two for a costume in blue and green. Talk to you tomorrow."

"Bye."

She appreciated his concern. To be honest, she was worried about her increasingly weird situation, too. If it got too bad, she could probably call him, and he'd come get her. Sarah could finish the spell by herself.

"How's Ruari?"

"He's fine."

"Good. Are you ready to learn some magic?" Sarah asked. On the dresser stood an odd assortment of objects including a charm pouch, some loose gemstones, and the metal toolbox.

She shrugged. "I guess."

Sarah's brows drew down over her hawkish nose. "That's not very enthusiastic. Look, I need your help. So you're going to have to fast track this one."

Marianne sighed and tried to put aside her jumble of feelings. If there were demons or other monsters involved, it behooved her to be more focused. "Okay. Show me what to do."

"Remember I told you that magic was just the name for manipulating the energy of objects and people, right? The first thing you have to do is be able to sense it. Here." She handed Marianne a charm pouch like all the others they'd placed that day. "This is a spell component. It has gemstones and herbs in it. Hold it in your hand. Focus on it. Stare at it. Feel it."

Marianne sat on the edge of the bed and held the bag in her hand. It was made of plain cotton and had a very slight weight to it. Other than that, it didn't feel or look like anything. She tried opening her mind to the possibilities the way she did when she was looking for ghosts. She closed her eyes and stared at her hand for about thirty seconds. Nothing. No matter how she looked at it, it was just an inert cloth bag. She could feel Sarah's eyes on her.

"I'm sorry. I've got nothing," she finally said.

"Okay. Now, I'm going to activate the charm and stir things up a bit magically speaking." Sarah plucked the bag out of her hand and held it cupped in her own hands. She closed her eyes, a slight frown creasing her brow, and murmured, "By Earth and Sky, Fire and Water, wake up." After a few seconds she handed it carefully back to Marianne. "Try again."

She held the little cotton bag in her hands again and stared at it. She closed her eyes and stared at it again.

"People feel magic differently," Sarah said. "It might be a visual thing, a color, a shimmer. For others it's a tone or a hum. For me, the object looks blurry. The more magically activated it is, the fuzzier it looks."

Marianne tried imagining if she heard a sound or saw a color or felt a taste. *A synesthete would probably be good at this*, she thought. After several more minutes she sighed and put the bag in Sarah's lap. "I don't feel anything. I understand ghosts, but this magic thing is beyond me."

Sarah took the bag and laid it on the dresser. She picked up a polished black stone that Marianne guessed was obsidian. "Try this." Sarah again murmured her incantation and 'woke up' the stone.

It lay cold in her palm. Nothing happened. They tried an assortment of objects including a black lacquer box that had come from inside the tool box. Sarah assured her the items were fully activated and were positively blurry with magic.

Ghosts sometimes felt like a buzzing in Marianne's ear, and she often read their emotions. But magical objects were complete blanks. After an unproductive hour, she just felt tired and stupid.

Sarah tucked them all away in her bag again. "Don't worry," she said, sounding upbeat in a forced way. "It takes time. Just keep at it, and you're sure to get the hang of it. When we're driving around tomorrow, keep trying to feel it. You'll get it."

"Here," Sarah handed her a cloth pouch that was substantially heavier than the others. "This is a protective amulet for you. You can wear it around your neck under your shirt or keep it in your pocket. It's got obsidian, turquoise, sunstone, selenite, and garnet for elemental protection. Angelica and plantain leaves for protection, and echinacea to power it all. I supercharged it for you," she said with a genuine smile. "Put it under your pillow. Maybe you'll dream about it."

"How does it work?"

"When it gets warm, it's warning you that Shadow People and other negative entities are nearby. It will provide protection against them as well. But it's like a shield, the longer it gets hammered on, the weaker it gets."

"Thanks."

Marianne brushed her teeth and climbed into bed. The bag felt lumpy under her pillow, and she surreptitiously put it on the bedside table. Sarah turned off the lights. Marianne lay in the dark listening to Sarah toss and turn in the other bed. She held Ruari's little cat carving in one hand and wished she was at home in her own bed with Oscar's comforting weight next to her. She missed Ruari's solid warmth. Guilt for cutting him off was a cold companion.

What was she doing in a motel far from home? She'd handed out a whopping four resumés since eight o'clock this morning. Over a dozen more sat in her backpack. Granted, it was unrealistic to imagine that Canopus had that many places she could offer her services as a historian, but she'd been hopeful. Sarah had no intention of helping her find a job. Instead, she had this whole other agenda. Magic spells and negative energies, whatever those were.

Sarah came across as serious and fact-based because of her job as a lawyer. That made her magic and ghost side seem more legitimate. What if Sarah was just a nut case? Or worse, making fun of her?

I could just call a cab tomorrow. Tell Sarah I'm sorry, but I can't do this. I need to focus on getting a paying job. Then I can be home and sleep in my own bed tomorrow night. Feeling like she had a solution, Marianne drifted off to sleep.

A jumble of images from the day passed by her waiting eyelids: cars, roads, hundreds of little white cotton bags, a dark opening framed by stones. Finally, she was walking through a meadow with Oscar by her side. She had bare feet and her pants were rolled up. She watched a dark red spot on her shin grow from pencil dot size to pea-sized. She must have nicked her self on something. She leaned over to wipe the blood off, but Oscar batted at the now grape-sized blob with his paw, and it dropped into the grass.

"Ew, a tick!" Oscar said in disgust.

Another dot of blood on her ankle rapidly swelled in size and dropped off.

"You should be wearing long pants and shoes!" He chided.

She pushed her pant legs down and realized there was another tick on the back of her hand. It fell off before she could knock it off. Something gave her a little pinch on the back of her neck and a hard little blue-gray bead fell into her hand. Her skin prickled all over. Revulsion coursed through her, and she thrashed wildly trying to brush every inch of herself off at once.

A hard jerk brought her awake. The motel room was dark, lit only by the streetlight outside. Sarah made a slow buzzing rasp in the other bed.

Dreaming of ticks counted as a nightmare in her book. It also had that edge of hyper-realism she associated with her clairvoyant dreams. Rats. She'd really enjoyed not having harrowing dreams over the last couple of weeks. She sighed. Okay, what do ticks mean in dream language? Is this supposed to be literal ticks or figurative ticks? Sarah had said something about going camping. Maybe she was supposed to watch out for ticks while camping? Wasn't it too cold for them at this time of year?

She got out her phone and looked it up. Ticks were not active below forty degrees Fahrenheit. That was good news. She checked the weather. If she stayed with Sarah, they'd be camping in temperatures in the high 30s. Yuck. Dammit, she hated being cold. Another reason to leave and go home tomorrow. Not feeling sleepy, she searched for information on demons (terrifying) and Native American legends for the area (frustratingly vague). Eventually, she felt her eyes burning and laid her phone down.

CHAPTER 6

$\mathcal{A}$ cold, gray drizzle accompanied them to Julie's café where they ate a hearty breakfast. They'd checked out of the motor inn already, and Marianne was trying to figure out how to bring up her decision to go home. Sarah was on her second cup of coffee.

"I always thought you were a tea drinker," Marianne said.

"This is a coffee trip," Sarah replied.

Marianne stared at her generic black tea that tasted like it had been made in the coffee pot. Maybe actual coffee wasn't such a bad idea. But it would make her heart race and feel like she was jumping out of her skin for the next six hours, so it probably wasn't worth it.

"Sarah, I've been thinking," she began. The waitress stopped by and laid their checks face down on the table before moving on. "I really need to concentrate on getting a paying job before winter. My savings are running out, and I'm going to end up waiting tables if I don't get something soon. You have this whole trip down to an art form and don't really need me. I don't want to derail you by asking you for a ride back to Maple Hill, so I could just call a cab from here."

Sarah stared at her, the light glinting off her glasses,

obscuring her eyes. She waited a moment or two before saying, "Is that it? Anything more?"

Marianne shook her head.

"First of all, I did hear you about your job needs. I'll help you work on that next week, make some phone calls. Sometimes other law firms need research done, and you don't have to be a paralegal to do it. My word will be enough, if they need someone. It wouldn't be steady, but it would be something. Second, this is actually a two person job. That's why Kelly and I normally do it together. She watches my back. Third, you can't leave without destroying the work we've done so far. Like it or not, you, me, and Natalie are all integral parts of the spell. If you leave, I have to start again, and I don't have time for that. So, stay. Please."

Marianne sat back in her booth seat in shock. All Sarah had to do was make a few phone calls? Why hadn't she offered that before? She'd promised history work on the trip and so far hadn't been interested in the outcome. A slow burn ignited.

"So I have to keep going because now I'm a spell component?" She narrowed her eyes. "Because you need me to watch your back?"

"Yes."

"I told you when the Trompenters were getting angry, and you pretty much ignored me. I can't do magic. What am I watching your back on? How can I possibly be helpful to you? What more are you not telling me about?"

Sarah pursed and moved her lips like she was rolling a hard candy around her mouth while she thought. "I promise I will tell you everything when I figure it out. But I need you to keep going until we're done with the project. I don't have time to start the whole thing again from Maple Hill. Even if you don't pick up magic this week, you can still be a huge asset to me. It's complicated. And dangerous. Please?"

"That's not good enough! I looked up stuff on demons. If you think they're involved, that's way out of my league. I don't want to have anything to do with that!"

Sarah put up her hands. "I don't think that's it at all."

Marianne raised her eyebrows.

"I truly don't think that's the problem," she repeated.

"Well, that's good. I also looked up some regional Native American lore, and it's really vague except some stuff about an evil twin from the creation myth."

"Thank you for looking that up. I don't think that's it either, though. I'm hoping my contacts at the next stop will have a better idea. Will you stay with me?" Sarah looked surprisingly vulnerable. "I think you can be helpful to me. That's why I asked you."

"Fine." Marianne exhaled in frustration. She'd give it another day. She could call Ruari later if she felt like she was in danger.

Marianne made one last trip to the restroom before getting into the car. Her solemn, unhappy expression stared at her from the mirror. She pulled out her phone, ready to find a cab company and call it anyway. She didn't want to bother Ruari at work, though she was pretty sure he'd come.

Screw Sarah. I should just go. Starting over is probably easier than she's letting on.

But, she said she'd make some calls. Sarah Landsman's word would be enough to get her some work. She said she needed me. *Please.* Twice. There was an edge of desperation to that word. Complicated and dangerous. How can I possibly help? Sarah was always so in control and in charge.

Marianne sighed and put her phone away.

I'm such a sucker for someone in trouble.

The old white Volvo needed two tries to turn over, and Sarah muttered, "C'mon *ma belle*. We have to do this." The engine finally engaged with a thrum. "Natalie doesn't like the dampness," she explained in response to her passenger's worried expression. "We're thinking of retiring her to Arizona."

All the beautiful colors of yesterday had been leached out by a damp chill that presaged the coming of winter. The flowery herb smell inside the car was fainter in the chill. They returned to the cemetery and placed charms there. Daniel Trompenter and his family were completely absent. Marianne did her best to feel something in the little charm bags, but she might as well have been tossing letters in a mail slot for all the feels they gave her.

They drove through the neighborhoods on the north side of Centerburg, leaving little protective charms behind. There were fewer old ones to recover, in fact only three, compared to the dozen or so they left.

"I thought you said your charms were safe. You made them invisible or something," Marianne commented.

"I do. Huh," Sarah said.

Marianne turned to her. "What is going on? First you said it was a cake walk. Now you're saying it's dangerous. Which is it?"

Sarah cleared her throat. "Normally it is pretty easy. We chat with my ghost contacts, and they agree to watch over Canopus for another year. Kelly and I lay charms across the county to protect people. We visit a dozen or so stone chambers and change out the closing charms. Then we adjourn to the Maple Hill Cemetery where we have a nice bonfire, activate the magical network, and close the spell. Then we drink mulled wine and call it good for another year."

"And that's it?"

"It's supposed to be."

"But something is wrong." Marianne held up her hand and ticked things off on her fingers. "Ghosts are missing from Maple Hill. The Wallaces talked about hunger and rumors. The Trompenters threw us out of their cemetery. You're missing charms. And my dream about blood sucking ticks which makes no sense. That doesn't sound normal to me."

Sarah looked at her sharply. "You dreamed about ticks?"

"Big, gross ticks. It felt like a true dream, but I have no idea what it means."

Sarah blew out a frustrated breath. "I agree with you that something is wrong. Believe me, I've been thinking a lot about it. I don't know what it means yet. All we can do is keep going forward and hope something ties all this together."

Not super helpful, Marianne thought, but at least Sarah had been honest about being mystified. "Maybe we should take some time to figure out what's going on and regroup before we go on."

"The veil is thinnest on Halloween night. We have to finish the protective spell by then or the county is defenseless, magically speaking."

Marianne blew out a frustrated breath. "Where are we headed?"

"Turner's Hope Mine."

At last, a chance to share her knowledge. She reached for her pack. "Great, what do you need to know about it?"

"Hold that thought."

They drove north and connected up with Route 401, the east-west road that crossed the county on the north side. Heading west toward the river, it was another twenty minutes before they turned off the road at a little brown state park sign that said, "Turner's Pond. Public boat launch." They bumped down a potholed road that became a wide gravel parking lot at the end. Sarah killed the engine. Several picnic tables and fire rings dotted the area. Though it was cold and empty now, Marianne could picture families spending a nice day by the water in summer.

As she stared out the windshield, Sarah said, "What do you remember about Turner's Hope Mine?"

Marianne didn't need her notes. She summarized from memory. "Turner's Hope was a working mine from the 1850s until the 1890s. They employed mainly Irish and Italian immigrants from the area and extracted iron ore in the form of magnetite and chondrodite which they sent to mills in Pennsylvania and New York. There it got turned into steel and then into rails for the booming railroad industry. For a while, it was the biggest open pit mining operation in the eastern U.S. It was six hundred feet deep and drilled into the ground at a steep angle. Thousands of tons of ore were removed during its heyday."

"Did you read why it closed?"

"Yeah. There was a disaster. One day in November after heavy rain, a huge chunk of the ceiling split off and collapsed into the pit. Thirty-five men were in the mine at the time. A lot of them escaped or were rescued, but thirteen people were buried in the rubble. It took them days to dig the bodies free. An inquiry determined that the mine owners were not at fault, and they swore no one could have foreseen the disaster."

"The survivors, and the widows and children who lost their husbands and fathers never really bought that," Sarah replied.

"Yeah, the inquiry commission probably got paid off by the owners to bury the problems and prevent lawsuits," she agreed. "Why are we here? It's a little cold for a picnic."

"The mine closed not long after the disaster. The owners used the nearby reservoir to flood it."

Appalled, Marianne looked out the window. "That's the remains of Turner's Hope Mine?"

"Yup. All three-hundred feet deep of it."

Beyond the trees, the water looked like a tarnished piece of pewter, flat and gray. Marianne shivered. The uneasy feeling she'd been ignoring crept into the seat with her. Thirteen people had died in that cave in, and it had taken days to recover their bodies. They'd never left. They were still here.

And they were not happy.

"You're not going to ask them to help you are you?" Marianne asked slowly.

"Yup." Sarah looked at her. "Are you coming with me?"

Walking into hostile territory was the last thing Marianne wanted to do. It would be like walking into a biker bar or one of Geoffrey's family holiday parties. There were angry ghosts here, maybe worse than George Rutherford. She never liked being in the same room as angry living people. But she couldn't ignore ghosts anymore, and she should probably learn to deal with the mean or angry ones as well as the nice ones. Sarah was taking point on this, not her.

'Kelly and I do this together. She watches my back.' She couldn't let Sarah go alone. If something happened, what would she say to Kelly?

Marianne nodded.

"That's the spirit. Do you have the amulet I gave you somewhere on your person? Good. Take one of these as well." She handed Marianne an herb jar with holy water in it. "It'll help protect you. All those Irish and Italians were good Catholics. They'll respect Father Williams' work." She stepped out of the car and zipped up her hood against the drizzle. She opened the back hatch, picked something out of a box and slammed the hatch shut again.

"But…"

Sarah was already striding away, a bottle in her hand. Marianne slipped her hand into her jacket pocket and found Ruari's little wooden cat. She squeezed it gently, thinking of Oscar. The little glass bottle was in her other pocket. Her jeans held the lumpy stone amulet. She had lots of protection. She'd dealt with her ex's horrible family, George Rutherford's mean ghost, and Vivienne, a thousand year old fey. How bad could it be?

A narrow stand of trees screened the road from a large pond or small lake, depending on your view. A rocky and precipitous shore with weeds and scrubby bushes ringed the water. A single boat ramp led into the water. Raindrops jostled the surface into a competition of rings. It looked completely unremarkable and innocuous.

However, a heavy pressure beat steadily against her ears the moment she stepped out of the car. Her sense of dread grew as she neared the water's edge and stepped gingerly onto the stony rubble beach. She fought the urge to go straight back to the car and shut the door.

I can't believe people go boating here and let their kids play near the water. I would never do that!

The rocky shingle was slick with rain, and she grabbed a branch as her boots lost their purchase and slipped out from under her. A few pebbles skittered away and fell into the dark water below, sinking out of sight.

"Watch your step," Sarah called from ahead of her. "You don't want to fall in."

Marianne joined her where she looked out over the man-made lake. Sarah stood there taking deep calming breaths, centering herself. Marianne braced her feet, her scattered thoughts unwilling to focus.

"Peter O'Meara, this is Sarah Landsman. I've come to speak to you and your men."

Her voice fell flat in the chill. She called several more times. "I've brought the libations." Producing a bottle of cheap whiskey, she unscrewed the cap and poured the contents into the water. It vanished as she poured it down the dark throat of the lake.

Marianne felt the pressure in her ears increase as if she were sinking into the water. The back of her neck prickled, and she spun back toward the parking lot.

You called us?

A man dressed in nondescript brown trousers and jacket over a dirty blue shirt stood behind them. He appeared to be alone, but when Marianne closed her eyes to focus on him better, she saw a ring of indistinct forms standing behind him. The miners radiated a simmering anger and menace.

Sarah faced them. If she was concerned that they stood between her and the car or that a three-hundred foot deep, cold pool of water was right behind her, she gave no indication. Marianne wondered if she was over confident or just oblivious to the roil of emotions.

"Peter O'Meara, thank you for coming. I think something in the spirit world is off kilter, and I've come to ask what you know, per our agreement."

Have you now? He carried a trace of an Irish lilt. *Where is your warrior woman protector?*

"Having her hair done," Sarah said in a tone that stopped all further inquiry.

He snorted. *Who is this?* He turned his fathomless black eyes on Marianne, and she shivered. It was not a friendly gaze. She was very glad Sarah was there, and she didn't have to face them alone.

"This is my associate, Marianne." Sarah turned to her and quirked an eyebrow.

Marianne cleared her throat and nodded once. "Hi, Mr. O'Meara, it's nice to meet you." Her voice sounded shaky.

He looked her up and down and dismissed her all in one gesture then turned back to Sarah. Marianne felt simultaneously relieved and ashamed of her own fear.

Sarah said, "Something is off kilter in the spirit world. What do you know?"

He tilted his head to one side. *All year you're absent, then you give us a wee drink and ask for our help. Is that how friends treat each other?*

Sarah showed no sign of embarrassment. "I buy a drink for you and your crew, and you keep an eye on this corner of Canopus County. That's our deal."

O'Meara stared at her. *Just business then. Well, lads, what do we think? Shall we accept this lady's drink and tell her what we know?*

Voices murmured, and he listened to them. Marianne couldn't make out what they said, but she became aware of another sound. An undertone below the voices. She tilted her head trying to hear it.

Peter O'Meara turned back to Sarah. *We can tell you what we've heard, but the price for further cooperation this year will be more than a bottle of cheap whiskey.*

"What are you asking for?"

Revenge.

"On whom?"

The curs who walked away from us and took no responsibility for what they did. For spending our lives like dust while they made money and built empires.

"Those people are long dead, O'Meara. They will no more recognize you now than they did in life."

You have some pull in the spirit world. You could force them to come back and grant us our revenge.

"Even if I could, I wouldn't do that, O'Meara. Even you know that's a violation of the rules."

Then you get nothing from us.

"O'Meara, you're the best watchers I have here." Her flattery held hint of desperation. "You're the only ones who can do this job. You're not scared of anything."

He grinned, his broken teeth betraying a lifetime of bad oral hygiene. *Then make me a better offer.*

Sarah made a frustrated noise, compressing her lips tightly. "Tell me what you know for the sake of the old agreement, and I'll think about what I can do for your other request."

His grin faded. *For the sake of the drink you brought, then. Something is pushing the barriers. They want to come to this side, and someone is opening the doors for them.*

"Is it draugers, Shadow People?"

He nodded slowly. *It feels like them.*

"Then our bargain is fulfilled. I will consider your new terms." She made to walk past them and the miners began to fade.

"Wait!" Marianne said. Part of her said, *what are you doing?!*

Everyone stopped. They'd forgotten about her completely. O'Meara and his men flickered back into visibility.

"Wait," she said again, feeling her hands shaking. "You asked for accountability from the people who ran the mine. Let me see what I can do."

Peter O'Meara looked at her with coal black eyes. *How? Are you a powerful witch?*

"No, I'm a historian. I can at least find out what happened and maybe that will help you. Please let me try."

"Marianne, we've talked about this," Sarah hissed. "You can't help—" she cut herself off before she finished the sentence.

"Why not?" Marianne said sharply. "History is what I do." She looked into O'Meara's fathomless black eyes and said, "Let me see what I can find out. I'll get back to you."

The men behind him murmured, and he said, *Very well. You have nothing more until you get back to us.*

Marianne nodded. That was fair. She couldn't be sure of what she'd find or how long it would take. "Deal."

Sarah said through gritted teeth, "Let's go before you promise anything else."

Together they skirted the insubstantial miners and scrambled back up the short bank to the parking lot.

They were barely out of earshot when Sarah lit into her. "I can't believe you offered to do that. After everything I told you!"

"I have an idea. While you were talking, I heard—"

"You can't just go promising people things like that! Especially someone like him."

Marianne raised her voice. "The men miss their families. They just want to cross over, but O'Meara won't let them. If I find something out, maybe he'll let them go."

"You're such a softie for a sob story."

"I know what I heard."

She muttered something Marianne didn't catch.

Marianne felt her heels digging in. Sarah didn't care about people, but Marianne did. They were almost to Natalie when Marianne felt the pressure in her ears again. The miners were still angry. "Sarah, they're coming. Let's get out of here!"

They hurried into the old Volvo, and Sarah turned the key in the ignition. All she got was a sad half chug. "C'mon, Natalie," she murmured, sounding less confident, "you can do it, *mon amie*. Get us out of here."

Marianne looked through the trees toward the cursed lake. She thought she could see pale figures rising out of the water and drifting toward shore, hands reaching toward them, wanting to pull them back. "I think they changed their minds about waiting. Hurry!" she breathed.

"Natalie is warded heavily," Sarah said sharply. "They can't get in. Don't worry." She turned the key again and pressed the accelerator gently.

O'Meara and his men flowed towards them like a malevolent fog.

Chuh…chuuuug.

Belatedly, the engine roared into life, and Sarah let out the clutch and pulled around in a tight turn, heading for the road in a shower of gravel.

❦

"That was close!" Marianne breathed as they swerved onto Route 401 again, Turner's Pond safely receding behind them.

Peter O'Meara wants revenge. She wasn't sure she could give him that, nor did she want to. *But maybe I can find out what happened. What if I could tell his story?* Maybe the county would be willing to put up an educational plaque or something? Hah. He clearly preferred to find the ghosts of the old mine owners and beat the crap out of them.

"Sarah, you said something about rules and not calling up spirits," Marianne asked.

"A powerful enough person can sometimes coerce spirits into manifesting on this plane. We don't do it because people deserve a rest after they've died."

"You mean like necromancy?"

"No, that would be raising the actual dead body and reanimating it temporarily with its spirit. Some traditions allow for that, but I don't do that. Calling up a spirit through a seance or a ouija board is risky, since you might call up other things as well. If the spirit is still on this plane, it's a little easier but also has its risks."

"Then what are we doing when we talk to your ghost allies?"

"It's a little different. I know what I'm doing. I contact spirits who haven't crossed over, and most of them still want to talk to the living." Sarah glanced at Marianne's face and said, "Okay, imagine spirits being in their zone, and we're in ours. We can call them with a spiritual equivalent of a telephone. If you're dead and you want to talk to the living, you pick up the phone. If you don't want to talk to the living, it's like getting spam phone calls. Annoying as hell."

That made some sense. Ghosts clearly had emotions. Jason had nearly faded from despair, O'Meara was furious, George had certainly had his agenda. They'd also had their issues like anchors, holding them to this plane of existence. But if you moved on or crossed over, then you were safe, right? The pain and ills of the physical body were left behind, and your soul or essence was safe in heaven or some kind of happy afterlife. A higher being existed there and protected you.

But if you were still on this plane, then maybe you weren't completely safe.

O'Meara said that something was pushing the barriers and someone was opening the doors. Marianne shivered.

"Sarah, what are Shadow People anyway? They sound like a secret society."

Sarah glanced at her. "Remember I said Kelly and I protect the county with a spell every year? We protect the county from negative energy. Draugers, or Shadow People, are the prime source of negative energy."

"But what are they? I didn't come across them when I did research on demons. Where do they come from? What do they want?"

"They're not demons. It's more like they're denizens or predators from the spirit realm. They don't really have intelligence or an agenda the way ghosts might. They're really just hungry."

"Hungry? That doesn't sound good."

"They exude their own negative energy and feed off negative energy of humans."

"What exactly do you mean by negative energy?"

"You know how when people are happy or in a good mood, they radiate a positive vibe and good energy? This is the opposite."

"So draugers are basically a bad mood that floats around like a miasma or something?" She meant it sarcastically, but Sarah didn't roll her eyes.

"Kind of. All I know is that if they're allowed to run rampant, the crime rate goes up, people who are depressed or angry get worse, and people with mental illness get much worse."

Marianne was skeptical. "So, basically we turn into New York City on a bad day?"

Sarah stared at the road but her profile was solemn. "Actually, yes. The city is way too big for one person to protect, and no one has ever claimed that territory or been successful in protecting it. So draugers exist there freely."

"It sounds kind of normal. Lots of people have problems."

"Yes, but Shadow People make them a whole lot worse. Maple Hill hasn't had a homicide in over a decade. Most of Canopus is rural and relatively sleepy. People come up here to get a break from all the crap in the city. Do you really want Maple Hill to turn into New York City?"

That would never happen. She wanted to laugh but couldn't quite. "So have you seen a drauger?"

"Yes."

"What did it look like?" Marianne couldn't suppress her own eye roll. "Please don't tell me they look just like people."

"Mature ones do. They look like the silhouette of a person with a hat on."

Marianne couldn't help herself, she snorted. "A person with a hat on?"

Sarah set her jaw and kept her eyes on the road. "That's right. A hat with a brim."

"How come I've never seen one? I can see ghosts."

"They're not that common, for one. Like I said, they're drawn to mental illness and negative emotions. So unless you hang around psychiatric asylums, prisons, or the worst places in cities, you probably wouldn't have. They also frequent places where the barrier to the Shadow Realm is weak."

"So what happens if you encounter a drauger?"

Sarah negotiated a turn onto another road before answering. "They step inside you and bring out the worst."

"They possess you?"

"Yes. That's why the murder rate goes up."

"So Shadow People are responsible for the crime rate?" The idea of supernatural creatures being the reason for the worst of human behavior seemed far fetched to her. Human history was full of wars, murder, theft, and horrible behavior without mystical instigators.

"Not completely," Sarah countered. "But the historic record shows a strong correlation between outbreaks of war and genocide and the appearance of draugers which the magical community tracks."

"Where do they come from?"

"A parallel dimension called the Shadow Realm. The stone chambers act like doorways at this time of year which is why we seal them magically." Sarah took her eyes off the road long enough to look at her. Her lips tightened. "Whether you believe me or not, I still need you to stick with me and finish the spell."

Marianne sat in silence, mulling over Sarah's explanation. This whole trip just got stranger and stranger. If she believed Sarah, not only the county but she was in danger if they failed in their magical mission. Something jumped out at her. "You said 'mature ones.' That presumes there are immature ones."

"I'm not well versed in the life cycle of draugers, but the little I've read says that the the silhouette kind may be related to more amorphously shaped beings. Those don't possess people. They hover around people's heads and get fat off the life energy of a person before the next one crowds in." She suppressed a shudder, making Natalie bobble on the road. "Those are associated with waves of sickness like fevers, wasting, and unexplained deaths."

A vivid image of a fat tick falling off the back of her hand came to mind, and Marianne shivered. Maybe that was the meaning of her dream. The draugers were like ticks. Yuck. Now she had to deal with spirit ticks sucking the energy out of her. Not wanting to dwell on it any further she said, "Where are we going now, anyway?"

"Peterson."

Marianne remembered Peterson in the south central part of the county. She pictured the old map with all the beautiful paintings in the margins. Peterson was one of the three oldest settlements, along with Crossfield and Centerburg. "What's in Peterson?"

"An old friend. How do you feel about funeral homes?" Sarah asked.

The pit of Marianne's stomach twisted with a lurch, and she felt her heart jolt. "I don't do funeral homes."

Sarah's eyebrows lifted in puzzlement. "You're okay with ghosts but not funeral homes? Most people are the opposite. Come on, I'd really like to introduce you to my friend."

A ripple of dizzy dread passed over her at the thought of entering a funeral home. She clenched her hands and tried to breathe calmly. She shook her head. "No, I think I'll stay out here for this one."

A frown of disappointment or disbelief creased Sarah's brow, and she looked like she wanted to insist. Instead, she pulled into a parking lot beside a low concrete building with "Balzac Funeral Home" in tasteful lettering. "Are you sure?"

"Another time." Breathe slow in and out. Count to ten.

Sarah shook her head. "Okay. I'll be back." She left, slamming Natalie's door.

SWIMMING

CHAPTER 7

Funeral homes brought back awful memories of her father's funeral when she was five. The sweet smell of cookies mixed with traces of formaldehyde. Her mother crying. Everyone dressed like black bats. She hadn't understood why people said her father was lying in the box at the front of the room. She'd last seen him in bed in the hospital. Why didn't mom take her there to see him?

Both her parents had small families, so there weren't many relatives much less children her age. Grandma Selene had been there, but she was too sad to pay attention to her granddaughter. People from her parents' work places were the main visitors. All of them ignored Marianne in her little brown dress. She raided the cookie table until someone moved the plate out of her reach. Bored, she wandered to the front of the room and got up on the step where the big black box was. People kept saying her father was in there. That was ridiculous. He was in the hospital. The edge of the box was over her head, so she dragged a chair over and climbed up to look inside.

Marianne couldn't remember what she'd expected. The man lying in a nest of white satin pillows wasn't it. He looked sort of like her father but more like a cartoon of him. She reached out and poked the side of his face. It felt like rubber. All at once, the enormity of the truth hit her. Her father wasn't in the hospital. He was here. She shook his shoulder, but he didn't wake up or smile or anything.

Death had turned him into a giant rubber doll.

Her screams brought the house down.

She'd avoided funeral homes ever since.

The cold glass felt good on her forehead, and Marianne breathed until her heart rate slowed to normal. Eventually, she was able to sit up. She felt hollow and shaky and opened a package of sweet chocolate rolls. Thank goodness a gas station yesterday had provided car snacks. The first two tasted like ashes as she washed them down with the luke warm remnants of her awful tea from breakfast. A second package of the little cakes tasted more like the waxy chocolate and cream she expected, and she felt better.

Rain ran in rivulets down the glass, and she noticed a man standing by the side of the building. He was in his sixties, balding, in a formal dark suit. Heedless of the rain, he stared at her. She looked away, hoping he hadn't seen her moment of panic. When she snuck a look in his direction, he was still staring. She stared back, and he made a small hand gesture for her to come over.

Go meet a stranger on the sidewalk but don't go inside a funeral home. It wasn't logical.

He gestured again.

It was a public sidewalk. She would be safe. Marianne got out and pulled up the hood on her jacket. She stopped out of arm's reach and said, "Yes?"

Could you take a message for me?

"What?"

He won't listen to me, but I need to tell him.

She looked more closely. It was cold outside and impossible to sense his temperature, but she was pretty sure anyway. The man's dark suit was dry in spite of the rain falling steadily. "Possibly," she replied.

He looked relieved. *Please tell my son I buried the box with the family heirlooms in the back yard under the cedar tree.*

"I can try, but you'll have to give me more information."

He looked so grateful. *Thank you. His name is Stephen.* He told her the phone number and address.

She fished a napkin out of her pocket and jotted the information down. "Like I said, I'll try. I can't promise he'll listen."

Tell him to sell all of it except the silver bracelet. I gave that to his mother on our first anniversary. She wanted him to have it. The rest of it will help pay the bills.

"Okay, Mr—?"

Benton. Carter Benton.

"I'll do my best."

A throat cleared. "Hey, Marianne. Let's go." Sarah stood impatiently on the sidewalk behind her.

Marianne nodded at her. "Just a moment." When she turned back, Mr. Benton was gone.

Sarah tightened her lips, shook her head, and said nothing. Marianne joined her in the car. "How is your friend?"

"Who was that?" Sarah sounded like Marianne was meeting with an unapproved boyfriend.

"Carter Benton. I think he passed through the funeral home recently."

"And?"

"He wanted me to call his son and tell him something."

Sarah gave a mirthless chuckle. "It's a classic. The dead guy with a message for the living. It's not our job to be a telegram service for them."

"But if it makes them move on and makes the living feel better, why not?"

"Because it doesn't work that way. Those left behind don't believe you, and half the time they accuse you of preying on them. It gets ugly. I don't do that anymore."

"So you used to?"

"I did. It worked out badly." She stared out the window and a muscle in her jaw jumped.

Sarah's experiences were her own. If she was as cold and awkward conveying messages to the living as she was now, no wonder people thought she was crazy or trying to take advantage of them. Marianne wasn't like that at all. She had decent people skills. Before she could chicken out or overthink it, she got out her phone and dialed the quickly blurring number on the wet napkin.

Sarah threw up her hands and thumped them on the steering wheel in frustration.

Sarah was pissed, but Marianne was discovering a perverse satisfaction in thwarting people who pushed her. Her marriage to Geoffrey might have turned out differently if she'd pushed back sooner. Or she might have called it quits with him way earlier. Either way, she was learning to stand up for herself. She could make her own decisions without Sarah butting in.

The dial tone purred several times before a man's voice answered. "Hello?"

"Hi, may I speak with Stephen Benton please?"

"This is him."

"Hi, you don't know me but I have a message for you."

"Who is this?"

"My name is Marianne, and I know this sounds weird, but I just spoke to Mr. Carter Benton. Is he your father?"

There was a silence on the other end of the phone.

"Hello?" She said, wondering if he'd hung up.

"Carter Benton is dead," the man said flatly. "He died three weeks ago. Is this some kind of sick prank?"

"No! I'm not pranking you. He wanted me to tell you that he buried the family valuables under the cedar tree in the back yard. He told me they would help pay the bills. You're supposed to keep the silver bracelet because your mother wanted you to have it."

"Who is this? How do you know any of this?" He demanded.

"I'm just trying to pass on a message. He said you'd know what he meant."

"You're crazy! Goodbye!" He practically shouted.

"I'm sorry to have bothered you. Have a nice day," she mumbled and hung up. She wasn't sure what she'd expected. Not effusive thanks but certainly not being told she was some sicko. Well, she'd delivered the message. Stephen Benton could do with it what he willed.

"He thought you were crazy right?" Sarah said. "Taking messages between the living and the dead is a thankless task."

Marianne twitched one shoulder in a shrug.

Sarah sighed and said more gently, "Never mind."

Sarah pulled the old Volvo into a gas station a few blocks away from the funeral home. "Natalie needs breakfast."

Feeling pretty low, Marianne was inclined to stay in the car, but a pressure in her bladder reminded her the tea had come due.

Marianne entered the little convenience store attached to the gas station and used their bathroom. She replayed the phone conversation, wincing at the son's sharp words. She'd made a mistake. Hopefully, he'd just forget about it. He didn't know who she was, so he couldn't go after her for harassment. Sarah was right, she should stop trying to interfere.

She wouldn't take on any more ghost messages or projects. The idea of a business centered on research for the dead and helping the living with paranormal experiences was ludicrous. She'd find out what happened after the Turner's Hope Mine disaster for O'Meara and do a little research for Astrid Delaney. Then she'd go back to getting a job in the living world.

She emerged and, spying Sarah washing Natalie's windows, took a moment to replenish her stash of snacks: chocolate roll cakes and a bag of nuts and dried fruit. At the checkout, she saw a Canopus County map for sale and added it to the pile. Back in the car, she dropped the bag at her feet with her backpack and pulled out the county map. She wanted to know where they'd been and maybe get a sense of where they were going next.

Sarah plunked into the driver's seat and turned the key. Natalie started up right away.

"*Ma belle Natalie.*" She smiled and patted the dash. "A little dry gas in your tank and you're all better."

Marianne only half heard her, she was so lost in studying the map. "Uh huh. Sarah, I'm looking at our route. We've been zig-zagging all over the place. Are you sure it wouldn't be faster to start at one end of the county and drive everything there, then gradually move to the other side? You're so worried about time."

Sarah glanced over. "You got a map?"

Marianne got out a pen and traced it along the roads they'd taken to Crossfield, Centerburg, and Peterson and circled with hash marks the areas where they'd left charms. As an afterthought, she marked the two stone passages with a little dot. "Yes, I can't keep all of this in my head. Besides, having a visual aid helps me remember."

Sarah frowned but said nothing more.

"Now what?" Marianne asked in some irritation.

Sarah shook her head. "Nothing. Just don't lose it or let someone else get ahold of it okay?"

They pulled into a gravel parking area on a lonely stretch of road some fifteen minutes later. It was one of those roadside turnouts that had about four spaces and a trail leading off into the woods.

"Still got your walking shoes on?" Sarah asked as she removed the empty coffee cup from the boot on the front seat and tossed on the floor behind her seat. She slid the boot onto her foot and tied it.

"Yeah."

"We're going for a little hike." She got out of the car and went to the back hatch. "I need you to carry some things."

"How long are we going to be?" Marianne asked, looking at

the cold gray day.

"Couple of hours at least. Be sure you have your amulets."

I must be crazy, like Stephen Benton said. It's raining and gross out. I should be at home on the couch in my jammies with Oscar. She loaded her back pack with water and snacks. She tucked the map in an outer pocket and put on an extra sweater and wool hat against the raw chill. Sarah added several small charms in cloth bags and some larger charms with bigger spell components. Marianne cupped them briefly in her hands before placing them at the top of the pack, trying to feel any sign of magic. She felt nothing except more weight in her pack.

"Leave your notebook and papers behind," Sarah said. "Nobody up there wants your CV, trust me."

Marianne swung her pack off her shoulder and dumped the papers face down on the dashboard. She was annoyed, but her pack felt lighter.

Aware of feeling like a grumpy teenager, she tried to shed her bad mood. "Okay, let's go." Her voice sounded reasonably enthusiastic.

The trail wound steeply up a hill through the trees. Rain dripped off the yellow, red, and brown leaves with a soft patter. Marianne followed Sarah glad for her hiking boots. More than once her footing slipped on the muddy incline. The trail leveled off after a bit. They walked in silence, saving their breath. The path branched left and right at a tee. Two signs with arrows pointed in either direction. "Maiden's Weep 2.1. Miles" went left. "Beehive 0.8 miles" went right. Sarah turned right.

"Beehive?" She pictured a domed rock formation with a scenic over look.

"It's a loop. We'll end up seeing both places and then go back to the car."

"What are they?"

"Stone chambers," Sarah said shortly and kept walking.

"Like the ones in Maple Hill and Centerburg?" Faint alarm wormed through her.

"Yup. We have to ward them differently than we do the rest of the county."

"Are they more like the one at the cemetery or like the one at the park?"

"Cemetery."

Marianne remembered the tingling vibration in the stones at the cemetery, and the faint sucking sensation as it tried to pull her inside. She shivered. She told herself they would be safe. Sarah knew what she was doing.

They walked further into the woods and higher up where conifer trees grew interspersed with the deciduous. Before they rounded the final corner, Marianne smelled a strong scent of dust with a sharp metallic undertone like a can of ten-penny nails.

They turned one last corner and were confronted with a low stone doorway opening into the hillside. Stacks of flat rocks, dry fitted, held up a larger flat slab. Scraggly vines hung around it. They stopped, and Sarah stood still for a minute, apparently listening or feeling for something.

The dark mouth felt like an undertow. The Beehive was either stronger than the Maple Hill cemetery opening, or Marianne was getting better at feeling it.

Sarah dropped to one knee and put her pack on the ground. Her eyes never left the opening as if she were watching a mountain lion. "Marianne, pull one of the bigger charms out of your pack will you?"

Marianne swung her pack down, retrieved one of the larger cloth bags, and handed it to Sarah. "Is it supposed to feel like this?"

She shook her head. "Something's wrong."

"It feels like something is pulling us in. What's down there?"

"Remember I said the stone structures act like portals between this dimension and the one the Shadow People live in? We shut them magically every year with charms. If you don't, they develop holes or leaks, and the barrier between us and the realm of Shadows gets porous. Draugers slip through." She loosened the strings at the top of the charm bag and showed her the contents.

"These charms have different herbs and bigger stones. This is how you activate them." She slipped things back into the bag and crushed it lightly, releasing the sulphurus scent of asafoetida, along with bergamot and echinacea. "By Earth and Sky and Fire and Water, close this portal and keep it locked. Let nothing pass through." She handed it to Marianne. "Now we go inside and place it."

Marianne couldn't think of a worse idea. "Are you nuts?"

Sarah looked at the opening. "Nope. I have a flashlight. Remember, our stone amulets will protect us if we run into draugers."

Marianne shouldered her pack again. It was as much a talisman as the holy water and Sarah's amulet. She braced herself and followed her mentor.

Crouching, she crept through the doorway, one hand steadying her. The stones buzzed with a disorienting vibration under her fingers, making her clench her jaw. She shook her head and snatched her hand back. The smell of old pennies and dry dust was stronger up close. Though she wanted nothing more than to wait outside, the thought of Sarah's scorn propelled her down a narrow, uneven stairway of stone.

The light disappeared very quickly, and she stood in twilight, letting her eyes adjust.

Sarah's flashlight beam glanced over a dirt floor and stacked stone walls in a circular room. Dozens of cobwebs crossed the ceiling, and Marianne flinched. The rough, flat blocks were stacked in a gentle curve overhead, holding themselves up in a perfect arch about seven feet from floor to ceiling. There was no mortar. Marianne was simultaneously impressed with the engineering and disturbed by the thought of tons of stone suddenly collapsing on her. A grating, subliminal buzz saw vibration set her teeth on edge and threatened to make her dizzy again.

Sarah played the light over the walls searching for something. "There you are you little sneak," she murmured. Sarah held out the flashlight to her. "C'mere. Hold this. See that opening? Hold the beam on that." She pulled a pair of old leather driving gloves out of her pocket and put them on. Standing on tiptoe, she thrust her fingers past the spider webs into the opening and fished around for a moment before pulling something out.

A little cloth bag fell to the floor. It was dirty and looked very much like one of Sarah's. Marianne leaned over to pick it up.

"Leave it!" Sarah said sharply. Marianne jerked her hand back.

Sarah cautiously picked up the bag and pulled the strings open. Into her gloved hand spilled dark brown splinters, a handful of black and red seeds that looked like little beads, and dried chrysanthemums.

Marianne looked at Sarah. "Is that one of yours?"

She looked grim. "No." She poked at each item in the beam of the flashlight. "The splinters are bone fragments and based on the rest of this, I'd bet they're from a cemetery. Fragments of human bone are often used in death magic and black magic. The peony seeds mean dissension and breaking. The chrysanthemums traditionally mean death."

"That doesn't sound good."

"Someone is trying to open this portal, not close it."

"Why? Who?"

"I don't know. But this acts like a wedge in a door. If I hadn't found it, our talisman wouldn't have worked."

"How did you know it was there?"

"Remember, magic looks blurry to me. I could barely focus on that area." She tipped the items back into their little bag.

"Wait, what's that?" Marianne pointed to the bag. One side was blank, the other had a symbol. Sarah held the flashlight over it. The letters TK inside a circle had been written in pen near the opening.

"Oh shit," Sarah muttered.

"Who's TK? Is that who put this here?"

"Yeah, I'm pretty sure that's Tristan Kitteby, the protector of Dutchess County."

"But why would he want to open the gates here if he's a protector?"

"He's protecting his county and diverting the draugers here, away from his own."

"What? That's terrible!"

"Yeah." Sarah tucked it into an outer pocket of her pack. "Let's finish and get out of here."

They wedged Sarah's closing charm into a different crack and tucked it completely out of sight.

"By Earth and Sky and Fire and Water, close this portal and keep it locked. Let nothing pass through," she murmured and Marianne joined in.

The buzzsaw feeling ceased as they spoke the words, and the stone chamber just felt like a dry empty vault. Marianne breathed a sigh of relief. Sarah placed her open palm over the new hiding spot and murmured again.

"There, that should keep anyone from finding it now."

The cold, damp dripping of the forest outside was welcome.

"Does this place vibrate to you?" Marianne asked. "And smell like old, rusty metal?"

"No, but that's good news." Sarah gave Marianne a faint smile of encouragement. "Maybe that's the way magic feels to you. Keep looking for that feeling when you practice with the charms. Let's get to the next one."

In silence, they continued their walk along the looping trail toward Maiden's Weep.

"Sarah, you said Tristan Kitteby was diverting draugers away from Dutchess County. Has that ever happened before?"

"Not that I know of. Byron told me the neighboring Protectors were callous at best. They looked out for their own counties but didn't care about their neighbors much."

"Yikes. That's not very friendly."

"They're not. We'll have to keep our eyes open from now on."

"Why this year, I wonder?"

Sarah didn't answer.

The low opening of the stone chamber at the other end of the trail angled into the hillside. A subliminal buzz saw vibration set Marianne's nerves on edge. Without saying much the two women crouched and prepared the next closing amulet before they entered the hollow stone room. The flashlight played over the damp back wall and Marianne saw the drip of a natural spring fall from stone to stone into a little pool.

"You should look for this one," Sarah said, "practice your magic."

Marianne took the flashlight and scanned the stones but gave up after a minute. There was just tight fitting stone with more spiderwebs. "I don't see anything."

"It's right there." Sarah pointed at a crack between two of the ceiling slabs.

Marianne saw nothing.

Sarah grabbed her hand and aimed the light. Reaching on tiptoe Sarah pulled out a second bone and peony seed charm with gloved fingers. She spoke the activation words over an asafoetida charm in its place and closed the portal down. Then she hid it from casual view with her 'don't look' spell. Marianne breathed a sigh of relief as the buzzing quieted and her head cleared.

Out in the daylight, they examined the cloth pouch and found another circled TK marking like the first. Kitteby had been here, too. Sarah tucked it into her pack with the other one.

They said little as they trudged down the path toward the parking area. Marianne was acutely aware of having failed Sarah's test. Her mentor's silence all but shouted, "You need to try harder. Kelly would have been able to do it." Much as she loved the bubbly, energetic woman, Marianne was beginning to resent Kelly big time.

"I'm sorry," she finally said.

Sarah shrugged. "At least we know you can feel magic. Keep

working on it. You'll get it eventually."

In a funk, Marianne trudged after her mentor.

In the parking area, Sarah opened the magical tool box and removed the black lacquered box. Grainy black sand filled the container, and Sarah used an old coffee scoop to put a couple of measures into two sandwich baggies. With gloved hands, she put an evil charm into each baggie and sealed them up. "That will neutralize their magic."

"Why black sand?"

"Salt, not sand. Salt is magically inert. White is good for protection, black is good for drawing energy out of magical objects. Kelly and I throw all our used ingredients into salt to reset them before re-imbuing them."

Marianne absorbed that information, then said quietly, "Holding the portals open would let the Shadow People in, right?"

Sarah looked grim. "Yeah, it would. It's time to make a phone call."

They drove to a diner in Deer Valley to get some lunch and better wi-fi. Canopus was rural enough with lots of hills that there were plenty of places with no cell signal. Along the way Sarah told Marianne about her mentor.

"Byron is one of the more powerful practitioners in New England. I told you he went to Europe to study magic more deeply. I didn't tell you why. Byron had a twin sister named Catalina. She was killed in a car accident when they were twenty-one, and he was devastated. You know how close twins are. They'd lost their parents when they were seven and bounced between different relatives' homes while they were growing up. It wasn't great. They pretty much could only rely on each other."

"That's so sad."

"It gets worse. Byron sees ghosts and draugers. He was able to reconnect with Catalina's spirit, and she stayed with him for many years. About five years ago, she disappeared. Byron had been studying magic and getting more accomplished. Doing that can generate rivals. He did some investigating and learned that his greatest rival, Riven Masters, had kidnapped Catalina's spirit and imprisoned her."

"Is that possible?"

"Remember I wouldn't summon spirits for O'Meara because there are rules? There is magic to compel a spirit to come to you and then trap them in a spirit jar. It's cruel, and something I would never do."

"So did he find the jar? What happened?"

"Byron went to Europe to learn enough magic to find Catalina and free her. He got back recently and told me he was close to finding out where Masters had hidden her."

"That's good. Why do you think the wedge charms are connected to that?"

Sarah looked at her grimly. "Before he left, Byron told me he suspected that the neighboring Protectors were helping Masters."

They pulled into the Deer Valley Diner parking lot. It was after two, and the lunch rush was over. Marianne was starving. Instead of going inside, they sat in the car while Sarah called Byron Mandell. She put it on speaker. Marianne leaned closer over the stick shift.

After several rings, the phone picked up. "Sarah, is that you?" A deep, theatrical voice answered.

"It's me. How are you?"

They passed through the pleasantries quickly. "My new assistant, Marianne, is helping me this year. Kelly's at home with a busted leg."

"I'm sorry to hear that. Is Marianne there with you?"

"Yes, you're on speaker."

"Hello, Marianne, it's nice to meet you." He sounded like a radio announcer.

"Hi, nice to meet you too, Dr. Mandell."

"Please, if you're a friend of Sarah's, call me Byron."

"Thank you, Byron."

"Byron," Sarah said, "I'm doing the protection round, and we just came across a couple of stone chambers with wedge charms in them."

"What?" He said sharply.

"Someone is deliberately trying to open the portals. We closed them, but they had TK in a circle on them."

"Dammit. I was afraid of this. Now that I'm back, Masters hopes to distract me. Which ones? How many?"

"Only two so far, Beehive and Maiden's Weep." She described the contents of the two bags.

"You're right: they would have canceled out your closing charms and held the portals wide open on Halloween night. What did you do with them?"

"I buried them in black salt."

"Good. Don't touch them with your bare hands. Maybe we can stop them before anything worse happens. Where are you?"

"We're at the Deer Valley Diner and could come by this afternoon."

"I'm not in town at the moment." He paused, sounding like he was weighing his options. "This is an emergency. I'll cut my business short and be back in two days instead of a week. Can you swing through again then?"

"I'll make sure to."

"In the meantime, follow the protocols I taught you. When did you start?"

"This is day two."

"Okay, I know where you are in the process. Keep going. You're doing the right thing. Is Marianne learning the ropes?"

Sarah gave Marianne a quick glance. "Yes, she's working on it. It'll take some time. She's new to everything."

"You're in good hands, Marianne."

"I'll try my hardest to learn." It was good to know that Sarah's mentor was just a phone call away.

"Good. Sarah, I think I know where Catalina is!" Byron's voice held a note of excitement.

"That's fantastic!"

"My work has not been in vain. I learned so much more. I'd rather tell you in person. See you in two days' time."

"Thanks, Byron. I knew we could count on you. Good luck. If there's anything I can do to help, just let me know."

"I will."

Over soup and sandwiches at the diner, Sarah said, "You know, if you're still struggling after this week, you might consider taking lessons from Byron. He's a really good teacher."

Marianne nodded. If she was still unable to connect, magically speaking, she would probably just stick with ghosts. They were more than enough for her.

CHAPTER 8

They spent the afternoon protecting communities with their charms, and Marianne enjoyed the Halloween decorations. She hadn't had time to put up her own and made a mental note to do them next year. They located two more stone chambers. Those didn't have wedging charms and were easily closed. They returned to Deer Valley for the night.

After a pizza dinner, they checked into the Sunshine Motel. It was run down, but Marianne was too exhausted to care that it wasn't the Ritz. No one greeted Sarah by name this time in the dingy, cigarette-smelling lobby. Instead, the parking lot was full, and they were lucky to get the last room. The manager eyed them coldly and handed them two keycards without a smile or comment. As they walked away, Marianne heard him mutter, "Fuckin' fags." It was pitched so they could hear it. She stiffened and started to turn in outrage, but Sarah put her hand on her arm and pulled her out the door.

"What? Didn't you hear that?" Marianne asked as they got back into Natalie.

"Yes, the manager's a homophobic asshole. Just let it go. Don't be like Kelly and make me have to restrain you."

Marianne pressed her lips together unhappily. For once, she

was with Kelly. The guy needed a good talking to. Given how sketchy the motel was, they unloaded the entire car into the room for safety and got ready for bed. It was then that Marianne realized there was only one bed.

"Do you mind sharing?" Sarah asked when she saw her look of dismay.

Marianne quickly shook her head and smiled. "No. Do you mind if I call Ruari?"

"Nope. I'd planned to call Kelly anyway."

Giving Sarah some privacy, Marianne put her coat back on and slipped outside to sit on the covered cement walkway in front of the room.

He picked up right away. "Mahri, where are you?" He sounded relieved to hear from her.

"We're at a motel in Deer Valley."

"How is your networking going?"

Marianne felt an uncomfortable squirm in her stomach. "Actually, the protection thing is turning out to be harder than Sarah thought. Remember the stone chamber at the Maple Hill Cemetery?"

"Yeah."

"Well, there are lots of them all over the county, and they're pretty scary even in daylight."

"Oh…"

"Don't laugh, but it turns out they're portals to another dimension."

"Really?" He sounded skeptical.

"Not only that but someone or something wants to wedge them open so bad things come through to our dimension."

He was silent for a heartbeat. "Like what?"

"Sarah told me there are things called draugers or Shadow People. They're not ghosts, they're beings from a neighboring dimension. They're attracted to negative emotions and people with mental illness in particular."

"Are they intelligent?"

"They sound more like mosquitoes or ticks, just mindlessly hungry. I didn't believe Sarah at first, but I'm beginning to think they're real."

"I'm afraid to ask, but what do they eat?"

"Us. Human energy. Sarah says they make people angrier and more depressed. They may even be the cause of crime waves and wars."

"That's bizarre. Well, if fey tree spirits are real, then maybe… It's strange. Erin's having a rough time."

"Sorry to hear that. What's going on?"

"I'm not sure. She's more snappish than usual, but she won't tell me."

"Do you think there's a connection?"

"I don't know. She still hasn't gotten a job offer, and her old friends have completely shut her out. Though personally, I don't think that's a big loss. They weren't very good friends in the first place. And I think her boyfriend is breaking up with her."

"Oh no! I like your sister. Wish I could be there to help out. I'll be back in a couple of days. Would it help if I called her?"

"I don't know if she'd talk to you."

"Well, if you think it would help, let me know."

His next words were drowned out by the roar of a car with a bad muffler. An old 1970s Pontiac, painted matte black, pulled into the space next to Natalie. Dozens of little rat skulls were glued to the roof and along the raised vee of the hood. A bigger skull of either a large dog or a wolf rode at the front like the figure on the prow of a ship, its fangs painted red. The car looked like it was advertising for the apocalypse.

Marianne plugged her free ear. "Hold it, Ruari, I can't hear you." She got to her feet and stood next to the room door, watching the newcomers warily.

Four huge guys emerged, wearing jean jackets with the sleeves ripped off, leather pants, and sporting beards and shoulder length hair done up in man buns or ponytails. They had clearly tied one on elsewhere. At the door to their room, the blonde guy fumbled with the key card, cursing when the door failed to let them in immediately.

"Gimme that," Man Bun said, handing a twelve pack of cheap beer to the first guy. He grabbed the card from his buddy's hand and inserted it into the slot again. It lit up, and he turned the knob.

The third man, also holding a twelve pack, laughed loudly, "Dickhead!" and pushed his way into the room. The last one caught sight of Marianne watching them and leered at her. "Want to party with us, babe?"

She shook her head, and he shrugged and stumbled inside. The door slammed shut on the loud conversation already going on in the room.

"Marianne? Mahri! Are you okay?" Ruari's voice jumped out of her phone in the sudden silence.

"I'm fine. The neighbors came home. It's going to be a fun night. I'm hoping they pass out by midnight."

"Do you need me to come and get you guys?" He sounded ready to jump in his truck.

"No, we'll be fine. It's a public place. We can always call the cops if we have to."

"Are you sure? I don't mind the drive. I could just hang out with you till the neighbors quiet down."

"Thanks for offering, but I think we'll be fine."

"Be careful," he said unhappily. "Not just with the neighbors but with everything."

"I will." She did her best to sound positive. "Talk to you tomorrow."

"Call me if you need me, okay? Doesn't matter what time." That warmed her to her toes. Her ex had never said that.

"You can count on it."

Ruari hung up the phone and tossed it onto the worktable in frustration. Marianne could be so stubborn! He appreciated her independence. She was a bit like his sister in that respect, but he wanted her to be safe. He still had a nagging suspicion that there was more to this trip than Sarah and Kelly had made it out to be, but there wasn't much he could do. Before she'd left, Marianne had made it clear she didn't want him to interfere in her life too much. He couldn't help worrying, though.

His own job was keeping him more than occupied. His boss, SueAnn Talmadge, had not been thrilled by his taking nine days off work recently, even though he had more than enough vacation time saved up. She'd rewarded him by scheduling several long-term maintenance tasks that made for long hours. His assistant Casey was slowly learning things in spite of himself but had made some messes when he'd been in charge while Ruari was away. They'd only cleaned up the last of them a couple of days ago. It would not be politic to take off work to go join Marianne and Sarah on a whim.

Erin had told him she was okay for now, though he'd detected an undertone of uncertainty. When he'd called her on it, she'd pushed back saying she was fine. Surrounded by independent, stubborn women he couldn't help made him edgy. He spent some time with Oscar making sure he was fed and indoors for the night. At least Oscar had appreciated his efforts, purring and rubbing his legs enthusiastically.

He retreated to his studio for the night. Better to channel his frustrated energy into a wood project. He pulled out some of his old drawings and leafed through them, looking for inspiration.

Having Vivienne out of his head felt weird. She'd been such a constant undertone in his life since Grandda had died, he'd become used to it. Well, he'd lived without her guiding him and teaching him new techniques for years before she'd come to inhabit his head. Time to see what he'd learned from her.

He glanced over at the intricately carved facsimile of a tree stump covered in animals, insects and plant life. It still took his breath away. He couldn't believe he'd made that. True, he'd been miserable while carving it since Vivienne had all but pushed him aside fully to use his hands. He'd been afraid he'd never be with Marianne again at the time. In spite of that, it was incredible.

That level of skill and focus was inside him somewhere. He pulled out a sketch for a table with carved legs. He could put leaves and vines on them. Maybe hide a little insect or animal face.

Yeah, this would keep him from stressing about whether Mahri was okay or not. And give him something to think about when Casey or SueAnn was being an ass.

He pulled his phone closer, just in case.

When Marianne stepped back into the room, Sarah was sitting on a chair by the bathroom. She looked pensive and far away in spite of the noise from next door. The room was cold even though the heater's blower was turned all the way up. An anemic stream of warm air tried to beat its way into the room without much luck.

Marianne looked at her companion with concern. "Is everything okay? Is Kelly doing okay?"

Sarah snapped out of her reverie. "She's fine. Her leg's bothering her, but she's hanging in there."

The party next door was in full swing with the men's voices carrying over the sound of a TV turned up to max. Marianne tipped her head to the thin sheetrock behind the bed. "Those would be the Vikings from hell."

"Great," Sarah acknowledged sourly. "Let's work on magic practice. Maybe they'll pass out."

Marianne doubted she'd be able to concentrate. If Byron thought she could do it, then she'd give it a try.

Sarah brought out the same objects she'd produced the night before, charm bags of both kinds, a nondescript knit cap from a thrift store, several polished stones, and the baggies with black salt with the remains of the evil charms.

Marianne gingerly picked up a baggie and shook it to make sure the bones and seeds were coated on all sides.

"Do you sense anything from it?" Sarah asked.

Marianne closed her eyes and held the bag in her hands. It might as well have been a bag of yesterday's leftovers. She shook her head.

"Good, you shouldn't. They won't be bothering us anymore."

She breathed a sigh of relief and opened her eyes. "Do we toss it in the trash?"

"No!" Sarah sounded offended. "We have a proper disposal system at home."

Marianne pictured radioactive waste being dumped in a lead lined container. "Does Maple Hill Garbage Disposal have an 'm-waste' day?"

Sarah gave her a look that said, don't be ridiculous. "No. We bury it and let the earth turn it into compost."

Marianne sat on the edge of the bed and tried to feel for any kind of magic in the various objects Sarah provided. According to her, they were infused with power. Between the goosebumps on her arms from the chill in the room and loud male voices vying to be heard over the TV next door, she was so distracted she gave up after about twenty minutes. Why could she feel the portals like a sledgehammer but these items not at all?

"It's not the best conditions," Sarah conceded.

Marianne was relieved her teacher was willing to let it go for tonight, though she still felt bad.

They turned the light off, crawled into bed with their clothes on for warmth, and tried to warm up their respective sides. The wall on the other side of the headboard vibrated and thudded regularly as the men partied next door. Sweaty sock aroma wafted up from the covers. After a fruitless half hour trying to find sleep and shivering in the dark, Marianne said, "Think we should call the front office and complain?"

Sarah's sleepless voice replied, "You can try, but I don't think it'll make much difference. They won't fix the heater tonight and probably won't do anything about the assholes either."

Marianne got up and dialed the front office. "Hi, this is room 130. The people next door are incredibly loud, and the heater isn't working. Could you ask them to be quieter? What? No, I— Fine, could you get us another blanket then? What?!" Frustrated and fuming, she slammed the receiver down. "Asshole."

"Told you," Sarah grunted.

"Do you know what he said?!"

"I can guess. No, he can't tell the neighbors to be quiet, and no, he can't fix the heater."

"And we can walk down to the front office if we want another blanket, but he's sure he doesn't have any more! The motel may be full, but I bet he has plenty."

Sarah sighed. "I wouldn't walk down there. We'll be fine. We can throw the sleeping bags over top of us."

Incensed by the manager's indifference, Marianne huffed indignantly as she replayed the conversation in her head. She planned to leave a very bad review when she had the chance. At least the sleeping bags added enough warmth that she began to thaw.

The phone next door rang. "Oh great, they're inviting more people to the party," Marianne grumbled. "Or maybe they're ordering out pizza and planning to stay up for another two hours."

Suddenly, there was an uptick in the noise. Fists banged rhythmically on the wall, and they heard drunken men's voices shouting, "Fag shag! Fag shag! Get it on, hoo, hoo, hoo!" followed by roars of laughter.

Marianne sat up. "Dammit!"

Sarah cursed quietly. "I suspect that the manager 'talked' to them."

"We should do something!"

The lawyer sounded resigned. "We can call the cops and make a noise complaint, but if they have more pressing issues, they won't come for ages."

Finally, the noise died down next door as the occupants passed out one by one. Mercifully, someone had turned the TV down. Their own pathetic heater gave up the ghost altogether, and the room suddenly grew even colder, pulling both women out of a fitful slumber.

Marianne's waking dreams of gangs and motorcycles chasing her through an endless maze of sleazy motel rooms turned into their own darkened room. The shadows seemed deeper than before, and her scalp prickled. There had been a noise in their room, she was sure of it. Extending her senses, she recoiled and pulled her head under the covers. There was something angry and resentful sitting next to the bathroom. It knew they were in the room.

"Sarah, do you feel that?" she breathed. It was a little like the old camping game of 'did you hear that noise?' If the other person didn't hear it, then you could go back to sleep confident you'd been imagining things. If the other person heard it too, then your fear jumped ten notches.

"Uh huh." She sounded as awake as Marianne was.

Crap. "Is it Shadow People? What do we do? I don't think the cops will come for this one," she whispered softly, trying to lighten the mood. The lumpy stone amulet in her pocket was body temperature. Maybe not Shadow People then.

"Can you reach my purse?"

Marianne lay on the side of the bed closest to the outer door. Their gear was in an untidy heap on the table and chairs between the bed and the wall. "Where did you leave it?"

"On the table. You're closer. Just get out of bed and grab it."

Loathe to leave the illusion of safety under the covers, Marianne forced herself to slip over the side of the bed as quietly as she could. The thing in the corner moved restlessly, and she stayed as low as she could. Keeping her attention on the shadowy thing in the corner, Marianne touched the slick covering of the tent, a rough cardboard box, the discarded case of a sleeping bag, and finally encountered Sarah's pebbled leather bag. Gently she slid it across the carpet and pulled it under the covers just as a low, hair-raising growl began in the corner of the room.

"Good job," Sarah breathed softly. "This is lesson number one. Be prepared." She pressed a glass jar into Marianne's hand and whispered, "When I tell you, sit up and hold the bottle in front of you. Don't be afraid. Don't be sensitive. Be strong. Be a hardass. Are you ready?"

Marianne nodded. "Yeah." The contents of the jar sloshed faintly.

"Go."

Together they threw the covers back and scrambled into a crouch, ready to jump if need be. They held their jars in front of them like shields, and Sarah spoke in a strong, steady voice. "By Earth and Sky, and Fire and Water, we are protected. Stay where you are."

The growling continued, but now it sounded uncertain.

"I don't know why you're angry," she continued, "unless it's because of the party next door. In which case, we're with you. We are not your enemy. All we want is a good night's sleep. So just settle down, and we'll be gone in the morning."

Marianne strained her eyes into the darkness and thought she saw the shape of a huge dog the size of a Newfoundland or a mastiff. She reached out tentatively with her senses and came in contact with it.

So thirsty. So hungry. Rita had been chained up and forgotten. Her people had never come back for her. Rita was still really angry about it.

"Sarah, I have an idea. Where are your keys?"

"Purse."

"Will you be okay 'til I get back?"

"Got it."

Marianne handed her the extra jar and groped in the purse for the car keys. She shivered violently. The air was frigid with the dog's presence. She wouldn't have been surprised to see her breath.

Unlatching the door, she squeezed out and made her way to the car. Although it was a little warmer outside than in the room, her stocking feet cringed on the cold cement. Shaking fingers unlocked the passenger door and raised the lock on the backseat door. She tugged on the back door latch without success. "C'mon, Natalie, let me in," she muttered. In desperation she threw her hip against the door and heard a little click. "Thank you."

Silently she retrieved the box from the backseat, locked the car, and ducked back into the room as quietly as she could. By the light peeking between the edges of the heavy curtains, she could see Sarah still kneeling on the bed. The hair on Marianne's neck stood erect at the sound of the escalating growl. The spectral hound was growing impatient, her frustration building. If they didn't do something soon, Rita would spring.

Marianne didn't want to find out if a ghostly dog could tear them to pieces or not.

"What are you doing?" Sarah asked in confusion. "I thought you were getting something we'd left in the car."

"I did."

Marianne opened the lid of the box, and the faint, pungent odor of garlic, sausage, and pepperoni rose up. Tiptoeing cautiously toward the corner of the bed, she kept her eyes on the hulking formless shape by the bathroom door. Laying the open box on the floor, she pushed it toward the bathroom area. "Here, girl, you're hungry." Her voice shook slightly. "You can have this." She leaped backward and fell onto the bed as something big rushed forward. She scrambled as far away as she could until she came up against the headboard.

Frenzied slobbering and tearing noises came from beyond the

edge of the bed. When they quieted, Marianne said softly, "Good girl. Feel better?"

A barely audible whine tickled their ears.

"How do you know it's a girl?" Sarah asked.

"She told me. Think she'll leave us be for now?" Marianne replied.

"Probably. I had a thought, though." Sarah handed Marianne the two bottles of holy water and addressed the spectral hound in a surprisingly playful voice. "Who's a good girl? Want to play fetch?" She squirmed around for a moment, then brought something pungent up in her hands and tossed it back and forth enticingly.

"Hey, girl! Are you ready?" The aromatic ball of socks went back and forth between her two hands.

Sounds of panting and a half stifled bark of excitement replied. She continued to toss the ball between her hands as the dog's whine ratcheted up. When Marianne was sure Rita was going to jump onto the bed with them, Sarah acted.

"Fetch!" She threw the ball as hard as she could straight at the wall behind the head board. The dark shape leapt in hot pursuit and passed through the wall as the wadded up socks bounced harmlessly off the wallboard

There was a brief silence, and then a frenzied barking and frustrated howling began in the room next door followed by the sounds of angry drunk guys roused from sleep.

"Did you really just do that?" Marianne asked in a choked voice. She was trembling from cold and adrenalin and began to giggle uncontrollably.

Sarah snorted and laughed. "I can't believe it worked!"

The sounds of anger turned to fright as the men woke, looking for the barking, growling dog in their midst. Several crashes and loud cursing suggested that lamps and possibly the TV had fallen to the floor.

Sarah and Marianne collapsed onto the bed laughing hysterically. Marianne's ribs hurt she laughed so hard. Wiping tears from their eyes, they pulled the covers back up and lay down again.

"Never piss off a paranormal lawyer," Marianne said with a last choking giggle.

"Or a resourceful historian. Damn straight. Pity we can't get the dog to go hang out in the lobby. Good call on the pizza, by the way."

"Thanks."

The noises eventually subsided next door, and as they dozed off, the blower started up again on its own, warming the room at last.

Instead of passing into a tired dreamless sleep, Marianne walked alone in a gray landscape. Oscar was nowhere to be seen. Little puffs of dust rose with each step. It had that peculiar hyper reality feel to it that told her it was one of her pay-attention-this-is-serious clairvoyant dreams. She was neither cold nor warm, happy nor sad, just neutral like the land around her. As she walked, she became aware of rounded, dark masses rising out of the ground, looming out of the gray. She stopped for a closer look.

The translucent bubble was about knee high, taut and smooth. The sac twitched and rocked slightly. Repulsed but fascinated, she peered closer and saw black blobs moving in the depths. As she watched, the bubble swelled, and she was reminded of the pictures of buboes from the Black Death. The exterior skin stretched and slowly parted with a sound of tearing paper. She stepped back as one by one, black pearls floated up like bizarre balloons. They hovered silently, smelling of dust and ten penny nails. With disgust she watched them bob above her. Then, like sightless newborns they oriented themselves on her and floated closer. She batted at them with her hands, retreating until she stumbled and fell over another swollen sac which burst with a sudden papery tear, releasing its black pearls into the air. They all turned toward her.

Scrambling to her feet, she ran, tripping over or dodging hundreds of dark masses, until she saw a light ahead. Oscar stood in the doorway with his back arched, fur bristled, hissing.

Looking over her shoulder, she saw a huge, slow moving mass of blobs following her. In desperation she flung herself through the doorway and kicked the door shut behind her.

With a sharp jerk she awoke.

"Hey," Sarah's sleep muddled voice said, "what was that for?"

Marianne was lying on a bumpy motel mattress with the sleeping bag over her. "Sorry. I was dreaming."

"Must've been a hell of a dream." Sarah rubbed her shin.

Time for sharing. "Sarah, have you ever been to the Shadow Realm?"

"No, thank the heavens."

"Have you read any descriptions of it?"

"A couple, why?"

"I think I was just there. Is it featureless and gray in all directions with lots of these round egg sacs all over the ground? When they break open, black blobs float up?"

Sarah turned on the bedside lamp. Not a trace of sleep was left. "That sounds like it. But the descriptions only mention seeing a few sacs."

She shook her head emphatically. "Not a few. Hundreds, thousands. I think they're baby Shadow People being born. They want to come here! They chased me to the door, and I just managed to kick it shut."

"You're sure this wasn't just a nightmare?" Sarah asked cautiously.

Defensive anger pricked Marianne. "You know what magic feels like. I know what a true-dream feels like. I was there. Thousands of Shadow blobs want to come through. It's like they're cicadas on a seventeen year burst. They're coming!"

Sarah put up her hands. "Okay, okay. I hear you. I guess it's more important than ever for us to visit all the stone chambers and close them off. Whoever wants the draugers here must know about the eruption."

"You know where all the doors are, right?" Marianne's heart was racing with the thought of thousands of tick-like draugers in the same world as she was. Nowhere would be safe.

Sarah said soothingly, "I know where all twelve are. Okay, change of plans. We'll prioritize closing them starting tomorrow and talk to ghosts afterwards. Protective charms will also have to be a priority. Maybe we can foil whoever it is and replace all their charms with ours. The good news is that Byron will be able to help us close the gates and complete the spell on Hallow's Eve."

Marianne nodded. The dream remnants were gone, but she was still wide awake. The dog had not returned. It was just the two of them.

Sarah lay back down and pulled the covers up over her shoulders. "There's nothing we can do about it for now. We'll get an early start tomorrow. Don't worry. We'll manage it. One of the first rules in magic is to stay calm and not get so wound up you can't think clearly."

Marianne took a deep shaky breath and let it out. "Okay. I'll stay up a little bit longer. Get some magic practice in."

"Good idea. Get some sleep, though. You're going to need it." She rolled over and slipped back into slumber in a few minutes.

Feeling anxious and driven, Marianne sat up, holding first one and then another of Sarah's magically charged objects. But try as she might, they still felt like nothing more than cloth bags, stones, herbs, and little bottles of water.

"Maybe your magic isn't very sensitive," Sarah suggested over breakfast the next morning.

Marianne slouched in the diner booth, nursing a bad cup of tea and feeling tired and depressed. Their momentary camaraderie over the spectral dog and rude neighbors had evaporated. The weird skull covered car was still parked next to Natalie, and they'd tiptoed their belongings out, hoping they wouldn't encounter angry, hungover guys or the horrible manager.

Sarah drank her coffee and tried to hide her disappointment, but it was plain.

"Yeah. Sorry," Marianne said.

"Maybe you only feel really powerful emanations, and anything less than that doesn't register. Kind of like being slapped by a cease-and-desist order. You can't miss it. Maybe more nuanced and subtle magic is beyond you?"

If Marianne couldn't detect ordinary magic, how could she wield it much less defend herself from it? She should just go back to her forté: researching the past and talking to the occasional ghost. When they got back on the road, she'd get on her phone and start working on O'Meara's problem. At least she could do someone some good.

"Never mind. It's only day three," Sarah said bracingly. "Just keep trying. You never know. We have our work cut out for us today. We have to close as many portals as we can and protect as much of the county as possible before Halloween. The old spell runs out when the veil is thinnest. That's when the draugers are most likely to break through."

Marianne gave a bleak smile. "All in five days? No pressure."

"I'm going to hit the restroom. We'll have to get Natalie's tank filled too."

"Okay." After Sarah left, Marianne pulled the county map out of her pack and spread it out on the table. She got out her pen and traced their route from yesterday, marking the two stone chambers they'd visited yesterday. She glanced longingly at Maple Hill and wished she could take Ruari up on his offer of coming to get her. It sounded like he had his hands full with work and trying to help Erin with her problems. Dealing with someone else's emotional issues sounded so much easier than doing this.

As she stared at the map focusing her eyes in and out on different parts, some puzzle pieces fell into place with a little click. The old towns of Peterson, Centerburg, and Crossfield made a familiar line. If she added in the dots where the stone passages were, another pattern emerged. She pulled the old map pictures up on her phone. She hadn't had time to download them to the library's computer system before she left.

There it was. The old linen map showed the three towns and several other communities that still existed including Maple Hill and Deer Valley. The overlain sepia lines connected a series of half ovals or rectangles sitting on a short line at the bottom. Four of them were in exactly the same locations as the stone chambers she and Sarah had visited.

Marianne gaped. The old linen map showed locations of the stone passages. She was sure of it. Someone had used this map to ride between them hundreds of years ago. Maybe that unknown person or persons had been doing the same job she and Sarah were doing now, closing portals. Her skin prickled with that sense of connection she got when she handled historical documents.

She counted the number of marks. Nineteen. But Sarah had only mentioned twelve. Seven were unaccounted for. If the unknown saboteur knew about all of them, it wouldn't matter if she and Sarah closed the twelve they knew about. Seven would still be open.

"Are you ready to go?" Sarah asked on her return from the bathroom.

"Sarah, you have to look at this." She explained her discovery, and Sarah stared at both maps for several minutes.

"Holy shit," her mentor whispered. "I never knew about these others. Byron only knew about the first twelve."

"We're going to have to find all of them, or it won't matter what we do."

For another half hour, they transferred the old map's chamber marks to the new map, annotating as they went.

The waitress stopped by to refill Sarah's coffee. "Where are you gals headed today?" She asked cheerfully.

"We're visiting historic parks and places in Canopus," Sarah responded with a practiced smile.

The waitress leaned over their map. "Looks very organized to me. It's supposed to be rainy again later today, so I hope you gals do your walking sooner rather than later."

"Good to know," Marianne said. "Could I have a Pepsi to go?" No crappy tea today.

"Sure, hon." She left to update their ticket.

"Do we have to worry about her?" Marianne whispered. Maybe Tristan Kitteby wasn't a waiter at a little diner, but he might be friends with people here in Canopus who could figure out what Marianne and Sarah were doing and alert Kitteby. "Now I'm all paranoid about this supposed magical intruder."

Sarah shook her head. "Nah, she's fine. We should head out, though."

Marianne refolded the map carefully and used the restroom before she picked up her Pepsi on the way out.

They gassed up Natalie and bought road trip snacks on the way out of Deer Valley. Marianne shook her head. Sarah bought Corn Nuts and Skittles every day and managed to eat them all. *Blech, so gross.*

"We have to make it to Minetto Point Preserve before the end of the day," Sarah told her.

"Isn't that on the Hudson?"

"Yup. It's a major focal point for the spell, and we have to rope it in early. Picking up the two extra stone passages in the south of the county is really going to slow us down."

"But if we don't, it'll be a huge hole."

"I know. We're just going to have to hurry. If we're lucky, we can find them quickly and bind them closed."

One of the stone chambers Sarah hadn't known about was located in the southeast of the county between Wixom Village and Deer Valley.

"We should head back to the river from here," Sarah said as they left the diner in Deer Valley, "but with all these new places, we're running out of time. We'll lay charms in Wixom on the way."

Wixom was no more than a hamlet in the shadow of the busy north-south Interstate 684. The lack of an on ramp to the highway meant the village was still small. A tiny post office and a couple of other small buildings constituted the entirety of the hamlet.

"Everybody else lives spread out on little country roads," Sarah told her. "We'll have to drive them to make sure they're protected before we move on."

The feed store doubled as a coffee shop, convenience store, and gas station. A handful of people in well-worn plaid shirts, stained caps, and muddy boots idled inside, drinking coffee or buying things from the practical side of the store. Sarah nodded at the man behind the counter and bought a cup of drip coffee and a couple of postcards.

"More coffee?" Marianne asked.

"These guys actually make *good* coffee. Here, have a postcard." She handed her one that said 'Historic Wixom Village' with a vintage photo of the store on it. The card looked like it had been printed a decade ago.

Marianne bought it in lieu of coffee from a solemn, bespectacled older man and put it in her pack. They stepped outside. "Where to now?"

"Keep a look out will you? Let me know if anyone comes by." Sarah casually walked down the alley alongside the feed store and stepped behind the old wooden building.

Marianne leaned against the weathered siding, trying to look nonchalant. Even though Sarah was doing something positive for the community, Marianne still felt vaguely criminal. A minivan drove up to the front of the store, and a harried looking woman with a baby got out and went in. Sarah came back empty-handed.

"I couldn't find the one I left last year," she said, looking worried.

"Did it disintegrate or did someone take it?" Marianne asked.

"I'm beginning to wonder if the missing charms are deliberate rather than random happenstance."

"Maybe we should assume it's deliberate and put them in different places than you usually do?"

She nodded. "Good call."

An old, ramshackle shed with broken windows became the new location. Sarah buried the charm bag along an outside wall, muttering the invocation as she kicked dirt over it. Back in the car, they consulted the paper map and the photo of the old linen map, trying to figure out where best to look for the new stone passage.

"I hate to say it, but these marks suggest it's in a swamp,"

Marianne observed, having zoomed in as far as she could on that corner of the photo before it blurred out. "Is there a swamp nearby?"

Sarah started Natalie who coughed a couple of times before roaring into life. They drove down a couple of roads, casting about for a swamp. Marianne used her phone to direct their search. Finally, Sarah pulled over on the shoulder and looked over the guard rail. Woods encircled an old marsh with skeletal dead trees in the middle. Marianne got out her phone and folded the paper map so that only the southeast corner showed.

"Looks like it's on the other side of those trees. Maybe we don't have to walk through the mud?"

The thought of having to slog through reeds and bulrushes made her cringe. Who know how deep it was? She laced her boots tighter and stuck her pants inside her socks before hopping the guardrail after Sarah.

They slid down a steep embankment about ten feet and began picking their way along the edge of the tree line. The boggy ground sucked at their shoes with every step. Cold water seeped in and crept through her socks. Marianne glanced at the leaden sky holding the promise of more cold rain and willed it to hold off a little longer.

After an hour of poking around, they came across a small mound back under the tree canopy. A pile of stone slabs half covered with dirt and overgrowth looked promising. They consulted their map and the GPS and concluded that it was most likely the remains of a collapsed stone chamber. Sarah walked around, viewing it from all angles while Marianne tentatively touched several of the stones, looking for a telltale vibration. They were as inert as the charms she'd tried to read last night. To be absolutely sure, she sifted through some of the dirt looking for more stones. Something poked her finger, and she yanked her hand back. No blood, but there was something sharp in there. More carefully she pushed the soil away and found a piece of wire. It was a human figure made out of twisted wire with a large bolt for a head and smaller bolts for feet. A long screw was affixed to one wiry hand. It looked very much like a little warrior with a sword.

"Hey Sarah, look at this!" She held it up and grinned.

Sarah joined her and scowled when she saw the figure. "I'd put that down if I were you. It's a poppet."

"What's that?" Marianne laid the little wire body against the collapsed stones.

"It's a magical device like an amulet that projects the power of the mage or witch."

"Oh." She recoiled a little and wiped the dirt off her hands. "Is it evil?"

"I wouldn't have thought so, but now I wonder. It's Paloma Xerxes' version of a protection charm."

The name rang a bell. "Paloma Xerxes? Isn't she a locally famous artist?"

"Yeah, she does 'art' based on found objects." Sarah's air quotes made it clear she didn't think much of it. "She's been in a couple of galleries in Putnam and Dutchess counties."

"She's also a guardian?" Marianne didn't think respectable professionals were likely to be into magic. Then again, Sarah was, so she shouldn't be so surprised.

"For Putnam county."

"Do you think she's working with Kitteby or Masters against Byron?"

"I don't know. Probably better to assume the worst at this point."

"Is there a Protector on the east side? That would be in Connecticut, right?"

"Fairfield County. Marette does string and knot magic."

Marianne raised here eyebrows. "String and knot magic?"

Sarah nodded. "Contagious magic can be very effective. Cast your intent into a piece of string, make it a knot, and throw it into the path of your enemy, and they will become confused and go in circles."

"And poppets?"

"That's based on imitation magic: create a figure doing the thing you want to do, and it will carry your intent and work on your behalf. I would have said that," she nodded at the little wire warrior, "was a guardian, but it could also be used to keep us away."

"But we found it, right? Can we neutralize it and put one of ours here?"

"Yup." She pulled out one of her own charms, activated it, and placed it under one of the collapsed chamber's stones. With a gloved hand, she picked up the little wire figure, carried it to the edge of the clearing and flung it into the swamp where it landed with a faint splash. "That should do it. At the very least it'll take the little bugger time to get back here."

A vision of the little wire figure walking along the swamp bottom, clambering over stones and logs to return to its post made the hairs on Marianne's neck stand up. The last thing she wanted to do was be here when it climbed back out of the water.

Sarah collected her pack. "Let's call it done and go back. We're already behind as it is."

As they slogged their way back to where Natalie waited patiently on the side of the road, Marianne asked, "Is there a Protector on the west side?"

"No, the Hudson is a very effective natural Protector."

"That's a relief. What kind of magic does Kitteby do?"

"I'm not sure. Clearly, he does bone and herb charms, so probably something similar to Byron's and my magic. It's called correspondence magic: stones, bones, herbs, flowers all have properties that affect other things. The Doctrine of Signatures falls in that category."

"I've heard of that. Like bleeding heart flowers are good for the heart because they look like little hearts. But that's been completely disproven."

"True. I would never make an ingestible medicine of anything based on how it looks, but combined with knowledge of their chemical and biological properties, herbs, stones, and flowers can have effective magical properties."

"So, it's a mix of chemistry and physics to cast magic and to be able to detect vibrations and energetic fields?"

"Exactly."

Marianne had barely scraped by in high school sciences. That did not bode well for learning magic now. She sighed and concentrated on keeping her boots on as they made their way through the mud.

They drove the rest of the winding, tree-lined roads around Wixom Village, leaving charms under little piles of stone, in the fork of a tree by the roadside, and behind random guard rail posts. Marianne thought of this now as fastening the spell to the locality. She drew hashed lines across the map where they'd been. They zig-zagged due west across the bottom of the county, detouring through Canopus Hill, another tiny hamlet next to a lake.

While she had a signal, Marianne did a search for the neighboring Protectors. Kitteby seemed to be a musician, his name appearing with several community theater shows over the last couple of years. He wasn't associated with a particular business, and there was no mention of magic. She'd hardly expected him to turn up under a search for "evil magician." Still, it would have answered that question.

There were many results for Xerxes, mainly connected with galleries and interviews in magazines. She looked like a glamorous hippie in vintage or thrift clothes that had been accessorized to look fashionable.

The only entry for Marette was connected to a knitting store in Fairfield. Marette seemed to be the owner. There was no photo, but the shop appeared to be in a modest strip mall near a deli and a boutique. Marianne had never been into knitting or crochet, having had no one in her life who was.

She typed in Riven Masters, but the loading symbol stayed stubbornly on the left side of the screen before saying "no connection." They must be out of range for now.

Marianne put her phone away. Sarah was still driving with quiet focus, her lips moving soundlessly. Marianne cleared her throat. "Where are we now?"

Sarah didn't answer.

She tried again. "Are you doing something magical? Is it something I can help with?"

Sarah finished her silent phrase and said, "I'm continuing the spell. Sure. Say it with me. By Earth and Air and Fire and Water, bind all our charms together and Protect Canopus County."

Marianne said it with her for several minutes, but the repetition felt silly after that, and she let her voice fade away. Sarah gave her a half nod and returned to her silent chanting. Marianne stared out the window as they drove the roads along the southern edge of Canopus. This southern route was more direct than most of the other routes through Canopus, joining the east and west sides, so the traffic was steadier than many of the places they'd been. At one point Sarah glanced in the rearview and muttered, "What the?"

Marianne looked in the side view mirror to catch a glimpse behind them and saw a large black sedan passing car after car behind them, recklessly crossing the double yellow centerline. When it was right behind them, Sarah said distractedly, "Look, our buddies are back."

It was the skull covered car from the night before. Sure enough, when the oncoming cars had passed, the sedan gunned its engine, and drew level. Marianne couldn't help herself. She leaned forward and looked past Sarah through the window. Man Bun was riding shotgun, his arm propped on the window frame. He looked over and widened his eyes in recognition. He bared his white teeth in a grin and said something to the driver. The driver revved the engine and pulled in front of them, barely missing Natalie's bumper.

"Fucking idiots," Sarah growled, braking.

The two guys in the backseat turned and faced them, leering and waving, laughing all the while. The matte black sedan hovered in front of them for a minute, and then the driver accelerated, pulling away with the throaty roar of a V-8 engine.

"As long as they keep going, I don't care," Marianne murmured.

"Did you get the license plate?"

"What? No, I didn't think to."

"Well, write this down." Sarah repeated the letter-number combination, and Marianne jotted it in her notebook, impressed. "Let's hope we don't ever see them again."

"Amen."

They pulled over a couple of times between communities, and Sarah planted charms at each location. Marianne strolled along the side of the road, keeping a nervous eye out for matte black cars. Her eye fell on a handful of random trash, bits of wire, bolts, an old nail, and a piece of red twine. They made her think of the little wire figure that Sarah had tossed into the swamp, and she shuddered. She was never going to look at the world quite the same way after this trip.

"C'mon, we have to get going," Sarah called.

Back in the car, Sarah returned to her quiet spell casting, and Marianne felt that conversation was out of the question. Her phone showed four out of five bars again, so she went back to researching Turner's Hope Mine and Peter O'Meara's problem. The memory of his coal black eyes and intense stare still gave her willies. He wanted revenge on the owners of the mine. Those men were long dead, so that was moot. If they'd died alone and penniless, maybe O'Meara would let it go. On the other hand, maybe recognition for the sacrifice he and his men had made would be a satisfying alternative? She had some ideas to explore and wrote them down.

If she could get some decent time at a library, she could make more headway. Given their deadline, that was unlikely. She'd have to wait until next week. If, that is, the world didn't end on Halloween night, filled with hungry black blobs.

When she lost signal she looked up again. Sarah was turning Natalie down another country road and the trees were giving way to fields outlined by stone walls. The grass was high, and it looked like no domesticated animals or agriculture had happened there in a long time. A particularly dilapidated barn with traces of red paint sat in the middle of one field. It leaned to one side as if one good sneeze would collapse the whole thing. Sarah bumped down a grass covered lane towards it. A small, rural cemetery lay across the track from the barn.

Sarah threw Natalie into park and killed the engine. Marianne hoped they could get her started again. The clouds were lower than before and a fitful breeze blew. If it rained, the old Volvo might strand them out here. Without a cell signal, it would be a long, miserable walk to get help.

"What's here?" She asked, looking at the neglected, overgrown cemetery. John Irving would be appalled.

Sarah was rummaging through the boxes in the back of the car. "An old ally. He's ornery, obnoxious, and mean as all get out, but he might agree to help us if it comes to a fight with the draugers."

"He sounds awful. How did you find out about him?"

"He was scaring the bejesus out of the locals. That's why the place is abandoned."

"Charming." Marianne prepared to hop the fence. "What's his name? I'll start looking for his grave."

Sarah slammed the back hatch shut, stuffing something in her pocket. "He's not in the cemetery. He's in there." She gestured to the rickety barn and started walking purposefully.

"Wait, you're not going in there? One wrong move and the whole thing will come down."

"That's where Adrian Vandermark resides. I need you to keep

watch. If it looks like it's coming down, tell me. Until then, I'll be busy calling up Vandermark."

Tall grass obscured everything, and Marianne tripped over boards and debris that had already given up their battle with gravity. Up close the old building looked even less stable. Swaying ponderously like an enormous shipwreck on a reef in a gale, the barn creaked and groaned. Sarah strode determinedly through the open door to the center of the space and knelt down. Scraping a shallow bowl in the dirt, she pulled a package from her pocket and poured a small quantity of something into the hollow. Marianne heard the clicking of a lighter and, a moment later, smelled the aromatic scent of tobacco on a gust of wind.

Sarah stood and called out, "Adrian Vandermark, come talk to me. I have need of your services."

Marianne leaned nervously on the doorway. The beam moved under her and she hastily stood up. As her eyes adjusted to the darker interior, she saw the remains of several old carriages and the outlines of horse stalls overgrown with grass.

"Adrian Vandermark, come talk to me!" Sarah called again.

Marianne felt the pressure on her eardrums grow as if she were sinking slowly deeper into a pool of water. It was accompanied by a faint howl that melded perfectly with the moaning of the wind through the broken teeth of the barn. Something angry and dangerous was coming. The hair on the back of Marianne's neck stood to attention, and she had a powerful urge to run back to the car.

Sarah stood calmly in the midst of the maelstrom of sound and feeling. "Adrian Vandermark, come talk to me!" She shouted. Marianne remembered how fierce Sarah had been in the face of O'Meara and his men and was reluctantly impressed again. Whatever Sarah's failings in the compassion department, she lacked nothing in the stand-up-to-bullies department.

The long wailing howl became a swirl of something dark. Marianne shut her eyes and saw a tall, angular figure materialize next to Sarah. In his hand he held a five foot length of thin, pliable wood with another five foot strip of leather, a gleaming spur at the tip. The carriage whip cracked, narrowly missing Sarah who stood stock still, staring at him defiantly. Marianne flinched involuntarily.

Get out of my barn! He bellowed.

"You don't scare me. I'm not leaving until I have what I want," she replied.

He hesitated looking disappointed then turned his hollow black eyes on Marianne.

That's not how she feels! He rushed at her with a scream that slid across two octaves, brandishing the whip.

Marianne flung up her arms and fled. Crouched behind Natalie, she had no idea how she'd covered the distance so fast. Her heart beat double-time and her arms wrapped tightly around her legs.

Don't let old grouchy pants get to you, a voice said with wry amusement.

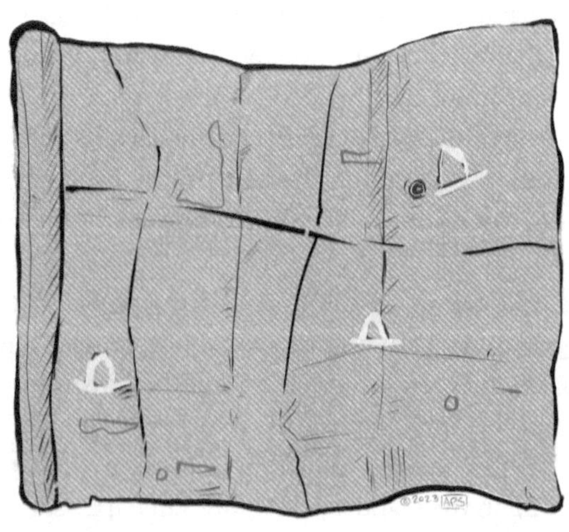

CHAPTER 10

Marianne hit her head on the side view mirror in surprise.

"Ow!" She clutched her skull and looked around for the owner of the voice.

Someone snickered.

"It's not funny. Where are you?" She snapped.

Here.

Marianne closed her eyes, and the smoky form of a young woman with thick, unruly hair came into view. She sat on the split rail fence of the small cemetery. The longer Marianne looked, the sharper the outline became.

Marianne stood up and dusted herself off. Cautiously she opened her eyes. The figure became translucent but didn't disappear completely. Once she'd fixed on a ghost, it usually stayed visible. Ghostly howling and Sarah's composed voice continued behind her. She sounded like she had things under control. The ghost in front of her looked more amused than scary.

"Sorry for snapping at you. I'm Marianne. Nice to meet you." She stepped forward and offered her hand without thinking.

The apparition raised her eyebrows and unfolded her arms enough to shake Marianne's hand. Marianne felt a cool touch.

Toni Woods. Nice to meet you, too. People don't usually see me.

Marianne closed her eyes, and the outline of the ghostly presence sharpened and took on more detail. Toni wore a pair of jeans, a blouse over a surprisingly broad pair of shoulders, white socks, and a pair of sneakers. Marianne raised her eyebrows.

The girl raised her chin defiantly. *Hey, no judging the clothes! My stepmom tried to bury me in a hideous dress. I pitched a fit until she put me in my favorite jeans.*

"She heard you?"

Toni flashed a feral grin. *No, I was so mad I ripped the dress right out of her hands!*

"She must've freaked out!" Marianne smiled, remembering her first encounter with an angry ghost.

She did. It was a shame I could only do it once.

The sounds of shouting continued behind her, and Marianne hoped negotiations were going well. She had no intention of returning until Adrian Vandermark was gone. Instead, she looked past Toni to the overgrown, neglected cemetery behind her. "You live here?"

Toni gave a one-shouldered shrug. *'Live' is kind of a strong word but yeah. Not my first choice, but no one asked me.*

"Mind if I walk around?"

Be my guest.

Marianne climbed over the splintery top rail of the fence and walked through the small burial plot. Toni glide-walked beside her. "Are you the only one here who's active?" Marianne asked.

Once again the broad shoulders shrugged. *Mostly. I'm one of the last people who came here. As you can see,* she gestured sarcastically at the waist high weeds and wind drifted leaves, *we're reeeeally popular. If people don't come visit, the residents tend to leave or stay asleep. My dad had family in the area and got me this cushy spot. Of course, his new wife made them move away, and they pretty much never come to visit anymore.*

"I'm sorry," Marianne said.

Toni's memorial had an open book carved on top with the inscription, "'Books were safer than other people anyway,' Neil Gaiman." Beneath that on the vertical face was an inscription: "Antonia Woods 1990-2007. Beloved daughter."

"If you don't mind my asking, why haven't you moved on?"

I don't know. She shrugged angrily. *I'm the oldest in my family. My mom died when we were little, and my dad married 'Chloe',* she spat the name like it was poison, *who came with four of her own kids. We never really 'blended' well. When I bit the big one in a car wreck, Chloe was relieved she didn't have to put up with me anymore.*

"I'm sure she was more upset than you think," Marianne temporized automatically.

No, she wasn't, Toni snapped. *I was there. She said some choice things to my two sibs. That bitch made my little sister cry.* Toni balled up her fists. *If I could've killed her on the spot, I would've.*

"I'm sorry your family is messed up," Marianne said softly. Anger and sorrow probably kept Toni restless.

Toni recovered herself, leaned back on the neighboring head-stone and folded her arms again. *So, why are you guys here? What did you want with him?* She tipped her chin toward the barn across the road.

She leaned against a neighboring headstone. "Well, Sarah, casts a spell every year that protects Canopus Territory from—bad things."

Toni gave her an incredulous look. *A spell, huh?*

Marianne bobbed her head in wry agreement. "I was skeptical too, but I've changed my mind."

Huh. Would that keep the shady people out of here?

"Shady people?"

Yeah. They're kind of like stringy shadows. Sometimes they check the place out.

Marianne looked around in alarm. "Are they here now?"

Toni grinned. *Nah. I give 'em hell. No shady people allowed in this shitty little backwater while I'm here.*

Marianne whispered, "You've met draugers?"

Toni sobered. *Is that what they're called?*

She nodded.

A couple of times. A guy who was buried after me had been an alcoholic and done some damage before he died. The shady people were attracted to him like flies to a corpse. She smiled mirthlessly. *I chased them off before they got too chummy and had a talk with Mr. Bottle. He agreed to lay low. His family never comes, so that helps.*

Sarah was right, Marianne thought looking at Toni's athletic, feminine form, *attitude was everything*. She was sad Toni was a shade. She wished she'd known her when she was alive.

Marianne glanced back toward Natalie. No Sarah yet. There was no more shouting, and at least the barn was still standing.

"Does Adrian Vandermark give you any trouble or attract shady people?"

Toni graced her with another feral grin. *When I first got here, we got into it a couple of times, but we worked it out. Your trouble is you let him chase you off. You can't let someone like him intimidate you.*

"Darn tootin' he's intimidating!" Marianne ducked her head with an embarrassed chuckle.

The young woman burst out laughing. *You can't win a meet or stand up for your little brother and sister if you don't take the right attitude.*

Marianne brushed the top of Toni's stone. "So, you like to read?"

Yeah. My dad put that on the stone. There's not a lot of great books out here, though.

Marianne felt a wash of loneliness and resentment. "What do you like to read?"

A shrug. *Mysteries, sci-fi, history, romance, pretty much everything.*

Marianne had a thought. "Just a sec." She walked back to the car and rummaged through her suitcase. She returned and laid a book in a ziplock baggie on the carved open book.

Toni brushed insubstantial fingers over it. *What's this?*

"I brought a book to read in case we had any down time. I don't think that's going to happen. I don't know how you can read it, but it looked good."

'My Grandmother Asked Me To Tell You She's Sorry,' Toni read. She said, *Thanks,* like she didn't get gifts very often.

"Let me know if you like it. What else did you like to do?"

I loved to swim. I spent every minute in the water I could. I won a few medals for my high school team. She pulled a couple of pale, round disks out of her pocket and showed them proudly.

"Wow, congratulations." Marianne cleared her throat, not sure how to ask and just went for it. "Um, did you have a boyfriend?"

Toni frowned, shoving the medals back in her pocket. *That's kind of personal.*

She felt her face heat. *Idiot.* "You're right, it was rude and presumptuous. It's just that I met a guy recently who's about your age."

She looked over Marianne's shoulder into the distance. *I didn't have a lot of time to date anyone between swimming and making sure my little brother and sister were okay. And then this happened.* She gestured at her translucent body. She was quiet for a beat then said, *Could he see me?*

"He's like you. He had a rough home life and a sudden…death. He likes loud music."

Like what?

"I think he mentioned the Melvins and Death Cab for Cutie."

She smiled. *Okay, okay. Probably not a total dweeb. Is he cute?*

Marianne smiled, remembering Jason's shaggy blonde hair and roguish smile. "Yeah, he is. I'll see if he can come by. No promises but I'll try."

Footsteps approached, swishing through the dead grass. "You

can come back now. We settled things." She gave Marianne a mocking smile. "Some back up you are."

"He surprised me that's all," Marianne replied with dignity.

"Huh. Who's your new friend?"

"Sarah, meet Toni."

They looked each other over with frank assessment. Marianne admired Toni's lack of deference. *I've got to learn how to do that.*

Marianne cleared her throat. "When I came back to the car to get a little fresh air, Toni introduced herself, and we got to talking."

"Did you tell her why we're here?"

"I was getting to that. Toni, would you be willing to keep the shady people out of here for the coming year? We're asking a bunch of people across the county to help us out, as well as leaving behind some charms to watch other places."

Like sleeping policemen, huh? Sure, what's in it for me?

"I could bring you more books, if that works for you. And I'll see if I can persuade Jason to come for a visit."

I guess that would be okay. She gave a shrug, but there was a gleam in her eye.

Marianne turned to Sarah. "She's met draugers before and chased them off."

Sarah looked impressed. "We think this year might be different. There might be more. A lot more. Are you still in?"

Toni narrowed her eyes and stared at Sarah appraisingly, then looked at Marianne. *Beats sitting in the locker room. How do I contact you?*

Marianne opened her mouth to reply, but Sarah interrupted, "She dreams. You could probably find her that way."

Toni said, *Sounds interesting. I'll see you there.*

They got back in the car.

"Well, she didn't seem too needy," Sarah said dryly as they bumped along the overgrown track back to the road.

Miffed, Marianne answered, "No, she was just lonely. What happened with Adrian Vandermark?"

"I explained the situation and offered him a chance to fight something other than punk kids daring each other to come to a haunted barn. He was up for it."

"Did you have to pay him like you did the miners?"

"He loves Captain Black Gold pipe tobacco. I brought him some."

"How on Earth did you figure that out?"

"You don't want to know."

"How am I supposed to learn if you don't tell me how you did it?" Marianne asked in exasperation.

"Figuring stuff out on your own is usually the best teacher."

"Bullshit!" Sarah's hands off style of mentoring was getting on Marianne's nerves.

Sarah chuckled. Her encounter with Adrian had left her in a good mood.

"Fine. I got the locals to tell me their stories of the haunted barn. I deduced Adrian was alive in the 1800s when this was all working farmland. There was a good chance he liked a smoke, so the next time I came out I brought a couple of tobacco blends. I lit them one at a time until he came to see what was going on. He showed up for Captain Black Gold."

"Did he ever scare the shit out of you?"

Sarah gave a wry smile. "The first time he showed up with that carriage whip, I admit I hightailed it back to Natalie. But I went right back and stared him down."

"I prefer Toni."

They left protective charms in secluded locations near houses as they headed west. Sarah's good mood evaporated as the she drove. They pulled over to hunt for another of the lost stone chambers along the way, but after thirty minutes without success, Sarah gave up.

"We have to get to Minetto before dark. If we have time tomorrow, we can try again."

They arrived at Minetto Point Preserve after three. As they pulled in, the only other car, a dark sedan, pulled out. The weather had turned for the worse and a light, cold rain was falling, promising to get heavier. Their map showed one stone chamber on the upland portion of the trail, but they would have to walk the entire four mile loop to lay charms and tie this corner of the county into the spell.

Sarah had asked her to research the history of the place, but Turner's Hope Mine had occupied Marianne's entire attention. She felt like a slacker for not doing the 'homework,' but Sarah didn't ask. Her guilt turned to annoyance. Sarah was like a professor who assigned tons of reading and then never asked about it.

"Park closes at dusk" read the sign.

"Don't worry, we can make it if we hustle," Sarah assured her. "It's paved and pretty flat."

I'm cold and lunch ran out an hour ago. I wish I was sitting in front of the fire with Ruari and Oscar. But Marianne put on her extra sweater, wool hat and gloves, and emptied her pack down to water, a dozen charms, and one of the closing charms. She patted her pockets: bottle of holy water, Ruari's carved cat totem, and the personal amulet of stones and herbs in her jeans and set out, following Sarah's lead. While they walked, she ate a granola bar. Maybe this wouldn't take too long, and they could go to dinner and find a nice warm bed somewhere, preferably without obnoxious neighbors.

They walked clockwise around the loop to cast a binding spell, pausing to step off the trail and bury charms near each mile marker. Sarah took extra time to find new locations so their mysterious enemy wouldn't find and destroy them. They found one empty cotton bag. Someone or something had been there and taken the rest. Grimly they picked up their pace.

Marianne stood watch while Sarah laid down spell components for the fifth charm. The wind rattled forlornly through the marsh reeds, and she shivered. Back along the way they'd come, she caught sight of two other hikers walking briskly.

Last minute visitors. They must be as crazy as we are.

Near milepost two the pavement became a wooden board-walk as the trail angled out over the marsh down near the Hudson. Whitecaps blew across the gray river. Their footsteps beat a quick tattoo on the boards as they hurried to the next paved section. Marianne joined Sarah in chanting the words of protection.

The light grew steadily dimmer as they wound their way up the steeper part of the trail into the upland section. The stone chamber was past milepost three along a little spur. They stopped to lay another charm just off the trail.

As she grew colder, Marianne felt a warmth in her jeans pocket. Glancing along the trail behind them, she realized the hikers were much nearer. They were catching up. Sarah's detours slowed their own progress. Her skin prickled with something other than the chill.

"Sarah, those two hikers I told you about are still behind us."

"Can they see me?"

"I don't think so, but they're getting a lot closer."

"Tell me if they get close enough to see where I'm putting things. Until then, don't worry about it."

"You keep saying that. It's not helping," Marianne muttered.

The light level dropped in half when they plunged into the trees. They nearly missed the trail, only catching sight of white letters on a sign saying,"Stone Mound 0.1 mile." They jogged up the winding trail as quickly as they dared in the gloom.

As they rounded the corner, Marianne felt the buzz saw vibration and clenched her teeth against the dizziness. Together they knelt and got out a closing charm and the flashlight. Mari-anne gripped the holy water and the wooden cat and took deep, steadying breaths before following Sarah into the hillside through the stone uprights.

This doorway was narrow, barely wider than her shoulders, and framed by two upright blocks of stone with a stone top. It looked more like Stonehenge than the others had, but the sickening magical vibration was the same. Marianne gulped and clutched the wall for support through a wave of vertigo. When it passed, she descended the three deep steps into the passage below. It was barely twice as wide as the entrance and about eight feet tall. It felt like a giant keyhole. Sarah was already playing the flashlight over the surfaces, hunting for the wedging charm. Marianne spotted a little flash of white in the ceiling.

"There! Is that it?"

The beam zeroed in. "Yup. You'll have to boost me up as far as you can."

Marianne ditched her pack on the floor, crouched, and grasped Sarah below her butt, counted to three, and heaved up. Sarah was thinner than Marianne but still weighed at least one-thirty and Marianne grunted and braced herself agains the wall. Another reason to take up working out. Sarah's wet rain jacket pressed into her face.

"Can you walk back a little?" Sarah directed her. "Okay, I can almost reach. Can you…just…a little farther."

Marianne took a deep breath and boosted her up as far as she could. "Hurry up, you're freakin' heavy, lady!"

"Almost…I got it!"

Marianne let her slide down and stepped back, panting.

"Another practitioner has been here for sure. Okay, get the other one ready."

Marianne crushed the bag holding the closing charm and got a sharp whiff of sulphurus asafoetida leaves. Together they chanted the words. They found a different crevice and wedged it into place, tucking all traces out of sight. Sarah put the toxic charm in a sandwich baggie and slid it into an outer pocket of her pack.

"Okay, we're done here. Let's—"

The stones in Marianne's pocket pulsed with a sharp heat like touching a hot pan. "Ow!"

"What's the matter?"

"Your amulet just gave me a hot flash!"

Sarah's head snapped toward the door. "Get out of here, quick!"

"What is it?"

"Shadow People!"

Marianne grabbed her pack, swung it up on her shoulder and bolted for the stair, Sarah right behind her. "But we just closed it! Nothing can come through!"

"Not in here. Out there. We don't want to get trapped."

Twilight had fallen while they'd been inside, and it was nearly dark. In spite of that, Marianne clearly saw two darker shapes on the path between them and the main trail. Unlike ghosts, they were tall and stringy like two smoky columns in the twilight. Where their eyes should have been, dull red coals glowed. Her heart sped with a surge of fear-laced adrenalin.

The two women stood just outside the opening, shoulder to shoulder. "You have no power over us here. Get out of our way," Sarah declared coldly. To Marianne she murmured, "Unscrew the top of your bottle of holy water and get ready. When I say run, throw the water at them and run like hell. Whatever happens, don't let them touch you. They'll make you crazy, then feed off the results."

Marianne gulped. "Okay," she breathed and forced herself to reach for the vial of water in her jacket pocket. She wished she had more than a couple of ounces. The two figures blocked their path. There was no way to get past them without making contact with them or crashing through the brush on one side of the path or the other. Her muscles tensed ready to run, but Sarah said nothing.

Marianne had thought the figures were silent, but as they slowly drifted closer, she heard a faint, ear curling sound of slowly tearing paper that was more menacing than all of Vandermark's bluster. It made her want to hide until they went away. What was Sarah waiting for?

"Run." The word dropped like a penny.

Marianne dashed forward, flung the holy water, bottle and all, at the dark figure on the right, and pushed through the bushes, stabbing her thigh painfully on a branch as she passed. The amulet pulsed with another hot flash. She got a fleeting impression of darkness, hunger, and a scent of dust and metal as she leapt down the path. Stumbling on the uneven ground, she almost went down, righted herself, and hit the pavement at a run. The sound of crashing next to her pushed her to run faster, and she flinched before she comprehended it was Sarah.

Together they ran pell mell in the pitch black darkness until Marianne thought her heart would explode, and a sharp pain cut her breathing in half. *I am so going to start a jogging program if I live through this.* No one followed them, and they slowed to a brisk walk.

"Are they going to come after us?" Marianne panted, clutching a stitch in her side.

"Holy water will slow them down. Parking lot not far." Sarah was out of breath too.

"That's good, 'cause I don't have a lot left."

They kept walking until the shape of Natalie's boxy white station wagon loomed in the deep twilight.

"This would be so much easier in mid summer. You'd have so much more light and time to get all this done," Marianne commented.

"Heh," Sarah replied, "solstice is good for many things but not the thinning of the veil between the worlds. Samhain, All Souls, All Hallows, Halloween is when you have to do this work."

"Figures."

Sarah fumbled for her keys, and Marianne flipped on the flashlight to give her some light.

"Turn that off!" Sarah snapped.

"I'm just trying to help!" Tired, feeling the shakes of post-adrenalin, Marianne snapped back.

"They're attracted to light! Turn it off!" Sarah ordered.

She switched it off, leaving her eyes mazed with dots for a few seconds. She heard Sarah's grunt followed by the click of the driver's side door. Looking back to the path, Marianne saw two dark figures pass through the fence as if it wasn't there and glide swiftly towards them.

"Holy shit! They went right through the fence! Hurry up!"

They flung themselves into the front seats and locked the doors.

Sarah turned the key, and the starter gave a sad half chug.

"C'mon, Natalie, start!" Marianne shouted. Their pursuers were halfway across the gravel lot.

"Don't shout at her!" Sarah snapped. "She's very sensitive. Come on, *mon amie*, I know it's rainy, but you can do it." Another half chug.

The draugers reached the car. Marianne braced herself, expecting them to pass right through the hood like an iceberg through a steel hull, but they stopped, unable to go further. The herbal scent of the protection charms intensified.

Chuh….chuuugg. The car turned over, and Sarah eased up the clutch and feathered the gas pedal. Natalie roared back in reverse, turned, and bore them away, headlights blazing a trail before them.

They returned to Peterson for the night. Dinner and a hot shower restored some of Marianne's composure. Already the feelings of fear were fading into unreality. Exhaustion weighed her down after a day of surprises and adrenaline. Sarah got on the phone with Byron again and conferred with him in a low voice in a corner of the room.

Marianne wanted to sleep for nine hours straight but needed

to call Ruari first. She desperately wanted to hear his voice and hear about his utterly normal life. She wanted to return to that normal life more than anything. Magical practice would have to wait until tomorrow.

"Hey, Ruari, it's me."

"Mahri, I was hoping to hear from you tonight! Where are you?"

"We're in Peterson at a motel."

"I thought you'd already been through Peterson?"

"We were, but the spell has to be woven back and forth, so we drive around a lot, leaving charms everywhere."

"I see. Have you been able to do any more networking for a job?"

"Not really. Unless you count meeting ghosts. I think I have to put job hunting on hold till we get back. How are you?"

"I'm okay, but Erin had a really rough night. I wish you were here, you could help us. She thinks her new place is haunted!"

"What?"

"For someone who doesn't believe in that crap, she's convinced there's a ghost here."

"What do you think?"

"I'm not sure. My big tough sister asked me to spend the night, so I'm couch surfing." Erin's indistinct voice shouted something in protest. "Okay, okay! She offered me a chance to sleep on her new pullout couch." He lowered his voice. "Honestly, Mahri, I haven't seen her this wigged out since she was a kid. Something has her spooked."

"She's not the only one. One of the maps I cataloged shows the locations of all the stone portals in Canopus. Unfortunately there are more than Sarah knows about, so we're trying to find all of them. Remember I told you about draugers? Two of them chased us at Minetto Point tonight. Luckily Natalie is magically warded, and they couldn't get us."

He sucked in a breath. "Holy shit! Are you okay?"

"Yeah. We threw holy water at them and ran like the blazes when they came after us."

"I really want to come get you."

"You have no idea how much I want you to, but I can't leave Sarah. Kelly is still not very mobile, and we've been walking a lot. According to Sarah, the spell will be null and void if one of us leaves, and she'd have to start all over again. There isn't enough time." She glanced up at Sarah's muted conversation. "We've been in touch with her old magic teacher, and found out that another magician? Magical practitioner? I don't know what the term is, but they've kidnapped his sister's ghost and is holding her captive."

"What?! That sounds crazy!"

"I know! But he thinks he's found out where she's being held and is all set to rescue her. I don't fully understand it, but he's promised to help us close the gates on Halloween. After the attack tonight, I'm scared. We need the help."

"I can be there. I don't know what I can do to help you, but I'll be at the cemetery on Halloween."

Marianne closed her eyes and gulped, relief flooding her. "That would be amazing. I have no idea what we have to do other than close the spell we're casting, but it would be wonderful to have you there."

"Text me when you think you'll be there, and I'll meet you."

She cleared her throat and tried to change the subject. "I haven't had any time to look for a costume yet, but I'll keep trying. Although at this point, I don't think we'll get to any parties given how things have been going."

"Tell you what, we can have our own private party. I'll share my costume, and you can share yours if you find one."

In spite of her gloom, the image of Ruari in a kilt flashed through her mind, and she grinned. "You're on!" She hung up a minute later feeling better than she had.

✿

Talking to Ruari had allayed some of her fears, and Marianne slid under the covers. She didn't want to think any more about the day, so she rolled away from Sarah's bed and pretended to be asleep. Sarah finished her conversation shortly thereafter and slid under her own covers and turned the light off.

"Marianne?" She called softly.

Feeling warm and drowsy and disinclined to hear something that would make her lie awake all night, she ignored her. Sarah let it go.

Marianne drifted into sleep and dream state. Roads and maps and snatches of conversation flickered by. Eventually, she found herself in a classroom taking an exam. The room looked like one from her undergrad days, and she looked up to see one of her old professors stalking around the room. Oscar sat primly on her desk, crooked tipped tail wrapped around his front paws. She looked at her paper. There were three questions, but she'd hardly written a word in her blue exam book. Alarmed, she read the first question.

"Psst!" The person in the seat next to her whispered. "Psst!"

Marianne looked up and saw a woman with thick unruly hair, her tee shirt stretching tightly across her broad shoulders. "Toni?"

The young woman put her finger to her lips and smiled. "Just making sure I can reach you!"

"There will be no talking during the exam!" The professor said sternly. "Miss Singleton, Miss Woods, do your own work! No cheating with cats!"

Oscar snickered and helpfully pawed the first question. Marianne tucked her head down and read it. "Do Victorian cravats change the nature of frogs and alter the state of the dirigible? Discuss in detail." She read it again and couldn't make heads or tails of it.

"You have five minutes left! Check your work!"

Panic blanked out any chance of recalling either the question or the answer. She was suddenly aware of the prof standing behind her. He leaned down and barked, "Check your work! Be sure you have completed your work! Go over your work and be sure it's right!"

"I need more time!" She wailed.

"There is no more time! Go back over your work!"

Marianne surfaced from the dream with relief. Drawing a blank during an exam had been her worst nightmare when she was in college. So strange to still have that dream even though she hadn't been in school for ages. Toni Woods had been there. It didn't have the clarity of her true dreams, but the professor's insistent voice was hard to shake. It didn't make sense, and she desperately needed the sleep. So she rolled over and let herself drift off again.

CHAPTER 11

They spent the next morning laying charms in small communities and the empty areas between. Sarah was clearly in her own world and either silent or chanting under her breath. Marianne's attempts to start conversation were rebuffed with terse answers. She was still jangled after their encounter with the draugers and guessed Sarah was as well, but her companion's silence made her feel isolated and scared.

Trying to distract herself, Marianne opened her pack. The stack of resumés was looking dog-eared. Marianne hadn't stopped to hand out a single one the day before, and it looked like that was going to be the case again today. She had rent to pay at the end of the month and all the usual expenses. Living with Geoffrey and his money for ten years had made her forget how hard it was to make ends meet. She could sympathize heartily with her mother's constant low-level anxiety while Marianne was growing up. She glanced over at her companion. Sarah stared straight out the window, driving down another long country road. When they were done with this trip, Sarah would be going back to her stable, well-paid lawyering job.

Sarah had promised to help her look for a job and then said

she could call in some favors with other law firms. That seemed to be the end of her promise to help. Well, Marianne still wanted to explore the historical society options. She got out her phone and searched.

Finally she said, "Sarah?"

Her mentor broke off her mutter and said, "Yes?"

"I'd really like to stop at another historical society or park with a history program today."

Sarah frowned. "Do you think that could wait? We have a lot to do to get these charms laid and find all the new stone chambers."

"This is really important to me, and you said you'd stop."

She blew out a breath. "Fine. There's a visitor center at Williston State Park. We have to go there today anyway. You can stop there."

"Thank you."

"Could you figure out how to navigate to some of the new ones?"

"Sure. Where are we now?"

Marianne got out the county map. There was one on the east side not far from where they were passing. She got them as close as she could before they had to park on the side of the road and walk into the woods.

The weather was no longer rainy, but the wind blew through Marianne's jacket, and she shivered as she pushed her stiff muscles up the slope after Sarah. They cast about for nearly twenty minutes, and Sarah had just talked about heading back to the car when Marianne felt a faint buzzing. She held up her hand to silence her companion and slowly turned on the spot. There, down in a little dell. She walked cautiously toward it, feeling the buzzing grow stronger. She also noted a faint trail of darker leaves. Someone had been there recently.

Sarah followed and said, "Hey, good going. I would have missed that."

They knelt and got out gloves and a closing charm. Only one of them could be inside at a time, the chamber was so small.

"You want to do the honors?" Sarah offered with a rare smile.

Marianne shook her head. "You go ahead. I'll keep watch out here."

Sarah shrugged and ducked inside. A couple of minutes later, she was back out holding another wedging charm.

"Tristan Kitteby again?" Marianne asked.

Sarah turned the bag over in her hands. "I don't see any marks. Let's take a look." She upended the bag into her gloved palm. Among the peony seeds, slivers of bone and flower fragments, there was a little piece of cherry red yarn. "Dammit," she said.

"What's that?"

"Marette. Well, it's official. It sure looks like the neighboring Protectors are trying to rid their own counties of Shadow People by pushing them into ours."

"She's the one who does knot magic?"

"Yup."

Marianne didn't think much of Protectors who saved their own territories by pushing bad stuff onto their neighbors. She wondered if they did that to each other, too and if it really was every county for itself, magically speaking. She voiced her disbelief.

"Byron made it clear to me when he turned over the Protection gig that this could happen," Sarah replied. "I have no idea if they push against each other, but it wouldn't surprise me at all."

"Have they done it before when you and Kelly were doing this?"

"No, but it's a weird year. If the draugers are coming through in large numbers here, they may be doing so in Dutchess, Fairfield, and Putnam too."

"What did Byron have to say last night?" Marianne asked

"He's close to finding Catalina and told me about a powerful talisman that he thinks could help rescue her."

"What do you mean? I thought talismans protected you."

"No that's amulets. The bag of stones and herbs I gave you is an amulet in the form of a charm. It contains items that inherently protect you. A talisman is a magically created item that projects your will and power."

"Like the charms we're laying or the little wire figure?"

"Yes. In this case, Byron found out about a sixteenth-century talisman from Spain which was created to close portals to the Shadow Realm. He thinks it's in the states, possibly even New England. If he can find it before Halloween, he can use it to close all the gates and stop the incursion of draugers. He may also be able to save his sister."

That sounded good even if it was extremely vague. Presumably he would know how to use such a thing, and they would be able to shut down the portals and protect Canopus County for another year. "What did he say about the extra portals?"

"He was upset and told me to focus on the known ones."

"But what about the new ones?"

"We'll just have to do what we can." And she lapsed into silence or murmured chanting.

Rather than stew about how many portals they had to go, the callous indifference of the neighboring Protectors, or Shadow People, Marianne checked her phone connection, and hallelujah it was there. She used her time to research Turner's Hope Mine. It wasn't easy getting access to library files, but she did what she could. She even called Mrs. Caldwell to look up a couple of things for her. The old librarian was terse but seemed intrigued when Marianne told her she'd been commissioned to create a memorial for the miners who'd died there. It was a little white lie but not entirely untrue. Peter O'Meara just hadn't promised to pay her for it.

When Sarah stopped the old Volvo in a new-looking neighborhood of mini mansions on quarter lots, Marianne put her phone away and readied herself to get out. Her hand was on the door handle when Sarah stopped her. "Wait."

"What?"

"Would you mind getting the maps out? Both on paper and your phone."

They unfolded the Canopus County map against the dash board. "We're here." Sarah pointed to a place outside Peterson. A small arch drawn by them indicated a stone chamber was nearby. Marianne pulled up the photo of the eighteenth century linen map and confirmed that they'd drawn the chamber in the right place. "Where is it?" She asked.

"That's just it. I've driven through the entire subdivision. I think they demolished it to build houses. Nothing looks familiar to me."

"Well, that's okay then. If it's gone, it can't be opened, right? It'll be like the collapsed one."

"Yeah, probably." Sarah sounded dubious.

"Maybe we should lay a closing charm as close to the original location as we can get?"

Sarah nodded, looking thoughtful. "And we need to make a note of this new subdivision."

Marianne annotated the map accordingly, and they drove around until Sarah stopped at a house that looked the same as all the others to Marianne.

"This is it," she declared.

"What is?"

"This is where the old chamber was."

"How can you tell?"

"The air between the house and garage is blurry. Can't you feel it?"

Marianne closed her eyes and extended her senses, searching for the vibration, but there was nothing. She shook her head, her earlier success negated. It had been a lucky fluke. Why did she think she could do this? Sarah's lips twitched downward, but she said nothing. Marianne felt a rush of guilt that she had disappointed her mentor yet again followed by a surge of annoyance.

It wasn't her fault if she couldn't feel magic at the same level as Sarah could. Being able to do magic seemed to be a completely hit or miss thing: you either had it or you didn't. As far as she could see, Marianne didn't have what it took, and she was reminded of Geoffrey's patronizing looks when he'd asked her to do something she couldn't do.

"No, I can't," she said flatly.

Sarah shook her head. "Never mind. I can see where to put it. Just hand me one."

Marianne rifled her pack and put a charm bag roughly into Sarah's hand. She said irritably, "I'll just stay here and look out for nosy neighbors, shall I?"

Sarah gave her a what's-wrong-with-you? look but nodded and said nothing. Instead, she got out of the car. Walking casually, she pulled a piece of paper from her pocket, looked at the house, and walked confidently up the driveway.

Marianne looked quickly around the neighborhood. The cookie-cutter mansions were all luxury-sized but lacking in anything like charm or character. Some had a car in the drive, others still had for sale or pending signs on them. Curtains obscured the windows of the nearest houses. If someone was looking, Marianne couldn't see them.

It would serve Sarah right if someone asked her what the hell she was doing and told her to get lost. But it was midday, and there was only one dog walker and a jogger who went past. Marianne scrutinized both for any unearthly signs of shadowiness but saw nothing unusual. Sarah returned a few minutes later and shut the door. She started Natalie up and headed back toward the main road.

"What's up with you?" Sarah finally asked.

By now a burning embarrassment had replaced her earlier anger and guilt. "I feel like I'm not much help to you. I'm not much of a magic student. If I could, I'd just go home and leave you to it."

"You can't."

"So you've said. I'll finish this trip with you, but I'm going back to ghost busting and history after this."

Sarah pulled over to the side of the development's road before they got on the main road. "Look, I brought you because I thought you had potential. It's still possible to learn to feel magic after all this. You'll just have to study harder than I did. Byron was a really good teacher, and I had a natural talent for it. Maybe you should get lessons from him. We'll finish this project, and maybe next week we can give him a call, and you can set something up. He's a good teacher. If you have any hidden talent, he'll find it and nurture it."

Marianne shrugged without enthusiasm. "I'll think about it."

Looking uncomfortable, Sarah put a hand tentatively on her arm, clearly trying to be sympathetic. "Your ghost handling is good and your clairvoyant dreams are a big plus. I think you have talent for magic in there too."

Marianne put up her hand, dislodging Sarah's hand. "Please stop. I don't want to do this right now. I'll think about it."

"Fine." Sarah put Natalie into first and let out the clutch.

Mid-afternoon they pulled into the Williston State Park parking lot. Marianne pulled out a resumé and walked up to the visitor center. A single park ranger was at the welcome desk.

"Can I help you?" He asked.

"I hope so." She smiled. "Do you have any job openings? I have a background in history that might be useful to you."

He smiled back. "I'm afraid we don't have any openings right now, but I can give you the name of someone to email, if you like."

"Sure. I have a resumé if you can pass it on to the appropriate person for me." She handed him the sheet.

He glanced at it and nodded. "I'll put this on my supervisor's desk. But your best bet is to go to our website."

Disappointed, Marianne returned to the car where Sarah was rummaging through Natalie's cluttered way back area. According to the map, there were three stone chambers in the park. They could probably be back to the car in time to go to a motel, but Sarah had another purpose. They had to camp out and wait for another of her allies. A mysterious person called The Leatherman.

"Is he related to Slenderman?" Marianne asked as they unloaded their camping gear.

"What is that?"

"An unnaturally tall, slender being, usually described as male, connected to the mysterious disappearances of people, particularly children. I'm pretty sure it's completely made up, but it's really creepy all the same." That particular research rabbit hole had given her nightmares for a couple of days.

"Slenderman sounds more like a Shadow Person sighting. The Leatherman was a real person, and now his spirit roams the same circuit."

"Are you sure he'll be there?"

"It's about the time of year when he passed through the park, but I brought his favorite things just in case: coffee and sweet rolls."

Marianne raised her eyebrows. She wished Sarah had told her to look him up while she had a signal. At least, that explained the enticing smell. Her mouth had been watering since the last gas stop when Sarah had picked the buns up. Sweet carbs were her stress food, and she was disappointed and annoyed at herself for wanting them in the first place.

Sarah paid the campsite fee at the trail head. They put on their fully loaded packs (clothes, food, cooking gear, magical gear, and extra warm things), hefted the tent and sleeping bags and started walking in. Marianne carried her pillow under one arm, trying to keep it clean. She hated dirt and schmutz under her cheek and wished she'd thought to bring a trash bag or something to keep it clean.

There were a few other hikers, but no one else was insane enough to be camping at this time of year. She watched them warily, but they seemed to be normal. Her cheeks and hands grew cold, and she knew she'd be shivering if she wasn't walking. Winter was the worst: she was always cold. Camping in October was completely bonkers, but this was Sarah's gig and she had no choice. At least they'd had a big lunch at a Greek diner in Williston and made plans for a big breakfast tomorrow. All she had to do was get through one night.

Under the sparse canopy, the leaf fall was thick with splotches of yellow, orange, and red among the brown. Sarah followed a trail map that took them deeper into the least traveled areas of the park, and they walked for over an hour. Thank goodness it was mostly flat and the trail was well traveled. The sleeping bag, pillow, and packs grew awkward, and they traded the tent back and forth between them. Finally, with a last check of her map and the surroundings, Sarah stepped off the trail and headed up a small rise. Marianne clambered up the slope after her, slipping on the leaves.

As she crested the hill she felt the familiar buzz saw vibration, this time coming through the soles of her feet. Sarah slid down the other side and held up a cautionary hand.

"Go around," she said, gesturing to the right.

Marianne realized they'd arrived on the soil covering the top of the chamber and half fell, half slid down the slope in her haste to get off, dipping the corner of her pillow into the leaves and dirt. She gritted her teeth, put her pack and tent down. She brushed the mud off her pillow and balanced it on top. From a pocket she pulled out a closing charm while Sarah got the flashlight. Getting through the barrier of vertigo and nausea was easier this time. She was ready for it. Maybe she was getting the hang of this after all.

They found the wedging charm easily, sticking out of a high-up crack between two slabs of rock. It wasn't nearly as well concealed as the others had been. Maybe they'd gotten better at finding and replacing them because they were out in record time, the evil wedge charm tucked safely in a sandwich baggie. Together they walked over the next rise and found two other stone chambers side by side.

The intensity of the combined magical vibration was like a physical blow, and Marianne had to stop and swallow her stomach's urge to revisit lunch. Nope, she didn't have this.

"This better be the last of it," she said through gritted teeth, "'cause I can't do this again today. It just makes me want to barf."

Sarah gave her a lopsided smile. "Good news, though. You can feel it."

"Great. Magic feels like stomach churning nausea. Very helpful."

"Maybe you can learn to channel it."

Marianne gulped and got out two charms. The wedging charms were as easy to spot as the last location. *If I didn't know better, I'd say our adversary was rushing. He or she is getting sloppy. Screw you Tristan Kitteby! We found your charms.*

She was very glad to put distance between her and the black openings. It was getting dark, and they had trouble finding the trail again. Marianne really didn't want to spend the night camped next to these three openings to another dimension. She wouldn't sleep a wink. A lucky flash of white paint on a tree trunk brought them back to the trail, and they headed deeper into the woods.

Marianne was stumbling over roots and stones in the path when Sarah said, "Here we are." She stepped off the trail and up a little hill. On the other side there was a depression. Once they'd stepped into it, the trail could no longer be seen. It had a broad flat bottom and looked like a large, natural bowl. Marianne felt like they were miles from Natalie's safety and worlds away from her snug home in Maple Hill.

"You want to put up the tent or get a fire going?" Sarah looked at her expectantly.

Marianne was cold, tired and hungry. The backwash of the magical energies still made her vaguely ill. "Sarah, I haven't been camping since I was a kid," she said bluntly. "I have no idea how to put up your tent, much less in the dark."

"Fine. You get some firewood. Our old fire pit is around here somewhere. It's a ring of rocks. Just dig it out." She sounded so matter of fact that Marianne wanted to scream.

Marianne dumped her pack and placed her pillow on top. The case was still relatively clean. She couldn't wait to curl up in Ruari's sleeping bag and be done with this night. Muttering, she collected an armload of dead branches and cleared the leaves out of the old fire pit. At least she knew how to make a fire. Geoffrey had been hopeless at it, and she'd treasured one of the few things she could do better than him. All the same, it took a lot more work out in the dark and cold to get a little flame coaxed into life but she managed.

Sarah finished erecting the two-person dome tent upwind from the fire and stowed their gear inside. "Is that all the firewood you could find?" She said flatly. "We're going to need a hell of a lot more if we're going to keep it going all night. Fire is one of the few things that keeps draugers at bay."

Not a single word of praise or thanks, just more work. *Dammit. After this trip is over, I'm not spending a minute more with you!* Sarah was easily the worst teacher Marianne had ever had and no kind of friend at all. Fuming, Marianne went back into the darkness to hunt for more firewood. It didn't help knowing at some level that Sarah was right, and the thought of draugers coming after them again made her flesh crawl.

She gathered a couple more armloads, but the wood was damp, and she doubted it would burn well. On her way back to camp, she tripped over a tree trunk and fell headlong, bruising her shin and arms where she landed on the wood.

"Shit!" She muttered.

"You okay?" Sarah looked up from her perch on a stone.

Marianne picked up the precious wood and returned to the small circle of firelight, limping.

"Just peachy." She dumped the armload next to the fire and grudgingly noticed that Sarah had added an armload as well.

"Don't get comfortable. We have one more thing to do before we settle in. We have to protect the area."

Of course we do.

Sarah lit two lanterns and handed one to Marianne. Together they walked clockwise around the raised lip of the depression in the enspelling direction.

"By Earth and Sky, Fire and Water, protect this place from evil," Sarah chanted. "May the Earth protect this place with her grace, her energy, her goodness. Guard us from evil and admit our helpers and friends," Sarah intoned as they walked three times around the rim of the clearing.

Marianne checked her pockets: a small bottle of holy water on one side, the cat charm on the other. The little bag of polished obsidian and herbs bulged in her front jeans pocket. She muttered the protective words without any conviction they would help against the inky shadows that had chased them at Minetto Point or in her dreams. She felt absolutely nothing magical when they were done. *This is so stupid and pointless.*

Together they brought the log Marianne had tripped over so they could sit. With the tent at their back and the fire on their faces, they settled in. Darkness shrank visibility to the area within the range of their little fire. It was the first night Marianne couldn't get a signal to call Ruari, and she wished with all her heart that she was at home.

Supper consisted of baked potatoes roasted in foil in the coals of their fire, a can of green beans, and a can of tuna apiece. The spuds took over an hour to cook and were burnt on the outside and hard in the center. The edible zone wasn't nearly big enough. Marianne was still hungry even after eating the overcooked parts. They warmed the beans and tuna over the coals.

I am never going camping again.

She imagined all the food she would bring if she were in charge. The only good part was there were no dishes or pots to wash. They only had about six quarts of water between them. Sarah brought out an old fashioned percolating coffee pot and set about making coffee, using some of their precious water.

"This is for your mystery guest?"

"Yes. Get the package of rolls out of my pack will you?"

Get this. Do that. Get your own stuff.

Teeth clenched, Marianne crawled into the tent and rummaged around in their gear with the flashlight. The stone amulet in her pocket pinched her thigh painfully. She pulled it out and dumped it on her sleeping bag. The package of store-bought cinnamon rolls was a little squashed but smelled like heaven. She was sorely tempted to eat one. Surely a ghost wouldn't mind having only five instead of six. As she hesitated, she caught sight of her pillow. A big dirty streak smeared across it with bits of leaf and dirt still clinging to it.

Fucking hell. I have to lay my face in that. Goddamn Sarah for dragging it through the dirt.

Sarah's pillow was still pristine, gleaming white in the flashlight. Marianne dug her fingers to the bottom of Sarah's pack and found the box of black salt. She grabbed a handful and smeared it over the clean linen, sprinkling more into Sarah's sleeping bag for good measure. She closed the box and tucked it back into the pack, smirking.

"Did you find it?" Sarah called. "I thought I left it on top."

"I'm looking."

Then she opened the plastic as quietly as she could and tore off a hunk. The sweet cinnamon pastry tasted amazing, and she consumed two big bites. She licked her lips and fingers hastily.

"Sorry," she called back, "the package got mangled when we brought it up here."

Marianne zipped the tent closed behind her and returned to the fire.

"Not to worry. Put them on the log, then come sit, and I'll tell you a story."

Oh yay, ghost stories by the campfire. Last thing I need.

The night enveloped them like a shroud. Above them the wind in the distant tree tops blew, sounding like a gale while only a slight breeze chased the sparks at ground level. Smoke from the fire fitfully blew in their faces, making her cough. Marianne pulled her hat on more closely and tugged her jacket around her, wishing she'd brought a warmer coat. She hoped Ruari's sleeping bag would be warm.

Sarah poked the fire with a long stick and added another few sticks to the blaze before settling back. "The Leatherman lived in the 1800s," Sarah began. "He was a nomad who walked a three-hundred-sixty-five mile circuit through western Connecticut and parts of Westchester, Putnam, and Canopus Counties. Each circuit took him about a month to complete, and he walked it for almost thirty years. He dressed in a handmade leather jerkin, breeches, and overcoat. His shoes had wooden soles like Dutch sabots with knee high uppers, and he wore a crooked stovepipe hat with a brim. He walked day in and day out, rain or shine, through cold and heat. Some people thought him frightening and threw stones at him. Others offered him a meal and a bed. He gladly took food and accepted gifts of tobacco and scraps of leather to repair his clothing, but he never slept in town, preferring to make his own shelter."

He sounded like a tramp. "Who was he?"

"No one is really sure. After he died in 1889, people found a French bible, a small cross, and a couple of journals written in a code no one could read. A newspaper reporter claimed he was named Jules Bourglay from France who had suffered a broken heart as a young man, emigrated to America and then took up his nomadic ways. But the paper retracted that story within a few days after printing it. Others believe that he was French Canadian because sometimes his wanderings took him to Canada."

"So he's one of your ghostly allies?" *He'd better not be like*

Adrian Vandermark. I don't have the patience for that kind of shit tonight.

"More than that. He was one of the first people to protect this area from the draugers. He walked his circuit to keep the protection up. Byron learned about the Leatherman's spell and vowed to continue it."

a whiff of coffee got Marianne's attention. Making coffee by campfire was not nearly as reliable as using a coffeemaker. Just as it was starting to smell slightly burned, Sarah removed it from the fire using her jacket sleeve as a pot holder and poured some of the pungent liquid into a cup and more onto the rolls. It soaked in. If she noticed the broken packaging, she said nothing. She offered Marianne a cupful and took one for herself.

"Now we wait."

Shivering, Marianne sipped her drink and gagged. It was bitter and sour, strong enough to keep her awake for a week. Even though she was cold, she didn't think she could drink it. Sarah pulled several sugar packets swiped from a restaurant out of her jacket pocket and dumped them into her cup. "Do you have any more of those?" Marianne asked.

"No."

Something inside her snapped. "Well that's typical."

"What?" Sarah looked confused.

"You make sure you're fine and leave me out completely."

Sarah stopped what she was doing and looked at her. "What is your problem? You've done nothing but bitch for the last couple of day, and I've done my best to overlook it. What is wrong with you?"

"Wrong with me? I've done everything you've asked of me even when I didn't really understand what the hell you wanted, and all you've done is criticize me, tell me how wonderful and perfect Kelly is, and ignore my contributions. You remind me of my fucking ex!" Her voice rose to a shout. The swearing felt good after containing herself for days.

"You haven't exactly been the best student or covered me when I needed it," Sarah replied evenly. "It was a mistake to bring you. You're too new at this."

"No shit! I've offered to go home a bunch of times, and you insist on me staying with you. You don't want me, but you make me stay. Again, just like my fucking ex!"

A muscle jumped in Sarah's jaw as she clenched her teeth and looked away. When she looked back, her glare was steely. "I told you, if you leave, I have to start everything from the beginning. There isn't enough time to recharge and lay all those charms again. The other Protectors are clearly sabotaging us. Byron's on the verge of finding the Navarro Talisman. He might also know a way to insert himself into the spell in your place. Then you can just go home."

Marianne's fury morphed into sarcasm. "The big secret weapon. He'll be lucky to find it in time, if it even exists. And if he doesn't, then what? I'm stuck with you till Halloween, and we're facing what? Blob-o-geddon? I don't want to be part of this!"

"If draugers break through, you're going to be part of it whether you like it or not. Get your feelings under control, or they'll be all over you like ants on a picnic."

"That's just like you. 'Do this or else.' No instructions on how, no help whatsoever. 'Just figure it out, Marianne.' Guess what? You're the worst teacher I've ever had! And you suck as a mentor!"

"You expect me to hold your hand and coddle you every step

of the way. Grad school must have been like grade school for you. If you'd been in law school, you'd have failed out at the end of first semester."

Contempt dripped from every word.

"I don't know what Kelly sees in you. Law school must have drained every ounce of compassion from you 'cause you're about as sensitive as a toothpick."

"Sensitivity gets you killed in this business."

"Why anyone would choose to work with you or be your ally is beyond me! They only come because you pay them," she spat.

"Spare me your niceness. Nice people don't fight. They run away from people like Vandermark," she sneered.

"Now I'm a coward as well as an idiot?!"

"You said it not me." Sarah pursed her lips in disgust and poked the fire with a stick before tossing it in.

Marianne was on her feet, boiling mad. Leaves rustled around them mixed with the curious, dry sound of tearing paper and a scent of dust and metal. She was oblivious, focused entirely on the person who'd humiliated and belittled her just like Geoffrey had done for years. A darkness gathered at the corners of her vision. No longer cold, a hot anger filled her that felt so damn good to lean into. She launched herself across the few feet that separated them and felt the satisfying thud as she knocked Sarah to the ground.

Sarah thrashed under her, trying to get a purchase on Marianne's bulky winter coat and push her off.

"Get off me!"

Marianne clawed at Sarah's face and grabbed a handful of her hair, feeling savage pleasure at her cry of pain. "I hate you, bitch!"

"Get off me!" Sarah grunted, twisting hard. Her free hand grabbed a stick and swung it at Marianne's head.

The wood connected with a solid thud, and Marianne reeled, losing her perch. Sarah rolled her off, scrambling to hold her down, panting, her glasses gone. It made her look entirely different. Pinned at the waist by the weight of a body, Marianne panicked. Geoffrey's face leered down at her. Marianne bucked and kicked wildly trying to free herself before his hands covered her nose and mouth.

"No, no, no!" Marianne gasped.

Sarah yelped as a lucky kick caught her in the back.

Marianne struggled out from under Geoffrey's bulk and shouldered him back to the ground. The only way she could survive was if she took him out first. Her hands closed over the exposed throat and she squeezed.

"Leave me alone! You don't get to do that to me!" Marianne yelled.

Sarah gargled and wheezed, her hands trying to pull Marianne's off her throat. Her face darkened and her struggles became weaker.

A distant deep voice said, "Peace."

What am I doing?! A small voice inside her screamed. *Stop! That's Sarah!* The spike of shock was like a bucket of cold water.

The ground shook with heavy steps, and she looked up in time to be bowled over by an enormous black bear. Its giant paw knocked her flat, and her head struck the edge of the log, setting off fireworks behind her eyes. Gigantic jaws opened inches from her. They were big enough to eat her face in one bite. Marianne's scream was lost in the roar.

A man's rough voice shouted, *"Allez!"*

The beast inside her cringed and fled, leaving only darkness.

Marianne roused to the smell of scorched coffee, and Sarah's hoarse voice. A deep male voice replied, but his words made no sense to her. Her head felt light and fuzzy, echoing her sore, bruised muscles. The back of her skull ached sharply, and she felt weak and queasy.

She put a hand up to her head and groaned.

Sarah came immediately to her side and gently helped her

into a sitting position. The queasiness became overwhelming nausea, and she turned to the side and retched until everything in her stomach was expelled. Shaking, she sat up again.

"Hey, are you alright?" Sarah rasped.

"I-I don't know. Something hit me, and I blacked out. What—?"

"One thing at a time. Can you drink a little something?" When Marianne nodded, a cup of bitter, sweet coffee was pressed on her, and she took a couple of bracing swallows. The hot scorch down her throat helped to clear her head and push some of the cobwebs away. Her stomach burned but stayed steady. It also brought her short term memories back on line.

She felt the blood drain from her face. "Oh shit! I-I tried to kill you! Oh my God, I'm so sorry!"

Sarah replied wryly, "You're not the first and probably won't be the last."

Marianne gave a few wrenching sobs and took a deep breath, trying to get a grip. "I was so mad at you. I thought you were Geoffrey. I thought he was trying to kill me."

Sarah gave her a brief, searching look. "I'm fine. Don't worry. Pull yourself together. We have company. I want to introduce you to a friend of mine."

"But..."

"First things first."

Marianne scrubbed her eyes with her hands and brushed the hair out of her eyes, feeling bits of leaf and twig. She drew her knees up and looked across the fire.

A curious figure sat on the opposite log. He was a big man with a matted thatch of dark hair and a bushy beard. A deep network of lines creased his face. His leather clothing was roughly sewn together with thongs, giving the appearance more of armor than of a coat and breeches. A worn homespun shirt peeked out at the neckline. His footwear looked more like cylinders of stiff leather than proper boots. Every time he moved, the leather creaked. He regarded her warily with piercing brown eyes. On the log next to him rested a crude stovepipe hat and a large leather pouch with a long strap. A walking stick leaned against his knee. He made Marianne think of Hagrid. Or a caveman. Or maybe a human rhino.

"Jean, this is my friend Marianne. Marianne, this is Jean. People call him the Leatherman." She gave his name the French pronunciation.

"Hi." Marianne gave a wan smile, and he nodded in reply.

Just then a huge black shape came out of the darkness behind Jean, and Marianne scrambled back. "Look out! Behind you!"

An enormous head, the size of a basketball nuzzled Jean on the shoulder nearly unseating him. He smiled and reached up under its chin and scratched its ear.

C'est mon ami, Jules. His voice was deep and rough from disuse. Even though his accent was strange, it clicked in her brain. French had been one of her grad school languages.

"Jules is a spirit bear of the First People," Sarah explained.

"He tried to kill me!" Marianne breathed, eyes wide.

"No, he attacked the things inside of you," Sarah corrected. "Between you and Jules, you drove the draugers away." Her face softened with unaccustomed shame. "Marianne, I apologize for putting you in danger."

Marianne stifled her urge to say, it's okay, because it really wasn't. So, she said, "What happened?"

"A couple of Shadow People got through our defenses and attacked us. They went into your mind and augmented your anger and fear. I should have realized what was happening and done more to protect you or deescalate the situation. I'm sorry."

Sarah's scared face flashed in front of her. *I tried to kill someone with my hands. If Jules hadn't stopped me, I might be staring at Sarah's lifeless body.* Her mind shied away.

"You didn't tell me the Leatherman walked around with a giant bear."

"He didn't while he was alive. After he crossed over, he found

Jules, and together they do what they can to ward their old territory against evil."

Marianne watched nervously as the monstrous bear paced silently around the campfire and approached her. She flinched as his wet nose snuffled her ear and hair. Tentatively, she reached out her hand and let him sniff it before touching the coarse hair of his chin. His black eyes peered at her with deep intelligence. He radiated a peace she wouldn't have imagined possible after his ferocious roar.

Il vous aime. Tu es en sécurité, Jean rumbled. *He likes you. You are safe.*

"Does that mean I'm safe from him or from the Shadow People?" she asked uncertainly.

"I imagine he means both," Sarah said dryly.

Jules snuffled softly and melted away from the firelight to prowl the darkness beyond. It was hard to believe he was a spirit, not flesh and blood.

"Do you meet every year to renew the spell?" She nodded toward Jean who was consuming the last of the coffee soaked rolls and washing it down with more of the bitter drink.

"Yes. While you were out, he told me something big was happening. He suspects there will be another attack before All Hallow's Eve."

"So the draugers will attack us again?"

Sarah shook her head. "I don't know. Your dream of Shadow People being hatched in their dimension and wanting to get here was pretty ominous. Did you dream of anything else last night?"

She frowned raking through her muddled mind. "Um, I dreamed I was in an exam at college, and the professor kept yelling at us to check our work."

Sarah smiled faintly. "That sounds ordinary at least."

She shook her head. "I think I was supposed to pay attention to it, but I don't know why. 'Check your work.' What does that mean?"

Sarah shrugged.

Glancing toward Jean, Marianne did a double take. The cup and package sat on the log. He and Jules had vanished. "Where—?"

Sarah shrugged. "He comes and goes as he pleases. Our business was finished, and he's always been restless."

Without the reassuring presence of the bear and the Leatherman, Marianne suddenly felt very exposed. "Will the Shadow People come back tonight?"

Sarah shook her head. "Jean and Jules are nearby, keeping watch until we leave."

Marianne felt both exhausted and taut as a wire. She drew her knees up and hugged them. "Sarah, that was the scariest thing that's ever happened to me. I couldn't stop myself hating you and wanting to kill you." Tears slid down her cheeks and a sob welled up in her throat.

Sarah replied mildly, "I'm not dead yet, I promise."

"But…"

"No buts," Sarah said firmly. "We all have feelings of anger and resentment. It's what we do about them that matters. In the end, we are the only people who can stop ourselves from doing evil by the choices we make."

Marianne sniffed and wiped her eyes on the knees of her jeans. "I feel so gross inside." She wished she could take a dozen hot showers.

"I know what you mean." Sarah stared into the fire for a few minutes. "You said something about your ex. Did he try to hurt you?"

Images flashed in front of her mind along with a sense of shame. She almost didn't answer, but it felt like a boil that needed lancing. "Sometimes Geoffrey thought choking enhanced sex," she whispered.

"You mean his choking you?"

She nodded.

"Did it?"

"Not for me. It only happened a couple of times." Embarrassed and ashamed, she gave a little one-shouldered shrug.

Sarah looked at her. "What he did to you was not okay. You can say that."

More tears slid down her cheeks. "No, it wasn't."

Sarah gave her a level stare. "You're divorced. He's gone. He can't hurt you anymore. You're okay."

Marianne's tears subsided. This must be Sarah's version of compassion. *That must be the part that Kelly loves so much.* She sniffed and sat up. "Thanks." She took a shaky breath. "Sarah, can I ask you something?"

"Sure."

"Why are you so tough most of the time? I don't think it would kill you to be a little nicer." *It might even keep me from wanting to kill you,* she thought.

Sarah's mouth quirked in half a smile. "Guilty. I'm not wrong about magic practitioners getting a disproportionate amount of cancer and autoimmune diseases. I guess between needing to be a tough advocate and defender as a family lawyer and wanting to avoid dying that way, I overcompensate."

"I don't think compassion and empathy are going to kill either of us." She took Sarah's hand and squeezed it.

"I'll take it under advisement." Sarah squeezed back and let her go.

Sarah tossed another couple of sticks onto the fire, sending sparks into the air. She pulled something out of her pocket and handed it to Marianne.

"By the way, don't ever take these out of your pocket again no matter how uncomfortable they feel." She pressed the little bag of protective gemstones into Marianne's hand and closed her fingers around it. "They would have helped you."

Marianne stuffed the pouch back into her pocket. She couldn't remember when she'd removed it. Now it was going to live there no matter what. "Do you think if Kelly had been here instead of me, you wouldn't have been attacked?"

"I don't know. Even after Minetto, I didn't realize how strong they were already. I really screwed up."

Marianne picked the bark off a twig before tossing it into the fire. "Do I have to worry about being taken over again now that it's happened once? I mean, can they get in more easily now?"

"No. I think now that you know what it feels like, you'll be better able to recognize them before they get a strong hold the way they did tonight."

Marianne was ashamed of the momentary pleasure she'd felt indulging her fury. She shivered. "I hope so. Have you or Kelly ever been taken over by Shadow People?"

Sarah stared into the flames for a a couple of minutes, clearly seeing some memory. "Once. When I was a kid I got fed up with being picked on and teased. Kelly and I laid an ambush for a couple of the girls who were my worst tormentors."

"Was one of them Erin?" Ruari had told her Erin had teased and bullied Sarah for years despite being younger than her.

"Absolutely. She should've been there that day, but she stayed late at school for some reason and missed us."

"What happened?"

"We heard them coming. They were talking about about us in very unflattering terms. I remember feeling a kind of ringing in my ears and being full of rage. I could tell that Kelly felt the same way by the look on her face. When they got close enough, we jumped them, threw their books to the ground and started in on them. They screamed and that was incredibly satisfying. Luckily, a teacher came running and broke up the fight. We were scratched and bleeding, but they were definitely the worse for wear. Kelly and I were suspended for fighting at school." She sighed. "I suppose we were lucky the parents of the girls didn't sue us or demand that we leave the school. Our respective parents gave us a severe talking to, and we were grounded for the rest of the semester. When we went back to school and saw the damage we'd done, we were ashamed."

"Did you know Byron by then?"

"No, we met when I was in high school. At some point I told him about the fight, and he told me about the Shadow People. From then on, Kelly and I were much more careful. We never let ourselves get out of hand like that again. And I learned to see them, which helped me understand why people sometimes acted crazy."

Silence descended between them except for the crackle of the fire. Marianne tried to sort through her jumbled thoughts. When she found a thread to follow she stared at the flames and spoke.

"Sarah, you asked me to come with you on this trip in exchange for helping me look for a job. I feel like you lied to me, or worse, that you were patting me on the head just to get me to come with you. When you said all you had to do was call a couple of friends at other law firms, why didn't you just say that at the beginning? Then you said you'd pay me to do research for you, but clearly you know all that stuff already." She lifted her head to look at Sarah. "It makes me feel stupid and used."

Sarah shifted uncomfortably. "I wasn't entirely truthful with you and that's on me. I needed and still need your help, but I wasn't sure you would come if I told you all the possibilities. I had no idea this would happen.

"Regarding the research I asked for, I wanted you to learn about Turner's Hope Mine so you understood some of the people we were meeting. I figured you'd connect to research better than just listening to me. Byron always had me do my own work when I was learning from him."

Marianne looked at Sarah over her knees and said, "I'm not you."

"Yeah, you're not. But you tend to teach the way you were taught."

Marianne replied doggedly, "No, you think about how you were taught and adapt to the audience."

"And that's why you'll be a better teacher than me."

The sting of losing the university job still rankled, but Marianne pushed it away. "I wish you'd been more upfront with me at the beginning."

"I honestly had no idea things were going to be this bad," she said defensively.

"I get that, but you don't tell me what's going on, you leave me in the dark. I end up imagining all kinds of things."

Sarah said softly, "I learned to do everything on my own, and lawyers aren't encouraged to share or be emotional. It's been a long time since I trusted anybody new."

"If I'm supposed to be your student, you're gonna have to change that."

"I'll work on it." Sarah rose and added a couple of sticks to the fire and poked it till the flames blazed up again.

Marianne brooded, feeling exhaustion dragging on her like an undertow. A little while later she said, "I'm turning in."

Marianne crawled into Ruari's sleeping bag fully dressed with her coat on. Away from the fire, she was freezing. Although she was utterly spent, her jaw clenched and her teeth chattered. The ground was hard and unforgiving as she lay curled on her side, dirty pillow under her head. She pulled her hat down, trying to conserve every last ounce of heat.

With no more distractions, images of Sarah desperately trying to breathe, clawing at Marianne's hands around her throat, mixed with Geoffrey's leering face. She'd wanted to kill Geoffrey for scaring her so badly and for every time he'd belittled her. She'd wanted to kill Sarah for her casually cruel comments.

She'd almost done it.

She'd nearly murdered someone.

She'd built her life on being a nice person. People liked her because she was a *nice person*. She felt bad if she inadvertently said something to hurt another and regretted it for days. And yet something lurked inside of her that used to whisper to her on the subway platform, "Just give them a little push." Sometimes she wondered if she could have killed Geoffrey with a kitchen knife while he slept and been free of his bullying so much sooner.

I am such a horrible person.

Tears leaked down into her hair, making a chilly spot on the hat.

How could I trust myself to be around Ruari? I would never want to hurt him, but clearly I have a part of me that could murder someone. How could he ever trust me? What if I lost control again or Shadow People took me over? What am I going to tell Ruari?

Her thoughts bit and chewed each other like junk yard dogs.

Murderer.

Thinking is not doing. Sarah had said, *In the end, we are the only people who can stop ourselves from doing evil by the choices we make.*

That seemed like such a flimsy barrier, but it was the only one she had.

At last she was aware of Ruari's musky, sweaty scent rising from the borrowed sleeping bag. It relaxed the lump in her throat, and she fell into an exhausted sleep.

Marianne woke some hours later, teetering on the edge between warmth and chill. Disoriented for a moment, she couldn't remember where she was. Then she heard a steady breathing nearby and realized her back was up against something warm.

Oh God, she'd smeared Sarah's precious black salt all over her bedding like some obnoxious brat. Marianne cringed and remembered doing worse. Yet, here was Sarah sleeping next to her as if it had never happened.

What am I going to do?

Leaves rattled in the wind outside the tent. A faint glow showed the fire outside flaring and dying back down. Something snuffled near her head on the other side of the nylon, and she tensed. Reaching out with her senses, she touched something enormous and calm.

Peace.

She woke again in a panic, images of choking Ruari in his sleep reverberating in her head. It was colder than before with no light outside at all.

Just a horrible dream.

She couldn't tell if it was a true dream or just her own conscience. It didn't really matter. She lay wide awake, afraid to let herself go until grey light began changing the blackness.

CHAPTER 13

When they emerged dirty and exhausted from the trailhead the next morning they stopped short, tent and gear slipping to the ground. Sarah's jaw dropped, and she stood transfixed. Marianne felt like she'd been punched in the gut.

Papers fluttered idly across the dirt and gravel parking lot like so many little birds. A scatter of colorful objects lay trampled next to a torn cardboard box amid something that glittered like diamonds in the weak morning sunshine.

Thousands of little cubes of glass sprinkled Natalie's hood and lay like a hail storm across the front seat. The back window was similarly smashed. Glass from her broken head and tail lights littered the ground. The wipers and antenna were bent into pretzels. Her blocky metal body rested on the rims within her slashed tires.

Sarah broke the spell first. Mechanically she walked around the vehicle, surveying the damage. Her face an impassive mask, she pulled out her phone, located a number, and dialed.

"Hello? This is Sarah Landsman. I'd like to report my car being vandalized at Williston State Park. Yes, I'll be here. Thank you." She drew up another number. "Hello? I need a tow." She gave them her name and location and then dialed a third time.

"Kells? Someone beat the crap out of Natalie." For the first time her voice wavered. Her face crumpled briefly as she listened to Kelly's voice.

All the while, Marianne stood rooted to the spot. Natalie had been their safe space and their ticket home. She wasn't going anywhere in this condition. Marianne started shaking. A bit of paper caught against her foot, and she bent to retrieve it with trembling fingers. It was a muddy copy of her CV.

Belatedly she registered Sarah's distress, and after she hung up with Kelly, Marianne approached her and put her arms around her. Wordlessly they clung to each other for a moment, and Marianne felt her mentor take several deep shuddering breaths. When Sarah stepped away, her face wore its usual controlled expression in spite of the glistening tracks along her cheeks. She wiped them hastily away and took a deep breath. Marianne did her best to pull herself together and present a calm exterior, though her hands still trembled.

"Natalie was protected from magical opponents. Her wards aren't good against a determined human attack, though. Don't touch anything until the police have been over it," Sarah said matter-of-factly.

"Who? Could it have been Kitteby or one of the others?"

"Possibly. I need to make another phone call."

Marianne nodded wordlessly and began collecting the scattered items from the car. It was completely useless, but the absurd impulse not to litter took over. When she finished, she sat on a railroad tie at the edge of the lot with their gear piled around her, feeling empty. A remote part of her noticed that the other three cars in the lot were undamaged. Maybe they'd arrived after the vandals had left.

A fragment of white on the ground caught her eye. It was broken but the little bone eye sockets were recognizable. It was an odd place for a rodent skull to be. She pulled out one of

Sarah's empty sandwich baggies and picked it up, careful to handle it with her gloved hands. Silently she handed it to Sarah who looked at the little skull with a grim nod.

Maybe the vandalism to Natalie was not connected to their magical journey. Maybe there was a more plebeian reason.

Sarah paced up and down, her phone pressed to her ear, arranging for repairs. A police officer arrived in a squad car from the hamlet of Williston, and Sarah conferred with him. What Marianne really wanted to report was being attacked by an evil entity. And possibly offer herself to be arrested for assault and battery. Instead, she pulled out her phone and called Ruari. She had no idea what to say, but she wanted to hear his voice.

He was on his way to work and had stopped to feed Oscar. "Hey, Mahri, how are you?" He sounded well rested and wonderfully normal.

Hey, I tried to kill Sarah last night with my bare hands, but a giant spirit bear stopped me. Then I dreamed I tried to kill you, too. And Natalie was destroyed by an evil mage, so we're screwed on spell casting. Other than that I'm fine.

"Not very good," she said shakily. It was such a relief to hear him after the vivid nightmare she'd had. "We camped last night, and I didn't sleep very well. And when we got back to the parking lot someone had vandalized the car."

His voice focused like a laser in his concern. "Are you all right? Do you need me to come get you?"

Tears sprang into her eyes, and her throat bunched up. She just wanted to be wrapped in his arms. Instead, she swallowed and said more firmly, "I'm okay. Sarah's okay."

"What happened?"

"While we were camping, someone came along with a baseball bat or something and broke a bunch of things and slashed the tires. It's going to take most of the day to fix, but Sarah's made all the arrangements, so we'll be okay."

"If you need me, I can call in sick. Talmadge still owes me sick time…"

More than you know. "I really appreciate that. I'm not ready to bail just yet. Knowing you could come really helps," she said.

He blew out a breath, sounding frustrated. "I'll keep my phone close, so if you change your mind, I'll be there."

"I will."

She closed her eyes, and took a deep breath. *I just need to be sure before I can trust myself around you, Ruari. I can't tell you what happened. Not yet. If Sarah can handle this, I can too. How would Toni Woods manage all of this? How do I turn this sickening guilt and fear into a strength? How can I still be me?*

She rose, dusted off her backside, and stepped over to Sarah and the officer.

Sarah's button up shirt had pulled away from her neck, exposing the livid bruising on her throat. Marianne cringed. She'd noticed it when they'd packed up camp that morning and begun another wave of apologies, but Sarah had brushed it aside.

"Are you sure you weren't attacked as well?" the officer was asking, staring blatantly.

"Yes, sir. I assure you I'm fine. I only want to report the damage to my vehicle." She gazed steadily at the man and spoke firmly, evidently willing him to let it go.

He glanced at Marianne who tried to look innocent. His eyes narrowed, and he pressed his lips into a straight line. His eyes traveled between the two of them, and he gave a little shake of his head as he shut his notebook and handed Sarah his card.

"Your evidence will help us with our inquiries. The station will call you if they find the culprit."

"Believe me, I'll be sure to press charges if you do."

Wiccopee Hamlet was too small to have its own repair shop, so Natalie was towed to Sheba Motors, a garage in nearby Peterson. Sarah negotiated with the head mechanic while Marianne, on autopilot, arranged for a hotel room. She needed a shower badly and wanted a place where she could lie in a bed for a few hours, even if she couldn't sleep.

They sat at Sheba Motors in Peterson while the man in greasy blue coveralls behind the desk searched for replacement parts for Natalie. The waiting room, paneled in faux wood and carpeted in a worn, gray outdoor rug, smelled of cigarettes. The contents of Natalie's trunk spilled over four plastic seats, sprawling onto the floor. Sarah jiggled her foot, teeth tugging on her thumbnail.

"What did the police say?" Marianne asked.

"They said Mischief Night had come early. There were several other reports of vandalism in the area they were following up on, but the attack on Natalie was the most serious. The other reports were things like toilet papering, smashed jack-o-lanterns, and egging people's doors."

"Why would those guys trash our car? We haven't done anything to them."

Sarah shook her head. "Bias against lesbians? Pure opportunism? No idea. Maybe they're just assholes."

"How long is it going to take to fix Natalie?"

She gnawed on the thumbnail. "I don't know."

"Miss Landsman?" The balding, heavyset mechanic beckoned them.

"Let's go find out," Sarah murmured.

Leaning on the counter like people at a nursing station, they waited to hear the bad news about their loved one.

"I can get you tires today, no problem. It's coming on to winter. Do you want all weathers or snows?" The name patch said Louis, and he tipped his chin down so he could look over the top of his glasses at them.

"All weathers are fine," Sarah answered.

Chin up, mouth slightly ajar, he peered through the bottom of his glasses and clicked something on the computer screen. He tilted his head down to look over the tops of his glasses again. "The headlights are problematic. It's an old model, and we don't have any in stock. But I checked around, and they can send me a couple from Brewster before the end of the day."

"Okay," Sarah acknowledged tersely.

"The tail lights will take a week or more to come from the central distributer. I can get a new windshield in, but I can't do anything about the back window or the bodywork. You'll have to go to a specialist."

"Can you finish the work you can do by the end of the day? Sooner if possible? We're kind of in a hurry."

He wasn't to be intimidated. He tilted his chin up, looking at his computer screen again. "I've got a few other cars in the bay, and my other mechanic is out sick. But," he looked impassively over his spectacles at Sarah's expression, "if the parts come, I can probably do the tires, headlights, and windshield."

She nodded tightly. "Fine. Do what you can." She turned away and then back again. "Thank you."

They stepped back to their pile of stuff.

"I got us a room down the road at a motel," Marianne said, feeling the fog of profound weariness descending.

"Thanks, I could use a shower."

For a whopping fifteen dollars a taxi took them and their stuff to the Home Fires Motel. Even though it hadn't rained, somehow the tent was wet. Once they spread everything out to dry, it looked like they'd rafted the rapids of an energetic river and gone overboard.

Sarah took one look at Marianne and said, "You first."

Mechanically, Marianne dug out clean, dry clothes and stripped out of her damp pants and shirt. In the bathroom, a stranger stared at her from the mirror. Tangled, dirty hair framed her face, and dark smudges underscored her haunted eyes. Purpling bruises splotched her hips and shoulders from last night's tussle.

The water was too hot on her chilled skin, but she made herself stand in the stream until her muscles unclenched. She shampooed and soaped a couple of times until the brown runoff cleared, and the room was filled with the scent of coconut.

Fragments of memory rolled by like a cruel magic eight ball: Sarah's struggling face, Jules the bear's enormous canines inches from her face, a feeling of fury and resentment. Geoffrey's dispassionate, intent face above her flicked by before she shied away from all of it. She shut the water off with shaking hands and toweled dry.

While Sarah showered, Marianne sat in dry clothes with the lingering scent of campfire rolling off her sweater. She felt shaky and hollow inside, and her limbs were like lead weights. She stared at the carpet unseeing until Sarah said, "Hey, let's get something to eat. You'll feel better."

A hot meal helped fill the space in her middle and steadied her. For once the tea was decent, and she drank two cups of peppermint. Sarah finished her third cup of black sweet coffee. She was wearing a turtleneck, and Marianne was grateful for the disguise over her handiwork.

"While Natalie's getting repaired, we'll go see Byron," Sarah told her.

Marianne looked away. "I was sort of hoping to take a nap."

"Trust me, you'll be better off meeting him than lying in a hotel room alone with your thoughts."

"What do you plan to tell him?"

"He needs to know everything."

Marianne blanched and flushed in quick succession. "All of it?"

"He won't judge. He knows all about that kind of thing."

Marianne gave a listless shrug of assent.

"Good. He'll pick us up in about twenty minutes. He lives here in Peterson."

Sarah reached out and gave Marianne's forearm a reassuring squeeze. "It'll be all right."

✿

Byron Mandell picked them up in his dark blue sedan outside the hotel. Sarah hugged him and hopped into the front seat. Marianne nodded a greeting and slunk into the back, where she wrapped her arms around herself, staring out the window as they drove through town. They pulled into his driveway and got out. Marianne pulled her jacket tightly around her with a shiver and stared at her surroundings. Byron's house was a two-story stucco sided house with a large front yard. The whole place looked prosperous and well-maintained. A sign swayed under the mailbox showing a stylized eye with rays coming out of it and the word 'Consultant' underneath.

"Psychic sounds too pretentious," he said in a smooth baritone when he noticed Marianne looking at the sign. "This lets people know that I'm willing to consult on matters of the spirit without evoking crystal balls and tarot cards."

Sarah's mentor was tall with silver gray hair brushed up in a quiff and wore a trim beard and mustache with lightly waxed ends. Laugh or squint lines radiated from the corners of his lively, perceptive blue eyes. A deep groove from habitual thought separated his bushy brows. He resembled an eccentric but kindly uncle.

Inside, Byron's house was orderly if very full. Marianne took her jacket off in the front hall and hung it on a coat stand next to a mud spattered wool overcoat and muddy boots. Apparently Byron was an avid walker. Perhaps he took long walks to help him think. Pictures and paintings filled the walls, and the mirror by the door had a dried sprig of something and a little necklace of Mardi Gras beads hanging on it. It was a stark contrast to their recent terror, and she was overcome with a wave of shyness. Sarah was already down the hallway, leaving Marianne alone with Byron.

He noticed her hesitation and said with a smile, "Come into the kitchen. You look like you need some tea."

Marianne followed Byron down a narrow corridor alongside the stairs to the second floor. The carpet underfoot was clean but a little threadbare, and the walls had old fashioned candy-striped wall paper. The kitchen was light and airy, reminding her strongly of her grandmother's house in Vandenberg. The only difference was the presence of protective charms over the windows and doors, the crystals dangling in the windows, and a collection of neatly labeled jars, tins, and bottles on rows of canning shelves. Marianne relaxed. Byron's house was well warded against Shadow People.

Sarah was already putting the kettle on the stove and rinsing out a ceramic pot for tea. She'd also put the coffee on. Slowly the room filled with the aroma of perking coffee, and the kettle whistled while Sarah and Byron chatted about inconsequential things. Marianne stayed out of the way. He carefully moved several stacks of papers and cleared half of the kitchen table so they could sit.

When tea and coffee had been poured, Sarah blew out a breath. "Byron, it's way worse than I thought. We always thought there were a dozen stone chambers, but Marianne figured out there are at least seven more."

Byron's eyebrows rose in surprise. "How do you know?"

"Marianne, it's your story, why don't you tell him?"

Surprised at being put on the spot, she swallowed and told him the story of finding the old linen map and realizing after she'd bought a county map that the old map marked the location of chambers. They'd transferred the information from one map to the other and successfully found both old and new stone piles.

"That's incredible," Byron said when she finished. "I was not aware of the other seven." He closed his eyes and pinched the bridge of his nose. "Well, I guess we've been lucky that our magic has been strong enough to protect the county so far. Hmm, I wonder." He looked up at them. "There was a Protector for Canopus many years ago, but he died without passing on his knowledge to anyone that I know of. I wonder if he knew about the extra portals? No matter. You'll have to try and rope them into the spell if you can. You said something about finding a wedging charm?"

Sarah took a sip of her black sweet coffee and said, "Yes. That's another thing. All but two chambers we've found so far has had a wedging charm in it."

Byron looked shocked. "So many? Can you tell who's been leaving them?"

Sarah nodded gravely. "Tristan Kitteby's circled 'TK' was on a couple of them, and we found a piece of red yarn in a wedge charm in an eastern chamber that sure looks like Marette's work."

Marianne added, "And I found a little wire figure at a new chamber near Wixom in the southeast part of Canopus. It was under a rock at a collapsed stone chamber."

"Paloma Xerxes," Byron said, placing his elbows on the table and resting his chin on his clasped fists. He looked pensive. "I was afraid of this. The neighboring Protectors have decided that we aren't strong enough to stop them from pushing their problems onto us. They've left us alone before, but this year is different. I think Riven Masters may be behind this."

Sarah nodded grimly.

There was that name again. Marianne was beginning to feel nervous every time he came up. Who was he? She'd tried to look him up but had no signal, then she'd gotten caught up in events. It would be rude to stare at her phone here, so she'd have to wait. She settled for asking, "Who is he?"

Byron answered, "He's another powerful magical practitioner. We've encountered each other a few times as we are often seeking the same knowledge."

"But why would he tell the neighboring Protectors to open all our stone chambers? Aren't you all on the same side?"

"It would be a distraction to me, for one. A few years ago, my sister Catalina's spirit disappeared. She and I were very close when she was alive. Our parents died when we were young, and we spent years going from one relative to another. We really only had each other. Then, she was killed." His face darkened in memory. "She was a brilliant mathematician but died in a car accident just months from graduating from college. Her boyfriend drove too fast, hit gravel on a curve, spun out, and hit a tree. He survived," he added bitterly.

"I'm so sorry to hear that," Marianne said softly. She was no stranger to loss.

He looked up gratefully. "I'm glad you understand. Sarah told me you can communicate with the dead. I, too, am a ghost speaker. I was able to commune with her over the years as her spirit hovered nearby. I'm sure Sarah has told you that our loved ones never really leave us."

Marianne nodded.

"About five years ago, her spirit disappeared. I was no longer able to reach her. I looked everywhere for her, delved into darker magic than I'd dared to before in my efforts. Finally, I went to Europe to consult with other practitioners and go through the magical archives there. That's where I learned about the Navarro Talisman."

"Sarah told me a little about it."

"Then you know how vital it is that I be the one to find it."

"But I thought it had to do with opening and closing the portals to the Shadow Realm? How is it connected with Catalina?"

His blue eyes shifted to Sarah. "Because I believe she's been imprisoned in the Shadow Realm."

"Oh no!" Sarah said aghast.

A vivid image of the flat, dead, gray land with hundreds of black sacs flashed in her mind. "But that's where the draugers come from!" Marianne blurted.

"Yes. I fear for her very so—"

"No, you don't understand," Marianne interrupted. "There's going to be a huge hatching of baby draugers, hundreds, maybe thousands of them this year!"

He looked taken aback.

Sarah spoke up. "She also has clairvoyant dreams that I believe to be true."

In consternation, Byron looked from one to the other. "Are you sure?"

Marianne felt she was on firm footing for the first time in a long while. "Very sure. I saw them. They're like black bubbles, and they hatched or are going to hatch out of these sacs on the ground. They came after me. I barely made it out."

Byron looked down and appeared to be thinking fast. "That can't be. I've done the calculations. There are cicada-like bursts of draugers every fifty-two years. The last one was in Canopus in 1958. It's why I believe the Navarro Talisman is somewhere in Canopus. The previous Protector brought it over from Europe specifically to combat the last outbreak. The next one won't be until next year. "

Sarah looked at Marianne, uncertainty shadowing her features.

"I know what I saw." Resorting to her new found stubbornness, Marianne insisted. "My dreams only tell me about things that are a few days or weeks out at most, never a year."

The look of consternation was replaced by resolution. "Well, there is a chance you are wrong." He saw her mulish expression and put his hand up. "If not, I'd better find the Talisman, and you had better close as many portals as you can."

Sarah's phone chimed. She looked at the screen and said, "I have to take this. I'll be right back. Hello?" She walked swiftly away

"But I can't do magic!" Marianne protested weakly. "I was sort of hoping you could take my place and finish the spell."

Byron shook his head. "I learned ways to do that, but I must concentrate on finding the talisman. It must not fall into Masters' hands. I will see my sister safely out of the Shadow Realm." He gave her a confident smile. "You'll have Sarah with you. She's a strong practitioner, in some ways stronger than me. You'll be fine. I'll meet you in the cemetery on All Hallow's Eve and help close the spell with you. We will succeed."

Marianne tried to feel better but failed.

Her worry must have been apparent because his face softened. "I understand your concern. Maybe I can help. Come to my study." He got up, and she rose reluctantly after him.

His study was off the foyer. Books lined the walls from floor to ceiling, framed in dark oak shelving. The volumes were neatly cataloged by subject, and she marveled at the array of historic and contemporary titles. She'd seen a number of them in the New York Public Library and thought Byron must've spent a fortune buying his own copies.

A rounded bay window extended off the side of the house, holding a generous wooden desk in its curve. Books and papers lay stacked on the surface, though in carefully organized piles. On the far side of the room, she spied a recessed alcove with a dark green drape and a photograph. A pair of small silver candlesticks stood on either side with half-used candles.

Byron rummaged in a drawer and pulled out an unbleached linen bag, opened the drawstring and selected an item. He tucked the bag back in the drawer and returned to her. He cupped his hands together, closed his eyes, and murmured something inaudible. Marianne wasn't adept at lip reading, but it didn't look like Sarah's favorite chant. Maybe it was more powerful. He opened his hands. On one palm lay a small polished pale brown charm about a half inch across. It looked like a little apple.

"Here." He handed her the tiny object. "I came across this during my sojourn in Europe. It's a protection charm, good against Shadow People. Put it in your charm pouch."

She rolled it between her fingers. It had substance, and weight for something so small. It might be made of ivory or maybe petrified stone. It didn't feel magical to her any more than Sarah's charged objects did, but she closed her fist around it. It had to help. "Thank you," she said, feeling a little safer.

"Let me show you what I'm looking for. As a fellow historian, you might be interested."

Sarah stepped into the room. "That call was from the police department looking into the people who hurt Natalie." Her eyes gleamed with satisfaction. "They found the bastards and arrested them on a charge of drunk and disorderly. If they're going to go around causing trouble, they should have a less obvious car."

"At least they're off the road," Marianne responded, relieved that she wouldn't have to keep an eye out for skull covered cars any more. She dug her gemstone and herb charm out of her jeans pocket and slipped the miniature apple inside.

"That's good news," Byron said. "I was just about to show Marianne what the Navarro Talisman looks like." He went to his desk and moved a couple of stacks, revealing a large, antique, leather bound folio. It looked to be at least a hundred to a hundred and fifty years old, Victorian era or earlier. He gently turned the pages, mindful of the fragile paper until he came to a lithograph.

It showed a bearded man holding something aloft while beams radiated from it. A stone portal stood in the background. A smaller image showed a double ended cross with a snake wrapped around the central shaft, engraved eyes at the junction of each cross piece. The scale suggested it was about six inches long and substantial enough to be held in a closed fist.

"Just think, we could close them all. No more draugers preying on the weak and sick," he said quietly, almost to himself.

Marianne thought of Raiders of the Lost Arc. *Don't look at the light, Marian. Close your eyes.*

"You think that's here in Canopus somewhere?" Sarah asked.

"Silas Coventry was the previous Protector for Canopus County," Byron answered. "As far as I know, he was the last known person to have seen it and used it. But it disappeared when he died."

He shuffled a few papers on his desk and pulled one out. "Coventry lived in Peterson, but he became paranoid in his old age and very secretive. He may even have lived under an alias. I've been eliminating possible names in hopes of finding the house he owned. With any luck the Talisman is hidden there."

"Marianne," Sarah said suddenly turning to her, "you're into research, maybe you can hang out here and look at Byron's work to see if anything jumps out at you. I need to call Sheba Motors and ask about Natalie's status."

They looked at her expectantly.

Marianne appreciated their confidence in her research skills but demurred. "It would take me quite a while to catch up with Byron's notes. I don't think I'd be much help to you."

Sarah looked disappointed. "I'll make that call." She stepped out of the room with her cell phone in hand.

Byron had taken a seat and was staring at the piece of paper in his hand. It looked like a list of names with some crossed off and notes written in the margins, rather like her own research trails.

"Do you mind if I look at your books?" She asked.

"Feel free," he said absently, opening another book that looked like an old city directory.

Marianne strolled around the room, looking at the titles. She recognized a few and itched to get her hands on some of the unfamiliar ones. Being Byron's student would have its perks if she could have access to this amazing library. She reached the little shrine in the alcove and stared at the picture. The woman bore a resemblance to Byron with the same eyes and sensuous lips. She looked shy but hopeful, and Marianne wondered what she'd been like. Byron clearly missed her a great deal. *I suppose if you've only ever had each other and you're twins, it would be hard to move on.* She hoped he could find Catalina.

Sarah returned. "Good news. Sheba got the parts, and Natalie's next in line. They should be done by late afternoon."

Byron closed the book and stepped around to give Sarah a one armed hug. "Excellent. I must continue my work, and you must continue yours as soon as Natalie is repaired. I'll let you know as soon as I find it. We'll meet two nights hence in Maple Hill and close the portals for good."

Sarah nodded solemnly. "We're on it, Byron. No worries."

"I'm sorry I can't offer you lunch, but I can give you a lift back to your hotel."

CHAPTER 14

As her mentor's dark sedan drove away from the front of the motel, Sarah asked, "Are you ready for lunch? We can't go anywhere until Natalie is fixed. We should probably get some rest too."

Absently, Marianne nodded and let Sarah lead her to a nearby restaurant. She believed that Byron and Sarah had things figured out and that everything would be okay, but, her researcher's mind kept gnawing on odd phrases and details.

Byron had said, *Our loved ones never really leave us.* But they do. Her own father had died when she was five, and she'd never felt his spirit anywhere nearby either when she was growing up or after she learned to be more aware of spirits. You'd think if he was worried about them, he'd have stuck by her and her mom. The truth was that a vast majority of people passed on after they died, her dad among them.

Sarah had said, *ghosts are people who have unfinished business.* Sometimes they stick around because they're angry, like Toni Woods, or lost like Jason Fargate, or scheming like George Rutherford. How old was Byron? He must be a well preserved sixty if he was a day, she guessed. So Catalina would have been around for almost forty years. What would have kept her here? Love and concern for her brother? Maybe. Although Byron was intense, he was oddly dispassionate. Why had he never moved past her death? Grief took people differently, she supposed, and it wasn't fair to judge others. It was a puzzle, though.

Byron seemed very focused on finding this mysterious talisman. He'd refused to help them close the portals even knowing there were seven more than before and that the timing would be very close. Sarah and she could use all the help they could get.

"What are you getting?" Sarah interrupted her thoughts, waving the menu a little to get her attention.

She realized she was very hungry. The waitress at the side of the table looked expectantly at her. "A cheeseburger, fries, and a Coke sound really good."

The woman scribbled on her pad. "Alright. And you?"

"I'll have the meat omelette, hash browns, and toast."

"Coming right up." The server left.

"You alright? You're very quiet," Sarah said.

"Sarah, do you think it's weird that Byron wouldn't help us close all the new portals?"

"Not really. He knows we can handle it, and he's the only one who can find the talisman."

"That's another thing. That thing has been missing for more than fifty years. Why does he think he can find it in the next couple of days? That's a lot to bet on when closing all the portals would be a sure thing."

Sarah smiled. "Byron taught me sometimes you have to take a big risk. If we close all the portals *and* have the talisman, we'll be able to rescue his sister and close all the portals in Canopus for good."

When Marianne still looked doubtful, Sarah added, "Look, Byron worked for Dalcon Chemical for twelve years as one of their top chemists. He's used to solving thorny problems and not taking no for an answer. We'll beat Masters at his own game and show the other Protectors we can't be pushed around."

"I don't want to push the Shadow People into the neighboring counties either."

"We don't have to. If we close the portals, the draugers will be trapped in their realm and a plague on no one."

Lunch came. The food helped body and spirit, but Marianne's mind still wouldn't let go. She Googled 'Riven Masters' with French fry greasy fingers and got ketchup on her phone screen. What she found surprised her.

"Sarah, did you know somebody named Riven Masters also worked at Dalcon Chemical? There can't be too many people with that name. He was there until 1983. When was Byron there?"

Sarah frowned. "Early '70s. Byron left in 1982 and became a college professor. That's how we met. I needed a chemistry tutor in high school, and he was recommended."

"Isn't that weird, though? They must have known each other."

"I suppose," she said slowly. "It's a big company, so they wouldn't necessarily have known each other. The world of magical practitioners is small, and they tend to keep their pursuits quiet. Other people tend regard them as charlatans or are fearful of them, so they don't go around advertising."

"Kind of a weird coincidence, though, don't you think?"

Sarah gave her a look. "What are you thinking?"

She shook her head. "I don't know. Just, it's weird."

Sarah shrugged. "Byron says Masters and he are both looking for the Navarro Talisman. If Masters wanted it badly enough, then he could have exiled Catalina to the Shadow Realm either to distract Byron from his search or to warn him off."

"I suppose. But Sarah," she swallowed her mouthful and said, "I've been there, even if it was only a dream. There's no way Catalina could have survived there for five years. If she did, by some miracle, she couldn't still be sane."

Sarah nodded. "He has to get her out of there."

"It seems like an incredible risk. Even I'm not that crazy to save people!"

She gave Marianne a piercing look. "Wouldn't you want to save a person you love if they were trapped there?"

If it were Ruari? Yeah, I would. Marianne nodded reluctantly. "But what if he lets loose thousands of baby draugers?"

"Byron's first job is to protect Canopus County. As long as he has the talisman, we'll be able to send them back or destroy them."

"And if we don't?"

"That's why we have to finish our protection spell, and as a last defense, our ghost allies will help."

Marianne polished off her meal and drained her glass. All the calories went a long way to making her feel better. She could feel bad memories hovering in the background, but the current problem was filling all her mental space for now, and she was grateful for it.

"Why did the skull car guys trash Natalie?" She asked. "Do you think they figured out we sent Rita after them?" The memory of the men thrashing around in their room searching for an invisible dog still made her smile.

"I've been thinking about that. The attack on Natalie seems more calculated than a crime of passion. I don't think they're smart enough to have figured that out. So, much as I'd like to believe they did it, I don't think they hurt Natalie."

Marianne felt a pang of guilt for calling the cops on them. "Maybe I jumped to conclusions over that little rodent skull. Do you think they'll be stuck in jail for a long time? Maybe we should tell the police we don't think it's them anymore..."

Sarah snorted. "Don't feel too bad for them. That's not the first time they've spent a night in jail, I guarantee it. There's no evidence, so they'll be out in no time. Don't worry about them."

"If you're sure." *If it wasn't the skull car guys, who was it?*

They paid for their meal and walked back to the motel.

Marianne laid down on the bed fully clothed, hoping to find sleep before her memories got in the way.

In spite of her weariness, sleep eluded Marianne. She spent the afternoon with Sarah sifting through hastily collected parking lot gravel, to find enough gemstones, dried flowers, and herbs to reassemble protective charm bags to continue their spell. They were able to recreate fewer than thirty.

"Is that enough?" Marianne looked at their pile of now dirty cloth bags on the hotel coverlet. It looked like a lot, but she remembered how many they'd started with and how often they'd gotten out to place them.

"It'll have to be. I'd rather have more. This means sparser coverage, but maybe we'll get a few in the places we haven't been to yet."

Marianne brought out their map, and together they pored over it. Sarah indicated where they still had to go and determined that maybe they could leave four or five in each place. They had visited a dozen chambers so far, which Marianne found encouraging. There was the new one they hadn't been able to find in the southwest of the county before they'd gone to Minetto and then six others.

"I know this one and this one," Sarah pointed. "This one is up an old fire road, and this one is easily visible at the side of the road. The other four are new to me, and we'll have to spend the time to find them."

"Do we try to find the one down by Minetto again?"

Sarah shook her head. "Only if we have time."

They consolidated the remaining items, folded the tent and its poles into its ridiculously small bag, and threw away the ruined cardboard boxes. After that Sarah gave Sheba Motors another call while Marianne lay down on the bed. She was just dipping into sleep for the umpteenth time when Sarah spoke.

"Natalie's ready."

Sarah paid over two thousand dollars to get her back. The car had four new tires, a new windshield, and one new headlight. The shop only had a left one so the right still looked sad and broken. New taillight covers hadn't been located and the rear windshield had a big, starred crack in the middle. Her body looked like it had been hammered by a precision drum corps. At least the front doors still opened and closed. The passenger door on one side was warped shut, and the other closed badly. The back hatch needed to be held closed with a piece of wire.

They took her to a gas station that had a vacuum and sucked up all the glass bits. Colored tape and clear plastic covered the remaining lights and patched the back window, so at least the interior wouldn't be soaked if it rained again. By the time they were done, it was too dark to continue laying charms or look for the next stone chamber on the map.

In spite of that, they loaded Natalie up again, paid for the use of the room, and set off for their next destination. They were way behind schedule, and Sarah looked frantic. They drove back to Centerburg and stayed in the Canopus Motor Inn. They ate at Julie's Diner again.

Over a gyro, Marianne said, "I've been thinking about that old anxiety dream I had about the test where the professor was telling everyone to check their work."

"Why?"

"Well, I got to thinking about all the dreams I've had on this trip. Two of them were about Shadow People. Obviously very important. The ones I had last night were horrible nightmares about killing things." She gulped and pushed away her daymares about hurting Ruari or Oscar. Better to focus on something else.

Sarah nodded.

"I think the 'check your work' dream is significant, too. I'm sure of it. My brain usually agitates about things when I'm really worried. I don't think it would just toss up a random thing. What if 'check your work' means go back to all the portals and places we left charms already? What if our adversary not only messed up your charms from last year but somehow went back after we were there and put up new wedge charms?"

"Now there's a horrible thought." Sarah blanched, her eyes looking a little wild. "We don't have time to go back and check everything! We barely have enough time to finish the regular job. We're going to have to cut corners as it is."

"I think we should check the portals at least. Maybe we have to go a little light on some of the communities in exchange."

Sarah sighed heavily. "I don't think I have enough closing charms to do everything twice, especially with all the new ones."

"Can you make more on the fly?"

"I need components: stones, herbs and time. Things like asafoetida are hard to get."

Marianne thought. "Do you have any more at home? Could Kelly or Ruari bring us the pieces?"

"That's a good thought. Maybe."

"The good news is whoever is trying to open the portals is under the same time crunch as we are. Did you notice that the wedge charms at the chambers in Williston were easy to find, as if the person was in a hurry?"

"You're right."

"Sarah, what happens if not all the portals are closed by Halloween night?"

"Then Shadow People can come into our world. We'd have to find each one and kill them individually."

"If there's hundreds or thousands of them, that's going to be really hard."

"Yeah. If we don't close them, laying charms to protect the neighborhoods will be more important as a line of defense."

"And we're running out of time."

In their new hotel room, blissfully free of ghostly dogs, spirit bears, obnoxious neighbors, and stale cigarette smoke, they made their phone calls. Sarah had a long, quiet conversation with Kelly, and Marianne called Ruari.

"Mahri, how are you?" He sounded tired.

"Hanging in there." She still didn't want to talk about what had happened. "It's been a long day. We got Natalie fixed so we can keep going tomorrow. We're in Centerburg tonight."

"I miss you."

"I miss you too. How's Oscar?"

"He's fine."

"Thanks for feeding him. Are you there now?"

"No, I'm at Erin's place again."

"How's she doing? Did you figure out if her new place is haunted?" Marianne felt guilty for not remembering until now.

"I finally heard the story of what's going on with her. Apparently while we were in Scotland, she had a close encounter with a poltergeist."

"What?!" Erin was a profound skeptic about the supernatural at the best of times and obnoxious about it to the point of being one of Sarah's childhood tormenters at her worst. For her to acknowledge a poltergeist she must have had a truly frightening experience.

"What happened?"

"Something invisible threw things around, spoke to her, and basically scared the shit out of her."

While Marianne was all for people realizing that the spirit world existed, she wished it hadn't been like that for Ruari's sister. She rather liked Erin even if she was a bit oblivious to other people's feelings. "Is it still there?"

"No and here's the oddest thing. She had to call Sarah and Kelly to help her get rid of it."

"Did they?"

"They did."

Marianne gave her traveling companion a sidelong look. "Wow. Why didn't she say anything when we got back?"

"Honestly, I think she was hoping to forget all about it." He sighed. "And then mom asked her to clean out her room at home."

"Clean her room?"

"She found her old diaries and started reading them for fun. She got reminded of something that had happened to her in fourth grade, and that triggered her memories. She's been been dealing with that and the ghost thing ever since."

"Oh no! What happened?"

"She was friends with a brother and sister her age and they spent a lot of time together. They met through summer camp or something. Anyway, she went to their house for a sleepover once and when she came back, she was different. I hadn't thought about it before, but I can see it now."

"Like how?"

"Erin has always been outgoing and stubborn. But she was really sensitive, too. After that night she started acting out more, got into fights at school, and became a little brat. Our parents thought she was going through a phase. She's four years younger than me, so it never occurred to me to ask."

"Did something happen at the sleepover?"

"According to her, the brother and sister were both a little weird. They liked creepy Halloween stuff all year round and liked scaring people."

"Sounds very 'Beetlejuice'."

"Absolutely. Erin told me that they'd made a haunted house for her to walk through that night. They told her a story of a family who'd lived there before them who was murdered by someone they took in out of kindness. He drugged them all one night and hanged them from the rafters in the big room of the house. They told her the neighbors found the bodies swinging the next day, two little ones and two big ones. No trace of the stranger was ever found."

"Ew! That would give me nightmares too. It sounds more like an urban legend than actual fact, though."

"Yeah, it probably was, but that's not the worst part. They

took her through their little murder maze, and at the end she was treated to four bundles of cloth hanging from the rafters." His voice shook with anger.

"That's nasty!"

"They laughed themselves sick when Erin screamed her head off. She told me she wanted to come home, but they convinced her the ghost of the murderer would follow her home if she didn't spend the rest of the night and let them do a ritual to keep her safe."

Marianne was outraged. "Where were their parents? Didn't they notice what was going on?"

"Yeah, makes me want to find all of them and punch them out for scaring my little sister so badly."

"So what happened next?"

"They did some kind of made up thing. The funny thing is that Erin remembered the ritual as clearly as the scare. They used a magic wand that scared her as much as the murder story."

"A magic wand?"

"She described it as a short rod with two cross pieces. The kids waved it around mumbling nonsense words."

Marianne felt the hairs on her arms stand up straight as a shiver ran up her spine. "How big was this wand?"

"I don't know. Small enough to be handled by a kid of nine, I guess."

"Ruari, please don't be offended but is Erin with you?"

"Yeah."

"Can I talk to her?"

"I don't know, she's been through a lot..."

"I wouldn't ask if it wasn't really important. Please? I need to ask her about the thing she saw."

He put his hand over the phone, and Marianne heard muffled voices in the background.

"Marianne?" Erin's voice sounded smaller and shakier than Marianne remembered, and her heart went out to her.

"Hey Erin. I'm so sorry you're going through a rough time. Ruari gave me a general idea of what happened to you. I hope that's okay?"

"Yeah. I'd've busted his chops if it was anyone else," she sniffed.

"Thank you for trusting me. I know this sounds weird, but could you tell me anything you remember about the magic wand the other kids used?"

"I was really wigged out at the time, so I don't know if this will make any sense."

"Go on, I'm listening. No judgement."

"They made me sit in the middle of a circle and lit a bunch of candles. They told me that the ghost of the murderer would follow me home and kill me and my family if I didn't do it. God, it sounds so stupid now! I can't believe I fell for it."

"Don't feel bad. You had no way to know. Little kids can be absolutely horrible to each other. Where were their parents?"

She snorted. "They were little shits," she agreed. "Who knows where the parents were. Watching TV probably, knowing their little darlings were entertaining their friend."

"Do you remember what the wand looked like?"

"It looked more like a short stick or a dumbbell. Lorette waved it around saying hocus pocus words while her brother Bruce walked around the circle."

A chilly frisson passed through Marianne. "Did you feel anything while they did their so-called spell?" Erin was one of the most skeptical people she'd ever met, so the chance of her being sensitive to magic was pretty low. It was still worth a try.

"Not really but..." she hesitated, "I thought I heard something."

"Besides Bruce and Lorette you mean?"

"Maybe. Don't laugh, okay?"

"I swear."

"I thought I heard someone screaming."

"You mean someone was shouting about something?"

"No."

"Could it have been the parents in another part of the house? Or the TV?"

Erin pushed back. "Definitely not! It was a small voice but very intense. Like it was coming out of a cell phone, but there were no cellphones in those days. It was someone in a lot of pain. That sound scared me as much as the whole murder story."

The hairs on the back of her neck stood erect. "Did Lorette or Bruce hear it?"

"They didn't act like they did. The wand was just another toy to them."

"Could they have borrowed it from their parents?"

"Maybe."

"When the spell was over, did you see where it went?" Marianne crossed her fingers, hoping against hope.

"Actually, I did. Lorette tried to distract me while Bruce hid it, but I saw anyway."

"Where did he put it?"

"There was a loose floorboard by the stairs. Lorette told me that was where they put all their treasures. She said the ghost of the murderer guarded it. Hah!"

Excited and full of dread, Marianne asked her next question very carefully. "Erin, I know it was a long time ago, and you were really upset, but do you happen remember where this house was?"

"Why do you want to know? If you're going with Ruari to chew the family out, I appreciate the thought, but I think they moved a long time ago."

"Not exactly. If it's still there, I think this magic wand might be very important. Until I see it though, I can't be sure. I know it's too much to hope for, but would you know what town or even the address?"

"It's in Peterson. That much I remember. It was a big deal to go play with friends outside of Maple Hill. I should've stayed home that night. I was such a dummy."

"Erin, you were in fourth grade and what? Nine years old? They were your friends. Of course you trusted them. You couldn't know they would be so mean."

"No, I kind of did." She sounded wretched. "They were always a little weird, like Wednesday and Pugsley Addams, you know? Obsessed with morbid things like ghosts and death and ouija boards. I thought they were dangerous and cool. I was actually flattered they liked me so much. Later, I realized they thought I was a sucker they could run their little scam on. Believe me, I never played with them again!"

"I don't blame you in the least! Do you remember where in Peterson they lived or what the house looked like?"

"It was a big, old, rambling Tudor-style house with white stucco walls and black vertical and diagonal trim. There were huge trees around it, and it was set back from the street."

There must be miles of streets in Peterson that looked like that. "Any chance you remember a house number or a street name?"

"No, idea. Sorry."

"That's okay. Thank you, Erin, for sharing all this with me. I hope you can lay your fears to rest."

"Me too. Thanks for listening and not calling me crazy."

"Any time. And, you're not crazy. Not in the least." She put as much reassurance into her voice as she could. "Could you put Ruari back on, please?"

"Sure. Thanks."

The phone was transferred.

"Hey, Mahri. Thanks for talking to Erin. She seems a little calmer. What was that all about?"

"I have a hunch that the magic wand she saw is important to our trip. I won't know for sure until I see it. I have to find the house and hope it's still there."

"How are you going to find it?"

"I don't know. We may be driving around a lot tomorrow."

"What is so important about this thing?"

She shared her suspicions and concluded, "I have to get off so I can do some magic sensing practice before I pass out from exhaustion."

"Mahri, please be careful. Sleep well. Let me know how it goes."

"You bet."

Sarah had climbed into bed but was still awake. "What was that all about?"

"Sarah, I think I know where the Navarro Talisman is." She gave an abbreviated version of Erin's story, without revealing Erin's personal angst.

Sarah looked stunned and excited. "You're kidding! That's fantastic news. Where is it?"

"Back in Peterson."

Sarah reached for her phone. Her tee shirt nightie pulled away from her neck exposing the purple bruising. "Byron will be ecstatic to find out!"

Marianne flinched and steeled herself for an argument. "Sarah, don't call him. Please trust me and don't call him. If we find it, we can bring it to the cemetery in two days. He can be excited about it then."

Sarah's brows pulled down, making her look hawkish, as she eyed her phone.

"Look, you promised to trust me. I have a feeling about this, but I can't explain it. Please?"

Reluctantly, she laid the phone back on the side table. "Okay. I guess we don't have anything definite to tell him anyway, and as long as it ends up at the cemetery, it doesn't matter who gets it there."

Relieved, Marianne said, "Thank you. Meanwhile, our plans for tomorrow have been changed again. I don't have an address, only a house description. The only way we're going to find this place is by driving the streets. With any luck we'll be able to talk our way inside. After that, I don't know how we're going to retrieve it. It may not even be there still. The kids considered it a prized treasure, and they may have taken it with them when they moved."

"Then set your alarm for six a.m. We have a lot to do tomorrow."

CHAPTER 15

*T*hey drove the streets of Peterson for an hour just after dawn under a chill light rain. Marianne hadn't slept well, and she was resigned to getting up. At least they could say they'd tried even if they turned up empty handed.

They spotted only one dedicated runner and the occasional dog walker out only to make sure their furry friend had accomplished a basic biological urge. All the same Marianne couldn't help thinking they looked like a couple of stalkers cruising the streets in a battered old car.

"We'll just tell people we're up from the city, looking to buy a house and only have a short time to look," Sarah suggested.

"You think we look like we can afford anything in these neighborhoods while driving your old Volvo? No offense to Natalie, but she's not exactly a Lexus or a Caddy. And her recent 'injuries' don't maker her look any better."

Sarah patted the dashboard in sympathy, murmuring, "She didn't mean it, *mon chéri*. You always look like a Cadillac to me."

Marianne snorted then pointed out the window. "Hey, slow down! Look at that place." They cruised past a three-story, Tudor-style house. The street looked like all the others they'd been through: upper middle class, old clapboard and Victorian homes from the early nineteen hundreds. Grinning jack-o-lanterns and faux graveyards decorated many front yards.

Mature trees crowded around this old house. Straw colored grass stood knee high and dry weeds crowded the walkway from the road. No car stood in the drive. No lights shone in the windows. It was easily more scary than all the other houses on the block without all the seasonal paraphernalia. A piece of paper fluttered on the front door. They couldn't tell what it said from this distance.

"What do you think?" Sarah asked. "Paper on the door is never a good sign."

Marianne shrugged. "It's as good a candidate as any we've seen. It also looks like no one's lived here for a while."

"Or they're not house proud and don't own a car."

Sarah cast a quick glance up and down the street, saw no one, and pulled into the drive, coasting as far back as she could go. They were in luck. The drive widened out behind the house, and she tucked Natalie's burly square back into the space. Hopefully, they wouldn't be visible from the street.

Getting out and shutting the doors as quietly as they could in the early morning stillness, they split up. Marianne peeked into the old carriage house garage while Sarah investigated the back door. The little building was dark, but she saw no sign of occupation.

On the back steps, inside a small entry way, Sarah pointed at the notice. "Private Property: Keep Out. Call Callahane Realty Managers for information."

"Do you think they'd give us a tour if we told them our story about wanting to buy a house here?" Marianne asked.

Sarah looked intrigued. "Maybe.

"What're our other options?"

"Breaking and Entering would shitcan my career, so unless it's our last resort…"

"Fine." Marianne looked at her phone. It was seven-thirty. Too early for the agency to be open. "Want to get breakfast?"

"I saw a place a couple of blocks away."

They adjourned and ate a good breakfast. Having made up her mind to be the one to call the agency, Marianne tried not to think too hard about it. An hour later, she washed her last bite of eggs and hash browns down with water, and took a deep breath. Sarah raised an amused skeptical eyebrow. Marianne dialed the number, pushing her nervousness away.

Putting on a bright, cheery voice, she said, "Hello, is this Callahane Realty? Hi! Thank goodness you're in so early! My partner and I are up from the city. We're looking to buy in Peterson and saw the perfect place. We wondered if you'd show it to us today? Uh huh. Yes, the address is 142 Martin Place. Uh huh. Oh, really? Just a sec." She put her hand over the phone.

"They said the place has been on the market for a while, it needs a little work, and are we sure?"

Sarah rolled her eyes and nodded.

"Yup! We're sure. We just love the Tudor style and want to see the interior today if possible. It has so much potential! Uh huh. I can wait." She put her hand over the phone again and said, "They're seeing if someone is available to show it." A moment later she listened again. "That's fantastic! We'll meet them at the house. Bye." She hung up. "All set. They're sending someone round at nine."

Sarah stared at her with both brows raised. "I'm impressed. Who knew you could spin such a good story?"

She shrugged. "It's hard for me to cold call people, but once I get going, I'm okay."

With steaming cups of coffee and tea, they walked back to the house on Martin Place. Natalie stayed in the parking lot after Sarah murmured,"Don't worry, *ma belle*. You rest here. We'll be back soon."

A young man with short, curly black hair met them at the curb in a red Subaru. Marianne guessed he was very junior in the firm and got stuck with the crazy ladies wanting to see the creepy, abandoned house.

"Hi, I'm Craig Johnson. It's nice to meet you." They all shook hands, and he said, "Well, shall we?" He handed them each a hastily printed spec sheet and told them a little about the house. "It was built in the 1920s and has had only a couple of owners. The old owner sold it to an investor about a year ago. The market has been a little slow, but things are picking up. This is a good time to buy." He sounded like he was trying hard not to oversell this white elephant.

They stood on the front step, and Craig pressed the code to the lock box and extracted the key. Inside, he turned on the lights and began the tour. Marianne followed him, only half listening. She opened her senses as far as she could, trying to get a feel for the place. Was this where Erin had had her big fright? Was the mysterious wand still here? Erin had said there was a loose board near the stairs on the second floor. She needed time to search for it.

"Excuse me," she interrupted Craig with an apologetic smile before turning to Sarah, "Honey, I'd like to feel the vibes upstairs. Will you take notes for me?"

Sarah replied after a beat, "Of course, sweetie. Take your time."

"Oh, but you should see the downstairs first," Craig protested.

"Marianne fancies herself a bit of a psychic," Sarah said, leaning in. "She likes to feel the Feng shui and the mystical flow of the building."

Marianne gave a dreamy smile and drifted back toward the entrance hall where she'd seen the stairs to go up.

Laying it on a bit thick aren't we?

If she was unsuccessful, she could take a turn distracting Craig with a repeat tour of the downstairs and Sarah could look.

At the top of the stairs, Marianne paused to get her bearings. The landing expanded into a large open space with a cathedral ceiling. It was dim up here between the cloudy day, the small windows, and the crowding trees. She strolled around, trying to feel anything magical. Dark brown beams crossing the space made her think of a large formal dining or living room space. It would have been an amazing rumpus or bonus room. Was this was where Erin had been told the urban legend? The beams would have been perfect to hang body-sized bundles of cloth for the final scare.

Just like the objects she'd held in her hands last night before bed, she felt nothing special. But she detected a low hum or buzz coming from somewhere. At first she wondered if it was coming from the kitchen down below, but the more she walked, the louder it became. It was like the buzzing she'd heard when George and Anne Rutherford were present but invisible in her own home. A prickle of anxiety rippled through her. Was someone else here?

She walked through the two small bedrooms off the big room. They were dusty and echoey. Sarah usually used a crystal pendulum on a necklace to speak to any resident spirits. Marianne hadn't figured out how to use one yet. Instead, she played hotter-colder: if the buzzing was louder, she figured she was closer to whatever it was.

It was loudest down a short hall to a little closet alongside the stairwell.

As she approached, the buzzing grew to a swarm of angry bees. It had a feeling of malice, and she felt a voice say angrily, *Go away!*

"Why? Are you hiding something?" She whispered.

She reached for the old fashioned faceted glass door knob. It rattled under her hand as if someone was on the other side. She jumped back, heart suddenly beating harder.

Was there a portal in the closet? Worse, was it full of draugers waiting to burst out? The protective charm of stones and herbs lay bumpy but neutral in her jeans pocket, so maybe not. She patted her pockets: Oscar carving in one, glass jar in the other.

Fighting the impulse to run down the stairs, away from the haunted closet, she clenched her teeth. If the Navarro Talisman was in there, she had to find it. Sarah had looked so disappointed when she'd run away from Adrian Vandermark in the old barn and all those times she'd felt nothing while practicing.

Squaring her shoulders, Marianne pulled the jar of holy water out of her pocket and loosened the top just in case. The facets of the old fashioned crystal knob pressed into her other palm as she twisted and yanked the door open.

A billow of dark fog reared up in the doorway. It coalesced into a vague humanoid form that wavered like heat over burning asphalt. It didn't radiate the hot fear and anger that had made her want to wring Sarah's neck. Instead, she felt a cold evil capable of killing the people who had offered him shelter simply because he could. There were many murders in this man's past, not the least of which was his own.

Every hair on her body stood up, and she froze as a cold cloud descended on her. It coiled and snaked around her, examining her with a dispassionate prospect of pain and death. Unable to breathe or move, she stood rigid.

Don't let them intimidate you...give 'em hell. No shady people allowed in this shitty little backwater while I'm here.

Toni's words gave Marianne a jolt. She gasped for breath, stumbled back, banging the door against the wall. She flung the holy water at the apparition, squeaking out, "ByEarthandSkyand-FireandWaterbegone!"

The foul miasma twisted and roiled as the consecrated water touched it and passed through it bringing with it all the power of Father Williams and his conviction. By the time the water hit the floor with a splash, the thing was gone.

She could feel it hovering close by as if it was on the other side of a glass wall. It squatted here and wanted to stay. A little jar of holy water was not enough to banish it permanently.

With shallow breaths and trembling hands, she dropped to her knees, tapping with her knuckles and feeling for mismatched boards with her fingers. Under the closet floor she heard the unmistakable sound of a hollow space. Feeling with her fingertips, she found the slightly raised lip of a board and tried to pry it up. Splinters jabbed her under her fingernails.

She felt in her pockets for something, anything to help, and found a pen. She jammed it in the crack between the boards.

"Honey, you okay up there?" Sarah's voice came from the bottom of the stairs.

"Yeah, sorry. I thought I saw a bat. You know I hate bats." Her voice sounded brittle.

"Do you need help?"

"Bats?" Said Craig, sounding worried. "Are you sure? We'll have to get an exterminator if you saw a bat."

Between her fingers and the pen, she slowly prised up the board. Just needed another minute.

"Nope," she called back, "I just scared myself. Silly me. I'll be down in a sec." The board came up with a creak and a pop, and she set it aside. With the flashlight app on her phone, she scanned the cavity below.

Jackpot. Lorette and Bruce had been little magpies. A dusty collection of shells, pretty stones, a gold bracelet with colored stones, the skull of a small animal, a pack of cigarettes with a lighter, and a black lacquered box.

"Hello, what's in here?" She murmured.

She lifted the wooden box out and tilted the lid back. Inside, on a bed of red satin, lay a cylindrical black rod about six and a half inches long with two shorter cross pieces, one at either end. A snake in tarnished silver wound its way around the central piece. A carved eye adorned the junction of each cross piece.

It was elegant, old, and powerful and sounded like hummingbird wings.

I see why Lorette and Bruce considered this one of their prized treasures.

She brushed her fingertips across the surface and felt a snap of static electricity prick her. She yanked her fingers back as a ripple expanded through her awareness like menthol clearing her sinuses. Her mind felt like a rung bell.

"What the hell?"

The holy water was wearing off. The murderous spirit hovered closer. He had every intention of hurting her if he could.

"We're coming to join you, sweetie!" Sarah called and the stair treads creaked.

Hastily she tucked the box into her jacket pocket. Slipping the board back into place, she stepped on it to press it flush with its neighbors. She closed the closet door as Sarah and Craig reached the top landing.

"How's the Feng shui up here?" Sarah asked lightly, giving her a searching look. Craig looked around surreptitiously for bats.

"Honestly, not great." She willed Sarah to open her senses. "I mean, I love the open space, but somehow it just doesn't feel right. I think there was a lot of sadness in this house," she babbled.

Craig's face fell. Sarah must have been buttering him up during their tour, getting his hopes up. Marianne felt sorry for dashing them, but there was no way she would ever live in a house whose central spirit was that of a murderer. No wonder it was so hard to sell.

The angry buzzing was back. "We should go." She gave a bright, brittle smile. "Now."

Sarah pivoted and went back down the stairs as quickly as she could.

Craig followed, oblivious.

"Is there anything else I can show you? We have much nicer properties just a couple of blocks over." He was still hoping for a sale.

"Gosh, I think we're going to need to regroup, isn't that right, honey?" Sarah put her hand on Marianne's arm. She nodded.

They apologized for getting Craig out so early in the morning and headed back toward the café.

"Who or what was that upstairs?" Sarah demanded as soon as they were alone on the sidewalk.

"Remember the story those kids told Erin about a murderer? Not an urban legend. Actual murderer. He was guarding their little stash of treasures, including this." She showed Sarah the corner of the black lacquer box in her pocket. "I'd be really worried about those kids having a pact with the ghost of a killer, if they still lived there. Hopefully, they haven't turned into serial killers or something. Erin was brilliant to dump them as friends. Should we tell Callahane Realty to get an exorcist?"

"Nope. We'd never be able to explain. There's a paranormal activity disclosure clause in New York. Any potential buyers will find out about it. That could be why the house hasn't sold in over two years."

Marianne reluctantly let it go. *Buyer beware, I guess. Maybe that's another thing I could add to my ghost business.*

Once in the safety of Natalie's front seat, Marianne took the box out and opened it.

"Holy mother of magic," Sarah breathed. "The Navarro Talisman." She looked at Marianne. "Good going."

"Now what?" Marianne asked.

Sarah reached for her phone. "We should give Byron the good news!"

Marianne made a face.

"What?"

"Could you not call him?"

"Why? He needs to know."

"Yes, but we can tell him when we meet up tomorrow night, can't we?"

Sarah brows drew down.

"I have a feeling. I don't know exactly what it is, but please trust me."

Sarah gave her a searching look and nodded reluctantly. "Okay, we'll play it your way for now. If you figure out what the feeling is, please tell me. So, now we do what we planned to do: close portals and lay charms. We have only today and tomorrow, and there's a long way to go." She reverently closed the box without touching the wood and silver and set it on the front seat between them. "First, I need another coffee to go. Can I get you something?"

Still feeling shaky after her encounter, Marianne said, "Hot chocolate? And a cinnamon roll? I think I need a minute to sit still."

"You got it. I'll be right back. Then we'll get on the road."

In the silence, Marianne relaxed a little. She was alive and had retrieved a powerful relic hundreds of years old. They'd bring it to Byron Mandel but not yet. She closed her eyes and took a deep breath. The Talisman sat on the seat next to her pulsing with a faint hum. As she relaxed, other little vibrations came to her attention.

That's weird.

Distracted by the sound of a fly trapped in the visor over head, she pulled the visor down to set it free and shoo it outside. She was not ready for a little gauze charm bag to fall into her lap. Holding it in her hand, she felt it buzz like a fly on the windowsill. She pinned it back overhead between the visor and the ceiling and turned her attention to the rest of the car. Marianne knelt on her seat and faced the back. When she closed her eyes, she detected other little buzzing fly sounds. Under her seat, under the back seat, in Sarah's visor, and a whole bottle of flies in the cardboard box in the way back.

Holy cow. I think I can feel magic.

Sarah pulled the door open with a cranky metallic creak and handed in a foam cup of sweet smelling chocolate and a hot sticky bun in a to-go container. Marianne turned around and sat again, waiting for Sarah to close her door.

"Sarah?"

"Hmm?" Her mentor was busy getting settled.

"I can feel magic."

Sarah stopped. "What? When?"

"I can tell you exactly where every charm is in Natalie including the ones in the visors."

Sarah stared. "How?"

"When I opened the box in the closet, I touched the Navarro Talisman."

Sarah's eyebrows contracted. "Haven't you learned anything about powerful magical objects by now? You don't touch anything without gloves."

"I think it blew my senses free."

Sarah gave her a penetrating look and said, "Let's hope it didn't do anything else." She turned to start the car.

Natalie lodged her protest at being left out of the haunted house trip by needing three tries to get her started. Or maybe she was just tired of the whole trip, Marianne thought, and wanted to go home. *Me too, Natalie, me too.*

Either way, Sarah patted her on the dash, "Hang in there, *mon amie*, just a couple more days." They gassed her up and went forward on their list.

The plan was to complete the protective spell as quickly as they could and pick up or revisit stone chambers along the way. They would connect with ghost allies when possible as a back up plan if they had to fight draugers, immature or otherwise, on Halloween night.

More to keep from thinking about the murderer's ghost and his every intention of making her his next victim, Marianne got out her map and continued annotating. The murder house got a big black X. When she finished, she dove back into research on Turner's Hope Mine with the idea of stopping and telling Peter O'Meara her plan. Hopefully, he'd love it so much, he and his men would help defend Canopus. It was worth a try anyway.

First they had to meet up with Kelly. She'd scrounged the house for supplies to create more of the closing charms but only found enough to make five. Driving up the incline into Maple Hill, Marianne felt a stab of longing. Her own little house was just a few blocks away. Oscar was probably out doing cat things, and Ruari must be out fixing things for Gloria's Hudson Valley Homes and Properties. Brown leaves, pumpkins and gauzy ghosts decorated the neighborhoods. Maple Hill looked charming, and she wished she could just be home to enjoy it.

Instead, they went to Sarah's house. Kelly met them at the door on her crutches. It felt like a hundred years had passed since that dinner party where the trip had been proposed. Kelly gave them each a fierce hug, adding a passionate kiss for Sarah.

"I know you can't stay. Here are the charms, and I made a couple of care packages for you too." She handed them paper bags and a cardboard box with five closing charms in it. "It was the best I could do."

"Kells, you are my hero. Thank you for doing this." Sarah hugged her again.

"Wish I could be with you."

"You are in exactly the right place. Thank you." They fell silent, resting their foreheads together for a moment.

Marianne peeked inside her bag. "Oh wow! This is amazing! Thank you. I am so sick of crappy tea." There were a dozen bags of tea, half caffeinated and the other half soothing. Under them was a sandwich, an apple and a bunch of candy bars.

Kelly gave her a broad smile. "I thought you would be. Sarah does flex fuel, but I knew you'd be hurting."

"Are these early trick-or-treats?" Marianne held up a candy bar.

"You know it," Kelly laughed.

"Time to go, babe," Sarah said. "I love you. I miss you. See you tomorrow night."

Back in the car, Marianne said a little wistfully, "Any chance we could see Ruari?"

"Do you know where he is?"

She shook her head. "I could call."

Sarah made a pained expression. "You could, but I'm not sure we have the time."

A couple of days ago, Marianne would've been seething, but she just nodded. "I'll call him later."

CHAPTER 16

The ghost of a WWI soldier met them on the road near Vandenberg. Ben Dixon cheerfully agreed to renew his help, his youthful, gap-toothed grin at odds with the Springfield rifle and bayonet in his hands. Marianne liked him immediately and was glad he patrolled the corner of the county near her Grandma Selene's house. As they drove past Grandma's road, Marianne insisted they divert so she could bury a protective charm at the foot of Grandma's mailbox. She longed to stop for tea, but they had no time.

Sarah had strapped her hiking boots into the seat between them, and a cup of coffee steamed in one, one of Kelly's tea bags dangled from a cup of hot water in the other. The black lacquer box was tucked up against the boots on Marianne's side. She could feel it vibrating against her hip. Her newly opened senses felt overstimulated and raw. She couldn't tone down the fly buzzes of Sarah's charms, but she could do something about the talisman. Surreptitiously she jammed her hat between them. It helped. She hoped her senses would calm down, and there would be a happy medium.

Searching for one of the stone chambers on their original list, they drove up an old fire road in the hills between the Taconic

State Parkway and the lakes of central Canopus. When Natalie could go no farther without serious damage to her undercarriage, Sarah made a labored turn and aimed the car down hill back toward the main road as a precaution.

"You never know."

They got out, and Marianne patted her pockets: jeans, left jacket, right jacket. Charm, Oscar carving, holy water. Sarah reloaded her pack with magical gear, and they continued up hill. They hiked through the quiet, dripping woods, looking for an elbow tree. Marianne had looked up these curious sign posts. To act as a pointer to a significant place, Native Americans and early settlers would weigh a branch from a young tree down. Over time the branch settled into that position and grew upwards at a right angle, creating an elbow pointing the way.

The track was overgrown, and crumbling stone walls peeked out from the drifts of leaves on either side of the road. Fifteen minutes later, they found an unmistakable branch bent at a right angle. They followed its pointer and left the track.

The buzz saw sound of an open portal was audible before she saw it. Down in a dell, a dark opening appeared. Marianne gritted her teeth, determined to push through the magical field and get the job done. Ahead of her Sarah dropped to one knee, pulled out her gloves and one of her closing charms.

"Are you ready?" Sarah asked. "Let's close this one quickly and move on."

"Got it."

They approached the doorway. Although it was narrow, it was tall enough for them to walk mostly upright. The familiar wave of vertigo and nausea rolled over her, and Marianne steadied herself. Sarah slipped inside, flashlight on and Marianne followed. Now that she knew what to expect, and perhaps with the new found sensitivity, she was able to push through.

As she passed through the opening, she detected another higher pitched sound like the whistling of a tea kettle buried in the teeth rattling sound of the wedging charm.

"Sarah? Do you hear that?" Marianne touched her mentor on the shoulder.

"No, remember I don't hear magic, I see it."

"Something is different. I don't know what it is but—"

Sarah reached up to grab the dirty white linen bag protruding from a crack between the ceiling slabs just as Marianne caught sight of another white bag wedged into the rock wall. The charm in her pocket gave a hot pulse. "Wait!" She shouted.

Sarah pulled the little bag free and all hell broke loose. Black blobs poured out of the opening and swarmed Sarah. Her mentor screamed and shook her head, batting at the baby Shadows. Either her charms were ineffective or the creatures were too hungry to care. They lodged onto her head and shoulders like ticks.

Horrified, Marianne yanked the holy water bottle out of her pocket, fumbled the cap, and emptied the contents over Sarah's head. The blobs silently writhed and twisted. Two of the five broke free and shrank into little raisins before falling to the ground, inert.

Sarah sank to the ground and lay unmoving, shadow blobs bobbing gently up and down on her head. Marianne rifled her mentor's pockets and came up with a second bottle of Father Williams' finest and poured it over the rest of the attackers. They too shriveled up and fell to the ground.

"Sarah! Sarah, c'mon, get up! They're gone." Marianne shook her hard.

Sarah moaned and twitched feebly. Marianne reached under her armpits and tried to pull her out of the chamber. It was like hauling a sack of wet cement.

"You gotta help me here, Sarah!"

Her mentor pushed weakly with her feet as Marianne lifted and pulled. Together they got out into daylight. Sarah lay on the damp leaves barely moving. Marianne sat panting next to her. The higher pitched sound was gone, but the buzz saw was still there.

She donned Sarah's old leather driving gloves, grabbed a plastic bag and a closing charm, and dove back into the chamber. Braving the jittery vibrations, she swung the beam of the flashlight around at the floor. The little desiccated shadow blobs had disappeared like ice on a hot sidewalk, but she had no time to worry about where they'd gone. She located the first cotton bag and out dropped a wooden splinter and a piece of bone into her gloved hand. She shoved them back inside for later consideration and threw the lot into a sandwich baggie.

She approached the second cloth bag very cautiously, not wanting to unleash another barrage. Through her gloved fingertip she felt something small and lumpy. Gingerly she pulled it free, ready to duck and run if anything happened. When nothing did, she dumped the second charm into another baggie. Both of them had a small circled TK on the cloth bag. *Dammit.*

Rolling their own charm bag in her palms lightly, she chanted the words to activate it and stuffed it into the crack in the ceiling. Mercifully, the grating buzz lessened and died down.

Outside on the ground, Sarah moved sluggishly, slurring her words like her tongue was too heavy. "Wha' happen?"

Marianne replied, "I think we were ambushed by a booby trap. Kitteby got here first. I don't know why they stuck it way up here not somewhere easier, but someone knew we were coming."

"That bastard. How did you…"

Marianne explained.

"Good. Have to keep going. Help me." She spoke like every word cost her.

Marianne shouldered Sarah's pack along with her own and helped her mentor to stand. Even with Marianne carrying most of her weight, Sarah walked like her legs were made of cooked spaghetti. Together they staggered back to the car.

"Why didn't your charm protect you?" Marianne asked.

"Maybe losing its charge. Been challenged a lot."

That made sense. Sarah had been the one to handle the evil

charms most of the time. At least Marianne's was still working as a warning bell.

"What happened when they were on you?" Marianne asked.

"Told you. Suck your energy out."

"How long are you going to be this way?"

"Dunno."

Marianne cleared the back seat and set up a sleeping bag for Sarah to lie on. She belted Sarah's unresisting form into place and slid into the driver's seat. It felt weird to be sitting on the wrong side of the car.

Feeling a little foolish, she addressed the dashboard. "Okay, Natalie, Sarah can't drive. The only way we're getting out of here is if you let me drive. It's been a long time since I drove stick, so I apologize in advance." She took a deep breath, depressed the clutch with her left foot and the brake with her right, and turned the key in the ignition. It took two tries but Natalie started up, and she released the brake and let out the clutch. The car jerked to a stop, and the engine died. She started the Volvo again and tried to remember how to balance the clutch and the accelerator.

Lurching and crow hopping down the bumpy road, Marianne stalled the engine and restarted it half a dozen times as she remembered the clutch-accelerator two-step from a brief couple of lessons many years ago.

"Stop killin' my car," Sarah slurred from the back seat. Marianne ignored her as they half rolled, half drove down the fire road to the intersection with the main road.

With the engine running, she threw it into neutral. Sarah lay on the back seat, either passed out or asleep. Who knew how long it would take Sarah to get her strength back. What if it was never? Better not think about that possibility. Let's hope a week of good food and lots of rest would do it. Until then, Marianne was on her own to finish the spell, locate and close the remaining portals, and get to the cemetery on time tomorrow night. And not run into their enemy along the way since she had no idea how to defend herself magically.

At least she didn't have to worry about meeting any other ghostly allies. All of those were Sarah's contacts. Now that she was up to her eyeballs in alligators, she had no bandwidth to make new contacts or deal with needy ghosts. If she could convince Peter O'Meara and his band to come, maybe that would make up for it.

It was just like grad school. Dissertation deadline: midnight tomorrow. Her committee had just dumped fifty more comments and necessary changes in her lap. The grad school was throwing roadblocks about formatting and paperwork at every turn. And Geoffrey had a big work-related dinner party she had to plan and host.

Piece of cake.

Marianne let Kelly know what happened, and although Kelly clearly wanted to have Sarah come home immediately, she agreed they had to finish the journey. Kelly promised to meet them at the cemetery.

The rest of the day passed in a blur. Marianne drove and laid charms until the box ran low, planning to save tomorrow for revisiting or finding the rest of the stone chambers. She only had a handful of closing charms, and she prayed she wouldn't need more. The weather was blustery but not rainy, and she thanked the universe for small favors.

When Marianne first asked Sarah for suggestions or guidance she got no answer. Pulling over in a panic, she checked Sarah's pulse. It beat slow but steady, and Marianne realized she was deeply asleep. Marianne was on her own. When she roused, Marianne fed her French fries and a cup of overly sweet, hot coffee. Sarah fell asleep again, and Marianne kept driving.

All day she was uncomfortably aware of the gentle thrumming of the Navarro Talisman in its box on the seat next to her. It weirded her out. She laid her pack over it to muffle the sound and did her best to ignore it.

She blew past twilight and into early night trying to finish laying charms in the last community. As she pulled out into the larger county road, Natalie's headlights caught the shape of a little four-legged creature darting across the road. Reflexes dulled after a long day, she swerved too late. A telltale thud shuddered through Natalie's body, and Marianne flinched. Pulling over, she jumped out and looked. The body of a fat raccoon lay on the road unmoving.

"Oh baby, I'm so sorry." She pulled her hands inside the sleeves of her jacket and gently lifted the critter off the road so it wouldn't get hit again. Its body heat warmed her hands. "I'm so sorry."

Murderer. A little voice whispered.

Her throat constricted, and she swallowed hard, biting back tears.

Sarah needed to get to a bed. They both needed to eat and rest. She climbed back into the driver's seat and pulled out, her spirits at a very low ebb.

At the eastern edge of Canopus Marianne pulled into a motel in Crossfield. Not the big, beautiful, expensive Pheasant and Tankard Inn but a poorer cousin down the road. She got a room on the first floor and helped Sarah inside and into bed. Marianne thought Sarah was walking a little better, but her friend passed out again almost immediately. She hoped that sleep was what she needed most.

What Marianne needed most was to hear Ruari's voice.

"Mahri, where are you tonight?"

"Crossfield again."

"What happened?" He said sharply. "Are you okay?"

"No, weird and crappy day." Her words tumbled out, falling over each other, while she did her best not to cry. She ended with the latest disaster. "He was just there in the road. I didn't see him in time."

"If you could've avoided him, you would have," he said gently. "You are a genuinely kind person, Mahri. It's not your fault."

He wouldn't say that if he knew everything.

Feeling utterly miserable, she drew a shuddering breath and said, "Ruari, there's one more thing. Something happened the night we camped out…" With halting words, she described nearly killing Sarah under the drauger's influence.

Ruari was silent when she finished.

More to fill the space than anything else, she said, "If you're having second thoughts about being with me, I completely understand."

"Considering that I was effectively possessed by a fey being, I can't be one to complain if something like that happened to you."

"But you didn't nearly kill someone."

"Okay, that's bad. But you didn't actually, right? Sarah's okay. I wish I'd been there. Maybe things would have turned out differently."

"They might have possessed you instead!" That thought scared her.

"Maybe, maybe not. I have some experience for what that feels like. What I'm trying to say is, I'm not going away. I wish I could be with you right now."

"I wish you could too. Thanks, Ruari." She took a shaky breath, feeling her shoulders relax. "I need some dinner."

"Want me to stay on the line while you eat?"

Her cheeks hurt as she smiled for the first time in ages. "That would be really nice."

She ordered pizza, and Ruari helped her wait for the delivery by telling her about Erin. She felt well enough to go out with him for coffee, but ducked back into her apartment immediately after, and curled up in bed under a pile of covers.

Dinner arrived, and several slices of sausage and mushroom pizza filled her belly. Ruari's story about teaching Casey, his self absorbed assistant, how to unclog a food disposer and pull the sludge out of the pipes below it made her laugh.

"Sounds so gross."

"Yeah, it was fun watching Casey deal with it."

After Ruari hung up, she felt better, not completely okay, but better.

Sarah slept, apparently undisturbed by the phone conversation or the smell of food. Marianne worried but felt her forehead and took her pulse. No fever and her heart and breathing were steady. With Sarah's collar pulled back, the livid purple bruising made Marianne wince. She pulled the covers all the way up.

Marianne put the last of the black sand from Sarah's precious stash into the baggies with the dark magic charms and shook it to coat them. She didn't know if that made it any more effective, but it seemed the right thing to do. How they were going to defuse evil charms after this she didn't know. If only she hadn't wasted so much in her childish prank.

Out of curiosity, while she was in Sarah's toolbox of magical stuff, she touched various items. Things that had seemed inert before now had a humming life of their own, making her nerves jump. Hastily she closed the lid of the box and set it aside.

She sat on the bed and reviewed her notes, wearily continuing her research on the mine. Kelly's thoughtful care package was nearly gone, but there were still several packets of tea. Two of the chamomile and peppermint teas disappeared while she stared at the map and planned out her last mad dash to finish the spell and close the portals.

When she caught herself nodding off with a jerk, she put herself to bed and hoped fervently for no dreams at all. She wrapped her fingers around Ruari's little effigy of Oscar and curled under the covers waiting to get warm.

Ruari is okay with me in spite of what happened, but I'm still scared. What if I attack him when I'm angry about something? What if I hurt Oscar? All those feelings of rage and resentment were mine. All the Shadow People did was push me over the edge. I didn't stop me. If Jules hadn't shown up, I wouldn't have stopped.

Now Sarah's sick. If I don't finish the spell, all of this will have been for nothing. I don't know how this is supposed to go, so I'll just have to make it up. Maybe something will be better than nothing. Byron's big on sticking to the plan, but I don't really want to call and tell him his star pupil is out of the action and Team Canopus is stuck with the rookie player.

She finally fell into an exhausted sleep. The Navarro Talisman on the bedside table between her and Sarah hummed softly to itself.

Marianne followed a voice in the dreaming darkness. It led her to a wall. Her fingers followed the smooth surface until they found a crack. The voice was clearer here.

"Hello?" She said.

+Who are you?+ The voice said.

She put her eye to the crack and saw a brown eye looking back. "I'm Marianne. Who are you?"

+Zorion.+

"What are you doing?"

+I'm stuck in here.+

"How did that happen? Can I help you get out?"

+It's a long story.+

He had an accent she couldn't place. Not French or German. Maybe Spanish with some overtones? Feeling oddly like she had all the time in the world, she sat down and leaned against the wall.

"Please tell me."

+No one has heard my story before.+

"I want to hear it."

+Very well. I was once a merchant of woolens, educated for my time. I ran a small business in Navarro, trading with many people. I had a wife and three children who helped me with my business. I should have been content. But trade was demolished by wars and petty religious fighting, and I lost goods to a storm and to highway men. My business struggled.

+A man who I called friend introduced me to his other friends. Together they made up a secret society dedicated to ending war and returning prosperity to our land. They showed me that human misery was made worse by the incursions of draugers from a neighboring realm, and if we could stop them, we might have a chance to restore peace to our land. I agreed to help, and they agreed to lend me money to start my business again. Please understand, my wife and children were hungry and I feared for their safety.

+These men initiated me in the mysteries of their beliefs, and I helped with their goal of eliminating the threat of draugers forever. Together we delved into darker and darker magic. I was not a devout man but attended church to keep the peace with my neighbors. My wife feared the church would find out and worried for my soul, but I assured her the risk was worth the effort. We forged a device, a talisman, that would be powerful enough to close the doors to the Shadow Realm and destroy legions of draugers.

+However, rumor of our work reached the ears of the church before we were finished. Witchcraft was greatly feared then, and they sent a warrior priest and a prelate to find us. We managed to remain hidden, but it was a near thing.

+All that was left was to imbue the talisman with the power to do its job. We gathered on a full moon night, in a secret place and raised the energy needed to complete our task. Unbeknownst to me, they'd schemed behind my back. They did not tell me until that night that they needed a life to complete the spell, and they had agreed that life should be mine.

+I argued, but my friend told me I was too kind and too trusting to continue. They worried I would betray them. They told me by my death I would become powerful. There were six of them. I could not escape or overcome them. Before they killed me, I begged them to look after my family. My friend promised he would, and they plunged a dagger into my heart.

+They stole my finger bone, burned my body, and bound my spirit into this device. The first time they used it, it nearly killed me again with the very pain of it. The device channels their magic through me, magnifies it, and closes doors to the Realm of Shadows but at great cost to me.

+I traveled through Spain from hand to hand, closing doors to save humanity for thirty generations, though at times it drove me mad. I traveled across the ocean to the new lands and did the same there. The man called Silas Coventry felt my pain and vowed never to use me again. He hid me in his house, and I rested for a long time, regaining my strength and sanity.

+Until you found me I had known mostly peace except for some foolish children who fortunately did not know what they had.+ He stopped speaking, and she let the silence hang for a moment.

She rolled onto her knees and looked through the crack again and the brown eye on the other side. Her heart went out to him. He'd been through so much. His wife and children must have been devastated when they learned he'd died.

I bet they didn't tell her how he died. I bet they made up some bogus story. I wonder if they even fulfilled their promise to look after them? Her specific knowledge of Navarro, Spain in the 1500s wasn't very detailed, but she remembered wars raging back and forth across the continent. Not a great time to be alive.

"Thank you for telling me your story. I am so sorry that happened to you. What do you want?"

+I want only peace and oblivion.+

"I wish I could help you."

+You have only to open or break the talisman, and I will be free.+

"Will you be able to join your wife and children in the hereafter?"

+I don't know. I would like to see them again and tell them

I'm sorry for abandoning them. But I have been part of such evil, I don't think I have a place in Heaven.+

"It wasn't your fault."

+But it was. I should have known my associates for what they were.+

"Zorion, did you know that we stand on the eve of another wave of draugers coming from the Shadow Realm?"

+There is always another incursion.+ He sounded bone weary.

"Yes. This time it's in my country, threatening my home and family. Would you stand with us and close the doors again?"

+I may not survive. Each time I am used, a piece of me is torn away. There is not a lot left.+

"Please, I would only ask if I had no other choice. I have been to the Shadow Land in a dream and seen hundreds of draugers pressing to get in. My friend was attacked earlier today, and they nearly killed her."

+Can you promise me oblivion if I do this one more time?+

"I promise."

CHAPTER 17

$\mathcal{M}$arianne awoke with her hand resting loosely on the black lacquer box on the covers. It had been such an intense dream. But maddeningly, it floated away from her memory. All she had was a lingering sorrow, but she didn't know why.

"Any tighter and Ruari's going to be jealous," Sarah croaked from the other bed. She was staring at Marianne with an unreadable expression. Tired? Curious? Suspicious? Marianne couldn't tell. The bruising on her neck looked like a vivid blue-black necklace, and Marianne winced.

Her hand reflexively tightened around the lid before she let go and placed the box back on the bedside table. "Hey, you're awake. How are you feeling?"

"Like I was hit by a truck."

"But you're better?"

"Conscious, sort of. Really tired, like I had the worst flu ever."

"Maybe coffee will help."

"Okay. No French fries though."

"If you're well enough to be picky, that's good."

"What's with the talisman?"

"I don't know. I dreamed about it, but I can't remember the details."

"Hmm. Highly charged magical objects have an effect on the people around them. Be careful."

Marianne got out of bed. "I finished laying all the protection charms we had yesterday. I plan on tagging as many stone chambers today as I can before heading back to Maple Hill."

Sarah remained under the covers. "I'll stay here until the coffee comes."

"You want anything else?"

"Omelette with everything and a cinnamon roll?"

"Too bad you have no appetite," she said with a wan attempt at humor.

In the bathroom, she dressed and brushed her brown, wavy hair into a ponytail under the cat charm's watchful gaze. Deeply shadowed eyes in a pale face stared at her from the mirror.

A splash of cold water helped, and she braced her hands on either side of the sink and took a deep breath. Then she gathered herself up.

"One more day. One more night. Then I can go home and sleep in my own bed for a week with my cat."

She laid Sarah's cell phone on the bedside table before heading out. "Call if you need me. I'll be as quick as I can."

Marianne scanned the parking lot. It was early and still pretty full, but there were no skull covered sedans in sight. *Good. Maybe they'll be in jail long enough for us to get this done. Maybe the sheriff will kick them out of the county.*

She pulled the bulky lacquered box out of her jacket pocket and put it on the seat next to her. She didn't remember putting it in there. *Why did I bring Zorion along for the ride? Why didn't I just leave it with Sarah?*

Wait. That's your name. We talked last night. A wave of sadness and anger washed over her. *What were you so sad about?*

There was no answer.

She took a deep breath and started Natalie on the obligatory third attempt. The clutch was an old friend after all the driving yesterday, and she eased the station wagon out of the parking lot. Take out from a nearby diner filled the bill.

When Marianne returned, Sarah was just laying her phone back on the bedside table. She was wearing a clean turtleneck, so she must've gotten up and dressed. "Kelly says hi."

They ate and got back on the road. Sarah opted to lie on the back seat again, drifting in and out of sleep, nursing her coffee. The paper cup sat in her hiking boot on the floor next to her. Marianne spread the county map out on the passenger seat as Zorion hummed softly in his box. She was relieved that she could tune out the faint fly buzzing noises of the other charms.

She located a couple of new stone chambers off a small side road in an old hillside. Sarah still felt too weak to do more than give advice. Hoping they weren't large, Marianne approached them warily, pockets bulging with her protective charms and two of the last closing charms. She felt the heavy buzz of the wedging charms and gritted her teeth against the nausea-vertigo barrier as she crawled in. At least if she fainted or threw up, she wouldn't have far to fall.

The roof was only four feet overhead, massive slabs weighing hundreds of pounds each, tightly fitted. The only place for a charm to be tucked was in the less well fitting rocks of the wall or the angle between the roof and wall. The good news was she didn't need Sarah's help to get to the old charms. The bad news was that their adversary was working off a more complete list than the one Sarah had started with. Marianne wondered if there were even more chambers than the old linen map knew about and pushed that thought away.

Using Sarah's flashlight, she found a little white cotton bag in each stone room and gingerly pulled them out with gloved hands. No booby traps triggered, but each one had a little snippet of red yarn. Marette had been there. Marianne jammed in the closing charms and activated them in each chamber, silencing the annoying buzz with relief.

Back at Natalie, Marianne dropped the toxic charms into a cardboard box and made a note to bury them in black salt later. She didn't know how to make black salt and didn't have time to coax the recipe out of Sarah or look it up on the internet.

Sarah slept the sleep of the dead on the back seat.

Marianne ran into trouble picking up the last known stone chamber between Crossfield and the little hamlet of Zaborowski on the northern border of Canopus county where it abutted Dutchess County. Pulling the car off the side of the road onto a grassy strip under the trees, she checked her pockets: two vials of holy water, the last closing charm, a pair of gloves, a plastic baggie, and Ruari's cat charm. Sarah's flashlight dangled on a bootlace around her neck. The protective ward of stones and herbs lay across her thigh in her jeans pocket. She stared at the black box on the seat, hesitating.

"Take it." Sarah's voice in the back seat sounded muffled. It was the first thing she'd said in a couple of hours. "You have a connection with it."

"Are you sure? You seemed worried about it before."

"I still am. But I can't watch your back. Maybe it can. I don't know how it works or how to work it. Byron's the one who's done all the research. Maybe you'll feel more confident, or it'll give you a little extra warning. You asked me to trust you. So I'm trying."

"Even after I nearly killed you?"

Sarah waved her off. "You need all the help you can get. Just don't touch it with your bare hands."

Flooded with a sense of gratitude, Marianne said, "Thanks." Sarah's confidence went a little way to repair the hole in her self-esteem. She tucked the black lacquer box into her pocket and hiked up the steep hill.

The old linen map indicated this last chamber was fairly close to the road. She was grateful that Canopus county had continued to use the old roads in many cases, merely paving and widening them, so the 1700s map was still useful. The one thing it didn't do was show topography: the hill was so steep she had to use both hands to pull herself up from trunk to root to bush. She arrived on a little plateau, winded. As she caught her breath she became aware of the low grating buzz of an open portal. After casting about for a minute, she followed the sound to its source.

A low stone wall crossed the hillside through the trees like stitching on a blanket interrupted only by a low opening into the dirt. The wet leaves were disturbed outside the entrance. Clearly their adversary had been here recently and had left a wedging charm and maybe something worse. She went down on one knee to get her things ready. Gloves on, baggie at the ready, she bent low and walked inside.

The flashlight beam passed over the stone walls and ceiling. She'd gotten better at passing through the magical barrier and looked for the tell tale white cloth bag. Buried in the buzz saw thunder of the wedging charm, she heard a higher tone that sounded familiar.

There you are, you little rascal, I see you. She scanned the walls and ceiling carefully and located the dirty white bag in a corner. But there was only one. In the other place up the logging road, there had been two separate charms. Sarah never said you could put both charms in the same bag. She never said you couldn't, but wouldn't they interfere with each other?

She was darned if she could see another bag. Cautiously, she reached up to tug on the corner. It fell out and all hell broke loose. Shadow blobs exploded from the hole like bats from a disturbed belfry. The protection charm in her pocket pulsed a hot spike of warning. Marianne leapt back and banged into the wall behind her. She hit the floor, landing on the box painfully, feeling glass and wood splinter under her. The hungry draugers followed her, bobbing around her head, trying to get a purchase on her skin.

Rolling, she tried to push or scrape the feathery touches of the blobs away with one hand and tugged the old leather glove off her other hand. She groped among the splinters in her pocket for the talisman, feeling the sting of cuts. The hummingbird wing vibration told her when she had it.

Fingers curled around the central column, she rolled onto her back and thrashed, waving the talisman around her head.

+Stop it!+ A voice cut through her panic and the cacophony of the wedging charm. +Hold me up so I can see. Say the words.+

"What words?"

+You know them. Say them.+

She thrust her arm up and said the only thing Sarah had ever taught her. "By Earth and Sky and Fire and Water protect me!"

A flash of brilliant, opalescent light lit up the small chamber, shriveling the blobs into raisins. They fell harmlessly in a patter around her. She felt them hit her face and jerked away, flailing frantically.

+Stop it! They cannot hurt you anymore. This hurts enough without you flinging me about like that. You're worse than those little children.+

She crawled out of the chamber and lay on the wet leaves. The noise was less awful out here. She looked at the Navarro Talisman. "I remember. You told me last night that it hurts whenever you're invoked. I'm sorry, Zorion. I didn't mean to hurt you."

+I understand.+

"I broke your box."

+Your pocket will do. I've been in worse. Though you might want to clear out the sharp bits. They won't do either of us any good.+

She dumped the glass and wood shards out of her jacket pocket. Ruari's little carving of Oscar had broken an ear but was otherwise intact. Then she put her glove back on and went back into the chamber. A second little white bag was stuffed further into the same hole.

Clever. And scary.

She put both evil charms in a baggie and sealed them up for decontamination later. Both of them had TK on the outside. Once she put the closing charm in place and awakened it with the right words, the buzz saw died down to blissful silence. She kicked the wood and glass fragments into a corner so no one would hurt themselves and left. Glancing at the stones on the way out, she saw a second TK in a circle done in blue paint, like a little bit of graffiti. She headed down hill back the way she'd come.

Sarah continued to sleep off and on. Marianne drove, refueling Natalie when needed. The floor on the passenger side grew littered with wrappers and paper cups from her own snacking. She stared at the map, trying to figure the best way to visit the most chambers and get herself to the dirt section of the Old Albany Post Road in western Canopus by evening. Although she had a powerful urge to check all the chambers they'd been to, there was no way she had the time to walk all the way out to the one at Minetto or the three at Williston. Beehive, Maiden's Weep, and the one up the fire road also took too much time to get to.

That left twelve she might be able to check or find. She'd save the Maple Hill Cemetery for last. The collapsed one by Wixom wouldn't be a problem, though the idea of a little wire figure climbing out of the swamp to destroy the closing charm she and Sarah had left gave her the willies. Then there was the one that had been replaced by the development. That left ten to revisit or find. She marked them on the map and plotted her route. She only had five of Kelly's quickly made closing charms.

The Crossfield stone chamber at the war memorial garden in the center of town looked more like a naked pile of stones than ever before. There were a couple of visitors taking selfies and talking animatedly. They ducked into the chamber for a couple of minutes and came out laughing. Marianne busied herself pretending to read the WWI memorial text. Sarah was still asleep.

When the pair had left, she approached the entrance to the

chamber. Someone had laid a couple of jack-o-lanterns on either side of the door, their grinning pumpkin faces turned outward. Someone's idea of humor or cuteness, no doubt, but they didn't disguise the familiar buzzing feel. It was amazing the tourist couple hadn't felt it. At least the wedging charms no longer made her dizzy and sick. She took one of the five closing charms she had left, entered, and looked for the fissure in the ceiling.

The string of the wedging charm's bag hung down a little, but it was still a good three feet overhead. She'd had to boost Sarah last time. She looked at the roughly piled rocks of the walls. If she wedged her toes in there and there, she might be able to climb up high enough to reach the crack.

It took a couple of tries, but she managed to brace herself between the walls at the corner and work her way up. Stretching at her farthest reach, she swiped at and caught the string before she lost her purchase. She fell, bruising her knee on the floor. In her hand she found a new wedging charm with a little piece of red yarn.

Dammit, Marette. Why are you doing this to us? To Canopus? Whatever bad fortune we have here because of draugers will eventually spill over into Fairfield. Pushing your Shadow People onto us won't help you in the long run. If I ever meet you, we are so going to talk.

She stuffed the evil charm in her pocket and pulled out the closing one, lightly crushed the herbs, murmured the activation charm and tucked it into a gap between the side and back walls as far up as she could reach, pushing it out of sight.

One down nine to go.

Marianne located the last chamber Sarah had known about before the linen map by the side of the road. It was squat and barely taller than the nearby culvert. She crawled in on hands and knees and found another wedging charm with a bit of red yarn. In the quiet of this chamber with only the sound of traffic passing by, she could feel a sort of trembling thinness to the air. She used another of her precious stash of closing charms to seal the portal, shutting down the potential. This one at least would be safe.

She found a new portal near Deer Lake and another on a farmer's land near a sugaring shed. Both had wedging charms with TK on the bags. She used two of the last three closing charms to seal them. There was only one of Kelly's charms left. She had to save it for the Maple Hill Cemetery chamber. That left five unprotected chambers.

There was nothing she could do about that.

She shifted focus and tried to lay the last of her protection spell charms in places they hadn't been to yet. The stash dwindled rapidly to nothing.

Sarah roused briefly to eat a calorie rich meal and down a coffee before falling asleep again. Marianne tried to update her while she ate a burrito. She wasn't that fond of Mexican, but it was fuel at this point. Sarah nodded but offered little in the way of comment or guidance. Marianne tried to be understanding, but it was a struggle not to be frustrated and scared.

When Marianne passed by a familiar turnoff, she braked hard. Natalie skidded to a stop. Turning down the road with a sudden idea, she pulled into the Holy Family Church parking lot. There were only a handful of cars, and Marianne supposed they belonged to people at work in the church offices. She sat for a moment, debating.

When Natalie had been attacked, their supplies had been upended in the parking lot at Williston State Park. A number of the glass jars of holy water had smashed, leaving them dangerously low on their one sure-fire weapon against the Shadow People. She could marshal about ten empties. If she could fill them again, that would give her a little peace of mind. She bundled them into her backpack and zipped it up. Sarah lay curled up on the back seat, looking small and vulnerable. Father Williams would understand.

She slipped into the sanctuary and scanned the room. There was a person kneeling in prayer up near the altar but no one else at the moment. A quick glance at Astrid Delaney's seat showed an empty pew. She hesitated and then headed down the hall to Father Williams' office. There was a light coming from the partially open door and she knocked gently.

"Come in?"

She entered. Father Williams' homely face smiled in recognition. "Miss Singleton, what a pleasant surprise. What can I do for you?"

"Well, Sarah and I had a break in on Natalie, her car, and lost a bunch of our things including a lot of your holy water. I was wondering if I might have a little more?"

He said in concern, "I'm sorry to hear that. Are you all right? Is Sarah?"

"We're fine," she said. *I'm sorry Father, please don't ask me more. I don't have time to tell you the whole story.* "We used what you gave us, and it was very effective."

"I have a little left over from a baptism the other day." He stood up and led her to a small chapel-looking room with a stone font at one side. "Please take what you need."

Gratefully, she pulled out the jars and began filling them. "Thank you so much, Father."

"It sounds like you've had trouble."

"Some. More than Sarah expected anyway. We have to be ready for tonight, and this will help a lot." There was only enough to either fill four dijon mustard jars fully or about six partially. She opted for splitting it into more, figuring it was better to have their best weapon spread among more people.

He regarded her solemnly. "If you have time later, please come back and tell me how it went."

She nodded and zipped her pack. Hoisting it to her shoulder, she said, "We will."

Later that afternoon, she bumped down the road to Turner's Hope Mine and parked. Sarah was dozing again. Marianne patted her pockets: Oscar carving, bottle of holy water, gemstone and herb amulet, check. Zorion lay comfortingly in her pocket next to the bottle. After rescuing her from the second booby trap, he'd been silent. She had the impression he was saving his strength. She took a deep breath, grabbed a pencil and small notebook and got out of the car. Natalie was parked facing the road, just in case.

This was the dumbest idea she'd had yet. Sarah would give her hell if she were awake to do it. Yeah, but they needed the back up, and Peter O'Meara and his men would make up for all the ghost allies they'd missed or who'd refused. She just had to convince him, or at least his men who might convince him for her.

Turner's Pond was flat and gray like it had been before. It had an air of desolation like all parks in winter without people and sunshine to light them up, but under that she could feel a steady menace.

The stones on the short beach were damp with moisture, and her feet crunched along to where Sarah had called the miners before. Keeping well back from the water, she eyed her escape routes. There were no great options if the miners decided to get mean. She might have to run right through them to reach the parking lot.

She cleared her throat and extended her senses. "Mr. O'Meara, are you there? Would you come talk to me?" Her voice sounded small in the stillness, unlike Sarah's commanding tone. She waited. He might be too far away to come, or still feel slighted and refuse to answer. She called again.

A dull pressure grew in her ears, accompanied by a sense of sullen anger, but he did not materialize. He stayed out of reach. Maybe ten minutes of calling into the silence passed without response. Her gambit had failed. The day was coming to a close. Time to move on to the next thing. She closed her eyes in a long blink and startled badly, losing her balance.

Men dressed in nondescript brown trousers and jackets over dirty blue shirts stood an arm's length away, staring at her in a silent ring.

Windmilling her arms, she steadied herself, heart beating suddenly loud in her ears.

"You called us?" Peter O'Meara stood front and center, his black eyes boring into hers.

"Yes," she cleared her throat. "I had an idea. You said you felt like no one understood your sacrifice. I'd like to create a historical marker that tells the story and put your names on it so everyone knows what happened."

He scoffed. "What about our revenge on the bastards who let the roof fall in? They got away scot free."

"Sarah's right about that: they're long dead, Mr. O'Meara. Over a hundred years has passed since you died, and they and their families are long gone."

"What about their children and grandchildren? We didn't get to be with our families, but they did. Tell us who they are, and we'll go haunt them!"

"I don't know who they are," she said.

"But you could find out."

She shook her head. "No, I won't."

"Then we'll come home with you until you do." His mouth split into a mirthless, bad-toothed grin.

Sarah had warned her about angry spirits haunting her. A little burst of fear washed through her, making her wobbly. But Toni had said, *You can't let someone like him intimidate you.* She drew herself up.

"I want to tell the story of what happened. Make a memorial to your sacrifice. The newspaper didn't print all your names. If you tell me your names, I can make sure they all get included." She looked past O'Meara to the less distinct forms behind him. "You're so much more than 'Italian no. 311.'"

Peter clearly thought the memorial was inadequate, but there was a murmuring behind him. Some of the men were interested.

"Tell me your names," she urged. If you were married and had children, I can include them. If you were single, maybe I can include your parents' names. Maybe I could find out how your families did." She was inventing wildly, promising more than she was sure she could deliver. But their cause was worthy, and she really needed their help. She'd find a way to fulfill her promise, or, she had no doubt, they would find a way to make her life miserable. She got out her notebook and pencil.

Peter O'Meara stared at her stonily.

Slowly, one by one, twelve miners stepped around their foreman and gave her their names and their families. They felt more weary and resigned than vengeful, and she tried to see each of them as they spoke to her. Most were blurry, but she caught a few faces and hands in sharper focus. She nodded at each one in turn. Marianne imagined holding an unveiling ceremony with the descendants of the men here in attendance. Maybe they could rest then.

When she was done, she made a show of closing the notebook and putting it in her pocket carefully. Her fingers brushed wood and silver on the way.

"Thank you. It will take me some time to convince Canopus County to do the right thing, but I'll do my best."

Peter O'Meara cast a cold look at his men and said, "What then? I want blood for the blood we spilled!"

"If you want a fight, there may be one tonight. You know of the Shadow People, the draugers? Someone is trying to let them into this world. You know what they do, right? They drain life out of people and drive them mad with their worst desires. It's my job to protect the county, and I'm asking for your help."

"You're no better than that Sarah Landsman who thinks she can buy us with a drink," he sneered.

"Maybe not. But the chance for recognition of what happened to you may be a worthwhile payment. I'll do it whether you come or not. Your descendants will know who you were and how you died. They will be able to tell their children. Just so's you know, at least some of those descendants, blood of your blood, still live in Canopus and they'll be in danger if the draugers invade."

The men murmured behind him. She thought they agreed.

"If I call you tonight for help, will you come?" She asked.

"We'll see."

"Either way, I'll do everything I can to tell your story to the world." She turned and walked the narrow path between the men and the dark water back the way she'd come, holding the little bottle of holy water in one hand and Zorion in the other. She wanted to run but refused to give them a reason to chase her.

"What's wrong, Ruari?" Erin asked. "I'm doing okay. You don't have to stay over again."

It was after work, and they were at her apartment over the florist's shop on Main Street. Ruari sat on the sofa and checked his phone for the twentieth time that day. No word from Marianne. He looked up. "Huh?"

Standing at the kitchen island putting guacamole and chips into two bowls, Erin said dryly, "I'm touched by your concern big brother, but I can see you're not worrying about me anymore. Is Marianne okay? Did she find the house?"

He shouldn't have come by tonight. Erin was right, she was doing much better. But he'd sought out company, consciously or not. Did he dare tell Erin what was going on? She and Sarah and Kelly had been mortal enemies throughout school and had an uneasy truce at best now that they were adults. Maybe their shared poltergeist experience had caused them to bond, but he was reluctant to put Marianne into Erin's category of ghost-talking weirdos. His sister could be a real bitch when she decided not to like someone, and Marianne didn't deserve that.

"She's had a rough couple of days," he said.

Erin brought the bowls of chips and guac and put them on the coffee table. Then she sat on the sofa and folded her legs criss-cross fashion. "Eat something. You're not going anywhere until you tell me." Her short red hair stuck out in all directions, unlike its usual confident cockatoo crest. Her expression was intent.

"What do you know about Marianne's trip?" He asked.

"I thought she was dropping off resumés on some kind of road trip with Sarah."

"She was. Things changed along the way. Please don't judge her, okay?"

"I'm not judgmental!" She gestured with a chip half way to her mouth. "Look, she didn't laugh at me when I told her about the magic wand thing. What does that have to do with resumés and history anyway?"

Ruari laid out the story as best he understood it. As she listened, Erin ate half the bowl of chips before pushing the rest of the dip and tortillas on him. When he finished speaking, he wolfed down the rest while Erin thought.

"If you'd told me this a couple weeks ago, I would have said you were out of your mind, Marianne was nice but clearly a nut job, and what did you expect of Sarah the weirdo." She sipped from her soda.

"But now?"

"After all the crap I've been through, I think Sarah has real ESP or whatever it's called. I would've been in real trouble without her and Kelly. If you tell me Marianne believes in ghosts, then she does. You love Marianne, right? The least I can do is give her the benefit of the doubt."

Ruari let out a breath he hadn't realized he was holding.

"So, you say she tried to kill Sarah because she was possessed by some kind of evil spirit?" She tilted her head back and forth. "I can sympathize since I've wanted to kill her and Kelly any number of times. But—" she put her hand up to fore-stall Ruari's protest, "murder is not cool, and Marianne is way too nice to do that under normal circumstances. So, I have to conclude that possession must be a thing. Gives a new meaning to being 'under the influence' doesn't it?" She waggled her eyebrows.

He rolled his eyes. "Be serious."

She gave him a lofty look. "I always am."

He ran his fingertip along the inside of the bowl and licked the salt off. "I'm worried something more happened to them. I haven't been able to reach her all day. I've left a bunch of messages and texted her."

"Cell service across this rural county sucks, you know that. If she's doing as much driving as you say she is, then she's probably incredibly busy. She's getting home tonight right?"

"Yeah, she and Sarah are going to be in the Maple Hill Cemetery tonight."

Erin grinned. "Then we'd better be there!"

"We?"

"Yeah, you don't think I'm going to go through all this stupid self-discovery shit and miss out on a genuine, spooky seance with bonus magic spell in a cemetery on Halloween night do you?"

He grinned. That was the fighting-Scot sister he knew and loved. "Guess it'll be more interesting than a costume party at the Dutch."

All Hallow's Eve had come at last. The night where the veil between the worlds was at its thinnest and spooks and draugers were at their strongest. Though people didn't remember the real reason, they carved pumpkins to protect their homes. Marianne had looked up the legend of Stingy Jack while munching a cinnamon roll and tea for fuel.

She'd bought a whole box of Cinna-Sweets for herself. The partial box left after their meeting with the Leatherman had been discarded days ago. It was weird, ghosts seemed able to taste food offered to them, leaving the physical food behind. But when she'd tried the coffee-doused rolls the morning after meeting the Leatherman, Marianne had only managed to swallow one bite. It had tasted bland and gray as if their essence had been removed.

As twilight faded Marianne saw groups of trick-or-treaters in their costumes going door to door. It was a chilly, raw night, and she felt sorry for the little ones. Sometimes they strayed close to the roadway, and Marianne remembered the soft thud of the car hitting the raccoon's body.

Murderer, a slippery little voice whispered in her mind. The voice sounded more like her own guilt than anything from outside of her.

Shut up, I am not, she thought firmly.

All the same she tiptoed in second gear through towns and floored it to make up time during the empty stretches. According to her map, most of the county had been covered, but there were still a handful of roads near Maple Hill that she'd left till last. The most crucial remaining road was the dirt section of the Old Albany Post Road near Maple Hill. That was the loop of the slip knot to the spell they were making. As she passed a roadside tavern, she spied a matte black sedan with white blotches across the hood and roof. She sucked in a sharp breath, goosed the pedal, and hoped they hadn't spotted Natalie's battered white body flashing by.

Ducking off the main road and along a series of smaller roads, Marianne relaxed her hands on the steering wheel. She pulled over at one end of the last bit of dirt road that marked the old colonial roadway. She climbed up the bank, and buried one of the last community charms at the base of a large tree as she murmured, "By Earth and Sky…"

Back in the driver's seat, she tugged the seatbelt tight, squeezed the little cat charm with one hand, and rubbed the stones in her pocket with the other. Sarah sat up on the backseat, wrapped in the sleeping bag for warmth. Marianne was glad of her wakeful presence for this part.

"Okay, it's time to tie up this spell." Sarah moved slowly,

conserving her energy. "As you drive, think of Natalie like a big white magic marker on your map, drawing all the lines of where we've been into a tight net of light."

Marianne eased onto the one and a half lane road and let the clutch out. The intermittent rain over the last several days had turned the hard packed dirt to mud, churned by dozens of wheels into ruts, and a local misty fog further reduced the visibility.

Perfect Halloween weather. Not ominous at all.

She'd driven this way once or twice in her own car, The Flea, but tonight it felt different. The starkly ancient bones of this road poked through the fabric of the universe. The track twisted and wound up, down, and around in dreamlike fashion. Berms as tall as Natalie bordered both sides in places, making it feel like a sunken lane. There was no shoulder to speak of, and runoff coursed down ditches on one side or the other. Stone walls, some in excellent repair and others collapsing into heaps, made a tenuous boundary against the trees and fields. Time seemed fluid. She thought she might be driving through the past.

Plain, square-built houses occasionally loomed out of the misty darkness, built at an angle to the road rather than face on, putting their shoulder to the public path. The early settlers wanted to be close to their one lifeline of supplies, news, friends, or militia. Newer homes were set farther back, screened by woods and fences, accessed by long driveways that isolated them.

On a night like this, closeness to the road, the link to other people, would have been her choice.

To hold the image of all the places they'd been in the last week, Marianne muttered them under her breath. "Pheasant and Tankard Inn, the chamber at the monument in Crossfield, the old falling down barn, Maiden's Weep and the Beehive, the fire road, that weird little suburb outside of Peterson, Wixom Village..."

The lights from another vehicle lit up the back of the car, and Marianne glanced in the rearview. It was approaching fast, disregarding the treacherous turns and slippery conditions. Her foot gave Natalie a little more gas. A bright light flashed in the rearview, and there was a sharp jolt as the bumper was tapped by the following vehicle.

"What the hell?!"

Sarah looked over the mound of stuff in the back and shouted, "Punch it! I think it's the skull car. They're trying to run us off the road!"

Marianne goosed the pedal and shifted down into second, concentrating on the rapidly changing road ahead of her. Stone walls loomed on the darkened right side of the car, and she jerked to the left. An oncoming car swerved out of the way. Her feet did a mad tango between accelerator, clutch, and brake. If they went off the road now, Natalie would be totaled, and their chances of survival were not good. Stopping was not an option. The skull car neo-Vikings were out of jail and had it in for them.

Another jerk shook her control, and she wrenched the wheels back on the road. Careening over a rise, the mist thinned a little, showing a long open stretch ahead of them. Shifting into third, she gunned it and pulled away from their homicidal pursuers. "C'mon, Natalie! I know you have it in you!"

They pulled ahead for a few hundred yards, and the mist thickened around them again.

"Kill the lights and pull over!" Sarah ordered.

"Hell no!" Marianne saw the rapidly approaching hill with stone walls close on either side and sailed up and over it, trying to widen the distance.

Sarah growled, "Find a place to pull over and kill the lights! They may pass us by."

"And if they don't, they'll stop and kill us in person," Marianne said through gritted teeth, continuing to race along, driving like a maniac. The skull covered car closed the gap each time they went over a rise until they were within a few yards of the rear bumper again. The twisting road kept revealing another turn, another farmhouse, and she barely missed the startled face of a person trudging along the side of the road. The only good thing about the narrow road was that their pursuers couldn't easily come along side them and force them into a wall or a tree.

They had to be satisfied by ramming them repeatedly.

Sarah clung to the backseat and muttered. It sounded like she was talking to someone on the phone. Marianne had no attention to spare to figure out what she was saying.

It was the longest six miles of her life.

Finally, she saw a streetlight ahead of her, and the rough mud transitioned into smooth asphalt under Natalie's tires like magic. Seeing the friendly lights of the gas station ahead of them, she hit the clutch and brake for the turn only to be smashed once again by the car behind them. Natalie slewed sideways on the wet pavement, mud in her new tires reducing the friction even more. Sarah swore and grabbed the back of the front seat. Marianne coasted the rest of the way under the well-lit awning next to the pumps before pulling up the hand brake.

There was no way their attackers would dare come after them in full view of a whole gas station.

The black sedan veered toward the cross street on the other side of the gas station apron but were cut off by a newly arrived patrol car.

The blare of an amplified voice said, "Stay where you are and put your hands out the window."

"Are you ladies all right?" The station attendant had seen and heard their wild entrance and come out to check on them.

Pulse pounding in her throat, Marianne managed a weak smile. "We're fine, thank you."

"If you're sure?" He sounded doubtful.

She nodded again. "The cops are already here. We'll fine."

He walked back inside, shaking his head.

"Sarah, do we have to stay and talk to the officers? 'Cause it's already eight o'clock. We don't have a ton of time. It's at least twenty minutes up to Maple Hill and another twenty to the cemetery from there."

"I think we can go. They'll have their hands full, and unless we want to press charges again, they can't hold those guys. We'd better be gone before they're free again."

"Right-o." Marianne backed out and left the way they'd come in taking the paved road that led up the hill toward Maple Hill and home.

Oscar. A roaring fire in the fireplace. Fleece jammies and a blanket. Ruari. All of it drew her like a homing beacon.

Too bad she couldn't just coast up to her own house. She had to bring Maple Hill into the protective spell.

A stab of fear as sharp as being rear ended bolted through her.

She had no more charms left.

She'd taken care of the entire county but left her home town vulnerable.

"Oh shit, Sarah, I used all the charms! I don't have any for here!"

Sarah's voice emerged from the depths of the sleeping bag on the back seat. "I figured that. Don't worry: Kelly laid them. All you have to do is drive the streets and activate them."

"But she's not part of the spell!"

"Kelly is always part of the spell. She helps make the charms and said a prayer for us every night we were away. All you have to do is drive through the neighborhoods and rope those charms in, magically speaking."

Marianne let out a breath. She could do that. Then her mind veered to another worry. "What are we going to do if Kitteby, Marette, and Paloma Xerxes show up at the cemetery?"

"We'll deal."

"What's your plan?"

"We make a ring around the fire and say the words that close the spell. We do it before they get there, and whatever they have planned will be moot."

"But Sarah, you're barely able to sit up straight. How are you—"

"That's why Kelly, John, and you are there. Hush and let me get one last nap." She closed her eyes and said no more.

It was too late in the evening for the little kid trick-or-treaters, but groups of older kids and costumed adults were still out and about. Marianne drove extra carefully and fretted the whole time.

She piloted the old white Volvo down yet another side street of homes with white picket fences and was shocked to see her own little white Cape Cod house at the end of the cul-de-sac. The windows were dark, and her mom's little Ford, the Flea, sat in the driveway under a drift of leaves from the big maple tree. She felt like Rip VanWinkle returned to his home after a hundred years' sleep. Had they somehow passed through the veil to an alternate version of Maple Hill? If she went to the door, would a stranger, or worse, another version of herself, answer the bell?

She shook her head and down shifted to first as Natalie swung around the circle, refusing to give in to dark fantasies. She'd sleep in her own bed tonight with Oscar and Ruari by her side. When she had a chance, she would bury a charm out by the gate. For now, she thought about her own charms on the windowsills and concentrated on driving.

Twenty minutes later she'd woven Maple Hill into the spell. With a pang she passed the turn off for Ruari's shop and continued down Main Street. The Dutch and its costume party was down a side street. She wished she was wearing a costume and dancing with Ruari in his kilt. Never mind. She hadn't found a suitable costume anyway.

She slipped out of the lights of Maple Hill, crossed the stone bridge over the Schukyll River which was little more than a rocky creek, and drove the last few miles out to the cemetery.

"Sarah, we're almost there. What now?"

"Park in the lot and help me along the road to the back of the cemetery. Kelly will meet us there. John'll have the bonfire going by now. "

The parking lot was empty. Marianne hip checked the dented panel of the passenger door and opened it for Sarah who said, "Grab the last of the holy water, any charms we have left, and the talisman."

Marianne patted her pockets in her ritual check for magical protection. Of the six bottles of holy water left, she took four and gave Sarah the last two. She hoped the charms they'd distributed across Canopus held the line if things went badly wrong tonight.

"We don't have any more charms," she reminded Sarah.

"Take Natalie's. We can use them in a pinch."

"But won't that leave her unprotected?"

"If things go well, she won't need them. If things go south and the other side is better armed, then it won't matter."

Marianne shivered remembering the black Shadows unable to get past Natalie's wards at Minetto Point as she pulled five charm bags from the glove compartment, the visors, and under the seats and gave them to Sarah. Then she put an arm around Sarah to guide her up the path. She spared a glance for the dark machine shop and wondered where Jason and Jesse were tonight.

Gravel crunched underfoot as they headed toward the glow of a fire. Marianne stumbled slightly under Sarah's weight. Her mentor was clearly struggling.

Rows of headstones led away to the left over the hill where the bulk of the cemetery lay. Marianne wondered whether the ghostly residents were still in hiding.

They rounded the corner, and immediately the warmth of the bonfire bathed her face. Two figures standing to one side looked up as they arrived.

"Sarah!" Kelly cried. Her crutches fell to the ground, and she hobbled as fast as she could to catch her partner in a fierce embrace. The women hugged as if they were the last two people in the world.

Marianne straightened up and stretched her sore muscles, wishing she could fall into Ruari's arms.

"Thank you for taking care of Sarah," Kelly said over her partner's shoulder. The firelight gleamed in her overly bright eyes. "She wouldn't be here without you."

"She's getting better but isn't great yet."

Kelly nodded and began speaking to Sarah in a low tone. Marianne spotted John Irving, the cemetery caretaker, on the other side of the fire and joined him. He was feeding branches into the blaze to keep it going. His gorgeous white Mark Twain mustache twitched as he smiled.

"You're back," he said.

"Yeah." The talisman gave a convulsive twitch in her pocket. Her eyes were drawn to the dark mouth of the stone chamber burrowing into the hillside. Zorion hummed in agitation against the sound of an open portal. The grating buzz was still dull, and she wondered if that meant it wasn't completely open yet.

John noticed her stiffen. "We'll be closing that for another year very soon, don't you worry."

"We have to. I've seen what lies on the other side. An army of baby Shadow People will come through this year if we don't."

His eyes widened slightly, but he didn't question her. "Well then, we'd best get started."

"Sarah said we have to join hands around the fire? We don't have enough people to get around something this big."

"More help is coming."

"Who?"

He tipped his head toward the road behind her.

Two pale figures flitted towards them, one taller and bulkier, the other shorter with a hoody over his unruly hair.

Marianne broke into a smile for the first time in a long while. "Jason!"

He blurred out of focus and reappeared suddenly a couple of feet away from her, having traveled fifty feet in a blink. She jumped. A mischievous grin lit his face.

Marianne! She heard his voice in her mind.

"Wow, you've been practicing!"

Yeah, my man Jesse is still way better than me. But I'm catching on fast.

She grinned back. "That's awesome!"

Jesse Carlton stood to the side in his overalls and cap. He and John nodded at each other by way of greeting.

The sound of another car arriving at speed as it pulled into the distant parking lot with a scrape of gravel cut her off. "John, who else are you expecting?" She asked.

He shook his head.

Footsteps hurried up the path, more than one set. She tensed. Was this the other Protectors come to disrupt things? She looked over at Sarah. She and Kelly broke apart and faced the path, ready to defend their space as best they could. Marianne hurried to join them.

Two figures burst out of the darkness into the light of the bonfire. One with a pale face, elegantly shadowed eyes, and dark green lipstick. Her red hair was spiked up on top. A black duster swept around her. A broad shouldered man with short, sandy red hair came up behind her, also wearing a leather jacket.

"Are we too late to join this party?" Erin said.

"Erin Allen, what are you doing here?" Kelly asked coolly, standing protectively near Sarah. Apparently the detente from the poltergeist incident had already worn off.

Erin stopped several feet away, hands on her hips. "Crashing this private party. Of course, if you don't want our help, we can always fuck off."

"Kelly, it's okay," Sarah said hoarsely. "Let her stay."

Kelly glared but let it go.

Ruari swept past the others and gathered Marianne into his arms in a fierce hug. "You're here, you're alright!"

She squeezed back. "I missed you so much."

Erin gave them a moment then cleared her throat. "Did you find it?"

"I did." Marianne smiled. "I wouldn't have without your help."

She nodded. "Cool."

"You look amazing," Marianne added in admiration. Erin and Toni would get along so well. Too bad Erin didn't want to believe in ghosts.

Erin grinned. "It's the first time I've felt like me in ages."

Jason slipped out of the shadows, glide-walked over to Erin, and looked her up and down appreciatively. *Love the trad look, lady. We should hang out sometime.*

Erin's eyes widened in shock, and she startled at the sight of his pale, slightly luminous form. "Who are you?"

Even better, you can see me! He crowed, straightening up and tossing his spectral locks. *I'm a friend of Marianne's.* He gestured to the other pale figure. *That's my man, Jesse.*

Erin stepped back several paces from both of them. Marianne could see she was badly spooked and said, "Erin, this is Jason. We met recently. He lives here now and is, um, apprenticed to Jesse who used to work here."

Erin nodded warily at them. It was a lot to take in for someone who hadn't had any positive ghost experiences.

Ruari touched Marianne's elbow. "Who are you talking to?"

She realized Ruari couldn't see Jason or Jesse. "Do you remember the hitchhiker and the former caretaker I told you about? They're here to help."

He stared at the empty space between Erin and Marianne and looked nonplussed. "Nice to meet you, I guess."

The sound of Jason's chuckle rumpled her mind, and Jesse remained solemn. Erin shifted uncomfortably.

The sound of more footsteps came up the path, and Marianne braced herself. If this was Tristan Kitteby, Marette, and Paloma Xerxes, or worse Riven Masters himself, she felt like they finally had enough people to keep them from interfering.

Byron strode into the clearing. "Thank goodness, I'm not too late."

He wore a dark, slightly muddy, wool coat, with a double row of buttons and large pockets. His beautiful upswept silver hair and perfectly groomed beard gleamed in the firelight.

"We must get started. There's not a moment to lose."

Looking vastly relieved, Sarah greeted him. "Byron, you made it!"

He looked shocked at her disheveled appearance and said, "Sarah, what happened?"

She grimaced. "I'm not one-hundred percent, but I don't feel like death warmed over anymore. Kitteby booby trapped the chamber off the fire road. I was attacked by draugers."

His eyes widened. "Damn! Sarah, I'm so sorry." Tightening his jaw resolutely, he said, "We'll get Kitteby, after tonight. We'll get him."

She shook her head. "Let's just get the spell done and worry about that later."

Aware of time passing inexorably to midnight and the likelihood that the neighboring Protectors could arrive at any moment, Marianne cleared her throat. "We should get started."

Byron stood taller and faced her. "We can't close the portals yet. First we must get my sister, Catalina, out."

The others gathered closer, Erin, Ruari, Kelly, John, Jason, and Jesse. Marianne frowned. "How?"

"We open the portal here and call her."

"But there are hundreds, maybe thousands of draugers waiting on the other side."

"I've done the calculations. The hatching is next year, and we'll be ready for them then."

"You're wrong," Marianne said flatly. "I don't know anything about calculations. All I know is that they've already come out. That's what attacked Sarah and nearly killed her."

He lifted his hands placatingly. "They are frightening, no question, but a few is not hundreds."

She lifted her chin and stared at him. "A bunch attacked me at another portal. I only got away with help."

He narrowed his eyes. "What help? How? Were your charms enough?"

"Holy water," her hand tightened around Zorion in her pocket before she pulled it out, "and this." The age-darkened wood with the silver snake wound around it gleamed faintly in the firelight.

Erin stiffened and gave a sharp intake of breath. She whispered, "Yeah, that's the one."

Byron shot her a sharp look before returning his gaze to Marianne. "So it's true. You did find it before I got there. Why didn't you call me the moment you found it?"

"Is that the talisman thing you were looking for?" Ruari asked.

He reached out to touch it, and Byron hissed, "Don't touch it!"

Marianne's fingers closed reflexively around it, and Ruari lowered his hand.

"How did you know?" Marianne asked.

"It's already spoken to you hasn't it?" Byron replied, appraising her thoughtfully. "It is said that the Talisman speaks only to a few. You are more fortunate than you know."

"Did you know I had it before I showed you?" She repeated.

Patiently Byron said, "I found the house in an old directory the day after you and Sarah left. I found the loose board in the closet by pendulum magic." He must have taught Sarah how to do that.

"What about the ghost who guards it? Did you meet him too?"

He shook his head. "There was no ghost. But I knew Silas Coventry had hidden the Navarro Talisman there. I could feel the magical residue. When it was gone, I assumed that Riven Masters had somehow beaten me to it." He smiled faintly. "I'm glad you have it instead. We can use it to open the door to the Shadow Realm. When it's open, we call Catalina. Let me have it. I have studied how to use it. Let me save her." He held out his hand palm up. "Please?"

Sarah spoke up. "Marianne, just give it to him, so we can get this over with. We're running out of time, and I don't have much energy left to pull the spell together and protect the county." She leaned against Kelly, looking wan in the firelight.

Truthfully, Marianne didn't know how to use the Talisman properly. Even if it hurt Zorion in the process, the cause was a good one: saving Catalina's spirit from the hands of a vicious magician who thought nothing of imprisoning a soul in the dead

Realm of Shadows just to hurt a rival. If they did it fast, the draugers could be contained in spite of the interference of the other Protectors. When they were done, she'd fulfill her promise to set Zorion free.

The pleading look in Byron's eyes melted her uncertainty. She laid the Talisman in his palm.

He stared at it for a moment before taking a deep, shaky breath. "Thank you, Marianne." He looked up at the ring of faces. "Let's get this done quickly."

With calm authority Byron had them link hands in a circle around the bonfire. Ruari took Marianne's left hand in his warm, strong grasp. Jason moved to grab her right hand, but Erin intervened firmly. "No way am I standing between two ghosts," she muttered. Her hand gripped Marianne's firmly.

Marianne smiled in spite of herself. Jason grinned and cheekily grabbed Erin's right hand, and Marianne felt her shudder, but Erin didn't pull her hand free of his touch. Jesse stood on Jason's right, followed by John Irving, Sarah, and Kelly. Kelly grasped Ruari's left hand and completed the circle.

Byron stood off to the side, facing the black entrance to the stone chamber. Slowly they began circling the fire as Byron began chanting. It sounded like a mix of Latin and something medieval. As his chant grew steadier and louder, Marianne felt the hair on the back of her neck rise. The buzz ratcheted up to a teeth rattling sound as the portal was finally opened.

"Catalina, I call thee. Come forth from the Shadow Lands. Come home to me," Byron called.

Marianne continued to circle the bonfire slowly, stepping clockwise around the flames. His compulsion was like someone pulling her arm insistently. She shook her shoulders and followed the tug of Ruari's hand instead.

Byron called again and again, more forcefully each time. Part of Marianne almost wanted break free and run to his side, but she squeezed Ruari's hand to keep herself anchored.

Byron's voice reached a crescendo, and he shouted in frustration. "Something is holding her back. I can feel her just beyond the gate, but she won't or can't come."

"What the hell is that thing?" Erin said.

The circle halted. The charm in Marianne's jeans pocket gave a half-hearted pulse and died. Marianne followed her gaze and saw to her horror a black bubble the size of a basketball float out of the mouth of the doorway and move slowly upwards. It stopped about ten feet off the ground and bobbed there. Marianne had the feeling it was orienting itself even though it had no eyes or face. In a few seconds it headed towards its favorite food source, them.

"Byron look out!!" Sarah called.

Byron lifted the Talisman before him like a shield. "By Earth and Sky, and Fire and Water, I destroy you!" He shouted. There was a sharp flash of light and a scream. The black blob shriveled and fell harmlessly to the ground where it vanished.

"There's another one!" Erin said.

"I can't see anything. What's happening?" Ruari said.

"Draugers are coming out of the open gate to the Shadow Land," Marianne said. "They look like black balloons or blobs about the size of a basketball. Whatever you do, don't let them touch you!"

"How the hell am I supposed to avoid them if I can't see them?!"

"They hate fire. We should be okay here."

"Is that talisman thingy the only way to kill them?" Erin asked.

"They also die if you hit them with holy water." Marianne let go of their hands and reached for her jacket pockets. She pulled out four bottles of water and handed two to Ruari and two to Erin. She kept the last one. "That's all I have."

Erin muttered, "You're fucking kidding me. We need a holy fire hose and this is it?"

"Make sure John Irving gets one will you? I'm pretty sure Sarah only has two."

"I'm on it." She ducked and headed around to the other side of the bonfire.

Ruari said, "Will these keep me safe?" He held up the bottles.

"No, this might help, though." She handed him a slightly squashed charm bag that had been under Natalie's back seat. "Put this in your pocket. If someone is attacked by the draugers, dump holy water on them. They usually go for the head so focus on that."

"Okay." He looked deeply unsatisfied with her answer. "I'm sticking with you."

She gave him a quick nod and turned to Jason. "I don't have anything for you. You'll be okay though, right?"

The young ghost looked up uneasily. Byron had zapped the second drauger.

I guess. Jesse didn't tell me anything about them.

"They latched onto Sarah and sucked the energy out of her. Just be careful."

He nodded.

"Sarah, I need your help!" Byron shouted. He raised Zorion and blasted another blob as it emerged.

With Kelly's help Sarah made her way to her mentor's side.

"I need you to go in and get Catalina," he said. "You've met her before. She's stuck and needs help."

Sarah nodded wearily, but Kelly threw her arms around her. "No! She's exhausted. If she goes in there, she won't come out again." She looked ready to defy Byron for the rest of the night if she had to.

"I have to stay here and guard the gate," Byron protested.

"She's not going," Kelly growled.

"I'll go," Marianne said.

"Wait, you can't go in there!" Ruari grabbed her hand. "If it's bad for Sarah, it isn't safe for you either!"

Byron looked at her with some surprise and seemed to recalculate.

Marianne explained. "I've been there once before, and I can see ghosts. I'll find her and bring her back."

Byron nodded.

"Mahri, I'll come with you," Ruari said.

She shook her head. "I can stay out of the draugers' way. You have to keep an eye on things here. Please? I'm the only one who can do this right now. I promise I'll be back as soon as possible." She leaned close to his ear and gave him a quick kiss. "If things get too crazy, take everyone back to the cars and get as far away as possible. We'll fight these things later."

He was not happy, but reluctantly nodded. "Be careful. I'll come after you if you don't come back."

She nodded, "I hope so."

Kelly gave her a grateful look.

"I'll hold them off," Byron told her. "Just bring my sister back to me."

Marianne touched the cat carving in one pocket along with the last of the herb charms scavenged from Natalie. The last bottle of holy water rested in the other. The stone charm lay cool and inert and wouldn't be of much help to her. She wished she had Zorion's comforting presence with her, but he was with Byron now doing the job he was created for.

She squared her shoulders and stepped into the stone chamber, ignoring the tooth rattling vibration.

Marianne had to duck immediately as another black blob sailed past overhead followed by another in what was becoming a steady stream. Crouching, she scuttled to the far end of the narrow passage. The stone wall was gone. Instead, a doorway opened to a dull gray land beyond. Before she could over think it, she held her breath and stepped over the threshold as if she were plunging into water.

She threw herself out of the way of the baby draugers in their exodus, hoping they wouldn't notice her. The buzz saw sound cut off, leaving her in blessed silence for the moment. The black bubbles ignored her and continued to stream through the portal. She breathed a sigh of relief.

A dusty, metallic smell filled her nostrils and made her skin crawl. It was just like her nightmare only more real. The dead plain stretched away in all directions, under a twilight sky. Light from an indeterminate source showed the collapsed remains of hundreds of black egg sacs. Over head, the cloud of black Shadows slowly dwindled.

She had to hurry. This was getting beyond their ability to fight, kill, or turn back the ones that had gone into her world.

"Catalina? Catalina Mandel? Are you here?" She walked a few steps forward, calling and looking around with her eyes open and then again with her eyes closed.

Go back to where you came from! You're in danger here! A woman's voice came from out of the dimness.

Marianne saw a patch of white against a pile of rocks.

"Catalina?"

How do you know my name?

"I've been looking for you! Come with me, hurry!"

Who are you?

"Marianne Singleton. I was sent to find you." She closed her eyes and the shape of a young woman in a sweater set over jeans, her hair in a pixie cut, peered out from behind the stones. When she opened her eyes again, the woman was clearly visible.

Who sent you?

"Your brother Byron. I'm here to save you and bring you back to our world."

Save me? What do you mean? As long as the black things are gone, I'm safer here.

"No, Riven Masters might come back anytime."

Who? Catalina sounded genuinely puzzled.

"Riven Masters, the one who imprisoned you here."

What are you talking about? I have no idea who that is. I came here on my own to get away from Byron.

It was Marianne's turn to be confused. "What?"

My brother is a selfish monster who won't leave me alone. This was the only place I could hide from him.

Feeling utterly confused, Marianne said, "You'd better tell me from the beginning."

Catalina told her in as few words as she could. Marianne was floored. She and Sarah had made a horrible mistake. Sarah needed to hear this, but Marianne knew Sarah would never believe her.

"Catalina, you have to come with me and tell everyone else what you just told me. We have to stop your brother before he destroys Canopus County."

She shook her head vehemently. *Byron is too powerful. I won't be able to resist him. He wants to put me into Sarah's mind to 'save me' from fading! I don't want that, and I'm pretty sure Sarah doesn't either.*

"That's horrible! We'd never let him do that. We'll find a way to stop him, but I need your help. We also have to deal with all the draugers—the black things—that have escaped into our world. Please come with me and tell everyone your story! All of us together will be able to stop him. We'll find a way to make him leave you alone. Maybe Sarah can help you cross over. Please come! We're running out of time."

Catalina hesitated for what felt like a million years, and Marianne struggled to let her make up her own mind.

Finally, Catalina said, *Alright, I'll come with you, but you've got to keep him away from me.*

"I'll do everything in my power to keep him from harming you," she promised. She took Catalina's ice cold hand in hers and turned back to the doorway.

Marianne would have sworn she'd only taken a few steps into the Shadow Lands, but the door was only a small rectangle of light a long way off. She pulled Catalina's hand and they ran. It felt like they'd been in there for hours. Everything could be chaos in the cemetery. Ruari might have convinced everyone to leave with him, and there might be no one left on the other side. Worse, they might run straight into a horde of hungry draugers, and she'd be drained dry.

Let's hope time is stretchy here the way distance seems to be.

The light grew brighter, and together they leaped through the doorway.

CHAPTER 20

Marianne ran four long strides through the stone chamber and bounded up the steps, Catalina behind her. They burst through the doorway into the firelight.

Near the bonfire, Sarah sat on the ground at Kelly's feet resting her head on her arms over her knees. John Irving tended the flames with Erin's help while Ruari paced a few feet away. His face relaxed when he caught sight of her. Dozens of ball-shaped draugers hovered ten feet off the ground deterred from their prey by the flames.

Byron stood off to the side, keeping a wary eye on the circling Shadows as he chanted softly. He held the Navarro Talisman like it was a lifeline.

He broke off when he saw her. "Did you find her?" He asked, expression tense and eager.

"I did."

"Where is she?"

Marianne raised her voice, "Sarah, Catalina's here, you have to hear her out."

Sarah raised her head and got to her feet. She looked bone weary. Kelly supported her, somehow managing her crutches with the added weight.

"What's going on?" Byron said suspiciously. "Catalina, where are you?"

Catalina stepped out from behind Marianne, keeping the living woman between her and her brother. Translucent and pale, she glowed slightly in the dark.

I'm here.

"Thanks be to heaven, you're safe at last from Masters' clutches." He stepped forward to welcome her.

Catalina retreated behind Marianne. *Stop right there. I have no idea what you told these people. There is no Riven Masters. I ran away from you and have been hiding in the Shadow Realm to get away from you. If you try to compel me again, I'll go right back.*

There was a moment of stunned silence.

Sarah looked to her mentor in utter confusion and disbelief. "Byron, what is she talking about?"

Everyone else turned to him for enlightenment as well, transfixed by the drama.

Focused on his sister, Byron said gently, "Cat, what are you saying? What lies has Masters been telling you?"

Byron, she said coldly, *I know what you did all those years ago. You sabotaged Ed's car so he would have an accident. You may not have meant to kill me, but you surely meant to hurt or kill him. All because I wanted to marry him and have a life of my own. I found love, and you took it away from me! You killed me, not him. Then you planned to force me into Sarah's body to stop me from fading!*

Byron's face went hard, and the blood drained out, leaving only fury behind. "Ed Barstow would have used you and thrown you away!"

No he wouldn't. You just couldn't stand to have me leave you.

"How dare you! Catalina, come here now." He raised the Talisman. "By Earth and Sky, and Fire and Water, I command you to come to me."

Marianne heard a thin wailing sound and knew it was Zorion. Erin clapped her hands over her ears. Catalina passed through Marianne in a cold ripple, dragged forward by the power of the talisman.

"Catalina, no!" Marianne tried to grab the woman's arm, but her hand passed through empty air.

Kelly swung her aluminum crutch at Byron and struck him on the arm. He broke off and grabbed the crutch with his free hand. Yanking it, he pulled Kelly off balance, and she cried out as she landed on her boot cast.

Sarah grabbed her parter's arm. "Kelly!"

Ruari gave a shout of outrage, "Hey!" and charged. He tackled Byron hard, forcing his upraised hand down. Marianne felt the compulsion slacken and saw Catalina falter only a couple of feet away from her brother.

Jason and Jesse appeared at Catalina's side and pulled her away. The trio vanished.

Ruari grabbed Byron's arm and brought it down hard across his knee to break his grip on the talisman. It fell to the ground, and Ruari grappled with the man. They were about the same height, Byron bulkier in his greatcoat, Ruari more agile. Byron's cold fury gave him the strength to pull away, but Ruari grabbed his arm and wrenched it behind the man's back. Byron cried out as Ruari forced him to his knees.

"Marianne," Ruari panted, "Grab my belt."

Ruari's voice broke her shock at the sudden violence. She dashed forward and fumbled Ruari's belt out of its loops. Meanwhile, he grabbed Byron's other hand and held his wrists together. She pulled the leather strap through the buckle around Byron's wrists and cinched it tight. Ruari pulled it almost tight enough to cut the circulation off and tied a clumsy knot with the rest of it. It was as secure as he could make it.

Byron knelt on the ground, his silver hair wild, his face contorted with rage. "You think you've beaten me," he panted. "I'll—"

"Shut up," Ruari growled.

Sarah drew closer. "Byron, what happened to you?" She sounded shaky.

Marianne said, "Catalina had never heard of Riven Masters. Everything Byron told us was a lie."

"The wedge charms?"

"I think he put them there," Marianne said.

"Byron, why?"

Her mentor and friend looked up, all traces of the kindly uncle gone. "I needed the portals to be open so I could find Catalina."

"No, I mean why did you tell us that ridiculous story about the other Protectors?"

A small, cruel smile touched his lips. "They have never liked me, and you were willing to believe it. It got me what I needed."

Sarah gulped a deep breath of air as if she were drowning. Stepping back, she nodded. "*Nemo nice stilts credit omnibus qui ei nuntiaverunt,*" she murmured. "And I'm a fool. You're not the man I thought you were. Maybe you never were." She turned and walked stiffly away.

No one but a fool believes all that is told to him, Marianne translated. *Poor Sarah. What else has he lied about?*

"Hey guys, watch out! The black things are moving again!" Erin called out.

Ruari stepped away from Byron and took Marianne's hands in his. His grey eyes focused on her. "Are you alright?"

His concern brought a lump to her her throat. *No time for that.* She nodded. "I'm fine. We need to get this spell done before anything worse happens."

"Maybe you can use this." He put the talisman in her hand and closed her fingers over it.

Ruari couldn't feel magic and maybe only believed in it a little, but he believed in her. She couldn't wait till this crazy night was over. She squeezed the wood and silver rod. Zorion fluttered in her hand. She knew he was in distress but could do nothing about it.

Kelly and Sarah stepped forward. Marianne was shocked to see how old and tired her mentor looked. Byron's betrayal had hit her hard. In spite of that, Sarah lifted her chin and clenched her jaw.

"We need more help," Sarah said. "With Byron down and Jason and Jesse gone, we can't reach around the fire. There are too many Shadows for us to handle while we try to close the protection spell. We need to call our allies."

"How?"

"You call with your mind, your words, whatever magic you have."

"Wait, you're calling more ghosts on purpose?" Erin said.

Sarah looked at her. "We don't have a lot of choices. We could use your help." Kelly looked unhappy at the thought. Sarah continued, "But if you don't feel comfortable, I get that. You should go now before things get any more dangerous."

Erin bristled. "Are saying I'm a coward?"

"No, I'm giving you an out."

"Fuck that. I can handle a few ghosts."

Sarah nodded. "Marianne, just call the ones you know, by however means you can." With that, she and Kelly backed off a few paces. Kelly kept a watchful eye, while Sarah drew into herself and began murmuring, her lips moving.

Classic. Sarah tells me I have to do a thing but doesn't tell me how to do it. Well, maybe it wasn't so different from her major professor in grad school pointing at the library and saying all the answers were in there.

Ruari looked at her quizzically. She shrugged. "I'll do what I can. I have no idea if it'll work." He nodded, trusting her to think of something. He stood watch while she centered herself briefly.

Zorion, we have to call our ghost friends. I have no idea if you know how to do that, and I don't want to hurt you. If you have any words of advice, now's a good time.

His voice was small and barely audible as if he was enduring great pain.

+Name them. See them. Call them.+

"Jason Fargate! Come back from wherever you went. Bring Jesse with you. The Shadows have come, and we need your help to fight and complete the spell!"

She imagined Jason's roguish grin and shaggy hair, and Jesse's stolid expression. "We need you, please come back!"

She pictured Toni in her lonely graveyard, short hair across her cheek and broad shoulders hunched over a book, her butt against her headstone as she read.

"Toni Woods, I need your help! We're in the cemetery in Maple Hill, and the shady people are attacking us. Come help us fight!"

She imagined Toni looking up, a feral grin stealing across her lips. After that, Marianne didn't know how to guide the woman to the cemetery.

"Come find us in Maple Hill!"

Astrid Delaney's sad, tear streaked face came to mind, but Marianne didn't have the heart to ask her to fight, and her mind raced on. She remembered the low cement building of the funeral home. What was his name…Stephen was his son…it was Benton.

"Mr. Carter Benton, I called your son. He didn't believe me, but I gave him your message. If you're still here, come help us fight against the Shadow People for the safety of Canopus County!"

The weather beaten face of the Leatherman and his shaggy ursine companion rose in her mind. He was Sarah's contact, but he'd spoken to her and saved her from the Shadows before, so maybe he would hear her.

"Leatherman Jules, Spirit Bear Jean, *je vous appelle. Venez avec nous au cimetiere de Maple Hill! Venez combative les Ombres avec nous!*" I call you. Come to the cemetery in Maple Hill! Come fight the Shadows with us!

She sent her call spiraling out into the ether, hoping against hope she would be heard, and they would come. Far away a dog whined. It was time to call Peter O'Meara and his crew. Would they come?

"Peter O'Meara, of Turner's Hope Mine, you wanted a fight. I offer you a fight! The Shadows are here. Your descendants are in danger. Come fight, if you care about anything at all!"

She pictured their cold, watery grave, felt their seething anger and desire for revenge. "At least fight a worthy opponent, O'Meara!"

She heard a dog whine again more closely and remembered the motel room.

"Rita! You good girl! Come get the Shadows!"

She felt Ruari's hands on her upper arms pull her back suddenly. "Mahri, come back." She opened her eyes. The firelight had died down some, and she sucked air into her lungs as if she'd forgotten how to breathe while she was so focused on calling people. Baby draugers were swooping slowly closer and there were more than she remembered.

They're starving, and we're their favorite food source.

The clearing was suddenly full of pale shapes churning among the ball-shaped draugers as they fought. The ghosts had arrived and understood their purpose immediately. The cloud of Shadows descended to ground level amid the strangely distant sounds of screams and shouts, the occasional muted crack of gunfire, and the growls and roars of large animals.

Able to sense them but not see them, Ruari tightened his hand on her arm, looking about him warily. Erin looked wild eyed.

"I wish you could see this," Marianne murmured. "Maybe go help John with the fire?"

"I'm on it." He cast a glance at their prisoner. Byron was still on his knees, head down, unmoving. Ruari collected his sister, and they began tossing sticks and branches into the flames.

On one side of the bonfire, a pale woman in full skirts and a mobcap with a white kerchief across her shoulders swung a long handled frying pan, batting at a shadowy bubble. Another black one bobbed behind her trying to latch on. Her husband in an open, long-tailed Revolutionary War coat took careful aim on that shadow blob with a flintlock pistol.

"Lean forward my good wife!" He shouted. The pistol went off with a loud bang, and the drauger attacking Mrs. Wallace disintegrated.

She rounded on him furiously. "Watch your aim, Mr. Wallace, or there'll be no chitterlings for you!"

Adrian Vandermark swooped about in his ragged frock coat, snapping the leather tip of his enormous carriage whip at Shadows. When the whip connected, a drauger burst with a dry pop. He howled ferociously and cracked his whip again, clearly enjoying being out of his lonely barn.

A dozen men in rough trousers and shirts slashed at draugers with pickaxes and their fists. O'Meara and his men had deigned to come. Marianne caught Peter's eye, and he flashed her a wolfish smile before stamping a bubble-like Shadow being with his hobnail boot.

Ben Dixon, the cheerful WWI soldier who patrolled the road up in Vandenberg by Marianne's grandmother's house, methodically stabbed draugers with his bayonet. Each one burst and vanished at the touch of his ghostly steel.

Marianne searched the clearing, but Toni Woods wasn't there. She hoped the young woman would find her way somehow. She didn't see Carter Benton either. Perhaps he'd moved on.

She heard a snarling whine and looked around. A big black dog snapped at any blobs hovering near the ground.

Feeling hopeful for the first time all night, Marianne muttered, "We need to get the spell going again. I hope Sarah is up for it." She collected Ruari and joined the others.

"Sarah, we have to try again while the Shadows are distracted."

Her mentor nodded as she and Kelly took up positions near the fire again. Sarah looked resolute. Ruari and Erin joined hands with her again on her left and right, but she felt a cold hand slip into her right. Erin recoiled and reluctantly took Jason's right hand. Jesse took her right, and Marianne suppressed a snicker as she watched Erin between the two ghosts. Erin looked like she was holding live snakes.

Sorry, babe, Marianne's my squeeze for tonight! Jason smirked.

"Jason, you're back! Is Catalina okay?"

She's safe.

Marianne breathed a quick sigh of relief for the beleaguered woman and began circling to the left again.

Sarah called out, "By Earth and Sky and Fire and Water," her voice hoarse but strong. "Let the warding spell be closed. Let all the points of light we laid be bound together in a net of protection. Keep Canopus safe for another year. Let every portal we spelled be closed against the Shadow Realm and proof against invasions by Shadow People."

Marianne added her voice and chanted loudly, encouraging the others to join in. The spell rose reluctantly. Marianne closed her eyes and let Ruari guide her as she mentally reached for all the little charms they'd left across the county. She pictured each cloth bag with its handful of stones, dried herbs, and flowers and imagined them lit up like little solar lights. Tension began building which she took as a sign the spell was coming together. Their voices rose in unison.

Something rammed Jason from behind, yanking his hand out of hers and Erin's. Marianne staggered, releasing the chorus of energy they'd been building back into the ether.

Hey! Jason cried. He turned toward his assailant. *Who the hell are you?*

You'd better run, Damian Brody is here.

A ghostly figure with wispy hair and a strangely charismatic face regarded him with a faint smile. Marianne's blood ran cold. She hadn't seen his full manifestation in the closet of the abandoned house, but there was no mistaking the eager anticipation of havoc to come. Jason stood dumbfounded for a moment too long.

The murderer's ghost grabbed Jason by the hair and yanked his head back, arching his neck. Jason's eyes flew wide, and he flailed his arms. Marianne watched helplessly as Damian drew a spectral knife across the young man's throat. Jason's cry of surprise was cut off as his ghostly windpipe was severed.

"Jason!" Marianne screamed. The young man's limp body disappeared.

An inarticulate shout of rage came from Jesse Carlton, who was usually little more than a waved hand. He grabbed Damian's free hand and twisted hard. Damian grunted in surprise but swung his knife around and plunged it into the man's belly. Jesse stilled then vanished.

Marianne stumbled backwards into Ruari's arms.

"What just happened?" He said.

A faint smile still on his face, Damian turned to the nearest living members of the circle and brandished his knife, rolling the handle expertly in his hand.

"Jason and Jesse are gone!" She panted. "Brody killed them! Erin, keep away from him!"

"Can he hurt us?" Erin danced back and shouted in alarm.

"I don't know!"

"Where is he?" Ruari looked around wildly, frustrated that he couldn't see what was going on.

Marianne pushed him back as Damian slashed at them with his ghostly kitchen knife.

She looked to where they'd left Byron. He was gone. The remains of Ruari's belt lay on the ground.

A string of Latin rose from the stone doorway. Byron stood

there, arms upraised, chanting loudly. Marianne didn't understand the words but felt the powerful magical pull of his call.

The specter backed toward Byron, arms out wide holding his kitchen knife, daring them all to stop the scholar-mage.

"Venite, Umbrae, venite nunc ad me!" Byron shouted.

Come, Shadows, come to me! Marianne thought. *Why are you calling them to you?*

"How the hell did he get free?" Ruari asked.

"I think he called on Brody." If Jason could focus his will and affect things in the physical world, then Brody with so many more years of trying might be able to call up that energy all the more quickly.

A smell of ten-penny nails and dust, accompanied by the sound of tearing paper, reached her.

"Oh, no," she breathed.

Two dark figures emerged from the stone doorway. Tall and stringy, like black candles made of smoke with dull red eyes, they glided forward. One headed for Byron. Full grown Shadow People. Ones like they'd encountered at Minetto and Williston.

Instead of warding it off, Byron opened his arms and stepped into the smoky column. It merged with his body and disappeared. Byron shook his mane of silver hair and his shoulders shuddered. When he opened his eyes, they glowed a dull red.

"What just happened?" Ruari said.

"You saw that?"

"Yes! His aura just went black like a void. Is he dead?"

"No, a Shadow Person went inside him. But I'm more worried about the other one."

"There's more?"

The other Shadow being cast about looking for a host. It looked toward her, and she stepped between it and Ruari. "I know what you are. You don't get to do that to me again, ever. Stay away!" She snarled.

It moved away and spotted a new target, accelerating.

"Erin, look out!" Marianne shouted.

Ruari's sister had been backing away from the murderous ghost of Damian Brody, a look of fear on her face. She didn't see the black smoky form until it plunged into her chest. She jerked sharply and shook her head. When she looked up again, her eyes held a dull red glow like two coals.

Damian laughed, a sound of pure delight.

"Erin!" Ruari cried in anguish.

Marianne grabbed his arm. "No, she's not dead, but she won't be in her right mind! That's what happened to me when I nearly killed Sarah."

He looked at her desperately. "Can we get it out?"

"Yes. I don't know how to do it, but it can be done."

A green lipstick snarl twisted Erin's pale face. She turned toward Sarah's voice and ran toward it.

"Sarah, look out for Erin!" Marianne shouted and prayed Kelly would be able to defend Sarah long enough for her to get Jules and Jean's help.

Marianne surveyed the battle, searching for the Leatherman and the bear. To her horror, she saw scores of draugers floating among the ghosts and the living. A dozen black pearls clustered around Mrs. Wallace. She'd dropped her long handled pan and batted at them with her hands as if she was trying to put out fires on her clothing. Mr. Wallace rushed to help her, a string of black things in his wake. Heedless of the danger, he pulled at the blobs, trying to rip them off his lady wife. Shadows covered them completely for several seconds, growing larger as they fed. When they drifted off, the Wallaces were gone. The engorged blobs bounced and rolled slowly along the ground, apparently sated.

Rita's pale shape bounded out of the darkness, barking and growling. She sank her teeth into a fat one and shook viciously it until it burst into dry shreds and withered. Barking, she lay into the others, biting and clawing at them. They exploded and dried up under her onslaught.

O'Meara's gang was surrounded by draugers, swinging fists and ghostly pickaxes, but there seemed to be fewer of the miners. Ben Dixon slashed his bayonet at three in front of him. As she watched, a miner fell to the ground mobbed by Shadows and was gone.

The ghost of Damien Brody darted after one of O'Meara's men, plunging his knife into the man's back. He arched and two Shadows descended on him. Brody turned to another target.

"Jules! Jean!" Marianne shouted, her voice cracking. She caught sight of the enormous spirit bear and the leather clad man on the other side of the fire, fighting their own drauger horde. "Jules, help Sarah!"

Someone grabbed her hand and yanked, wrenching Zorion out of her grasp.

"I'll take that!" Byron stepped back from her in triumph, red eyes glowing.

Zorion shrieked in her mind as the Shadow being burned around his talisman body. She clapped her hands over her ears instinctively even though it did no good.

Byron pointed the Talisman at Brody and said, "Brody, get back here!" The murderous ghost flinched and returned to Byron's side

"Mahri!" Ruari stepped in front of her, but Byron had already retreated to the stone portal.

"He took Zorion!" She panted.

It was all falling apart. The ghosts were losing, Byron was free, the Shadow People had possessed the living. Kelly or Sarah screamed from the other side of the bonfire. Ruari stiffened.

Marianne tried to think straight. *Pick a course of action. Don't just stand here and let it all happen.* "Ruari, go save Erin!"

"What about you?"

"I'll be fine. I have to get Zorion back."

He looked at her incredulously. "I can't just leave you!"

"There's only two of us left. We need to get Erin back on our side. Jean and Jules can handle the Shadow Person in her, trust me. But you have to be there when it goes out. I'll try to distract Byron and slow him down. We have to get Zorion back, close the portals, and seal the spell. Go!"

With a last anguished look, he ran off.

Summoning up her determination, Marianne approached Byron cautiously.

Sarah and Toni can do this 'fearless' thing. Just pretend I'm them.

Damian Brody stood between her and Sarah's old mentor, and she cast a wary eye on him. She didn't know if his spectral knife could hurt her, but if she was afraid of him, he'd certainly be able to do more damage. It was impossible not to be afraid.

Byron stared at the silver chased black rod in his hands.

"Hey Byron!" She called.

He looked up.

"Why did you booby trap those portals? You nearly killed Sarah, you know. Your own student! She worshipped the ground you walked on and you nearly killed her! Why?"

"She's too good. I had to slow her down. I thought you were useless, but you're better than I thought."

Bad line of thinking. She didn't want him focusing on her. She reached for the most outrageous thing she could think of. "So why did you pay those guys to trash Sarah's car?"

He snorted contemptuously. "*I* did that! Amazing how good it felt to smash that old pile of junk. Never understood why Sarah didn't haul it away and get a real car. You were both so pleased with yourselves for catching the vandals, I almost gave it away."

"Then why did they chase us?"

"Did they? Excellent!" He laughed again, sending shivers up her spine. "I posted bail and told them where you'd be. It was a fifty-fifty shot they'd lose interest and leave."

Anger flushed through her. All the time they'd wasted undoing the wedging spells, blaming the other Protectors. She had to get Zorion back. If she could get rid of Brody and delay

Byron until Ruari came back, maybe the two of them could take the older man down again. Her hand brushed the cool hard glass in her pocket. Marianne loosened the lid.

A scream of pure terror came from behind her. It sounded like Erin facing the worst thing ever. Good, maybe Jean had chased the Shadow Person out. Brody's eyes flicked away from Marianne, a hungry expression on his face.

She pulled the jar out, tore the top off, and splashed Father William's blessings across Brody's face and chest.

"Byron, stop it!" Someone called out. Catalina was back.

CHAPTER 21

*E*rin's week had been shitty in the extreme. She'd managed to forget the encounter with a poltergeist in her own home a couple of weeks ago, but seeing her childhood diaries had torn all the bandaids off. Horrible memories had overwhelmed her, making her feel like a helpless child all over again. Ruari's support kept her from drowning, and giving Marianne important information made her feel better. Going to the cemetery tonight was her way of taking her power back. She didn't know what she'd do, but by God she was going to fight all the things that had scared her.

Sarah and Kelly's presence made her edgy. The old habit of antagonizing them kept intruding. It figured that Sarah's mentor turned out to be an evil old prick, too scared to go after what he wanted himself and making others do his dirty work. That didn't make Sarah look too good.

The appearance of actual ghosts and then the freaky black balls coming out of the stone chamber had momentarily scared her enough to want to run away. She'd kept her shit together, but it was touch and go. The appearance of knife wielding murder ghost was more than she could take. Ruari and Marianne had things under control. She was going back to the car and wait this out. Before she could step away to get her bearings, she'd been ambushed again.

When the smoky black Shadow knifed into her body, everything changed. The little charm Sarah had given her flared like a match in her pocket and died. Clean, sharp rage replaced her fear. Relief from uncertainty felt so much better. Rage had hovered protectively on the edge of her life for as long as she could remember, and she welcomed its strength now.

What was she doing in a cemetery at night on Halloween? She ought to be at a party dancing the night away. It was like that travesty of a haunted house she'd been subjected to as a kid. Only this time it wasn't dubious friends she'd wanted to impress. Instead, her old enemies Sarah and Kelly were responsible for this whole fucking gig. If they hadn't sucked Ruari and Marianne into it, Erin wouldn't be here.

Erin finally had a chance to kick their asses for all the times they'd bullied her or spouted their ridiculous mumbo-jumbo. She spun on her Doc Martins and headed around the fire where she'd last seen them holding hands for this idiotic circle.

Kelly leaned on one crutch, her leg crooked up in a cast, supporting Sarah who looked gray and tired as she mumbled some new bullshit. Christmas had come early, and it was time to dance on their graves. Erin let out a harsh, guttural cry and launched herself at them. She had the satisfaction of seeing Kelly's eyes go wide.

"That's right, bitch!" Erin growled.

Kelly shoved Sarah out of the way and started to raise her crutch when Erin tackled her around the middle. The crutch went flying. Kelly was tall, athletic with an Amazon's physique, but her leg was only two weeks into healing from a fracture. Erin was a head shorter and stockier. Her impact knocked both women to the ground with a mutual oof.

It had been awhile since Erin had been in full contact grappling with anybody, but she remembered all the scratching, hair pulling, and skin gouging and went at her enemy with a will. Kelly fought back like a wildcat trained by three older brothers. Kelly brought both hands up sharply against Erin's head, catching her a ringing blow against the ears.

Dizzy and momentarily disoriented, Erin flailed against the other woman's arms. Kelly twisted out from under her and groped for the metal crutch. The pain in Erin's head made her angrier, and she screamed as she flung herself full length over Kelly's extended body and tried to pin her arms.

Something grabbed the back of her leather coat and lifted her high enough for Kelly to squirm free again. She felt the seams part.

"Erin, stop!" Ruari shouted, trying to get a better grip.

"She's not in her right mind!" Sarah warned.

"Let me go!" Erin snarled, swinging clawed, black painted nails at Ruari. She raked his cheek, leaving blood in her wake. He let go of her jacket and tried to catch her arms.

A growling roar came from somewhere behind her. The primal sound raised the hair on Erin's head. She half turned in Ruari's grip and saw a gigantic bear, maw wide, white fangs gleaming, leap over the bonfire and land an arm's length away from her. She brought up one leather clad arm to shield her face, and a massive paw batted it away. Its jaws rushed forward, and Erin screamed in pure terror as it roared.

Her rage fled as fast as it had come, leaving her awash with fear and pain, expecting sharp teeth to close on her face and tear her head off. Instead, a large wet nose sniffed her, leaving damp trails across her cheek. The bear snorted and turned away.

Dizzy, Erin felt the ground strike her shoulder hard.

"Erin! Erin!" Ruari's voice penetrated her haze. "Are you alright?"

She flailed her arm defensively before he caught it. Her big brother's worried face looked down at her.

"It's okay," he said, "whatever that was, it's gone. The thing inside you is gone."

"Is that bear thing gone?"

He looked blank then hugged her fiercely. She melted into the safety of his arms for a much needed moment. Then she pushed him away.

"Okay, already! What the fuck happened?"

"You were possessed by a Shadow Person," Sarah said, holding Kelly in her arm.

Erin saw the bloody streaks on Ruari's face and Kelly's disheveled hair and scratched skin and felt the stirrings of shame. She had been so busy avoiding the murder ghost that she hadn't been able to stop the black flamey thing from taking her over. The feel of things under her nails made her want to wash her hands.

"I'm sorry," she said.

"Forget about it. You're okay now," Ruari replied.

Kelly gave her a baleful look, still panting.

"Do this later," Ruari said. "Marianne needs us now. Byron got free." He offered her a hand and pulled her up.

She wobbled for a moment, tugged her leather duster straight. She'd deal with Kelly and Sarah and that humiliation later.

Anything to put it off. "Let's go."

Brody screamed and jerked as if she'd dumped acid in his face and vanished. Marianne dashed forward and grabbed Byron's arm. He pulled it away, raising it and the Talisman out of her reach. His other hand grabbed a handful of hair on the side of her head and yanked her painfully up on her toes. She yelped and grabbed his hand trying to ease the pain.

"This is mine, you little wretch. You could never know its true power. My dear sister will come when I call this time. No more hiding for her."

Catalina stepped into his view. *What happened to you? What happened to the brother I loved?*

"He left when you left him for another man," Byron said coldly. "Now you will serve me. Us. With the power of twin magic I will pay back everyone who disregarded me or stole from me. Starting with Ed Barstow."

I won't let you! Catalina said.

Marianne twisted and kicked in Byron's grip. Her hiking boot connected solidly with some part of her captor, but he ignored her and tightened his hold.

"Zorion, don't do it," she gasped, feeling sharp pricks where hairs separated from her head.

"The Navarro Talisman will do what I want. By Earth and Sky, and Fire an—"

A projectile flew out of the darkness and struck Byron squarely in the face. He staggered back as a small bottle fell to the ground.

Ruari charged up and punched Byron in the face. The man let go of Marianne's hair and howled. She reeled away, scalp throbbing. Leather-clad arms steadied her.

Erin looked terrible. Her smeared makeup gave her a macabre look, but her eyes were earnest. "You okay?"

Panting, Marianne nodded.

"Good." She whirled away and ran to help Ruari.

Marianne steadied herself. Byron was using both hands to fight off Erin and Ruari. Where was the talisman? Beneath the churning feet, she caught a gleam of silver on the ground. She waited for an opening and hoped it wouldn't be trampled and broken.

Byron was winning with the added power of the Shadow inside of him. Erin tried to get an arm around the man's neck, but she was shorter than he was, and it was hard. Byron landed a fist on Ruari's torso, making him grunt. He elbowed Erin, trying to shake her off. His nose bled like a waterfall down his face.

Three pale, translucent figures coalesced and mobbed Byron.

A tall, athletic woman with short, unruly hair leapt onto his back, shrieking like a banshee. Toni Woods had arrived at last.

At first, Marianne thought Byron was treating the ghostly swimmer as if she had physical weight, but when she plunged her hands into his body at the junction of his neck and shoulder, Marianne realized she was trying to reach the Shadow Person inside him.

"No shady people on my watch!" Toni screamed.

Two more ghosts, one in a hoody, the other in overalls, swung spectral tire irons at Byron like they were at batting practice. Although they passed through the man's clothing, they seemed to come in contact with something solid a couple of inches inside. Toni managed to grab the edge of something and started to pull it, as if she were teasing a whelk out of its shell.

Erin had hesitated when the ghosts arrived, then redoubled her efforts to put Byron in a head lock. Ruari worked to immobilize his arms. Marianne started to reach for Zorion, but scuffling feet blocked her.

Another ghost materialized next to them, wielding a long spectral knife. Damian Brody was back. He swung it toward Toni's unprotected back. The downward arc was stopped short by a ghostly tire iron.

No way! Jason held the blade away from Toni with both hands. Damian Brody let out a high-pitched, maniacal laugh and let the blade slide off the tire iron with a distant shriek of metal on metal.

I didn't kill you hard enough last time. He shifted his grip and swung the blade upwards toward Jason's gut. Marianne gasped.

It never made contact. Jesse caught the murderer's ghost on the side of the head with the full swing of his own tire iron. Brody looked stunned for a second and vanished. Jason gave his mentor a quick nod, and they both turned back to help Toni.

Marianne took that opportunity to dart in and grabbed the talisman. Her hands closed around the wooden rod, and she leaned back unsteadily. Her foot landed on something hard, and she fell on her butt. She looked down and saw the bottle of holy water. Its top was still on. She snatched it up as well.

Toni held a dark, stringy mass with both hands, and Marianne was reminded of the cheesecloth ectoplasm of the spiritualists. But unlike cloth, it was fighting to stay in its host. Jason and Jesse both dropped their ghostly iron and sank their cold hands into Byron's torso and grabbed hold of the Shadow Person. Byron bucked and twisted. Marianne wasn't sure if he was trying to escape their icy cold hands or if it was the Shadow Person's attempt to writhe out of their grip.

Twisting the lid off the jar, she splashed the water on Byron's face. He roared a guttural sound and nearly thrashed out of Ruari and Erin's grasp.

Five against two proved to be enough. The ghosts drew the black entity out of the man's body, and Byron collapsed on the ground, panting and half-sobbing.

The three ghosts hauled the writhing mass to the remains of the bonfire and threw it in. In the brilliant heat of the fire, it withered into nothing.

Without the adrenalin fueled rage of the Shadow, Byron's body let him know about every pain all at once. He cradled his broken nose, cracked ribs, and crotch in a fetal position of misery.

Catalina stood to the side, her arms wrapped around her torso.

Ruari and Erin bound Byron's hands behind his back again with the soft leather belt from Erin's duster.

Marianne said, "We have to close the portals and finish the spell before it's too late."

Speaking of late, sorry, Toni said with embarrassment. *Apparently I still get lost easily.* She stood next to Jason who was staring at her with a goofy grin on his face.

Marianne gave her a tired smile. "You showed up just in time. Thank you." She widened her gaze.

The draugers still clustered thickly in the clearing. The protective charms were doubtless exhausted by the constant use. There were fewer of the miners, Ben Dixon was gone, and the Wallaces had not returned the way Jason and Jesse had after Damian Brody had stabbed them. The murderous ghost was also missing.

No time to think about that.

"Sarah, we have to do something about the draugers. If we don't, we'll be overwhelmed."

Sarah nodded. She looked beyond exhausted.

Marianne said, "How about you work on bringing the bonfire up again? I'm going to ask Zorion to help us."

Sarah nodded once more, and she, John, and Kelly started tossing sticks on the bonfire.

"What can I do?" Ruari asked.

"Can you watch over Byron?"

"Absolutely."

"Erin, can you warn me if Shadow People get too close? I have to talk to Zorion, and I get distracted."

"You got it. I have one left." She raised a small bottle that had once held capers and now held Father Williams' special sauce.

Marianne stepped back a pace and held the black and silver, double ended talisman in her hands.

"Zorion, are you there?"

She felt his pain, exhaustion, a desperate desire for it all to end.

She closed her eyes and stared at the wood, willing herself to see him in there.

"I hear you, Zorion. I promise to release you, but we are overwhelmed with Shadow Beings and need your help. Can you help me one more time and banish or destroy the draugers and close the portal here?"

+...don't want to... so tired...+

"I am too, but we'll be overrun if you don't help us."

Acknowledgement. +...I will try...+

"Thank you."

She faced the clearing and held up the talisman trying to encompass as much as she could see in her eye. "By Earth and Sky and Fire and Water," she said, "destroy the draugers in this clearing, in this cemetery, and as far as you can reach."

She felt Zorion's hummingbird vibration in her hand as he powered up. A light like a dozen halogen spotlights arced out of her hand, bathing the clearing in brilliant white light. Zorion shrieked in agony as if a hundred hot pokers seared his flesh.

"Whoa!" Ruari exclaimed.

She slammed her lids shut but was temporarily blinded by the brightness anyway.

It was over in a moment. When she opened her eyes, the menacing black blobs were gone. She blinked and saw negative images that slowly faded.

The draugers were gone. Zorion lay trembling in her hand.

"You did it! They're gone. Thank you."

He wept.

She brought the talisman to her lips and kissed it, imagining kissing his cheek as he lay on his deathbed. Then she twisted the barrel. Age had stiffened its joints, and it didn't want to move. She struggled for a moment.

"What are you doing?" Byron's hoarse voice said. They ignored him.

"Let me help," Ruari said. He took it gently from her and twisted each cross piece. Though his hands were bruised, he coaxed the old pieces apart. "Here."

Marianne gave it a last turn and upended the contents into her palm. A sliver of fragile, ivory-colored bone fell out along with tiny, sparkling grains of coarse sand that once might have been gems.

"You're free. You've served the world a hundred times over. Find your family and be at peace," she said, tears prickling her eyes. She tossed the bone, wood, and silver into the fire and felt Zorion depart.

"No!" Byron shouted in outrage.

Marianne and Ruari jerked their heads toward the sound. Byron stood, his eyes a furious, dull red, his pain blotted out.

The Shadow Person who'd been driven out of Erin had found a new host.

CHAPTER 22

"Not again!" Erin eyed him in disbelief.

Byron only had eyes for Marianne. He gave her a look of pure hatred. "You fool!" he spat. "You've destroyed one of the greatest talismans ever created."

"It was time," Marianne agreed.

Byron glared at her through swollen eyes over a nose that looked like a melon as if he was memorizing her inside and out and contemplating how best to destroy her. Ruari stepped between them, fists bunched, ready to put him down again.

Catalina looked at her twin with revulsion.

Toni let out another banshee howl and ran for Byron a second time, Jason and Jesse on her heels. This time Byron was faster. He reached for the ghostly figure of his sister, and Marianne thought she could see a second pair of dark arms reach out of him as well. They fastened on Catalina's struggling form, and she melted and disappeared.

Unable to evade his pursuers, Byron gave a frustrated grunt and dove straight into the stone doorway. Toni, Jason, and Jesse halted unwilling to follow him.

"Hah!" Erin cried. "Outta my way, ghost people." She darted after Byron.

She returned a few moments later empty handed, looking puzzled. "Did he come back this way?"

"No," Ruari replied.

"He's not in there."

Sarah croaked, "He went into the Shadow Lands. Quick, form the circle and finish the spell before he's back with more draugers or worse."

"What about Byron?" Marianne protested.

"Later. Do this now," Sarah said.

Even though she'd already spent her last nickel of energy, Sarah summoned up reserves from somewhere and began her spell casting a second time.

They walked clockwise around the bonfire, Sarah chanting raggedly, "By Earth and Sky and Fire and Water, let the spell of protection be closed. Let all the points of light we laid be bound together to keep Canopus safe for another year. Let every portal we spelled be closed against the Shadow Realm. Let all the Shadows be banished through the portals back to their own land."

Kelly, Erin, Ruari, Toni, Jason, and Jesse joined in. Marianne forced her fatigue aside along with her fears and tried to remember the old linen map.

The memory was so far away. Images of the dead grey Shadow Realm and Byron's look of pure hatred kept intruding. Just when she'd gotten rid of her stalking ex, she'd have to watch her back again.

Stop. Deal with that later. Focus on the now. She listened to the chant. Her feet kept moving. Ruari's strong hand pulled her forward around the fire. Erin urged her from behind. She needed to close the spell by remembering everywhere they'd been.

They'd left Maple Hill a lifetime ago, Sarah driving like a maniac down the hill. Marianne had driven like a maniac along the Old Albany Post Road to draw the ribbon of the spell back to the beginning. They'd walked in the woods and along highways and swamps to get to stone chambers marked on an old map. They'd buried charms of herbs and stones in every community they could reach. The magic of the little charms sounded like a chorus of voices singing wordlessly, and she hummed faintly in her throat trying to catch the tune of it. The chorus created a web of light, and she augmented its glow in her mind.

"Send the Shadows back into the nearest portal and close the gate." The chant around her had changed as the magic grew in intensity.

The distant chorus of voices gave the circle momentum. Her feet moved faster. She held the glowing web of light around Canopus County in her mind.

A full Metropolitan Opera Chorus swelled and coalesced on a single shouted note and fell silent. The portal behind her was quiet.

The circle stopped moving. Marianne shook herself, feeling a lingering buzz in her body like she'd been driving all day. She opened her eyes.

"Is that it?" Ruari asked.

"I think so. Sarah, did we do it?"

Sarah unzipped her jacket pocket and dragged her cellphone out. She looked for a moment and shrugged. "I'm not sure. It's five after midnight. We might have made it or might have just missed it." Her voice was barely audible.

"How strict is the time limit?" Marianne asked uneasily.

"Not sure. We never missed it before. Let's call it good for now."

Marianne sagged in relief. "Okay."

Erin released her hand.

Marianne said, "I think Byron grabbed Catalina. And he was still possessed."

Sarah lifted her shoulder in a minimal shrug. "He chose that."

"But he has Catalina."

"Deal with it later." Sarah had nothing left.

"He was totally evil," Erin declared. "Good riddance."

"He was my teacher and friend for a long time," Sarah said. "He lost his way."

Marianne sympathized with Sarah's loss, but she agreed with Erin's assessment. Byron had allied with a murderer and welcomed the Shadows with open arms. Twice. You had to be more than a little lost to let that happen.

"Jason," Marianne said, "I saw you and Jesse get killed by Damian Brody. What happened?"

Jason looked unsettled for a moment. *I thought I was a total goner. Felt the knife and everything. But I woke up back in the shop. Jesse turned up a few seconds later. He told me I couldn't die like that unless I let myself. So we came back.* He gave Jesse a fist bump. Toni looked impressed, and he ducked his head with a smile on his face.

"I'm so glad you're both alright!" Marianne said. "Toni, are you going back to your cemetery?"

She tipped her head to one side and looked at Jason, who grinned. Then her gaze slid to Erin in her leather clad duster.

Nah. I'll hang out here for a while. I like being seen and heard. She looked at Erin. *Wanna come by sometime?*

Erin looked startled. "I guess I could."

Toni gave an off-hand shrug. *Yeah, I'll stay.*

Cool! Jason said. *Can I show you around?*

I guess. Toni winked at Erin before she vanished along with Jason. Jesse faded.

Erin looked startled, staring at the place where Toni had been.

Marianne looked around the clearing. "So where is everyone else? I hope Zorion didn't hurt them."

"Jean and Jules went back to their territory after the portals closed," Sarah answered. "Adrian Vandermark went back to his barn."

"Where are Peter O'Meara and his men?"

We're here, a rough voice with a touch of Irish lilt replied. He stood just outside the ring of firelight. *I lost six of my lads today.*

"Lost?" Marianne asked. "Didn't they just go back to Turner's Pond?"

No, they were consumed by Shadow People. They will never see their families again.

"What? How can ghosts die again?" Once you were dead, nothing worse could happen, right? She looked at Sarah with growing dread.

"When larval Shadow People latch on to a living person," Sarah explained in a flat voice, "they suck their available energy out, leaving the person exhausted and weak. But their living body has enough bio energy to keep them alive and recover. Ghosts are made of pure energy. When that's consumed, they're gone."

Marianne rounded on her. "You knew this? When we called them here, you knew they could be obliterated?"

Sarah looked tired and resigned. Her silence said it all.

Marianne turned to the head miner. "Peter, did you know this?"

Aye, we knew it was possible.

"And you came anyway."

We'd been sitting in that lake for so long. You offered us a chance to go home to our families. We all agreed to come.

Marianne's eyes burned. "I'm so sorry."

O'Meara flashed an angry look. *Don't you dare pity us. Just do what you said you would. Make people remember us. We'll tell their families what happened.*

She nodded, and he and his men winked out.

"What did you agree to do?" Sarah asked suspiciously.

Marianne lifted her chin, defiantly. "I told them I'd get them a plaque commemorating the mine collapse and list all their names so no one would forget them."

"Huh," Sarah said. "That's a good idea."

Sarah's admiration was welcome but Marianne was too tired to care at the moment. She turned to the rest. "Does anyone know what happened to the others? I was so busy focusing on Byron I didn't see."

"Ben Dixon was fighting alongside the miners," Sarah said, "and I think he's gone too."

"Did anyone see where Damian Brody went?" Erin asked.

No one had. With any luck he'd been consumed by draugers, but they couldn't be sure.

"Where's Rita?"

"Who's Rita?" Ruari and Erin chorused.

"The big black dog from the motel."

Sarah shrugged. No one seemed to know whether she'd gone back to her motel room or been consumed by Shadows. Marianne knew it would take time to mourn the people who'd ceased to exist on any plane.

Erin broke the silence with an impatient sigh. She tipped her head toward the scratches she'd inflicted on Kelly. "You should wash that out with soap and water and put some antibiotic on it. I'm sorry." It looked like it cost her a lot to make that apology.

Kelly gave her a disgusted look, relented a little, and nodded. She turned to Sarah who leaned against her. "You ready to go home, love?"

"Yeah. One more thing," Sarah said, turning to Marianne. "I need to take a break. I need some time to regroup, take care of Kelly, focus on my day job. Marianne, would you take the Protection gig?"

Taken aback, Marianne said, "What? No way, I don't know how to do all this!" *I've just killed some of my friends for good, and I'm pretty sure Byron wants me dead.*

Sarah said, "Fine. Think about it at least."

"Maybe. Not right now."

Sarah had to accept that. She and Kelly limped down toward the parking lot with John Irving's help.

Marianne looked at the bonfire that was still burning brightly. "Much as I want to go, I don't think we should leave this unattended."

Erin, Ruari, and Marianne poked and tended the flaming pile, watching the sparks fly up. The weariness that she'd kept at bay crept back, and she had visions of crawling into bed. Soon.

Ruari came up behind her, and she heard the creak of leather as he put his arms around her. He was warm and comforting.

Erin looked up from her moody stare with a grin. Her makeup was smeared badly, but Marianne was too tired to decide whether she looked comical or disturbing.

"Well, that was refreshing," Erin announced, her red, spiky hair a wild mess.

"Are you kidding?" Marianne replied.

"I've been moping around the house for a couple of weeks feeling like shit. I finally feel like me again."

Marianne felt Ruari shake his head. "Figures. So, Goth Girl, are you all into ghosts now?"

Erin tossed her head from side to side, considering. "Guess they're not all bad."

Ruari chuckled. He squeezed Marianne gently. "Did you get any leads on a job?"

"Between meeting ghosts and running away from Shadow People? Not really. Guess I have work to do. Monday though. I'm taking the rest of the weekend off."

"Hey, I have an idea," Erin said brightly.

"Uh oh," Ruari murmured. "Look out."

She stuck her tongue out at him and said, "How about this? We could go into the ghost busting business!"

Marianne raised her eyebrows.

"No, really. You could do the background research, I'll do computers and the books, and we could exorcise them together!"

"And what would I do?" Ruari asked.

"You've been wanting to start your own woodworking business. You could do that. Maybe we can make space for an office in your studio."

"I don't know." Marianne had strong misgivings. But part of it had a nice ring to it. Not the whole county though. That was too much. Maybe she could feel her way into this? Astrid Delaney and Peter O'Meara could be her first clients. That still left her with no income. Starting out broke and doing everything pro bono was not a good business model.

Silence descended for the first time in a long time. Marianne breathed in cold air, tinged with leaves, woodsmoke, and a hint of rain. The fire crackled and snapped.

After a time, John came slowly back up the path. His mustache drooped, and he looked as tired as Marianne felt. Erin walked over and took his arm.

"How are you feeling?" She asked with more care than she'd shown all night.

Marianne was surprised by her level of concern.

Erin looked at their expectant faces. "What? I'm not totally evil. We saved each other from being blob food."

John patted her arm. "I'll be fine. Thank you for attending the fire."

"Did they get off okay?" Marianne asked.

"They did. You might call her in a couple of days and check in on her."

They watched the fire steadily burn down for a few more minutes.

Finally, John said, "I can manage this from here, if you want to go."

"Are you sure?" Marianne yearned for nothing more than to go home to her bed, her boyfriend, and her cat.

He nodded, and they moved off down the track back to the parking lot. Ruari's hand was warm and comforting around hers.

Erin turned and walked backward so she could face them. Her makeup looked less crazy away from the firelight.

"Hey, can I come stay with you guys?" She asked. "There is no way I'm going back to that haunted apartment!"

"That's not my call. I can always clear a space next to the band saw if you want to stay at my place," Ruari offered.

She snorted loudly. "No way, big brother. I'd rather sleep on

Mom and Dad's couch before I sleep next to your band saw. But seriously, can I sleep on your couch, Marianne?"

Marianne tightened her hand around Ruari's and smiled. She had a sneaking suspicion it was going to be a busy year. At least she had help.

ACKNOWLEDGMENTS

Bryan Adams once said you can write a song from a mumble when asked how he came to write music for "Spirit: Stallion of the Cimmaron." You noodle around with a tune and wait for the words to come to you. Turns out you can write books that way, too. I wrote "Hallowed Dreams" from a mumble. I knew I wanted to write a third book in the series, but I wasn't sure what the story would be. I tried a couple of ideas, and the one about a buddy-road-story stuck with me. The development of the plot, the Shadow beings, and the antagonists emerged over time. Initially, Ruari had a full story going on in Maple Hill too, but my writing group rightly pointed out it was its own story. That story will be book 4, "Legends and Dreams."

I revised an early draft with the help of a workshop hosted by Daniel David Wallace (https://danieldavidwallace.com/). I met some wonderful people there and need to thank Daniel, Allison Saft ("Down Comes the Night"), Cara, and Helen for their thoughtful suggestions. On the subject of thank yous: the care, attention, and time of a number of people helped this book come into focus. My amazing family Austin, Kelton, and Orion took time out of their busy lives to read and provide invaluable comments and suggestions. Penny, you've been with me on this journey since we met, thank you as ever for your support and comments! DeeDee, thank you for your suggestions and legal advice for Sarah. Angela, Sanan, and Miles provided feedback on early drafts, and Jenny read the final draft and assured me it was good enough. Any flubs or flaws after that are entirely my own.

This book brought a new adventure. It started when one of

my beta readers said, "Hey, I'd love to see what a coffee cup in a hiking boot looks like," and I thought, I know a guy….Collaborating with artist Andy Slaughter of Pilcher Illustrate has been an absolute gift. Andy embraced the concept of illustration immediately, and we chose illustration subjects together. He is such a talented, smart, beautiful human being, and I loved having an excuse to meet with him regularly as the images developed. If you like them too and want to see more of his work, go to his website www.pilcherillustrate.com. I look forward to collaborating further with Andy on "Legends and Dreams."

"Hallowed Dreams" let me create and explore fictional Canopus County. I grew up in the Hudson Valley and have loved creating a place that is a composite of familiar and imaginary places from the history of Dutchess County and Putnam County. What is real? The Leatherman was a real person. I gave him a purpose for his wanderings, and who knows, maybe it's not that far off? The Old Albany Post Road dirt section is real. It contains a beguiling mix of old and new as you drive its winding path. The stone chambers are real. They can be found throughout New England. Their origin is a mystery, and that mystery lends itself to interpretations and musings. To my knowledge, there is no Shadow Lands on the other side of the stone wall, nor are their Shadow beings waiting to break through. The chambers are fun to wonder about, though. If you choose to explore them, please stay on public property.

The towns, businesses, and geography of Canopus County, Turner's Hope Mine, Williston State Park, and Minetto State Park are entirely fictional, serving the purpose of the story alone.

If you enjoyed this book, please look for my other books, visit my website PalouseDigitalPress (http://palousedigitalpress.com/), sign up for my newsletter, and find me on Instagram @elizabethralix. An author's readership grows when people like you leave a review on Amazon or Good Reads. If you're not sure what to say, tell someone why you picked up the book. What did you like or not like about it (no spoilers)? Would you recommend it to someone else?

Thank you.

ABOUT THE AUTHOR

I have been writing all my life. My first story was in fourth grade complete with crayon illustrations. Since then, I've written fan fiction, short stories, novellas, and novels set in a variety of fantasy worlds. Getting a Masters and PhD in anthropology from Washington State University allowed me to spend summers camping and doing archaeology in Alaska and the Aleutian Islands. I spent twenty years being a taxi-mom, reading aloud, telling stories, and sneaking in a little writing when I could. My husband reads my drafts, challenges my thinking, and always makes my stories better. I currently work as a professional archaeologist in Eastern Washington. In no particular order, I love to sing, knit, garden, role play, play board games, and spend time with my family and friends.

Maple Hill is a fictional town nestled in the hills of the Hudson Valley, New York. It's a composite of several places I've lived in or visited. I loved creating this world and look forward to returning in the future to tell more stories with familiar faces and introduce new ones. Look for news about upcoming stories at palousedigitalpress.com/

If you like my work, recommend me to others.

Find me on https://www.amazon.com/ in paperback and e-books. Leave a review and help others find my work.

Contact me at ERAlix@turbonet.com if you want to say hi.

Visit my website, palousedigitalpress.com/ where I promote other local or regional authors and publications. Sign up for my occasional newsletters.

Follow me on Instagram @elizabethralix where I occasionally post pictures of the Palouse.

DREAMS OF FIRE (BOOK 1)

Marianne Singleton flees her obsessed ex-husband to the sleepy town of Maple Hill, hoping to start a new life. She doesn't find a safe haven.

Plagued by nightmares and eerie occurrences, Marianne quickly learns the charming older home she bought is filled with a strange, spectral presence. When her ex-husband follows her to Maple Hill, she suddenly has more trouble than she can handle.

With the help of some new friends, and her cat, Oscar, Marianne attempts to unravel the mystery of who—*or what*—inhabits her home. If only her new friends could help her deal with a stalker ex-husband. As he menaces ever closer, she must find the courage to face him down.

Sadly, she's always been better at fleeing than standing her ground…

Available at Amazon.com in paperback, and on Kobo, Barnes and Noble and Apple Books in digital format.

SYLVAN DREAMS (BOOK 2)

Marianne Singleton has defeated both her horrible ex and the ghosts in her house. Her prospects for a job are promising, and her love life is back on track. Life is good.

But she's still seeing ghosts. When she picks up a hitchhiking ghost who won't leave her alone, she has her hands full. To make matters worse, her new boyfriend starts missing dates, and that may be more than her bruised heart can stand.

Ruari Allen is at a crossroad in life. His job is thankless, and he longs to start his own woodworking business. Marianne makes his heart sing, but, having broken someone's heart in the past, he's afraid of hurting her. When he starts seeing colored haloes and smoke around people, he worries about his sanity. Especially since he's also started dreaming of a mysterious red-headed woman who claims to have known his dead grandfather.

Relationships are hard enough without supernatural forces getting in the way. If Marianne and Ruari's relationship is to stand a chance, they'll need to take drastic steps.

Will a desperate journey to Scotland bring them together, or forever cast them apart?

Available at Amazon.com in paperback, and on Kobo, Barnes and Noble and Apple Books in digital format.

HALLOWED DREAMS (BOOK 3)

Wake your ghostly allies, All Hallow's Eve is coming…

Marianne, a fledgling clairvoyant, embarks on a road trip with Sarah, her mentor in all things ghostly, to protect Canopus County from supernatural danger. As Marianne struggles to learn magic, the trip becomes more perilous. Needing to prove to herself she can stand on her own two feet, Marianne refuses to bail out and go home.

Frustrated by her stubbornness, Marianne's boyfriend Ruari cools his heels at home in Maple Hill. When his fiercely independent sister, Erin, asks for his help out of the blue, something is really wrong. A trauma from Erin's childhood might just hold the key to Marianne's dangerous journey.

As the clock ticks toward a showdown in the Maple Hill Cemetery on Halloween night, Marianne will have to learn magic and convince some rowdy ghosts to help her or doom Canopus County to suffer from an ancient, malignant hunger.

Illustrated by Andrew P. Slaughter of Pilcher Illustrate.

Available at Amazon.com in paperback, and on Kobo, Barnes and Noble and Apple Books in digital format.

LEGENDS AND DREAMS (BOOK 4, FORTHCOMING)

Everyone knows the Avery Theater in Maple Hill is haunted.

The latest production of *The Legend of Sleepy Hollow* is supposed to revive the failing old theater, but ghostly doings are disrupting rehearsals, and people are getting way too into their characters.

Marianne's new business as a historian for hire isn't exactly a financial success. Her first jobs are for ghosts who are notoriously short on cash. Ruari struggles to get his new woodworking venture off the ground. Separately, they are drawn into the mysterious events at the theater. Can they save the play?

As opening night draws closer, the past and the present begin to merge. The last time *Sleepy Hollow* was performed the theater burned down…

Illustrated by Andrew P. Slaughter of Pilcher Illustrate.

A fifth book is planned for this series.